FULL ASSAULT MODE

ALSO BY DALTON FURY

Tier One Wild

Black Site

Kill Bin Laden

FULL ASSAULT MODE

DALTON FURY

ST. MARTIN'S PRESS ♏ NEW YORK

This is a work of fiction. All of the characters, organizations, and events portrayed in this novel are either products of the author's imagination or are used fictitiously.

MAY 1 3 2014

FULL ASSAULT MODE. Copyright © 2014 by Dalton Fury. All rights reserved. Printed in the United States of America. For information, address St. Martin's Press, 175 Fifth Avenue, New York, N.Y. 10010.

www.stmartins.com

Design by Omar Chapa

The Library of Congress Cataloging-in-Publication Data is available upon request.

ISBN 978-1-250-04048-0 (hardcover)
ISBN 978-1-4668-3585-6 (ebook)

St. Martin's Press books may be purchased for educational, business, or promotional use. For information on bulk purchases, please contact Macmillan Corporate and Premium Sales Department at 1-800-221-7945, extension 5442, or write specialmarkets@macmillan.com.

First Edition: May 2014

10 9 8 7 6 5 4 3 2 1

To the 10,000-plus armed nuclear security officers throughout the homeland who strap it on every day to prevent radiological sabotage on their watch

AUTHOR'S NOTE

Jamiat-ul-ulema-i-Pakistan Identification Card and Document

We had just climbed the Madrassa's high dirt wall on a moonless summer night. With my teammate, codenamed Happ, and our Air Force Combat Controller, we quietly but smoothly cleared the three upper floor rooms before we heard the tell-tale signature of three rapid-fired supersonic 5.56mm rounds from outside the compound.

They know we're here now.

Thinking over the options, maneuvering to help or holding what we had, I thumb-pressed my hand mike.

"You good out there?"

"Roger, we're good!" said another operator from outside the compound.

It was a suspected layover spot along a known al Qaeda rat line just a couple of miles from the Pakistan border in the lawless border town of Shkin. My boss, Colonel Gus Murdock, wasn't too keen on green-lighting the hit that night, but he understood our concern and, like all good commanders, he always trusted the guys on the ground. And even though he yielded, giving us execute authority a half hour earlier, I think he knew we would have figured out a way to launch anyway.

From the second-story balcony, Happ and I spider-dropped into the compound and headed across the soft sand for the open door. We buddy-cleared several rooms before confirming the presence of al Qaeda fighters in the last one. We rat-fucked their sleeping bags, secured their left-behind hand-held radios, and easily noticed the wind-blown curtains half covering the window they squirted through. We back-cleared the rooms, taking opposite sides in each as we flowed back to the open-air compound.

At the still-locked front gate, Happ lifted the deadfall lock out of the wooden holder, allowing the large metal door to swing open.

"Eagle, Eagle," Happ said as he led us outside, then hugging the outer wall as we moved north.

Now kneeling over a white-robed heavy-set body, I gently placed two fingers alongside his neck, level with his Adam's apple and under his beard, to check for a pulse. I looked at the man's white turban and followed his forehead down to his locked-open eyes. They were distant, pupils motionless, locked on paradise above. I reached up with my gloved hand, fingers extended and joined, and slid my palm from his turban down to close his eyes. I had never done that before; it's the kind of thing that stamps your soul, never leaves you.

I looked up to see his opponent standing close by holding a foreign pistol. At the time of the radio call, I had no idea the operator on the other end was the shooter. Had he not been on his game, he could have been the one horizontal on the blood-puddled, sandy soil.

This head master made two bad decisions.

His first mistake was choosing to harbor al Qaeda fighters entering Afghanistan to kill Coalition troops. Our intercepts of enemy radio transmissions two hours earlier were spot-on, but we would have been happy enough to flex and fly the guy up to Bagram airfield.

His second mistake, the really dumb one, was he chose to pull a Makarov

9mm semi-auto from his leather shoulder holster after he jumped out the window. The radio intercepts drove the late-night visit, but it was the pistol draw that initiated the combat rules of engagement. For certain, the last thing he saw before being martyred was the fuzzy image of a combat-clad American Delta Operator under nods at roughly ten paces.

It was a high-noon showdown he was never trained to win.

Happ knelt next to me on the opposite side and pulled the AQ facilitator's pocket litter from his left breast pocket. He was a card-carrying member of Jamiat-ul-elema-i-Pakistan, and his bloodstained ID card and half-folded papers bore the marks of the three-round shot group, the size of a half-dollar, we had heard earlier while on the wall.

I looked up at the shooter. "Good hit!"

"You're a little rusty," Happ said. "I'm used to seeing this the size of a dime."

We could have left it alone that night. We could have stayed in our rat-infested quarters and minded our own business. Instead we kitted up, bumped knuckles, and turned the target.

It was more than simply the *commando cocktail* kicking in; a term coined by the über-talented former Delta commander Pete Blaber to describe the entirely intoxicating mixing of the thrill of the hunt with the thrill of the kill. No, it was much more than that. It was also about commitment to each other and to our countrymen, and sure, on the heels of 9/11, there was a little vigilante justice running through our blood.

And that, folks, after a dozen years of war on terror, and as our nation winds down our involvement in Afghanistan and moves to the Horn of Africa or Syria, is still the fundamental motive that drives the full assault mode mindset of one Delta Force Major Kolt "Racer" Raynor.

Back for the third time in this Delta Force series, Kolt Raynor still has not learned a single thing about listening to authority since he hung it out in *Tier One Wild*. But, hey, when you save POTUS's ass, your pad speed skyrockets in a second. This time, though, he should have let it go, he should have aborted the op.

But Racer has always marched to his own drummer with a wrecking-ball attitude, and when a mate is in the shit or a high-value individual is in his sites, the word *abort* isn't in his vocabulary.

No, in times like that, Kolt Raynor defaults to *execute, execute, execute*. Besides, as you'll see inside, some targeted tier one personalities are just more important than others.

Most black specops outfits, like Delta Force, SEAL Team 6, or even the British 22 SAS, can afford maybe one or two maverick operators through the life of the organization. More than that, and they are likely to have their operators dispersed into the conventional ranks and the headquarters shuttered, like Dick Marcinko's Red Cell or the Canadian Airborne Regiment.

But rest assured, the ones that can keep it together long enough to turn target after target, zig and zag intuitively, and consistently get the drop on the skinny in the shadows tag themselves as action hero operators. The kind of guys you want in your foxhole or clearing corners with you. You can't ask for the moniker, it just happens. Sure, running with men like Kolt Raynor is scary shit at times, more often than not resulting in someone shoving Kerlix to the bone in your bleeder or even pulling your dog tags and zipping up your body bag. And yes, sometimes pinning another worthless medal on your chest.

Why do men and women do it? Why do some American men and women aspire to serve the ranks of the most elite top-secret organizations where your every move is analyzed, every shot counted, and every hit a pressure cooker?

Why would a small team of Delta operators conduct a high-risk day-time hit in the middle of Tripoli, the Libyan capital, to roll up Abu Anas al-Libi in October 2013? Sure, the scumbag was a senior al Qaeda member and was wanted by the United States in connection to the bombing of American embassies in Tanzania and Kenya in 1998, with at least a $5 million bounty on his head, but was it the cocktail talking again, or something else?

More so than ever, the Full Assault Mode mission is filled with subtle first-hand experiences, both from my military service as well as my post-retirement career. Things I've witnessed a small band of unsung men and women voluntarily do again and again, from one battlefield or protected area to another, and done sans fanfare.

In *Full Assault Mode,* I try to shed light on the *why,* while continuing to protect the *how.* This issue, naturally, remains extraordinarily important to me.

Commercial nuclear security is a big deal in this post-9/11 era we live in, which is why I enlisted two trusted subject matter experts in identifying and protecting Safeguards Information—the government-protected, highly sensitive details on what is vulnerable and what is not that is protected by the Atomic Energy Act of 1954. To Richard H. and Allen Fulmer, two of the best, your enthusiasm, knowledge, and attention to detail are very much appreciated.

Most writers will tell you that to craft an edge-of-the-seat thriller in today's ever-changing technological era, it takes a team of experts behind the scenes. The people who understand the unique details of how a droid functions, what's deep in the bowels of a nuclear reactor, or how the best helicopter pilots find their target in a tsunami-induced blackout. I'm deeply grateful to the handful of friends who set my left and right limits, and then adjusted my azimuth to keep me true. Most important to me was the insight that Chris Evans brought to the table. A super-talented and accomplished writer, Chris's uncanny ability to gently massage chapter after chapter, adjusting my shot group from time to time, was extraordinary, timely, and entirely cherished.

Fans of Racer will recall that he is a recovering alcoholic, having fallen off the wagon in his debut novel, *Black Site*. Now back in the Unit, and back for the hat trick, most would agree that it's wise to keep his old buddy Jack Daniels out of the single-wide. But if Kolt was to belly up to the bar again, maybe after coming down from the commando cocktail high, he'd certainly buy the rounds for my editor, Marc Resnick, from St. Martin's Press and my agent, Scott Miller, of Trident Media Group. Even though Kolt might consider them SEAL Team Six groupies at times, he would learn very quickly how savvy, supportive, and aggressive they are in the publishing biz, and how the thrill of the find is just as exciting as the thrill of the sell.

So here's to Rich, Allen, Chris, Marc, and Scott! Five world-class guys on top of their game and, very fortunate for me, in my corner. But, as usual, Kolt's longevity really rests not only with the readers, but also with the three ladies in my home. Always supportive but lurking just outside the squared circle for signs that Kolt Raynor might be taking center stage, or believing his own press, I'm very grateful they allowed Kolt to stave off enough arm bars and dirty leg sweeps to get through round three.

Ding, ding, ding.

I'm not the killer man, I'm the killer man's son. But I'll do the killing 'til the killer man comes.

—*Ronald Reagan, 40th President of the United States*

FULL ASSAULT MODE

ONE

Eastern Afghanistan, early February 2013

A menagerie of animal-named armored vehicles trundled along a rutted dirt road deep in Taliban territory near the Pakistan border. The temperature hovered around freezing, not bad for early February, and dusk was only two hours away.

The mission was simple enough—clear ten klicks of heavily mined road leading to a Taliban-controlled village that was acting as a hub for three rat lines funneling Taliban and Haqqani fighters infiltrating into Afghanistan. It was an important mission, and its success would severely hamper the Taliban's spring offensive, but there was zero chance it would make the six o'clock news back home. This was no Thunder Run, the rumbling charge of M1 Abrams tanks and Bradley fighting vehicles that blew through Baghdad like metal hail through lace during the invasion of Iraq in 2003. It couldn't even compare with the Syrian armored runs of T-72s and BMP armored fighting vehicles through the Damascus suburb of Daraya. No, this was an excruciating crawl, where progress was measured in feet, sometimes inches.

It was day 5, and the column was still a klick out. Leading the way on this godforsaken goat path were a pair of ten-ton, two-man Husky 2G armored vehicles equipped with four large electronics-bay panels affixed to their fronts. Each vehicle swept one side of the road using the Niitek Visor 2500 ground-penetrating radar set housed within the panels. They were looking for IEDs. They'd already found three today, for a total of twelve since the mission began. Seven of the IEDs had had enough explosive power to easily kill the heaviest vehicle in the column. Finding them before they could be detonated had been a major success, but as the saying went, you only needed to miss one IED to have a very bad day.

It was an arms race, pitting sophisticated electronics and up-armored vehicles against guile and ever-increasing explosive power. It seemed criminal now to think troops had once traversed these roads in nothing more than standard Toyota pickup, but then you went to war with what you had, and back in 2001, IEDs weren't an issue.

As the armored vehicles slowly rolled forward, a herd of seven Buffalo armored vehicles followed. Tipping the scales at over twenty-three tons apiece, the six-wheeled Buffalos looked and sounded like growling metal monsters. Their sheer size and power were so ferocious that one even made an appearance in a blockbuster movie as a shape-shifting warrior-robot.

Fearsome or not, a bundle of four 155mm artillery shells left over from the Soviet invasion of Afghanistan and buried two feet below the ground could turn fierce, blowing up and scattering bits of metal . . . and flesh. And so the column inched forward, the Huskies scanning the dirt for hidden death while, following from a safe distance, were the Buffalos, each carrying a complement of four dismounts—a cold term for the soldiers that would, if necessary, leave the protection of the Buffalo's heavily armored V-shaped hull and patrol on foot.

Forty klicks away at Jalalabad Airfield, Kolt "Racer" Raynor sat perched uncomfortably on a cardboard box full of MREs in his Bravo Assault Team's lounge area and watched the progress of the armored column on a fifty-inch flat screen. The feed came live from a UAV loitering some fifteen thousand feet above the column. A small box on the upper left of the screen showed an infrared view of the same area. So far, the only hot spots were the column's vehicles and a trio of donkeys huddled on the leeward side of a rocky hill a hundred yards in front of the Huskies. It wasn't as sexy as a Tier One high-value individual, but the hot spots would get Kolt and his men out the door. Tonight, they were on tap working a TST—time-sensitive target. Specifically, they were focused on the triggermen. While some IEDs were rigged to detonate on contact via a simple pressure plate, others were remote-detonated, the explosion set off by the thumb of a triggerman. For that to work, the terrorists would need to be within a couple hundred meters, hidden from the naked eye somewhere in the rocky outcrop. Kolt could have contacted the gunners in the Buffalos to tell them to forget the damn donkeys and sweep for two-legged asses, but the young army officer on target didn't need white noise from someone back in the rear, even if it was Kolt Raynor. Besides, Kolt stiff-armed micromanaging as a practice himself.

"We should be out there, not here," Kolt said under his breath. Forty klicks, even by helo, was far too long for a so-called rapid response. Kolt looked around the room. He was an invited guest here, and so he kept his thoughts to himself. Yes, he was their commander, but sometimes the smartest thing you did in command was to do nothing at all. Besides, he wasn't going to gripe to the men about how it should be. It was important to keep that subtle separation between the commander and the commanded. After a decade plus of war, everyone in the room was war weary, and the hunger to mix it up with the bad guys had abated years ago, something certainly not lost on Kolt.

Kolt accepted his fate, for the moment, and turned away from "Thunder Turtle's" agonizing progress to look around the tent. All four of Kolt's assault teams lived in tents that had once been green. They were now covered by a half inch of brown dust, which clung to everything, even the interior. Between the dust and the clutter, it could have been a cave.

The operators chilled out on green nylon, squeaky, foldout army cots, whose aluminum legs never seemed to balance correctly on the plywood floors. Individual shelves were fashioned out of half-inch plywood and two-by-fours with small head-high walls placed between each bunk to give an impression of privacy. There wasn't any really, unless they considered their five-by-six-foot space an island.

Kolt stood up and walked over to the door and cracked it open. He reached into the cargo pocket of his Crye Precision G3 combat pants and yanked out a half-empty pouch of Red Man. *It's going to be dark soon,* he thought as he pulled three fingers of leaf and slipped it between his cheek and gum. Another day come and gone with little to show for it. Too many days had gone like this for the thirty bearded Delta operators. Sequestered in relative secrecy inside a small area of Jalalabad Airfield, it was easy to imagine being stranded on a very desolate island. Worse, rescue did not loom on the horizon. With the United States and Afghanistan signing a security agreement years earlier, control of military operations was moving over to Afghan forces. American troops and equipment were departing the war zone at a rapid rate. But not for the EOD troops out on Thunder Turtle, and definitely not for spec-ops troops like Delta. Like it or not, they were here to stay. And as long as al Qaeda still threatened either the fragile Afghan government or, more importantly, the security of the United States, operators would be sticking around.

A noise made Kolt turn. Bravo guys were hooting and pointing at something on the screen. Kolt squinted to get it into focus, then shook his head. Based on the blurred heat signature, it appeared as if one of the donkeys was getting it on with another one.

Kolt checked his watch and figured they had about another hour or so to go. One more hour of this mind-numbing sitting and waiting for something to happen before dusk fell and Thunder Turtle turned and headed back to their FOB. This was his life at J-bad. Hours followed by days of boredom, punctuated by sporadic short-notice, quick-strike missions in the more dangerous and unforgiving parts of Afghanistan. It had been that way since their first deployment after 9/11. Even with a decade of Groundhog Days behind them, and Osama bin Laden taken out two years earlier, not much had changed.

In Afghanistan during the twenty-first century, just as during centuries before when Alexander's legions were there, adrenaline rushes could be served up in a moment. One minute the troops could be watching a column of armored vehicles crawl across a lunar-like landscape, and the next they could be engaged in a bitter firefight with insanely reckless insurgents. If it came to that, Kolt knew he had a hell of an advantage.

There was a lot of experience inside the tent that night. Four of the five members of Bravo Team had spent close to twelve years rotating back and forth from the States to Afghanistan as part of Operation Enduring Freedom. The newest operator on the team had just done over four years of combat time. Moreover, in between the months of hunting the ghost-like Taliban and al Qaeda fighters, they all had seen years of harsh urban combat in Iraq and had eaten plenty of brownout in east Africa. Along with the valor awards, most had TBI (traumatic brain injury) from eating too many IEDs or wall-breaching charges to prove it. And most, if not all, figured they were sure-bet candidates as future sufferers of PTSD.

Unlike Afghanistan, Iraq was an operator's paradise. There was always something to blow up, someone to rescue, someone to kill. Intel nuggets uncovered from one raid dominoed to the next raid and then the next raid and so on. More times than not, almost before they returned to their sleeping quarters, savvy intel analysts had added some previously unknown individual to the link-analysis poster of foreign fighters and Shia militia leaders. For most the war, pace in Iraq was missed, but for some the lines between right and wrong were blurring, and killing had become either too sport like or numbing.

Now, on this cold late-winter night in northeastern Afghanistan, all but one of the team members sat on their asses. The only one earning his hazardous-duty pay, Shaft, was three hours and forty-five minutes away.

Unlike the rest of them, Shaft was working the sexy Tier One target—the one with National Command Authority attention.

"Shaft make his last comms window?" Slapshot, the burly troop sergeant major asked Kolt.

"Last check he was still looking for jackasses," answered Kolt, barely turning from the screen. He tilted his head, placed his upper lip delicately over the open end of the empty water bottle, and deposited a stream of Red Man leaf-tobacco juice.

Without looking up from the latest copy of *Maxim* magazine, Digger jumped in. "Shouldn't have trouble with that in the Hindu Kush."

"Dude, the four-legged kind. It's a long walk down the valley," Slapshot answered as he shook his head in mock disgust. "Although if that pair become a ménage à trois, who knows?" he said, pointing at the flat screen.

"A ménage à what?" Digger asked.

"A frickin' three way, dumbass!"

"Yeah, the number of appendages is about the only difference," Digger quipped back as he dropped the magazine to his chest to steal a look at his troop daddy.

Kolt chuckled, careful not to appear to take sides between two assault-ers exchanging jabs.

"Think Ghafour is there?" Slapshot asked Kolt with an obvious change in tone. He was referring to the sixty-four-year-old Pashtun elder Haji Mohammad Ghafour, a terrorist they were keen to get their hands on.

"Who the hell knows, Slapshot? I guess I better believe it, or I should never have sent Shaft," Kolt answered.

"My money says he ain't, but don't start second-guessing your instincts now, boss."

"If you didn't think sending Shaft was smart, why didn't you pipe up?" Kolt asked.

"I've known you too long, Racer. It wouldn't have mattered what I thought," answered Slapshot.

Kolt didn't answer, turning his attention back to the plasma screen and Thunder Turtle. He knew he pushed it more than most. It had gotten him in trouble more times than most, and many an operator could credit their Silver Star or Purple Heart to one of Kolt's impetuous command decisions. He knew some of his calls hadn't played out as planned. Several of his mates whose names were engraved on the unit-memorial wall in the garden were daily reminders to everyone who walked the Spine of Delta compound. Even so, his men knew he was an action magnet, drawing fire exponentially more times than most troop commanders, and if you were still in Delta after ten-plus years of war, you pretty much recognized two absolutes: you were either divorced or about to be, and running with Kolt would guarantee trigger time or a body bag. It was still a volunteer organization, and selection was an ongoing process.

With the war in Afghanistan still going after twelve years and counting, and with the most wanted man in the world, the al Qaeda chief Osama bin Laden so much fish food, the targets for Tier One outfits like Delta had changed. The new number 1 on Delta's target list was the Egyptian doctor Ayman al-Zawahiri, Z-man as he was known in SOF circles. He'd taken the reigns of al Qaeda soon after bin Laden was killed and was still at large. Ghafour, a relatively unknown entity until recently, had rocketed up the list because of his long-term relationship with Z-man.

Despite the intelligence, no one knew where either man was. Rounding up former acquaintances of targets had long been an operational method for American special operations forces. Some referred to the targets as the "low-hanging fruit." The hope, and it often was more hope than anything else, was that they would reveal something about the targets above them. Over the years, the technique had mixed results.

Finding Ghafour could very well mean finding Zawahiri, but recent intelligence had revealed that finding Ghafour was becoming crucial for an entirely different reason. The CIA no longer considered Ghafour simply low-hanging fruit.

After nearly a year of combing through the treasure trove of computer files, hard drives, thumb drives, and handwritten documents in Arabic that SEAL Team Six had taken out of bin Laden's hideout in Abbottabad, Pakistan, information about Ghafour had surfaced. Hidden within Osama's extensive pornography collection, an analyst with insomnia discovered encrypted general plans linking Ghafour to the planning of attacks on commercial nuclear power plants. Two of the plants were located in Europe, but three others were only referred to by a crude code using the letters X, Y, and Z. The analyst and Kolt agreed one hundred percent, figuring X, Y, and Z were almost certainly in the U.S. of A.

It was enough to get the president's attention, as well as the attention of every leader of America's allies. And since the recent international uproar, when the rogue Syrian regime used sarin gas on its own citizens, showed that there was only a limited appetite from the "coalition of the willing" for responding to international incidents, POTUS couldn't afford to be soft on a potential attack on American soil. Unlike much of what was discovered in Abbottabad that night, which was declassified and shared with the world, every important acronymed organization or agency that listed national security as one of its core responsibilities agreed that the MTSAK files, curiously pronounced "empty sack," should remain top secret. Truth be told, just as he didn't with the civil war in Syria, Kolt didn't give two shits about Haji Ghafour, until the connection to the homeland was uncovered. Otherwise, he would never have asked Shaft to hang it out on a singleton mission in the Pakistani badlands.

"Maybe we should roll up and squeeze those donkeys," Kolt said, watching as the animals finished their afternoon delight and set off on a path that would intersect with the column of armored vehicles. "Did they get a good look at those animals?" Kolt asked Slapshot, knowing he had an earbud in while monitoring the Thunder Turtle radio transmissions.

"Yeah, Racer," Slapshot said. "Just three run-of-the-mill donkeys. Nothing strapped to them, and there's no way they'd get enough explosives in them and have them move around like that."

"Rog, I guess not," Kolt said, growing uneasy all the same as the donkeys wandered down from their rocky rendezvous and out onto the road being cleared. The Huskies, fifty yards away, slowed, not that you could really tell.

The lead Buffalo edged over to the right side of the road, no doubt because of the top gunner's begging to get in a shot at the animals, at least to scare them off. The image on the flat screen blossomed into a roiling white cloud, obscuring the entire column.

"Fuck!" Kolt shouted, gripping the water bottle so hard it cracked, spilling the tobacco juice over his fingers. As the cloud dispersed, the Buffalo could be seen nose down in a large crater a full five yards wide.

"Damn, that one is gonna hurt," Digger said, easing forward until his nose almost touched the screen. "The Buffalo looks intact, I mean, probably lost the right front wheel, but the tub looks solid. Any casualties, Slapshot?"

"Stand by. They're trying to unfuck it now."

Slapshot was bent over, his right hand pressed against his ear as he listened in. He looked up a half minute later. "No criticals or KIAs. Driver probably has a broken ankle, and the rest are pretty banged up, but otherwise they're good to go."

Kolt relaxed. A thousand yards behind this column was a second one composed of three more Buffalos and a pair of twenty-nine-ton MRVs, mine-resistant recovery vehicles. They were essentially wreckers on steroids, each heavily armored and sporting a huge thirty-ton lifting boom in addition to recovery and drag winches. Thunder Turtle might not be fast, but it was well prepared.

The second explosion marked the last moments on earth of the three donkeys.

"Damn, the donkeys were rigged. Triggerman must have gotten jumpy and hit the button too soon," Slapshot said.

Kolt was about to agree when tracer fire crisscrossed the screen. A lot of tracer fire. Several smaller explosions appeared among the column of armored vehicles. One appeared on top of a Buffalo. Several secondary explosions from within the Buffalo followed, ripping the armored beast to shreds.

"They're dumpin' mags and frags," Kolt said, confirming to the others that they'd met their trigger to launch.

"Christ, it looks like they landed a mortar round right through the gunner's hatch!" Slapshot said as he scrambled out of his bunk.

Kolt was already racing out the door. "We launch in ten!"

TWO

"Kit up!" Kolt shouted, already moving to the door to get back to the ready room.

Slapshot held up a hand as the men of Bravo Team began to move. "I've been keeping tabs on the flight status, and we're in for a wait. They launched the ready birds an hour ago on some support mission for the ANF. And then a CASEVAC flight took fire and one of their Black Hawks declared lame duck and had to sit down. Flight ops launched two Black Hawks to assist. They are saying it'll take at least an hour to get a couple more preflighted and spooled up."

Kolt stopped and turned to face Slapshot. "I don't care if they have to use duct tape and rubber bands, but I want another Black Hawk ready."

"On it, boss!" Slapshot said as Kolt left the tent, the rest of Bravo Team in his wake.

He ignored the cold as he quickly trudged across the compound to the ready room. He started to bitch about the half-baked planning that had left Thunder Turtle in this predicament, but he stopped himself before he got worked up. Recriminations could, and did, come later. Right now, he had to focus; he had to get switched on.

Kolt stepped through the door and made his way to his plywood cubicle at the far end of the room. He chose that spot because it let him look over his mates as they got ready. If anything, or anyone, was having trouble or having second thoughts, he'd spot it. He quickly began the ritual his muscles knew by heart. It didn't matter if it was training or the real deal like tonight, kitting up was always done the same, and with intense focus. It was a bit like a superstitious ball player who always laced up his cleats the same way while chewing four pieces of spearmint gum, tapped his cleats with the bat barrel, or opened and closed the Velcro on his batting gloves between each pitch. The big difference in a Delta operator's case, however, was that lives, not batting averages, were on the line.

Kolt took a moment to survey his kit, making sure everything was where he placed it after the last mission out the door. Sitting upright in the middle of the cubicle were his assault vest and body-armor plates, which, like a Roman soldier's breastplate, were heavy and sturdy. They didn't shine, but they were impressive all the same.

His rifles and hoolie tool were leaning against the back of the cubicle, rifles muzzle up with the Magpul rifle magazines loaded and stacked neatly against the sidewall. His tactical tan Gen4 Glock 23 pistol sat unloaded on its side with tan hard-ball-loaded magazines next to it. Handheld OD green smoke canisters, thermite grenades, frag grenades, and nine-bangers were stacked on top of each other in cardboard boxes. It wasn't pretty, but it was practical, and after all these years it still brought a smile to Kolt's face.

His two radios in their chargers blinked green, indicating fully charged batteries. The quickest way for a Delta troop commander to step on it was to launch with tits-up radios. To Kolt, that was almost as bad as having a weapon with no ammo. If you couldn't communicate with your assaulters or snipers on target, you weren't leading shit.

Spare batteries for everything from the weapon optics to NVGs to GPS to Peltor (ear pro) were neatly taped or otherwise secured to the appropriate piece of gear or stuffed in a pocket on the vest. Door charges, both rubber-strip charges and an eighty-four-inch ECT charge, were rolled neatly and secured with a rubber band. Fuse igniters were on the opposite side of the charges until ready to be connected. Kolt made sure to put the igniters in pockets opposite the strips, just to be extra safe.

He paused, letting his eyes unfocus as he listened to the bustle of Bravo Team kit up. This wasn't the loud, flashy scene of a sports team. The men were quiet, their conversations low and to the point. Hollywood and the moviegoing public would definitely be disappointed if they saw this. Satisfied that shit was straight, Kolt patted his left shoulder pocket, making sure there was at least a third of a pouch of Red Man tobacco there. He also felt the CAT tourniquet and hoped he wouldn't need it again. Letting his hand slide down his body, he felt in his left trouser pouch for the silk escape-and-evade map of the surrounding area, along with three hundred dollars in gold coins and his "blood chit," written in a half-dozen local languages, including Arabic, Farsi, Urdu, Pashto, Russian, and Hindi. In the age of jihad, you had no idea whom you might run into, and depending on their affiliation, the prevailing winds, and the mood of whatever god they prayed to, it could all go south in the blink of an eye. Gold, however, had a tendency to put a twinkle in any man's eye.

Kolt unfastened his black nylon utility belt and retucked his shirt into his Crye combat trousers before retightening his belt. Next, he secured the looped end of his elastic safety line to his belt buckle and ran the nylon around his waist before securing the snap-link end to the belt loop in his lower back area. In the event of a helo crash, hard landing, or abrupt maneuvers by the pilot of whatever aircraft he was in, Kolt was assured he'd ride that baby all the way to the ground, as long as he clipped in.

He heard the door to the ready room open and the sound of running boots. Slapshot arrived, a smile on his red-bearded face. "We got a bird! We launch in six minutes!"

"Good deal," Kolt said, before thinking about Master Sergeant Jason "Slapshot" Holcomb's physical condition. It had been about a year since the two of them had wrecked the Durango SUV during a high-speed chase of Daoud al-Amriki in northern Mexico. Slapshot took the brunt of it, leaving him with a broken cheekbone and left arm, as well as massive internal injuries. He spent six months in a medically induced coma, and nobody was entirely sure he would pull through.

"You wanna sit this one out, Jason?" Kolt asked.

"Kiss my ass, Racer," Slapshot shot right back. "If I wanted to sit it out, I would have stayed in Fayetteville and been closing down Huske's Hardware House about now."

"Your call, bro."

Kolt nodded his approval and went back to his kit. He didn't want to launch without his troop sergeant major, but he wanted to be sure Slapshot was good with it. Putting the thought behind him, Kolt picked up his call-sign patches with their luminous letters and affixed them to the Velcro on his shoulder pockets. He bent down and picked up his assault vest by the shoulder pads and spun it around. He pushed on the CamelBak water-reservoir sleeve to ensure it was full and then lifted the vest over his head, sliding his arms through the armholes. He grabbed the Fastek buckles on either side and connected them before pulling the running nylon ends tight to snug them to his body. He wondered if all those centuries ago Roman centurions experienced the same reaction he did when the armor went on. He suspected they did.

Kolt grabbed his two MBITR AN/PRC-148 radios, pulling them from their chargers and checking to ensure the frequency of the one he placed inside the radio pouch on the left side of his vest was on the troop internal net, or lower frequency, while the one he slid into his right-side pouch was set for the upper squadron command frequency.

"I could be an astronaut after this gig," Slapshot said, scrambling into his gear.

"Astronauts eat powdered food, Slapshot. You'd suck at it," Digger said.

Kolt hadn't thought about that, but with all the kit they strapped on, it did remind him a bit of the suit-up procedures he'd seen on documentaries before a space walk. He brought the mouthpiece of his CamelBak up to his lips and took a sip. Flat, warm water entered his mouth. He knew some guys put in Gatorade and even Red Bull, but he was old-school, and plain old H_2O was his drink of choice when turning targets.

"They're still swapping fire," Slapshot said, monitoring Thunder Turtle's firefight while getting dressed. "RPGs, mortars, and AKs. And . . . ah, shit! It's starting to snow."

The ready room got quieter. "How bad?" Kolt asked, amazed how easily Slapshot could see that a thermal screen. Despite all the tech and all the advances, snow was still a bitch to fly in. If it got too bad, the bird wouldn't be cleared to take off.

"Not a lot, but it's only going to get worse."

Kolt cursed under his breath. "This just gets better and better." He turned back to his cubicle and grabbed two mini frag grenades and two nine-bangers from the box and placed them in the pouch custom sewn over his soft-armor V-shaped groin pad. A dozen years ago, the first time he did that, he felt a bit queasy, but now he didn't think twice about it.

He picked up his tan 5.56mm thirty-round Magpul magazines and placed them into the four single-mag pouches on his stomach, bullets down and facing to the right to facilitate a fast mag change with his rifle. He left one mag on the shelf for his rifle. Grabbing the two extra .40mm fifteen-round Glock 23 mags, he put them in the two pistol-mag pouches, again, bullets down and facing to the right.

"How's Thunder Turtle?" Kolt asked, fitting his Peltor ear protection in place over his long brown hair. He pressed the ON button on the rear of the right earpiece and then clapped several times close to his ear to ensure they worked properly. They did.

"Holding their own, but they've got three seriously wounded," Slapshot said. "A Pedro flight has been launched, but they won't get clearance to land until the LZ is safe. They're already talking about loading the wounded and driving them, but that would take hours."

"Then we need to be airborne ASAP," Kolt said, routing the Peltor radio cables through the Velcro fasteners and attaching the push-to-talk to the nonfiring shoulder area of his vest.

The door to the ready room burst open. "Helo is ready in three mikes!"

Kolt picked up his Glock 23 and power stroked it three times, bringing the slide to the rear firmly each time to ensure the pistol was unloaded and spread the thin lube across the slide grooves. He raised the pistol and put the front site on a one-by-one-inch piece of black tape on the wall to his front and dry-fired the trigger. In one fluid motion, he inserted a magazine of .40mm, power stroked the slide to allow the first bullet to move into the chamber, and then thumbed the mag release and dropped the magazine into his off hand. He set the pistol in his holster, inserted another round into the mag to top it off, and then unholstered and fully seated the mag until he heard and felt the distinct click. Then he holstered the pistol again.

Kolt reached for his helmet, patting the subdued American flag attached with Velcro to the right side and the call-sign patch affixed to the rear. He turned the helmet over and smiled at the picture he carried of his grandfather during World War II in its webbing. It was comforting to have his grandfather looking over him. He flipped the helmet right-side up and pressed down on the IR glint tape to make sure it was firmly attached, then placed the helmet over his Peltors and fastened the chin strap.

He pressed the release to lower his NVGs in front of his eyes to make sure they activated automatically and that the compass function set itself. Satisfied, he raised the NVGs back up, locking them into place, then removed the black plastic dust covers from the ends of the two lenses and placed them on the shelf.

He paused, taking a deep breath and then slowly exhaling. Focus was the key. Details mattered. Rushing around like a chicken with its head cut off would get you a similar fate. Centered and calm, Kolt reached for his HK416 rifle, thumbed the selector switch, and then put two fingers on the charging handle and pulled it to the rear three times to ensure the weapon was clear. He knew it would be, but he did it anyway. You always checked a weapon when you picked it up, always.

He picked up the last 5.56 mag and inserted it firmly into the magazine well, giving it a tug to ensure it was fully seated, then pulled the charging handle to the rear one more time and let the bolt slam forward, pushing the top 5.56 Hornady TAP 75 grain bullet into the chamber. He tapped the forward assist with his right palm before moving the selector switch to the safe position and closing the ejection-port cover.

Kolt raised the rifle and powered on his EOTech optics to ensure that they worked before powering them back off. Looking around the room again, he removed the infrared cover from the tactical-weapons light secured to the right side of the upper receiver and pressed the ACTIVATION button to ensure the light worked before placing the cover filter back on. He did the same with the IR laser and floodlight on the top side of the upper receiver.

Bravo Team was almost ready. The men were going through their final checks, every one of them intent on his weapons and gear. Kolt nodded and tugged on the sling to ensure it fully extended, checked the setting on the collapsible stock, then slid his left arm into the sling and held the rifle just off his chest while he adjusted the sling to snug before releasing the rifle.

Kolt keyed the push-to-talk button to make a radio check with the team and confirmed all radios were working and everyone was up on net. He turned the top-sided channel selector on his higher radio one click to

the right and made a check on "Helo Common" with the air-mission commander.

"Baller Two-One, this is One-One. Over"

"Go for Baller Two-One," replied the chief warrant officer 4, Bill Smith,
a longtime buddy of his.

"Smitty, how's the snow?" Kolt asked

"Racer, if there wasn't an active firefight with wounded, I wouldn't be
launching," Smitty said.

Kolt knew it had to be close to blizzard to hear that from Smitty. He
decided not to push it.

"Got it, partner. We roll till you pull. Your call as usual," Kolt said.

"Roger, ropes pinned and stowed, ready for customers," Smitty said.

Kolt pulled his quarterback armband over his left forearm and opened it
to reveal the GTG, grid target graph, of the target area. Reaching the end of
the ritual, he turned back to the cubicle and removed the three-by-four-inch
full-color, red, white, and blue American flag velcroed to the plywood shelf
and affixed it firmly on the Velcro portion on the midchest area of his vest.
The large Old Glory was a throwback from the early Delta operators, and
Kolt and many of his men felt obliged to follow their lead. Finally, he walked
over to the fridge, grabbed a Red Bull energy drink, turned to the men who
also had cans or bottles of their preferred energy drink in their hands, and
toasted, "Here's to us and those like us—damn few left!" They chugged,
then tossed the cans in the corner trash bin.

Kolt looked around at the black-clad warriors and then turned for the
door—then uncharacteristically hesitated, turning back to his men.

"Anyone think Shaft has a better deal tonight?"

THREE

The Black Hawk carrying Kolt and Bravo Team put them down on a rocky hill six hundred yards to the west of Thunder Turtle's position in a swirl of snow. Kolt was already unclipped and out the door before the helo's balloon tires gently touched the ground. Nine times out of ten, helos got you where you wanted to go, but they were just big fat targets when they landed. Every second on an unmoving helo in a combat zone was ass puckering.

Ricocheting tracers bounced into view over the low ridgeline that blocked Kolt's position from the Taliban ambush site. An eerie orange glow marked the location of the destroyed Buffalo. Kolt had had the pilot put them down in a downwind position from the Taliban ambush point behind the cover of a small ridge. He kept his eyes on the ridge, searching for the telltale spark of enemy fire, but the Taliban had focused all their energy on Thunder Turtle.

The Night Stalker's custom MH-60M Black Hawk's twin General Electric T700 engines whined as the pilot poured on the power and launched the helo skyward while the last assaulter exited the bird. Kolt buried his head and closed his mouth as stones and sand pelted him. It was never a good feeling for those few seconds when tons of whirling death hovered over your head.

"I'm betting they didn't see us come in," Slapshot said, coming up beside Kolt and tapping him on the shoulder as the windstorm created by the departing Black Hawk dissipated into the cold mountain wind.

Kolt looked up at the ridge, flipping down his night vision goggles. The Taliban must have figured the snow would keep any kind of immediate rescue from reaching Thunder Turtle. Or they simply planned to make a mess and melt back into the village before American air power could get on station. Either way was good.

"The helo just radioed Thunder Turtle our position. They know we're here," Slapshot said.

"Rog," Kolt said. "Now, let's let the Taliban know we're here."

Kolt, Digger, and the team's sole sniper, Stitch, took off, moving down the hill into the small gully before the ridgeline. It would have been a suicidal move in daylight, but in the dark and with the enemy blind and focused elsewhere, it was a calculated risk. Actually, it sucked, but it beat the hell out of trying to put the helo down on the X. That had been tried before, and a lot of good men paid the ultimate price. Still, if the Taliban had even a single spotter on the ridge watching their rear, Bravo would catch hell. Kolt, impetuous and even reckless at times, wasn't stupid. Half of Bravo remained on the hill covering the other half as they made their way down the hill and then up the ridge.

Slapshot whispered over Kolt's earbud. "Racer, movement on the ridge, your eleven o'clock."

Kolt froze. AK fire mixed with the heavy pounding of a 40mm grenade launcher on one of the armored vehicles while a gunner blazed away on a loud-ass .50. The rest was lost in a wind that was picking up speed and, with it, more snow.

"Shit, lost it."

Kolt eased his head back and looked up and to the left. Blowing snow and wavy shadows from the flames of the burning Buffalo on the other side were all he could see.

"Well?" Kolt asked, easing his HK416 into a more comfortable position against his shoulder. He looked out of the corner of his eye and saw the two other Bravo Team members with him had frozen in place as well. Stitch's nearly six-foot frame with superwide shoulders cast a long moon shadow several feet in front of the larger Digger, who was humping a twenty-two-pound M249 light machine gun with a MultiCam soft bag loaded with two hundred rounds of linked 5.56mm and his twenty-six-pound black medical-aid bag.

"I was sure I had a head and upper body, but I can't see shit now," Slapshot said.

"Can you rifle lase the spot for us?" Kolt asked from under his nods, wanting Slapshot to activate the IR laser on his rifle and put the narrow unseen beam on the enemy position.

"Marked. You got it?" Slapshot asked.

"Got it."

Kolt kept scanning the ridge, but if the Taliban spotter was there, he'd gone to ground.

"Fuck it. Let's move," Kolt said, pumping his legs to climb the last sixty yards to the top of the ridge where Slapshot had focused his IR laser. If there had been a spotter there and he'd seen them, then there was no time to lose.

The snap of rifle fire echoed over his head, and he knew it wasn't a stray round from the firefight on the other side of the ridge.

"Three Turbans on the ridge—your ten o'clock!" Slapshot shouted as Digger opened up with the M249 LMG. Expended links and brass from the rapidly fired 5.56mm rounds zipped through the air above Kolt's head, the copper bullets stitching the ridgeline, which was now just eight yards above him.

Kolt dropped to his knees and grabbed a frag grenade. He yanked off the tape tab, pulled the circular pin, counted to two, and airmailed it up and over the ridgeline to where the Taliban should be.

There was a sharp bang and the whir of stone and dirt flying through the air. "We're moving up the ridge," Kolt said into his mike, standing up into a crouch and running the last eight yards. He didn't go directly at the Taliban position but angled to the right, hoping to flank them, reaching the ridgeline fifteen yards to the right. He flopped down onto his stomach and stuck his HK416 over the edge and looked over.

The bodies of two Taliban fighters lay sprawled on the rocks. Brain matter hung out of the back of the head of one of the fighters while the other was faceup, his sightless eyes staring into space. Kolt thought about eye-thumping the other one but opted instead to hold what he had and put two suppressed rounds into him for insurance before turning to scan for the third Taliban. He spotted him thirty yards away, scrambling down the ridge like a scalded ape, his left hand clutching his right shoulder. Out of the corner of his NVGs, Kolt saw Digger fire a short burst, all three shots hitting the fighter between the shoulder blades. The fighter went facedown and didn't move, impressing Kolt given Digger's main job in the troop was medic.

"Slapshot, three crows down. We're good," Kolt reported as he studied the two lightly clad dead fighters nearby. It always amazed Kolt how the Taliban were acclimated to the freezing temperatures—how they lived and fought in the same thin layers of clothing, seemingly oblivious to the seasons.

"Rog," Slapshot whispered back.

"Push up a hundred yards to the north on the ridge. That'll give you cover and a good view of the road and the gully behind us."

"Got it, Racer, moving!" Slapshot said.

"It's like a fucking circus!" Stitch said, cutting in over the net as he deployed the bipod legs underneath his custom semiauto sniper rifle and settled in behind it.

Kolt saw what he meant. The road below was awash in light from flaming wreckage. The Buffalo that took the mortar round had ripped in half, strewing its contents over forty feet in every direction. There was no way the crew survived that, and Kolt knew it must have been something a lot nastier than a single mortar round. The Buffalo that tripped the IED tilted nose down in the crater caused by the explosion, but a gunner was manning the weapon in the turret, so that crew looked as if they'd be OK. The rest of the vehicles appeared intact and were pouring out a heavy stream of fire as tracers zipped over their heads.

"Those guys obviously brought a shitload of ammo with them," Kolt said, surprised that the troops in Thunder Turtle were still firing a cyclic rate well into the ambush.

"Sounds like they brought their balls, too," Stitch said, obviously impressed with the combat tenacity and guts of the American troops below them.

Two mortar rounds landed on the road between a Buffalo and a wrecker but did no damage beyond scratching the paint. That was the horror of mortar rounds. With a little cover and distance they were harmless, but if they impacted on you, it was lights-out.

Kolt knew immediately this wasn't going to be the typical drop-in visit. If the three Taliban they smoked and left to freeze in the snow didn't convince him, what he saw now certainly did.

"Slapshot, this is One-One. Push up and tie in to our north. Over."

"Rog. Moving," Slapshot sarcastically replied, as if to say, *It's about time.* Kolt didn't take it personally, and he knew he would laugh about it later at the hot wash. Besides, operators like Slapshot, or any Delta operator for that matter, didn't strap it on and hang it out just to sit in overwatch on a distant ridgeline.

"Boss, I've got an RPG team moving toward the convoy," Stitch said.

"Be sure, Stitch," Kolt said, subtly reminding his sniper to positively identify friend from foe before he squeezed. Master Sergeant Clay "Stitch" Vickery was one of the top snipers in the unit for sure, but Kolt didn't need a blue-on-blue out here.

"PIDed, boss. I'm taking the shot."

Kolt didn't see them, but he didn't have Stitch's 20/15 vision. He did wonder why he hadn't heard from the Joint Operations Center. The ISR feed into the JOC back at J-bad from the circling Predator B drone at ten thousand feet above the ridgeline should have picked up the fighters before Stitch.

"It's all yours," Kolt said, focusing his attention on an AK flash some two hundred yards away and getting radio comms established with the Thunder Turtle commander.

A solid thwack marked Stitch's first shot exiting the suppressed end of his Heckler & Koch PSG1 7.62 mm sniper rifle. Two more shots followed in rapid succession.

"Three done. Confirmed," Stitch calmly said over the radio.

Kolt cycled through several frequencies, counting the clicks to the correct channel, looking to reach Thunder Turtle.

"Any station, any station, radio check. Over," Kolt said into his mouthpiece.

"This is Thunder Turtle. Who is this?" a very obviously scared and lower-ranking voice said.

"Thunder Turtle Actual, this is friendly American unit, call sign Mike One-One, on the ridgeline to your immediate east. We've got IR strobes on. Can you identify?"

"This is Private Ahrens. Our commander is dead. We need to get out of here."

Kolt quickly keyed the mike, but paused and released the button. He wasn't sure why. If for no other reason than to make the mental adjustment that the troops firing rapidly in front of him likely had less command and control than he thought. And that made things a lot less warm and fuzzy for Kolt and his mates.

Kolt keyed the mike a second time.

"OK, Private Ahrens. We're here to help. Listen carefully. This is what I need. Break," Kolt calmly said as he released the mike for a second, then pressed it to talk again.

"We've cleared the high ground on this side. Tell your squad leaders to look for our IR strobes and make sure they understand we are friendly. Over."

"OK. Yes, sir. We've got serious wounded, and we're getting low on ammo."

"Got it, partner. Now confirm to me ASAP that you guys have eyes on our strobes. Over."

Dirt and snow kicked up a few feet away from Kolt, and a fraction of a second later he heard the sizzle of the ricocheting bullet. The Taliban were aware they no longer held the high ground all to themselves, but Kolt was more worried that the troops from Thunder Turtle were mistaking Kolt and his men for the enemy.

Kolt thumbed the button to transmit over the troop internal net.

"All elements, sounds like the Turtle commander is KIA. His RTO is up on comms but pretty shook up. They haven't PIDed us yet, so hug the rocks," Kolt said, tracking another muzzle flash and firing several rounds at it. The hammering whine of talking SAWs told him Slapshot's group was now on the ridge as well.

"One-One, this is Slapshot. We're in position, and we copied your last. Holy shit, there's bad guys everywhere!"

"Focus on the north end of the ridge," Kolt said, following a shadow through the snow that looked to be carrying another RPG. He ran his mag dry and reloaded. He couldn't tell if he hit him or not.

"One Mike Mike, we're picking up a lot of Taliban chatter. They have decided to back off."

Kolt ignored the kid's inaccurate use of his proper call sign. The young soldier was amped up, and understandably so. Kolt turned his eyes up to the top of the far ridge and trained his HK416 on it. The Taliban were fierce fighters, but they no longer had the upper hand. Every moment they stayed meant risking American air power and artillery raining down on them. They'd set out to do what they meant to do and now wanted to get the hell out of Dodge.

But they weren't moving up the ridge opposite Kolt. Under nods, Kolt quickly scanned both sides of the valley floor, looking for signs the enemy was actually bugging out. Nothing. Kolt wondered whether the chatter Private Ahrens had reported was bullshit. Before he could overthink the problem, movement at the bottom viewing portion of his nods grabbed his attention.

"Shit! They're coming at us!" Kolt said aloud to himself before grabbing his push-to-talk and sharing the word with the others. Immediately, Kolt switched radios and keyed into the Turtle frequency.

"Turtle, Turtle, Cease fire. Cease fire!" Kolt said. "Hold what you got. They are bugging out."

Through Kolt's other ear, he heard the last part of a question.

"Last calling, you were stepped on. Say again. Over," Kolt said.

"Boss, what's the call. I count three dozen, minimum. We bolting or what?"

It was Slapshot. Slapshot, like everyone else lying on that snowy ridgeline, anticipated Kolt's giving the order to unass the high ground.

"Stand by!" Kolt said quickly. It was a common tactic of his. Put everyone, and everything, on hold while he ran the options and the risk through his head. He'd been here before, dozens of times. Hell, every one of the wide-awake Delta operators on the ridge had. Five against three dozen? None of them liked to run from a gunfight. Kolt knew that much about his men. But what were the odds?

"Kolt, fast movers are on station, but the CG wants you to come up on Green SAT first. He sounds a little bent," Slapshot said.

Kolt fingered the knob on his higher radio and turned it three clicks clockwise, picking up a transmission already in progress. The voice was familiar. It was the JSOC commanding general.

Great timing. What the hell does he want? Kolt thought.

A silhouette of a man appeared thirty yards below on the ridge through Kolt's NVGs. Kolt activated his lime-green infrared laser and put the tip of the invisible beam on the figure's chest, center mass, but before he could break the five-pound trigger, the man threw his head back and collapsed to the ground as blood gushed white from the wound in his neck.

Nice, Kolt thought, traversing his rifle farther along the lower part of the ridge, looking for more targets. He spotted motion and began pumping rounds. The falling snow was making it increasingly difficult to see.

More Taliban broke from cover and raced farther up the ridgeline. Kolt saw three more Taliban go down.

Kolt swapped out his magazine for a fresh one before turning his attention back to Admiral Mason and Green SAT.

"I'm seeing a lot of Taliban," Slapshot said with obvious emphasis on the graveness of the situation. Kolt didn't respond, keying the mike to engage the commanding general.

"Capital Zero-Six actual, go for Mike One-One. Over," Kolt said firmly, conscious of the inflection of his voice and controlling his nerves.

"This is Admiral Mason. Put the officer in charge on the radio. Over," Mason said with an obvious frustration in his voice.

Kolt thought it was an odd request. *Who the hell did he think he was talking to?*

"This is. I'm a little busy. Send it," Kolt said clearly, in no mood for giving a lesson on radio protocol to the new JSOC commander.

"I have cleared hot close-air support. Move your men four hundred meters to the south to reach safe standoff," Mason directed.

Kolt did the math. Big bomb, danger close. Not only the Taliban on the lower crest of the hill would be vaporized, but he and his men would be toast as well. And very likely the men of Thunder Turtle, especially if the GPS-guided bomb was even slightly off mark, which they were notorious for. Moreover, moving away from the ridgeline, and away from the approaching Taliban, would surrender the high ground to the enemy. Within minutes, they would be at the mercy of the enemy, who would be plunging fire into the valley floor as they retreated.

"What's the call, boss? We gotta do something!" Slapshot said.

"OK, here's the play. Slapshot, contact the fast mover. Wave him off; check his fire. We go online here. The moonlight is to their back; mass our fire toward the enemy," Kolt said before releasing the push-to-talk to think about the next step.

"Fuck, Kolt, I advise against that. You wanna reconsider?" Slapshot said with a little irritation in his voice.

Actually, Kolt wasn't sure. It seemed doable. It was basic infantry shit. Everyone get shoulder to shoulder at double-arm interval and mass the entire group's firepower to the front. But that potentially left their flanks unprotected, and certainly their rear. But if Kolt knew anything about leading hardened Delta operators in war—and few would disagree that he knew more than most—he knew enough to trust his instincts. Only once, and it was bad, did he make the wrong call. He lost men on that op, and he paid a dear price himself. He wouldn't let it happen again.

"Negative. We are holding here. Check the fast mover. Prep frags and hold your fire till I make the execute call. Let them think we bugged out, get about ten meters from the crest, then we'll unload on 'em," Kolt said, hoping like hell it didn't sound like he was making this shit up as he went. If he was out there flapping, the response from his men would confirm it.

He patiently waited for responses. He knew the troop's sergeant major, Slapshot, was the key. If Slapshot supported the call, the rest surely would.

"Kolt, you're jacked up. But I'm too old and cold to run away now. I'll check the fast mover," Slapshot said.

"I'm in," Digger said.

Stitch followed. "Let's knock the ugly off plan A and make it work. No time for plan B."

Kolt smiled. Proud of Slapshot. Proud of the entire team. Hoping like hell he hadn't bit off more than he could chew and condemned more of his men to death. The unit wouldn't accept it again, nor could he live with himself if, for a second time, he had the blood of his mates on his hands.

Kolt and his men didn't have long to worry about it. Thunder Turtle had stopped firing minutes earlier. It was eerily quiet, short of the sound of the howling winds at altitude. And the hushed Pashtun voices that could be heard well within hand-grenade range.

The Taliban were talking. Either they thought Kolt and his men had left the area, or they simply didn't care. Their voices were frantic and loud at first, several men either arguing with each other about what to do next or discussing how in the world the coalition hadn't shown up with the attack helicopters or bombing planes yet. And then, moments later, twenty something enemy fighters stood from behind the rocky outcrops, slung their AKs over their narrow shoulders, and began walking directly up the hill, heading for the house and morning prayers.

"I think we are all seeing the same thing," Kolt whispered into his mouthpiece. "Keep it simple, basic ranger-school shit. Wait for the command, then dump two mags each in your lane, then lob your frags. Slapshot, you throw long; I'll take short. The rest take center mass, key your mike if you understand. Over."

Kolt listened for four distinct breaks in squelch. One, two, three, four.

The enemy closed on Kolt and his men, completely oblivious to the Americans' presence, stepping on one rock after another as they delicately placed each foot as they ascended.

"Execute, execute, execute!" Kolt said.

The five Delta operators unloaded simultaneously into the group of enemy fighters. They watched through their nods as their green IR lasers settled on the torsos, dropping two and three at a time—some falling backward down the ridgeline and out of sight, a few slumping forward to lay facedown and lifeless on the large rocks they had hoped to safely negotiate.

As Kolt and the others reloaded to dump a second mag into the group, faint cries and moans could be heard from the mass of enemy lying to their front and below. One fighter yelled out, *"Allah u Akbar!"* Then a second fighter followed suit. *"Allah u Akbar! Allah u Akbar!"* Kolt couldn't help but be impressed with the enemy's dedication and commitment to their cause as he emptied his second magazine into the group and yanked the safety pin from another frag.

"Allah u Akbar my ass, motherfuckers!"

Kolt tried to listen for voices or signs that some of the enemy survived the ambush, since he gave the "cease fire" command about a minute earlier. There was no more of the distinct sound of AKs or Thunder Turtle's gunners raking the ridge.

As the last operator-tossed frag detonated among the rocks, snow, and ravaged enemy fighters, the mountain grew strangely quiet. The sound of the wind took on an eerie quality. Echoes of gunfire still rattled around in Kolt's head, but he couldn't hear anything new.

"Racer, it's Slapshot. I've got Baller Two-One. They've got a CASEVAC helo inbound. Twenty minutes."

Kolt nodded. "Good. Take your team and push out another two hundred yards on the ridge. I don't want any Taliban sneaking back to take a shot at the helo."

Kolt listened in on his radio as Thunder Turtle talked to Baller Two-One. Four dead, another four wounded. Kolt heard movement behind him and turned to see Slapshot approaching from his rear. The veteran warrior's thick beard was obvious in the ambient light as he dropped to his right kneepad near Kolt.

"Happy birthday, sir!" Slapshot whispered. "Forty is old as hell."

"You would know, Slap," Kolt said.

"Nobody buys the farm on their birthday, but you are a crazy man. I wasn't sure that would work," Slapshot said.

"Thanks for the vote of confidence, and for the record, I wasn't sure either."

Slapshot laughed quietly, shaking his head side to side. "You call the CG back yet?"

Kolt hadn't called Admiral Mason back yet. He wanted to, sort of, just was too busy to think about it.

"What now?" Digger asked over the radio, breaking Kolt's train of thought.

Kolt looked at his watch and then at the snow-filled sky. "Now, we stand watch over Thunder Turtle until dawn. Think warm thoughts."

FOUR

"It's gonna take two days for my ass to thaw," Slapshot said, walking stiff-legged around their lounge area back at base. "That was the coldest damn night I've spent in years!"

Kolt sipped his mug of coffee and smiled, wondering if Slapshot was still suffering from the severe injuries he'd sustained a year ago while chasing Amriki in northern Mexico. It had been cold. His cheeks were still burning, probably a touch of frostbite. Still, compared to those four poor souls in that Buffalo, he and Bravo Team were fine. Stiff, cold, and tired, but fine.

"Twenty-eight confirmed dead," Stitch said for the fourth time. "Twenty-eight Taliban fucks in the ground."

Kolt nodded but didn't engage. Snipers were an odd lot. Maybe it was all the attention to detail, but numbers mattered to them in a way that only accountants might understand.

"Maybe that'll get us a mission now," Slapshot said to no one in particular. "They got any Taliban in Tahiti?"

"We'll be off our butts and busting Pakistani airspace in a day or two," Kolt answered with a bit of nervous confidence. He was proud of last night's work. They'd kicked serious ass and come out intact. They were ready. But the final word wasn't yet in from Admiral Mason about how things went down out there. Sure, twenty-eight was a helluva score. Kolt knew it. Everyone knew it. Even so, whether the new commanding general was impressed or pissed at the perceived insubordination was yet to be seen.

"Still optimistic after all these months? I think I recall hearing that from you a couple of times before," Slapshot said, rubbing his butt as he walked.

Kolt didn't blame him. The odds of their ever receiving authority again to launch a Delta assault force across the Afghan-Paki border were slim.

"I don't know, I doubt the commanding general will pull the trigger and actually send us," Digger said, sitting up and throwing the *Maxim* toward Slapshot. "All yours."

"Yeah, what's the new admiral now, one for thirteen with execute authority?" Slapshot added.

"Would have been two for two with Team Six by now, though," Stitch added, simply to remind everyone, as if they needed reminding, that admirals are to the navy as generals are to the army. The implication being that Admiral Mason favored his high-strung, hard-drinking, throat-punching SEALs over the army's more reserved Delta Force.

"That's bullshit," Kolt said, before cautioning them all. "Besides, don't say that too loud. Shaft might hear you."

Shaft, Bravo Team's second in command, was a Green Beret medic prior to being selected for Delta's ranks. Even though he was a full-fledged Delta assaulter now, the guys around the compound often spoke of his skill with the scalpel. He had a knack for it. Medicine was his true passion. Sure, it was completely contradictory to his current job as a counterterrorist operator. He was paid to kill, not paid to heal. But, nevertheless, his Delta buddies weren't complaining.

Shaft was from Boston, Massachusetts, where two things were preordained even for those born in the Back Bay neighborhood: One, the hot summers of a boy's formidable years were spent pretending to slug walk-off grand slams over the Green Monster in left field of Fenway Park, home to the Boston Red Sox. The Red Sox were heroes the equal of the mythical Odysseus or venerable Zeus around all parts Boston. But it was largely seasonal devotion.

Two, as soon as the pennant race ended and the World Series was decided, the ball bats and gloves were traded for hockey sticks and pucks. And if things didn't go the Red Sox's way, the Garden, home to hockey's Boston Bruins, was conveniently set up with beer maids, testosterone tests, and fellow fans that placed a premium on yelling until hoarse and on generally making complete asses out of themselves. For some reason, even when the Sox had a banner year, things inside the Garden never changed when "the Bs" cut the ice.

Several members of Bravo Team now lounging in their tent could practically kiss Shaft for giving up his hockey dreams as a kid. Instead of slashing and cross-checking to inflict as much pain as possible on an opposing player, the urge to heal his fellow man became irresistible. He was better at baseball, anyway, and because he was a black boy, albeit a light-skinned one, growing up in the Northeast, the neighborhood troublemakers tagged him as Shaft. The early-70s action-hero film about a New York private eye seemed to fit just right. The nickname stuck. And, like any code name in Delta Force, it's never a personal choice.

When Slapshot took a 7.62 mm round through his right hand in Syria while aiding the Free Syrian Army in early 2011, it was Shaft's quick thinking and care that doctors ultimately credited for saving the limb. Sure, the world-class pistol shooter had to switch shooting hands, which he had bitched about, of course, but the hand stayed.

Just a few months later, back in Afghanistan, the team was on a quick-reaction mission to rescue a compromised Canadian reconnaissance patrol when the helicopter was struck by a rocket-propelled grenade as it searched for the embattled troops. The helicopter was forced into a controlled crash-landing, and Shaft went to work

The helicopter pilots had few good choices for where to put her down and tried to stick a landing in between some high rocks on a rocky ridge-line. A flying piece of a main rotor blade sliced a crew chief's left leg clean off above the knee. Had Shaft not immediately noticed, the young sergeant would have bled out within a minute.

Today, however, while the others recovered from their firefight on a chilly mountain in northern Afghanistan, Shaft's medical skills were in high demand 123 miles away in a remote village nestled in the deep bowels of the

Goshai Valley in Pakistan. It would take another twenty-four hours, though, for the villagers to realize they'd need him.

"To be honest, I'm not convinced the admiral should give us the green light," Stitch said suddenly. "Ghafour doesn't rate in my book."

The comment wasn't entirely unexpected from one of the operators in the tent. Nor was it exclusive to Stitch. And that last point certainly wasn't lost on Kolt Raynor. Kolt knew to let it go, chalking it up to the valued and time-tested uniqueness of the Delta selection process. Everyone, regardless of rank, was required to think, to contribute, to excel. They were also required to both speak their mind and maintain thick skin.

"It's just another HVI, fellas, no better or worse than the hundreds before him. We roll till our tour is up and we pop Ambien on the freedom bird back to CONUS," Kolt said, keen to not single out Stitch, but sure to let his men know he was still pushing the optempo even on what seemed like their hundredth deployment to the badlands.

HVIs, high-value individuals, was JSOC's way of saying "most wanted." In a way, Stitch was right. Delta was trained to go deep, go dark, and terminate the very baddest of the bad. But not to kill and tell. At the moment, the fact that Haji Mohammad Ghafour topped that list didn't impress Stitch. Ghafour's position there was remarkable, since he had been an unknown person to the CIA or even inside the SCIF at Joint Special Operations Command in Fort Bragg, North Carolina, just a few weeks before.

Along with roughly eight hundred other residents, Haji Ghafour called the deep Goshai Valley home. Located in the upper stretches of the North-West Frontier Province, almost eleven miles due east of the very northern tip of the notorious Konar Province in neighboring Afghanistan, it wasn't exactly a hot vacation spot featured in the latest edition of *National Geographic*.

Transportation was limited. Locals rode donkeys or walked. American commandos might choose the same or take their chances inside a helicopter. But the vast rugged terrain, similar to that in the mountains of neighboring Afghanistan, offered few flat and level landing spots larger than the size of a living room rug. Naturally, nobody was pushing the idea of infiltrating by parachuting in.

It took a few days to flush out the tactical plan. Sure, Kolt and the boys could be wheels up on an air-assault raid within thirty minutes if the intelligence was good enough. But a mission to build that intelligence packet required covert reconnaissance and thus more delicate handling and a great deal of patience.

Shaft was the obvious choice. The color of his skin didn't hurt either. Under the cover of darkness, a helicopter inserted the seasoned operator high in the snow-covered mountains roughly three miles northwest of that godforsaken and forgotten village known by mapmakers as Drosh, Pakistan. From the JOC back at J-bad, Kolt was following his progress as best he could on the terminating end of Shaft's daily updates when they were available. Kolt was impressed that Shaft had successfully walked to Drosh and presented a letter signed four months earlier by Haji Ghafour himself. The meat of the letter was a request for humanitarian assistance for the villages up and down his valley. In a major coup, the CIA had intercepted the letter a week ago. It provided a solid cover for Shaft, and everyone back at the JOC, except Admiral Mason most definitely, knew he could pull it off successfully.

Traveling solo and masquerading as a non–government agency doctor, Shaft had packed accordingly. From his helicopter insertion point, Shaft humped a large civilian backpack filled with basic medical supplies, a wad of rupees, a small Glock 26 9mm, a single hand grenade, a small digital camera, an infrared pointer, a Thuraya cell phone with spare battery, and an iPad 4.

Now, three days into the operation, Shaft was making sufficient progress—just enough to keep everyone on their toes back at J-bad. From the JOC, the J-staff was able to monitor Shaft's exact location via a satellite link to the iPad 4 in Shaft's bag. The technology is similar to the conventional military's Blue Force Tracking system, but the GPS module is embedded in a new highly secretive program known as Raptor X, the U.S. government's version of GIS mapping capability with multilayer application capability. If Google Earth was classified and on steroids, it would be called Raptor X. And that logic module was fully embedded in Shaft's iPad 4, allowing Kolt to at least track the iPad 4 down to ten meters' accuracy, as long as it was powered on and registering, which would be enormously valuable if they had to launch an in extremis rescue of his man on the scene. If something got ugly for Shaft, as long as he kept the iPad 4 with him, Murphy's Law could be managed.

Although unsuccessful in obtaining pack mules or porters to accompany him to the target valley, he linked up with a few armed locals who offered to escort him to Haji Ghafour. Allah may provide a cure for every disease, but everyone loves a medicine man.

Kolt's cell phone rang. The ringtone was the theme to *Shaft.*

"Everyone shut up!" Kolt shouted, grabbing the Thuraya cell phone and pushing the little green button to answer. The team crowded around him.

"Hello?"

"Steak and lobster tonight, isn't it?" Shaft asked with his typical ice-cold demeanor and quirky sense of humor.

Kolt smiled wide. "Ha! Not till the night after tomorrow, bro, but it's good to hear you have things under control." Kolt knew Shaft wouldn't be wisecracking unless he did.

"Yeah, well I'm sure the rest of the team is already standing in the chow line."

Kolt smiled and nodded in agreement but ignored the comment. "Status?"

"My friends and I have reached the mouth of the valley," Shaft said, passing the official word that all was well and on track.

Kolt figured he must have caught one of those overloaded but colorful Jenga trucks on the Chitral–Dir road. The ride would have been backbreaking, but it would deliver him to the mouth of the Goshai Valley. From there, however, the next five miles to Ghafour's village was all on foot.

"Yeah, we have a positive track on you. That was quick!" Kolt stated, letting Shaft know that the iPad 4 location was pinging just fine.

"Saddle sore?" Kolt asked.

"Nope, the public transportation out here works smoother than New York City. You don't even have to tip the driver."

Kolt smiled. "Good to hear. Save your juice. Talk to you tomorrow at seventeen hundred hours," Kolt answered as he made eye contact and bumped fists with the team members standing around him.

"Enjoy the steak!" Shaft shot back as Kolt removed the phone from his ear and mashed the red END CALL button.

Fayetteville, North Carolina

Sergeant Cindy "Hawk" Bird was becoming paranoid. So she thought, anyway. She was certain she had seen the black four-door Mercury Grand Marquis three times now while she had run some errands on the military base and hopscotched Fayetteville while shopping. The gorgeous day was much welcomed, one of her few days off over the last several months. After three weeks of mind-boggling TDY in Rockville, Maryland, home of the Nuclear Regulatory Commission, where she reviewed pressurized and boiling water reactors, the fission process, and what exactly were the key components that Delta would need to take out should POTUS order a covert attack on Iran's nuclear program, she hoped for a long weekend to unwind and snuggle up with a good love story around the fire.

With the ongoing conflict in Syria escalating for Delta, she, along with a select team of fellow unit members, was swamped. This was exacerbated because of her formal military training as a chemical, biological, radiological, and nuclear specialist. The sarin-gas issue ensured she would be knee-deep in the mission analysis. She wasn't bitching—she knew part of the deal with the unit was maintaining her quals in everything nuke or internationally banned chemical weapons. Truth be told, though, she yearned to be overseas in Afghanistan doing something to help with the war effort. She didn't know what exactly that would be. There wasn't a lot of operational or tactical necessity for someone with her skill set or looks, but she figured she'd learn something new just the same.

Thumbing her iPhone 5 as she passed through the food court before exiting the main entrance, she marveled at how glorious a day it had become. If the sun held, she thought she might take in an hour or so poolside to even out her farmer's tan after hours of flat-range pistol work at the secret Delta compound located in the upper left quadrant of the sprawling nineteen square miles of Fort Bragg, North Carolina. Nothing bugged her more than the distinct tan line separating her biceps from her wide, muscular shoulders. But that would have to wait for much warmer days because, even though the sun was strong enough to make her slide the white Costa Hammerhead sunglasses off her head to protect her eyes, February in Fayetteville usually floated between a frosty 33 to a cool 47 degrees.

The vehicle seemed a little out of place in the Bragg main-exchange parking lot, where she first noticed it. Late-morning Wednesdays weren't a busy time for the exchange, which typically meant the parking lot was fairly empty. The vehicles usually seen there at that time of the week were dated pickup trucks, complete with prominent black-and-white stickers of U.S. Army Airborne wings, or the red, white, and blue AA stickers showing they were a proud former member of the famed 82nd Airborne Division. Retired military personnel who chose to remain in the Fayetteville area liked to represent. Besides retirees, military spouses driving family-focused minivans, with some of the better-off spouses tooling around in a full-size Chevy Tahoe or GMC Yukon, populated the parking lot before the normal lunch crowd.

She hadn't been able to get a look at the occupants, though, since the Mercury's windows were tinted, but the not-so-discrete government license plate gave her pause. When she first saw the Mercury, she had been more concerned with finding her keys in her loaded purse and with checking for a text message about lunch from her Green Beret boyfriend. But it was only about five minutes until she had spotted the same black Marquis a second time. Heading south along Bragg Boulevard, she slowed her vehicle to let the Marquis pass. Hawk watched in her rearview mirror as it slowed its pace as well, maintaining four to five car lengths behind but in the fast center lane. She checked her speedometer, making sure she wasn't getting too crazy and offering an easy speeding ticket to a bored Fayetteville police officer. Her gas gauge was showing just over a quarter tank, so she gunned it through the yellow caution light to cross two lanes of traffic and took a hard right into the Citco station on Shaw Road. She looked back toward Bragg Boulevard and watched the black Marquis continue south and out of view.

As she squeezed the pump handle and filled her tank, she zipped up the front of her pink sport fleece to take the chill off her neck. She brought her shoulders up toward her ears to further protect her from the strong winds coming from the east over Bragg Boulevard. Settling the gas pump back in its cradle, she realized she was missing something important.

"Shit! The damn bracelet," she said, not caring if anyone heard her. "Troy's gonna freak!"

Her 5th Special Forces boyfriend Troy was a gear Nazi and dedicated prepper, always good for a story of how the world is coming to an end and how it's important to be ready. Sure, the end of the world one day is a possibility, she reasoned, but she figured worrying more about her obstacle-course times and getting her Mozambique drill time under a respectable eight seconds were more pressing and realistic problems.

Troy had hand woven a bracelet out of pink and lime-green parachute cord, complete with an integrated whistle and flint fire sparker. Cindy wasn't all that impressed with it, but the colors weren't bad, so she vowed to wear it for Troy. She had no idea why or when she would ever need it. If the world came to an end, she was thinking she'd need more than a pretty bracelet to survive, but it's the thought that counts.

As Hawk turned from the pump and her attention back on her shopping day, she looked over the hood of her Beetle and watched the Marquis slowly drive past again, this time heading back north toward Fort Bragg and the main exchange.

Sure, Hawk had the advanced countersurveillance training under her belt. And she knew, simply given her sensitive position as a female unit member, that she was special. But out and about, away from the unit compound, she was just another hot brunette with olive skin and a tight ass. Out in the real world, she was simply Cindy Bird, not a commando code-named Hawk.

Even so, she vividly recalled Major Kolt Raynor hammering her on the finer points of countersurveillance shit as she rode shotgun with him in the narrow streets of Cairo last year, yet another Middle Eastern hotbed demanding attention. Kolt's incessant lecturing on the importance of looking for patterns, erratic driving maneuvers, U-turns or odd lane changes and the like annoyed her just as much as she knew it educated her. And now with the black Marquis six car lengths behind her again, she rapidly moved her eyes from the roadway to her rearview mirror at a speed-zone-respectable 62 miles per hour down Skibo Road and whispered Kolt's exact cautions.

"Same face and ride twice was a coincidence. Three times and it was a pattern, and patterns ain't coincidence."

But she chided herself for even worrying about it, shaking her head as much to break her paranoia as to move the side-swept bangs out of her eyes.

And it was kind of annoying that she was thinking about Kolt when she was off duty. *Get it together, Hawk. This ain't Cairo.*

Hawk looked up again and saw the Marquis slow, then turn north off Skibo and into a neighborhood side road. She would have been happy to leave it alone and refocus on her search for wicked pumps that would make Lady Gaga jealous if not for the light blue Ford Focus she was now observing through her rearview mirror. That car, with two clean-cut-looking gentlemen wearing dark sunglasses in the front seats, seemed to swap out with the black Marquis. The Focus followed her south, pretty much tailgating her, as she left Skibo, and it eased off her as she passed behind Luigi's restaurant on North McPherson Church Road. She watched the Focus close the distance again, practically rear-ending her as she turned west on congested two-lane Morgan-town Road before passing Carrabba's Italian Grill on the right. Hawk drove underneath the uber-busy All American Freeway, then north into the Cross Creek Mall entrance, and finally clockwise around the perimeter mall road. By the time she pulled her metallic-gray 2013 Volkswagen Beetle into a lucky vacant spot up front inside the crowded Macy's parking lot, her spider senses were at full ping.

Assholes!

Hawk knew one of two things. Either they were tailing her for un-known shady reasons or they wanted a piece of her tail. Either way, *it ain't happening,* she thought. She shook her head. She was being crazy.

If I'm about to get rolled up on one of those Delta training exercises, they could at least wait until I'm on government time.

The fact of the matter was, none of the males in Delta questioned Hawk's ability to take care of herself or even to take a punch. No, not after she breezed through female selection and assessment for the pilot program two years earlier. She was a quick study back then and since then had proved herself in hot spots like Libya and on target. This was put to the ultimate test when Major Raynor pulled a wild stunt during an AFO stint that quickly went from a simple mission to collect intelligence and atmospherics to a hastily planned low-visibility hit in the heart of Cairo. She had been tested. She had taken a man's life, two probably. Her classified personnel records even included a Defense Meritorious Service Medal with a citation mentioning the fact that she had saved the life of a fellow soldier—Major Kolt Raynor. Some of the die-hard graybeards weren't convinced she should be knighted as an operator, so the jury was still out. But, so far, she had been found not wanting by most of her male mates.

Hawk stepped her white sport heels down on the asphalt and lifted herself out of her Beetle. Out of habit, she checked her text messages again, kind of wishing Troy would have given her a nice set of fur-lined leather gloves instead of the prepper bracelet she'd left in her apartment, before slinging her patch-knit purse over her right shoulder and thumbing the wireless key fob. The reassuring audible double horn sounded behind her as she turned away and dropped her keys in her purse. She threw her shoulders back and tossed her bangs out of her eyes, wrapped the long scarf around her neck, and stepped off at a determined pace for the certain warmth of the women's department and the sale racks.

Jalalabad Airfield, Afghanistan

The members of the task force knew there wasn't much they could do for Shaft if things went to shit in the Goshai Valley. Kolt figured Shaft had enough battery power to last about three days or so; a few seconds daily to check in with enough juice to make the final Hail Mary call to get Kolt and the others on the helos and in the air to finally capture a key link to Ayman al-Zawahiri.

It suddenly occurred to Kolt why Admiral Mason might want to string him up by the ears. By charging off to rescue Thunder Turtle, Kolt had essentially removed himself from the operation to retrieve Shaft. Sure, other operators were briefed and equally capable of pulling Shaft out, but it was Kolt's op and Kolt's responsibility. And, true to his maverick nature, Kolt hadn't bothered to inform Mason beforehand.

Fuck.

The shit would have really hit the fan if things had taken a turn for the worse while Kolt was unavailable. Any unplanned calls could generate a lot of attention back at J-bad and would have the helicopter blades spinning in short order on an in extremis recovery of Shaft. Kolt had actually strong-armed those birds for the rescue mission last night.

The dark possibilities were starting to make him sick to his stomach, but Kolt had faith that Shaft could live his cover as a medical contractor and be anything but a seasoned Delta operator. As long as he remembered that his cover was the truth, and the truth was his cover, he would be OK. So far, so good. Things were clicking along as planned.

The following evening, Kolt was still sweating it out waiting for a summons from Admiral Mason when the *Shaft* ringtone lit up his Thuraya. He grabbed a pen and a pad of paper and sat down on one of the chairs in Bravo's lounge, which had become his new home. Shaft's voice was hurried. It was obvious to Kolt that the extreme cold was kicking Shaft's butt.

Shaft was all business. "Jackpot!" he said, passing the standard Delta code word signaling the targeted personality had been located, "with a nice family photo."

Kolt scribbled the letters quickly on the paper, raised it in the air, and showed it to the others standing nearby. "Got it! All OK?"

"Nothing big. I have a new roommate. Uh, er, more like shadow."

Kolt practically felt Shaft's violent shivering. He could hear teeth chattering through the Thuraya.

"Compromised?" Kolt asked. He felt more than saw the other operators tense up when he asked. To a man, they all preferred a straight-up firefight to all this cloak-and-dagger shit.

"They say my watch looks like the kind that American commandos wear," Shaft answered.

"Tell them American commandos only wear Rolexes," Kolt said, trying to calm Shaft's nerves a little. Everyone looked at Kolt: The smile kept them relaxed, but the comments confused them.

Sensing Shaft's nerves, Kolt tried to pump in some confidence. "Remember, you are the best damn dentist those folks will ever see."

Shaft didn't answer, but the comment generated more odd looks.

"Hey, real fast, weatherman predicts more snow in your AO," Kolt relayed.

"Is that what they call that cold white stuff that has been falling all day?" Shaft jabbed back with sarcasm, letting Kolt know his head was still in the game. The weather report was a little late.

"Alright, doctor, as soon as the moment is right, give a ring." Kolt ended discretely, reminding him to trust his cover for action and to call back as soon as Ghafour's residence was positively identified.

Kolt hoped they were a GO for the mission that night.

The good news was that Shaft had located Ghafour. And even though the experts couldn't produce a photograph of the tribal chief after four years of looking, Shaft made it look easy. But after several months dealing with the relatively new and risk-averse JSOC commanding general, Kolt worried that Shaft's job would be easy compared with trying to pull execute authority from Admiral Mason.

A short time later, an e-mail popped up on Kolt's phone. In living color, plain as day, it showed Shaft cross-legged and barefooted on the floor of a small clay house, a spread of lamb, rice, walnuts, and dried fruit laid out to his front. Book-ended by a smiling young Afghan boy to his right and a larger, more sinister-looking gentleman under a white turban to his left. *In honor of the visiting western doctor,* Kolt thought. Shaft was apparently showing one of the villagers his phone and how the camera function worked because three more photos popped in shortly after. All four showed Shaft smiling with several youngsters while Ghafour sat comfortably and unaware in the background.

It was the first known picture of their target.

Jackpot! It was a great start.

Nonetheless, even if he was the first American in years to lay eyes on the shifty and mysterious elder, they were still a long way from scarfing him up off the battlefield.

Of more immediate concern to Kolt were Shaft's hints at trouble. From the short daily cell phone updates, Kolt could tell Shaft feared the locals were on to him. Sure, Ghafour and his tribe had welcomed him with open arms. That was a regional cultural imperative, for sure. But the Pakistani elder also assigned him a roommate, who stuck around in the shadows. Watching—no, more like studying—the Delta operator's every move.

The fifth and final photo confirmed Kolt's suspicions. Three Pakistani men armed with collapsible stock AK-47s sat against one wall in the house. They weren't threatening Shaft, but it was clear they were keeping an eye on him and everyone else in the house. Kolt knew at once they would be Ghafour's personal bodyguards. Shaft was relaying fantastic intel. Now he just had to stay cool. Shaft wasn't asked to capture or kill Ghafour all by himself. He didn't have to invade Ghafour's personal space. He just needed to pass a building number per the grid on the satellite map.

"That's got to be enough for the admiral," Digger said, looking over Kolt's shoulder at the computer screen that showed a tiny bright-blue icon identifying the exact location of Shaft's iPad 4.

"We still don't know which house," Kolt replied. The intel had already narrowed down the possibilities to a dozen, any one of which could be Haji Ghafour's house. Shaft knew that going in and had now succeeded in making direct contact with their target, but that wasn't his house, or Shaft would have said so.

"Looks like building number seven to me, Racer," Digger said.

"Could be. But with the pictures Shaft sent, and assuming he has the iPad 4 with him, that might be just the party room. An old goat like Ghafour probably beds down out of hearing distance of the after party," Kolt said.

The hand-wringing and ambiguous decision makers back at the JOC would require a lot more than "he might be in one of several different compounds" before they gave the green light to Kolt and the boys to go on a cross-border air-assault raid. Hell, they almost didn't go after Osama, and they'd narrowed that down to one compound. Bottom line was that the intel had to be near perfect for a cross-border mission to get the nod.

"Shaft knows what he's doing," Slapshot said. "He'll get us the intel we need. You wait and see."

Kolt hoped Slapshot was right. The key was Shaft's iPad 4. To any villager or suspicious Haqqani, it looked innocuous enough and, more importantly, nonmilitary. To make sure no one tried to take it from him, Shaft had been drilled in using it in the open, showing villagers lists of medicines he was compiling to bring back on his next visit. It was a way to ensure he had their medical needs recorded and sanitize them to his constant use of the strange device. Rumors had been rampant for years on both sides of the border of targeting beacons discretely placed near enemy personnel or buildings to guide U.S. smart bombs to the target.

Kolt knew that Shaft would still end up fielding a lot of questions about it. To backstop his cover story, the iPad 4 was filled with medical charts, anatomy diagrams, and even short commercial videos of various drugs taken straight off the Internet and TV. What the villagers wouldn't see was the encrypted black-and-white satellite photo saved in the iPad 4. The photo was a very recent shot of Ghafour's village with bold white numbers super-imposed on top of each dark, shaded building. Once Ghafour was located and his bed-down spot pinpointed, all Shaft had to do was give Kolt a call, pass a single number, and then make tracks for the mouth of the valley and a black landing-zone pickup spot.

Shaft's latest phone call gave Kolt an uneasy sense as he waited. He had a bad feeling about this one. The Goshai Valley was a long way from Jalala-bad. He marveled at Shaft's individual courage. Only the best Delta opera-tors were selected for singleton missions, and Kolt had no better choice than Shaft. Guys had to be completely comfortable with their abilities. Outside help couldn't be relied on. A certain amount of conniving was necessary. A certain amount of "calm, cool, and collected" was a must. Lastly, the job required a whole lot of badass. Kolt knew he was unfit for the duty. It didn't really matter, though, as Delta officers weren't welcome in the singleton business, anyway. Solo operations were saved for the most seasoned Delta sergeants. *Just the way it should be,* Kolt always thought.

FIVE

Isolation Cell Black—Black Ice—undisclosed location

Cindy "Hawk" Bird's four-by-four-foot box leaked from the top. It leaked bad. But she was as comfortable in the water as a Navy SEAL, so water drops she could handle. Now, waterboarding—that was a different matter. She hoped it wasn't coming to that. But she knew she had been stubborn throughout her seventy-two hours in the box, including during five interrogations, for which she was strapped to a chair in a very cold and musty room. She couldn't be sure. Some of the bruises were certainly from her struggle with the two gorillas from the light blue Ford Focus outside Macy's. Others were from the interrogator, including the severe pain she felt near her floating left rib. But it wasn't the box, the raindrops, the hard interrogation tactics, or the awful stench of her own urine that was driving her crazy. No, those were unsettling, for sure, but it was clearly that damn baby crying for her daddy.

Hawk tried to adjust the angle of her long, unshaven legs inside the tiny-ass plywood box. She palmed both ears to drown out the loud screams of the wailing babies. Over and over, the same tape played. And it played loud. The only relief was the intermittent but unpredictable spurts of Middle Eastern music. Hawk recognized the variety of songs praising Liwa'a Abu Fadl al-Abbas, Syria's pro-Iranian Shia "International Brigade," which

43

curtly insulted nonbelievers and blatantly threatened the Syrian rebels. But given a choice, she'd take the music over the crying babies.

If this was the Delta-operator life she so wanted to be a part of, or "living the dream," as she so often heard the boys in the Unit say throughout the Spine, she was certainly having second thoughts. *How long have I been here. Is this just training?*

Actually, it had only been just under forty-eight hours since Hawk was rolled up. It's easy to lose track of time when you are in the box. Your ability to think clearly is conceded early. Tracking time is a bitch. Simple arithmetic is compromised. Trying to stick to your cover story while scooting away from your own shit is even dicier.

But it wasn't like she hadn't been warned. No, her superiors at Delta had made it very clear to her that selection was an ongoing process, and even though she had proved valuable to the command on several occasions now, she wasn't entirely accepted. There were still some naysayers. Older, very seasoned operators that had been around for decades, by nature, didn't impress easily. Old-school mind-sets that never believed the pilot program was a smart idea in the first place. Women had no place in the unit or on the battlefield, they argued. More so, in their eyes, women just got in the way of the male operators actually, well, operating. But the Delta commander, Colonel Jeremy Webber, saw it differently. From his perspective, Cindy Bird had validated his long-held assumptions that a female could help an operator ensure a successful mission. Webber wasn't looking for female operators, nor was he arguing that the Unit should even consider female operators. He just wanted the eye candy, but from a performance perspective only. No airheads. They had to be switched on. And as far as Webber was concerned, results mattered most.

Hawk's performance in Lybia at the fall of the Ghadhafi regime two years earlier, and the unique help she provided to Major Kolt Raynor and his AFO cell on the streets of Cairo, had been commended. Moreover, the fact that her performance had been widely talked about and debated inside the halls of the Unit validated Webber's every assumption.

In fact, Cindy Bird was the first female guest at a place called Isolation Cell Black. To the guards it's known simply as Black Ice. And, yes, it was training, vital training, for sure, but it was the kind that nobody really got a kick out of. You don't sign up for Black Ice; you don't put it on the training schedule. No, you don't find Black Ice; it finds you.

There were no time-outs at Black Ice. No potty breaks, no lawyers, and no phone calls home. And Black Ice, for the time being anyway, was still as big a secret to the members of Delta as the exact standards required to enter the ranks in the first place remained after thirty-five years. Guests at Black Ice had to sign a Special Access Program nondisclosure agreement, or NDA, when they were released. That is, if they could still steady a pen long enough to sign it. Speaking about it, the experience, or even its existence was forbidden. And, so far as Webber knew, after six out of the seven operators enrolled had survived, or graduated somewhat, the secret still held.

Hawk's wooden box offered no amenities—short of plenty of privacy, that is. Outside the box, pointed at odd angles, four large spotlights illuminated the hard right angles of plywood and cast long shadows on the dirty and paint-chipped walls. It did come with a single lightbulb cut into the center of the roof. Not that anyone was concerned about a detainee having enough reading light at night. The light was just part of the package deal. It never turned off, ever, and cast a short seven-inch-long shadow off the side of her half-gallon tin coffee can that held an inch of warm potable water. She had debated to use it as her personal Porta-Potty. But anticipating that the guards wouldn't find it amusing, and knowing that without water she would become delirious and rapidly lose strength, she opted to simply let nature take its course where she sat.

The package also included a twelve-inch-long metal chain secured to a heavy eyebolt in the roof. Just enough chain so that when the accompanying shiny handcuff was placed around Hawk's wrist, it kept her in an agonizing position. At some point, and she couldn't be sure exactly when, Hawk's left arm had become numb from her shoulder to her fingertips. Reaching up with her right hand to take the pressure off her wrist created by the cuffs was her only source of relief.

A small six-by-six-inch sliding window at the very bottom of the box provided her only view of the outside world. It also served as the entry point for the two lukewarm bowls of chicken broth she had received so far.

Most men don't come out of Black Ice with the same mental state as when they entered. The place wears on a man, any man. Hawk had no way of knowing this, of course, but inside her own box, she realized she was just as human as the rest of them. Black Ice wasn't picky about who it broke. It wasn't specific about religion, nationality, or even sexual orientation. No, Black Ice was an equal opportunity torture chamber.

Black Ice became a necessity after several Delta operators were captured in Pakistan years ago, when the MI-17 they were in was shot down by Taliban fighters in the mountains northeast of Gardez. The leader of that rescue team was LTC Josh Timble. Timble had been Kolt Raynor's mentor for years in Delta, and, in fact, it was Raynor's screwup across the border in Pakistan that led to TJ's and the others' capture. Black Ice wasn't around back then for TJ to benefit from, but thanks to his efforts and doggedness after his repatriation, the command recognized the importance of preparing Delta operators for captivity before they needed the skills. It was an insurance policy that, God willing, they would never cash in.

Hawk's mind was near collapse. She argued with herself internally about the importance of Delta, and even about how committed she was. Sure, she took a big step when she actually killed a man at close range in Cairo. That changed her, just as it changes every male operator. But she wasn't an operator. That had been made very clear to her by the command. Even Kolt Raynor had reminded her of that one night inside the Cairo safe house.

Maybe this Delta stuff is just as insane, just as inhumane, just as crazy as this fucking box. Is all this shit still worth it?

With her left wrist secured to the chain in the center of her isolation box's roof, weighing four pounds fewer than when she tried squeezing into the size 6 skinny jeans at the mall, and covered in dried shit from her earlier bowel movement, she wondered why she signed up for Delta in the first place. She could have just finished up her enlistment in the army like normal people do. *I think I made a big mistake.*

Jalalabad Airfield, Afghanistan

A few hours after taking Shaft's latest situation report over the phone, Kolt leaned over a large black-and-white satellite photo sprawled out on a wooden table. He had left the comfort of Bravo Team's tent, gained the wooden palette walkway that kept troops out of the mud during the rainy season, and half jogged the forty meters or so across the frozen dirt ground. He slipped around a short maze of concrete T-walls and sand-filled Hesco barriers designed to protect the place from incoming enemy mortar rounds before stepping up two steps and pulling aside the first of two large nylon flaps that served as the entrance to the Joint Operations Center.

Kolt moved quickly to the nearby long table to grab a cup of coffee. He emptied the GI-issue silver pot, giving him just half a cup, all the while ignoring the handwritten sign prominently posted just behind the half-opened boxes of Christmas care packages from home that read LAST CUP REFILLS THE POT.

Kolt balanced his Styrofoam cup, careful not to spill what little hot coffee he had, as he walked across the uneven floorboards toward the unwelcoming makeshift planning bay located toward the back of the tent. He passed behind five rows of tables, each crowned by a half dozen of the latest Dell laptop computers, perfectly aligned and alive. On the far wall, six large plasma flat screens played *Kill* TV on different frequency feeds. Somewhere in eastern Afghanistan and western Pakistan, a dozen armed drones captured every move of unsuspecting ant-size people of interest. Their every move opened to the sky was piped hundreds of miles into this single headquarters.

The JOC was the working domain of the joint staff officers that did the lion's share of the work. A 24-7 operation, the staff developed target decks, analyzed mountains of raw intel in search of a golden nugget, and assessed risk and monitored the entire battlefield—all with a single goal in mind: get Delta operators out in the badlands turning targets as fast and as often as possible. Pushing the operations tempo, or optempo, was the sole purpose of the J-staff. A unique mix of the distinct aroma of a Best Buy showroom, fresh plywood flooring, and sweaty, overworked adults on reverse schedule who rarely see the sun could be detected as soon as you opened the second flap.

Standing around him in the tight quarters and surrounded by plywood walls covered with giant maps of the major fighting spots across Afghanistan and western Pakistan, Admiral Mason and his staff listened intently.

"Buildings two, three, four, five, and possibly seven," Kolt stated with authority while pointing in succession with his unfolded Spyderco blade. Admiral Mason and the others hung on Kolt's every word with a focused gaze.

"We need to do better than that," Mason rhetorically stated as he shook his head side to side. "Your man needs to pinpoint the exact location, or I'm not authorizing a launch. I thought that was perfectly clear, even to you, Major."

Kolt was dumbfounded. He squinted in disappointment. *Fuck*. Fine, it wasn't perfect, but it was actionable. He looked first at Admiral Mason, conspicuously taller than the rest in the room, with a full head of brown but graying hair that never seemed to need a comb, before shifting to the others around the table, the task force planners, the JSOC Command sergeant major, and the helicopter force's air-mission commander.

It was the first time Kolt and Mason had been in the same room together in weeks. In fact, Mason had kept his distance from Kolt for the last few months. So much so that folks were starting to realize that the admiral wasn't Kolt's biggest fan. It was an astute observation and something not lost on most of the force, particularly after the admiral skipped the hot wash after the Thunder Turtle mission.

Kolt didn't necessarily have anything against the admiral. Well, besides the fact that he was a Naval Academy graduate, a fact not lost on anyone else in the tent since his obnoxious 1982 class ring stood out like a Dallas Cowboys Super Bowl ring on a newborn baby. More than the gaudy ring, most annoying to Kolt was the admiral's noticeably brand-new set of pressed Multi-Cam camouflage fatigues he always wore.

Midshipmen don't become flag officers by spending their formative years with their fatigue pants not bloused in their boots properly or their fatigue top sleeves not rolled down correctly and buttoned at the wrists. No, the quickest way to nonselect for promotion was violating military regulations on uniform wearing and appearance. Kolt often wondered if this was why very few former Delta commanders were ever given the reigns of the Joint Special Operations Command.

Mason had served the last four years holding down a desk job in the Pentagon. It was a two-star special operations billet requiring a bright white and pressed service uniform daily. Both the billet and the uniform fit him like a glove. It was one of the very few senior staff jobs that ensured he was read on to all JSOC operations. And, in turn, to Delta's top secret ops.

Which meant, of course, that Kolt Raynor's antics over the years were no secret to him.

Admiral Mason knew all about Raynor's stupid move in Pakistan that got several of his teammates killed and captured years earlier. He knew about the shady redemption operation, an unsanctioned operation, to locate and rescue his Delta teammates, including his best friend, Lieutenant Colonel Josh Timble, from a black site in Pakistan.

Mason was an action officer detailed to brief the National Security Council when the hijacked Boeing 767-400 jetliner tried to take off from an airfield in New Delhi. After hearing the details of how Kolt Raynor and three other Delta operators landed on the wide-body fuselage while it was moving, breached through the roof hatch, killed a half-dozen Pakistani Lashkar-e-Taiba terrorists, and rescued over 140 hostages, Mason knew that the army major needed a breathalyzer, piss test, and full psych workup.

And most recently, just six months ago, Mason had been part of the entourage when the president secretly visited the Delta compound at Fort Bragg, North Carolina, to thank them for taking out American-born terrorist Daoud al-Amriki. Of all Delta's successes since the war on terror began after 9/11, this operation was personal. Kolt and Josh Timble, in another off-the-books operation, this time on U.S. soil, prevented Marine One from being blown out of the sky just outside Andrews Air Force Base as the president returned from overseas. The president openly thanked the unit, yet everyone knew it was all Kolt and his buddy TJ. And Josh Timble didn't make it home.

Yes, Mason knew all about Kolt fucking Raynor. And nothing about the maverick Delta officer was to his liking. In fact, he wasn't too comfortable in Kolt's presence even now. Sure, Mason knew Kolt had a reputation for getting shit done, but it was Kolt's colorful past that made it all the more difficult for him to approve the mission the Delta major was presently seeking his approval on. Cross-border raids into Pakistan require POTUS approval, and even though most of the J-staff knew the president had pushed the authority down to Mason for the time being, Mason always seemed to play it like the call was still way above his pay grade.

In fact, if it wasn't for the incessant pestering from Washington, D.C.

about the status of finding Haji Mohammad Ghafour, Admiral Mason would have never approved Delta's plan to send Shaft into the Goshai Valley in the first place.

Kolt did a round of square breathing—fifteen seconds inhale, fifteen seconds hold, fifteen seconds exhale, fifteen seconds hold—before risking opening his mouth. He motioned a lazy circle with his knife. "Admiral, these five buildings are all within the length of a football field. We can land on both sides and clear each as we move to center." He wanted to add, but didn't, that it wasn't that much bigger than Osama's compound.

Almost as if he ignored Kolt's reassuring comments, Admiral Mason nervously tugged at his belt line. He didn't even bother to address Kolt by name.

"If we can't get more clarity on Ghafour's exact location, we'll have to wait for another opportunity," Mason said.

Kolt knew the admiral would be looking for an excuse not to approve the mission.

"Besides," the admiral continued, "the helos can't wait around that long. They will be out of gas before you ever get those five buildings cleared."

And that's based on your extensive ground combat experience.

Everyone froze. All eyes shifted toward Kolt. They knew Kolt was the assault force commander for this mission. They knew Shaft was his man. He had the most invested. None of his peers around the table dared say anything for fear of the admiral's wrath. Kolt recognized this. He wisely remained laser-focused on the facts and shied away from making this a personal confrontation with Admiral Mason. He swallowed noticeably hard.

Playing it as if he hadn't detected hesitation in the admiral's voice, he said, "Sir, our contingencies are clear. You approved them the other day. If we can't find Ghafour before the helos have to depart, then we'll clear them out of the area and we'll keep looking for Ghafour."

"You're suddenly very glib about the use of helos," Mason said, finally giving vent to his anger over Kolt's impromptu mission of Thunder Turtle.

Kolt didn't rise to the bait. "It's an acceptable risk, and it makes sense. The helo's can"—

"I don't want the helos having to make a second turn into that area," Mason barked as he tapped his long narrow fingers on the deep Goshai Valley area of the map. "Twice is a pattern. They will be sitting ducks for enemy rockets or crew-served machine guns a second time in that valley."

Kolt took a deep breath. "The plan, again, sir, is to walk back out the valley with Ghafour in tow." Then he piled on a bit. He scanned men around the table, pausing to momentarily lock eyes with each of them. "We all agreed on this the other day."

An uncomfortable silence filled the briefing room. Kolt felt this operation slipping away. He assumed attack formation.

Kolt looked up at the air mission commander, the same special ops pilot that dropped them into Thunder Turtle's AO, helicopter pilot Bill Smith, a longtime friend of his. "Smitty, can you get us in there or not?"

Smitty was a professional and not easily intimidated. "I'm pretty sure we can," Smitty said confidently. "At least the first time."

Kolt looked back at the admiral. He tried to curb the admiral's uneasiness a bit by pushing off his own assumptions and opinion as fact.

"Sir, we have a Delta operator alone in the Goshai Valley. He believes they may be on to him. Narrowing Ghafour's location down to five buildings in that shithole village is already a major success."

It was clear Admiral Mason wasn't too keen on trading comments with the Delta troop commander. But the Delta commander, Colonel Webber, was back stateside with the unit command sergeant major to chair the commander's board at Delta's selection and assessment. To join the ranks, you had to get past these two guys first. Webber would be back in country in a few days, but the mission would be long decided by then, one way or another.

In these circles, which were night-and-day difference from the halls of the Pentagon, Mason knew Kolt had a lot more pad speed than he did. The Delta officer had been running with this crisis-planning tactical stuff for many years now, starting well before 9/11. Mason also realized he had next to zero ground combat experience, much less any commando work on his résumé.

Most important, though, Kolt knew guys like Mason tended to be severely risk averse, and their personal indecision and discomfort with risky commando tactics took the wind out of a lot of sound missions before they were ever launched. Mason had only been in command of JSOC for about five months, but he already had the rep among the Special Missions Units and the Army Rangers.

In contrast, Kolt thrived off the challenge, but hated guys with the rep, realizing more often than not that the key to success was not the obvious actionable intel presented but rather stroking the ego.

Admiral Mason suddenly changed tactics by changing the subject.

"We are late for the twenty-hundred daily battlefield update brief. We'll take another look after tomorrow evening's phone call. Your man is prepared to walk back out of the valley the way he came, isn't he, Major Raynor?" Mason said before turning toward the tent flap and walking out of his makeshift office. It was the admiral's way of reminding everyone who was in charge.

No shit, sir! Kolt thought. *Shaft ain't hanging out for shits and grins.*

SIX

Nearly twenty-four hours later, Kolt was rapidly losing that warm and fuzzy feeling. Shaft had missed the commo window. More worrisome for Kolt and his mates was that the iPad 4 was tracked moving northeast up the Goshai Valley floor earlier in the day. The blue icon hugged the east of the river for several miles, jumped to the west side for a half mile or so, then back over to the east side for another eight miles before stopping for most of the day in a smaller village.

Shaft was three hours late by the time the key leaders met again in Admiral Mason's makeshift office. Again, they huddled over the map Kolt had brought with him.

"Anything new, Major?" Admiral Mason asked.

Kolt shook his head. "He missed his commo check tonight, sir. I'm not sure what's going on," Kolt answered, trying to maintain confidence. "Raptor X has his beacon strong, but it moved about fourteen miles down the valley."

"Hmmm," Mason mumbled. "Do you think he already initiated the exfil plan and is heading back out of the valley?"

Don't tell me he is actually holding in a grin about this.

"No chance of that, sir. His exfil route should take him west, not east, and he would have called first. He has at least twenty-four more hours of battery life," Kolt answered. "Something unexpected must have come up."

Admiral Mason traced his finger over the map as if in deep thought. Kolt looked at where his finger was pointing, but it wasn't anywhere close to the valley.

Mason looked up at the group. "Well, let us know the minute you hear anything. I suspect this one is in the bag."

Kolt could feel the mission slipping away. He wanted Ghafour bad. Ghafour was the key to potential strikes on U.S. soil. It was also the task force's best chance since Tora Bora of locating Z-man. Everyone turned and left the room without another word, leaving Kolt staring distantly at the map in front of him.

Life in Jalalabad continued at a maddening pace while Shaft risked his life on a solo mission in Pakistan. It wore on Kolt, but he had to keep up appearances for the troop. If he was antsy, that would only amp them up. Most of the operators hit the gym after breakfast. They waited for the weather to warm a bit before taking in some marksmanship practice on the flat ranges not too far from the tents in the afternoon. But Kolt had been on edge ever since Shaft inserted. He had spent the entire day inside the Joint Operations Center staring at either the Raptor X blue icon denoting Shaft's iPad 4 or the dedicated Predator B and MQ-9 Reaper feeds on two of the half-dozen flat plasma screens that lined the wall of one side of the JOC. If nothing else, Kolt was relieved that the iPad 4 had returned to Ghafour's village and was pinging almost equidistant between buildings 2 and 3.

Kolt noticed a lot of movement in the village. Nothing looked out of the ordinary for a Friday. Locals tended to their livestock, chopped the spindly sticks they used for firewood, and appeared to meander back and forth from one cluster of houses to the next or to and from the local mosque. Kolt assumed the lack of enemy activity was a result of the cold and snow.

Shaft's exact location was anyone's guess, but Kolt hoped to get lucky. Maybe he would pick up on a sign of the Delta operator if he just concentrated harder. Kolt didn't dare leave the screen. He even enlisted the imagery analysts to keep him stocked with hot coffee and spit cups.

Kolt also stared at the clock. Even more frequently as 1700 hours—the opening of Shaft's daily commo window—neared. He nervously checked the Thuraya's battery, resting quietly on the desk in front of him a dozen times. *Ring damn it!*

It had been almost thirty hours since he had spoken to Shaft. If he missed another commo window, Kolt feared the mission would certainly be aborted. Admiral Mason would demand it. More so than losing the chance to nab Haji Ghafour, Kolt worried about Shaft. Why hasn't he called? *C'mon, Shaft, help us help you, will ya?*

The *Shaft* ringtone startled a dozing Kolt. He knocked over an old spit cup reaching for his phone. "It's him," he said as the intel analysts came running over.

"Shaft." Kolt spoke first. "Are you OK?'

"My last battery is about out of juice," Shaft quickly but softly said. "I got tied up with a pregnant woman."

Kolt's shoulders slumped with relief. "That's gr"—

"Listen," Shaft said, cutting Kolt off. "The PC"—precious cargo—"sleeps in building five. He is tired and there now. There are a lot of guns here. I'll mark the helicopter landing zone with my infrared pointer." Shaft was calm and deliberate, but obviously hurried. "How soon until you guys can get here?"

"We're working on getting launch authority now," Kolt said, cringing at how pathetic that would sound to Shaft. "I'll check again as soon as we hang up."

"What?" Shaft was obviously shocked by Kolt's last comment. "Don't tell me I came all the way over here and . . ." The connection died.

"Shit!" Kolt looked at the LED screen on the phone, then quickly back to his ear.

"Shaft?"

"Hello, hello?" Nothing.

"We're coming, Shaft. We're coming," Kolt said into the phone, as if the line had not gone dead, staring intently at the static blue icon on the computer screen to his front.

It took fifteen minutes for the key leaders to gather in the admiral's sleeping area. Kolt paced the room looking for something to punch. The lack of urgency was killing him. He resisted the urge to remind folks about the single

Delta operator risking his ass while they enjoyed steak and shrimp night at the chow tent.

Not everyone had arrived yet, but Kolt couldn't wait another second. The others would have to catch up.

He leaned over the large satellite photo. Remembering he left his knife back in the JOC, he reached for a mechanical pencil and turned his head to Admiral Mason. Before he spoke, he detected a little steak sauce on the admiral's fatigue top and around his bottom lip.

"Admiral, Shaft missed tonight's commo window by a couple of hours," he stated with a slight pause. "But he did make it. Seems he had some trouble with a pregnant woman. Not sure what." Kolt could already see Admiral Mason wasn't impressed.

Kolt pointed to the satellite photo with the eraser end of the pencil. "Ghafour is in building five tonight. I request authority to launch immediately."

This caught everyone's attention in the room. All eyes shifted from Kolt to the admiral.

"How can he be sure of that out of all the buildings out there?" Admiral Mason asked in a condescending tone.

Kolt's blood started to slowly boil, and it had nothing to do with the admiral's personal space heater keeping his quarters uncomfortably warm. "It's why he's there, sir. He was tasked to find out where HVI number two was located and give us the building number. He's done that. It's time to act."

"Get him on the horn again," Admiral Mason ordered. "I need him to confirm the location before we execute this thing. We are pushing the envelope on this already. I must be sure before entering Pakistan."

Kolt's restraint snapped. "We can't, sir! His phone battery died while we were talking. This is our shot, right here, right now."

"I'm not comfortable with what little we have here, Major."

Kolt knew his mouth was wide open, but he couldn't believe what he was hearing. "Sir, are you serious? You have a Delta operator in harm's way that completed his end of the bargain. He successfully located the targeted personality. He successfully pinpointed his sleeping quarters. He has confirmed he is asleep in building five right now, tonight." Kolt paused for effect and to mentally gauge how many of Admiral Mason's buttons he could push before it all blew up in his face.

Mason locked eyes with Kolt. "Major, I hear you, but it's not actionable enough."

"Sir, this is probably more actionable than the bin Laden hit was, and the *empty sack* files pulled from Abottabad are pretty clear that Ghafour is more of a threat to the homeland than bin Laden was since September eleventh," Kolt said, trying to reason with the admiral and subtly remind him of how high the stakes were.

"Speculation!" Mason blurted.

Kolt continued. "Sir, we have a responsibility here to execute this mission. If Haji Mohammed Ghafour was important enough to send Shaft on a singleton mission four days ago, then how can the target not be important now?" Kolt took inventory of his inflection. He took a deep breath and broke eye contact with the admiral. No need to push it.

You could have heard a pin drop. Kolt looked around the room and could see that his passionate comments startled the others. All of the other leaders in the room knew who Kolt was. And most actually liked his aggressiveness and thought he was in it for the right reasons. But this didn't keep them from becoming shocked by Kolt's tone with the admiral. Well, everyone except the guy in command of the assault helicopters. CW4 Bill Smith stepped up.

"Admiral Mason, sir," Smitty said, his voice characteristically even-toned and without emotion, like all good pilots. "The aircraft are one-hundred-percent full-mission-profile ready. We are fully prepared and willing to execute this tonight."

Admiral Mason stared at Smitty for an uncomfortable ten seconds or so. It was clear Mason was searching for the guts to launch the force. Or the balls to court-martial everyone in the damn room. He turned to the JSOC command sergeant major, Sergeant Major Castor. Castor had been typically back-row quiet up to this point. He knew when to interject and when to let a subordinate commander like Kolt speak for himself. Castor served with Kolt in the Unit years ago before making too much rank and moving up to JSOC, scratching and bitching the entire way.

"Sergeant Major?" Admiral Mason asked as he turned to the senior and most seasoned noncommissioned officer in the command.

"I recommend we go, sir," Castor answered in his characteristic relaxed tone.

Kolt could barely hold back his delight. Smitty and Sergeant Major Castor were about to change the admiral's mind. They were going to execute after all. He could feel the tide shifting.

Admiral Mason finally spoke. "Damn it, gentlemen!" he barked. "Ghafour better be in building five."

Kolt pushed his luck a little. He rose up off his palms and instinctively reached down to his cargo pocket to pull out his chewing tobacco.

"We'll get him, sir," he said before turning to exit the admiral's quarters. Over his shoulder, he added, "Smitty, we'll be at the helos in five minutes, ready to load." He moved quickly for the door, leaving the others to work the final details and to deal with an aggravated commanding general. He also wanted to get out of there before Mason changed his mind.

SEVEN

Goshai Valley, Western Pakistan

It was a few minutes after 0200 hours by the time the two black twin-rotor MH-47G Chinook helicopters reached the entrance to the high-walled Goshai Valley. Wicked and steady crosswinds forced the pilots to gorilla grip the joy sticks as the crew chiefs kept a keen eye out the open-door gunner hatches for rocky outcrops and thermal signatures of enemy fighters. Either one could bring down the vulnerable birds in a second.

Just like any valley in Afghanistan, the horizontal snow flurries played tricks on night-vision-laden pilots as they pierced the airspace at 130 knots just a few meters off the deck. Visibility was only a hundred, maybe two hundred, meters. Since it was also under twenty degrees out, the weather made it about the worst possible night for an air-assault raid.

Piloted by air operators from the black 2nd Battalion, 160th Special Ops Aviation Regiment, the two lumbering Chinooks, affectionately termed Dark Horses by those in the community, came in from the northwest low over the first set of outlying mud-walled buildings. Snow-covered ridgelines peaking at fourteen thousand feet boxed them in from the north and south. The sketches on their knee boards told them there was only one way in and the same way out. But seeing it firsthand, away from the comforts of the planning tents, had a way of ripping your gut out through your throat.

After making the final left-hand bank into the village, the pilots eased off the sticks to slow the aircrafts' approach speed. Their motto, "On time, on target, plus or minus thirty seconds" was being put to the test once again. Smitty, running with call sign Ghost Two-One, now that the mission called for the larger, more powerful MH-47Gs instead of the smaller and sleeker MH-60M Black Hawks, strained under his night-vision aviator goggles to identify Shaft's green infrared laser that was to mark the correct landing zone.

There was a problem.

"Negative signal from ground," Smitty said over the radio.

Kolt looked back to the tinted minilaptop screen on the aircraft floor showing Shaft's iPad 4 location still strong and steady between buildings 2 and 3 before replying. "Rog, that."

Kolt checked his watch. The Night Stalkers were true to their motto once again, but their man Shaft was behind schedule.

Kolt tried to imagine Shaft's situation. He had to know they'd be coming, regardless of the fact that the authorization hadn't been given when they were on the phone. Maybe he decided to leave the iPad 4 behind for some reason and move to the landing zone without it? Shaft had to know Kolt wouldn't leave him hanging . . . he hoped.

Shaft's adrenaline button kicked in as he heard the telltale sound of helicopter blades powered by 4,868-shaft-horsepower Honeywell engines carrying on the cold night air. He smiled, but he wasn't able to enjoy the sweet sound alone for long. His roommate, the twentysomething Paki man that had been assigned as his minder, startled awake and opened his eyes wide. He didn't sit up; he just seemed to listen with one ear as the other rested on the dingy yellow covered pillow.

Shaft knew instantly what he needed to do. But he hesitated. The man was unarmed. He wasn't displaying any hostile intent just yet. But Shaft knew that would change in a second as soon as the kid realized the noise of the helicopters weren't just routine Pakistani resupply runs crisscrossing the mountain passes. Shaft stopped thinking and started to execute.

He quickly grabbed his backpack with his left hand, reached into the top flap with his firing hand and found the familiar handle of his Glock 26. Without taking his hand out of the pack, he shoved it with both hands hard against his minder's mouth. He tried to line up his aim, forced to guess the correct angle to the minder's face. Rapidly, he broke the Glock Ghost 3.5-pound trigger twice.

Two Remington HTP 9mm lead bullets tore through everything in their way inside the pack before slamming into the Paki's face. One entered just above the left eye orbit. The other one went through the right cheek. Both bullets pinballed around his skull but failed to exit out the rear. The man's body went limp in a second. The backpack hadn't muffled the gunshots as well as Shaft thought it would. He had never actually tried that before. But it did the job.

Shaft yanked the badly frayed wool blanket off the dead Paki, revealing his folded-stock AK-47 lying next to his torso. He grabbed it, placed the stock tight under his right arm, and dropped the banana magazine with his left hand. He press-checked the mag to see how many bullets he had, then rocked and locked the familiar metal magazine into the mag well and tugged firmly to ensure it was fully seated. Shaft tilted the weapon, took the safety off, and dropped his left hand underneath the receiver, finding the charging handle. He power-pushed the handle to the rear before releasing it, driving the top 7.62 × 39 full-metal-jacket round of the mag into the chamber. Better safe than sorry, he pulled the handle back just over an inch until he saw shiny brass, confirming the weapon was loaded, before releasing the handle.

Shaft patted the dead man's pockets, looking for any identification that would show affiliation with the Pakistani Taliban, Haqqani network, or Hezb-i-Islami. He felt something small but hard in his front breast pocket and pushed two fingers in to secure it. He looked at the white plastic-covered thumb drive, debated whether or not to take it with him, then decided to keep it and slid it in his backpack along with the Glock 26. Shaft threw on his wool hat and reached deep into his pack, fishing for the buried PVS-14 night vision monocular and the IR laser pointer.

"Shit!"

Shaft felt small pieces of sharded glass inside his pack. He opened it wider and saw the damage. Before both 9mm rounds tore into the minder's head, they had bored through the iPad 4.

Shaft closed the pack and pulled the drawstring tight. Holding both items in his left hand, he right-shouldered his pack and held the rifle in his right hand as he moved toward the doorway. He left the medical supplies he had brought all the way from J-bad sitting in the neat piles separated by type and size. He slung open the rusted door just in time to see the dark purple shapes of two low-flying helos against the snow-covered ridgeline over-shoot the landing zones by two hundred meters or so.

"I'm late!" Shaft whispered.

Shaft watched as the helos started into a hard left-hand turn. Without an identifying laser marker and with the extra foot of fresh snow on the ground that hid dangerous landing obstacles, he knew the helo pilot had little choice. Shaft knew they were positioning to execute a go-around and make a second attempt to find his laser mark and the landing zones.

Shaft began slogging across the snow-covered ground like a man in molasses. He was surprised at how difficult it was to run in the freshly fallen snow. It had been snowing since they returned from the complicated birth hours earlier, and he thought about dumping the AK or the pack, or both, before quickly reconsidering. The fierce and raw high winds pushing against his chest only made it all the more difficult with each step forward.

He reached Ghafour's mud-walled sleeping quarters and peered around the corner. He fumbled to activate the laser marker as he eyeballed the exact spot he wanted to land the assault helos. There wasn't any room for error. It was going to be a tight fit for both. But Shaft knew speed and location were essential. He wanted the assaulters to exit the back end of the helos right next to Ghafour's house. The last thing he wanted was for Ghafour to squirt out the back door and hide out in another of the three dozen buildings in the area. If that happened, he knew they were in for a long night of me-thodical searching. And if it hadn't been destroyed, he might as well throw his iPad 4 in the village well. Even if they got lucky and found Ghafour before he escaped, they faced even longer days and nights of walking back out of the valley with a noncompliant shackled man in tow.

"Holy shit!" Shaft intuitively hit the deck. His body practically flopped on the ground as if he were a kid again back home, turning somersaults in the snow. A rocket-propelled grenade had soared from a nearby rooftop, barely missing the tail rotor of the slow-moving lead helo by several meters. The warhead impacted harmlessly against the valley wall some fifty yards away. It was close. Too close. If Shaft had a radio link with the pilots, he would have aborted the infil immediately and been happy to walk home. Even Ghafour wasn't worth losing a helo full of teammates. But he didn't.

He watched as the lead helo flared then steadied over the small open area off the southern tip of Ghafour's two-story house. He placed his green spotting laser off the starboard side, sparkling the center of the landing zone. The pilot was in the right place, but Shaft wanted to confirm their good judgment. He figured it might be smart to let them know he was in the area, too.

Shaft nervously watched the helo as it seemed frozen in the air. He knew the pilot was desperately trying to ease her down without striking the rotor blades on the uneven terrain and adjacent buildings. Shaft pulled his PVS-14 night vision to his left eye and aimed it at the back of the lead helo. He could make out one crew chief on a knee on the tail ramp looking out the back. He knew that guy was the pilot's eyes in the rear.

Shaft also knew the operators were on their feet in the back of the helo up against the thin metal skin. As per standard operating procedure, they would be maintaining two lazy but separate lines facing the rear ramp, unable to do a damn thing from up there until they exited the aircraft.

Kolt could feel the erratic wobble in the rear of the helo, telling him Smitty was struggling with the controls, trying desperately to hold her steady in the middle of a man-made blizzard. The fresh snow was whipping up and turning on itself in a violent manner. The operators tried to look out the side bubble windows to orient themselves. The door gunners provided their only protection at the moment, but like Kolt and the other operators, they couldn't see anything but a white wall of flurries.

Kolt knew all the rear crew chief needed was the call from the pilot to drop ropes. Once received, two Delta operators would step toward the edge of the tail ramp and reach up to release the cotter pin to free the two coiled green nylon fast ropes that hung lazily from an adjustable I beam. Both sixty-foot ropes would unsnake from their loose coil, and gravity would extend them all the way to the ground.

But after two minutes of hovering, the radio call hadn't come yet.

Kolt watched some of the operators drop back to a knee as they held onto the side rails. Kolt joined them. They just felt safer than standing until the helo touched the ground. It was one of those lessons an operator just has to learn the hard way.

Kolt turned to look at the pilots. *What is taking so damn long?* They were a sitting duck for even a novice rocketeer.

On the other side of the helo, Kolt noticed the dark fuzzy outline of Admiral Mason. *Un-fucking-believable!* The admiral was still sitting on his rear end, still under the headset, ostensibly communicating with the pilots. His basic-issue tan-colored body armor and slick, freshly painted Kevlar helmet contrasted heavily with that of the operators on board, whose kit contained dozens of tools of the trade in various colors.

Kolt was beyond perturbed by the admiral's last-minute demand to clear a spot on the manifest for him, but getting the execute order for the mission softened the pain a good deal. Kolt figured the admiral wanted to be able to report directly to the president that he was personally on the target and thus a very hands-on type of commander. After a couple of recent former JSOC commanders had done the same thing in Iraq years earlier, the pressure to equal their courage was significant. Kolt didn't like it, but he got it. He shrugged the thought off. Besides, if the wide halls of the Pentagon and the plywood office space inside the circus tent were Admiral Mason's domain, out here in the wild badlands it was Kolt's. Kolt knew that as soon as he and his men could get off the damn helo things would happen so fast that there was nothing the admiral could do to stop them.

"What the fuck, Smitty?" he yelled, knowing he couldn't be heard over the engine roar. "Is your crew chief gonna drop the ropes or . . . ?"

Kolt couldn't finish the sentence before he overheard Admiral Mason's voice break into the radio net.

"Ghost Two-One actual, this is Capital Zero-Six. Heavy enemy resistance. Abort the infil. RTB immediately. Over."

Kolt then noticed the helicopter crew chief giving the abort signal with his knifed hand, moving it quickly as if he was cutting his own throat. Kolt turned back quickly toward Admiral Mason. He was still under the radio headset but now making the same abort motion as the crew chief.

"Shit!"

Kolt knew the enemies' green tracer fire seen out the side windows through the whiteout and off the back ramp made folks nervous. But after twelve years of war, the world-class crews and pilots from the 160th had learned to fly with ice in their veins

Kolt was only a few feet from the hinge side of the ramp. He thought about simply reaching up and out and pulling the damn cotter pin that kept the gathered fast rope connected to the helicopter. A quick yank, and gravity would do the rest. In a second, the end of the nylon rope would be lying in the snow-covered valley and ready for ropers.

No way he could pull that off, though. He knew that would be the craziest thing he'd ever done. If the admiral says abort, then that's what they would do. And in a normal situation, if this could be called normal, the decision would stand. But what about Shaft?

Kolt hoped his mate had maintained his cover as the two Dark Horses made the hour-plus flight to the target area. He hoped he hadn't done anything stupid. Nothing to be a hero. But there was no way to confirm his safety. Not from a hovering helo that was about to abort the mission and fly away. And not even over the cell phone. Shaft's batteries were dead.

But if Shaft maintained his cover as a medicine man and went with the flow, Kolt figured he could safely work his way out of the situation. If the helos left the area, sure, things would be in full frenzy for a while with the locals on the ground, but Shaft was there to help them, not kill them.

Quickly, Kolt looked down at the Toughbook laptop screen. Seeing the liquid crystal display had gone into sleep mode, he reached down with his gloved firing hand to swipe the pressure pad to bring the screen back to life.

Where the hell is the blue icon?

Kolt slapped the Toughbook's magnesium-alloy case slightly in the side, hoping it was a simple glitch and the blue icon would flash back on the screen in all its brilliance. Nothing. Kolt knew immediately that was too much of a coincidence to be, well, a simple coincidence. No. The blue icon had been strong and steady the entire time Shaft had been in Pakistan. Raptor X had been spot-on this entire rotation to the box. No. Something was definitely jacked up on the ground.

From underneath his headset, Kolt heard Smitty's response to Mason's order.

"Abort! Abort! Abort!" Smitty had made the net call, confirming to everyone listening in from Jalalabad to Tampa to Fort Bragg that the mission was aborted.

Kolt couldn't blame Smitty. The order had been given. Maybe if Admiral Mason was hours away back at the JOC watching things unfold on screen from a Predator B drone feed, Smitty could ignore the order. Maybe Kolt could maintain some control of the situation and keep Smitty focused. Enough focus, at least to get Kolt and his Delta operators on the ground.

But Mason wasn't warm and safe in the circus tent listening to the radio traffic. He was front and center. And, as such, was in as much danger as anyone else in the back of the helicopters.

And then the black sky lit up like a rock concert stage. A massive fireball erupted only ninety feet to their four o'clock. Kolt instinctively turned away from the trail helo and lifted his arm to shield his face from any flying debris tearing through the sky at treacherous speeds.

Kolt's helicopter shook violently for a second before it bounced back to level. Everyone standing had been thrown to the floor and toppled over those that had maintained a knee. Kolt turned back. He watched the flaming trail helo counter-rotate slowly, drop its tail uncharacteristically but then correct and level off as it struggled to move south down the valley on the front end of a massive smoke trail.

Kolt had no choice. The decision had been made. The mission to grab Ghafour had to go now. A downed helo full of operators? The blue icon of Shaft's iPad 4 beacon gone? The admiral had pushed him at every turn.

If Kolt lived, what he was about to do would certainly get him booted out of the special-ops community for the second time in his life. Or, worse yet, it might come with a stay in Leavenworth federal penitentiary. Either would be worse than death to Kolt. But Shaft would never make it out alive now without help, and losing the lead on Zawahiri would push back years of effort.

"Fortune favors the bold," whispered Kolt.

He dropped the radio headset, stepped over the legs of several kneeling teammates, and reached for the silver cotter pin. He yanked it out and watched the dark nylon rope fall freely toward the snow-covered ground. He didn't bother to wait and ensure the infrared chemlite taped to the free-running end of the rope had stopped moving. The sign that the rope was actually on the ground. No, Kolt Raynor simply grabbed the rope with his two gloved hands and jumped out into the darkness before the ninety-foot fast rope had time to fully extend.

He'd work it out with Admiral Mason later. He'd have to.

EIGHT

Isolation Cell Black—Black Ice

The sliding open of the six-inch window at the bottom of the box startled Hawk. She knew the routine. She could set her watch by it if she had one. The visit was too early for breakfast. It didn't matter, though; she was too weak to resist anything by now. She tried to open her two black eyes as the Middle Eastern music stopped, but severe swelling had closed her left one completely.

"Rise and shine, little lady," the rent-a-cop said. "Gonna tell us what your real unit in the military is today?"

No response.

"I'm going to ask you one more time, Miss Bird. Why has your boy-friend, Troy, been spreading a rumor all over downtown Fayetteville about you being in an organization called Delta Force?"

Bird had ignored this question a dozen times on day 1 and at least a half-dozen times on day 2. As far as she could tell anyway, she had long ago lost track of time and numbers. Not sure if it was Saturday or Monday, and only believed it may have been morning from the asshole's greeting. This time she figured she'd answer the question. In fact, she'd do almost anything to get out of the box. But not to serve as a punching bag again for the cops—not that she believed they were real cops—but rather to stand up straight and stretch out. Short of that, Hawk prayed someone would put a stop to the incessant loud playing of jihad music or the blood-curdling cries of baby girls begging for their daddies.

"Troy is a dumbass," Bird said. "He doesn't know what the fuck he is talking about."

Or does he? She wondered if Troy might have spouted off to one of his buddies about her outfit. She knew for sure he had no idea that she was anything more than a garden-variety 74D, a chemical, biological, radiological, and nuclear specialist by trade. She was certain she had not violated operational security about her true position in the slightest. In fact, as far as she knew, Troy thought all she did at the Unit was clean and issue gas masks.

But then again, Hawk knew Troy had a hard-on for anything Delta related, particularly after attending tryouts two years ago and being dropped on Bloody Thursday.

I'll cut his balls off.

She couldn't see her interrogator since her box was pitch-dark, and even trying to steal a peak through the spots where the plywood was fastened just revealed the powerful bright lights aimed at the box. But she knew the jerk talking was one of two dirtbags who had been doing the questioning, dishing out the beating, when they didn't like her response.

Yes, this asshole was either the short dumpy guy who smacked her across the face with a closed fist outside Macy's, ruining her Costas, or the taller bald guy who landed an upper cut to her rib cage the last time she didn't answer the same question. Either way, Hawk had just stepped outside the circle. It was a major mistake. She admitted to knowing Troy, confirmed their relationship, and showed she still had some fire left in her to resist. It was the slip the interrogators were waiting for.

"Is that so?" the cop replied, knowing she had slipped up but still not buying it in the least. It was the tall bald cop. But he wasn't alone. Hawk didn't know that Webber was standing just outside her box.

Webber was surprised by Hawk's tone and response. After three long and full days, this was the first sign of her willingness to play. So far, she had diverted into irrelevancy when under questioning or even feigned sickness and cowered away as if she was scared of being beaten or slapped anymore.

"Should we play the tape? Your Troy boy sounds pretty proud of you," the interrogator asked.

"Bullshit!" Hawk said.

The cop laughed as he looked down to read from the three-by-five cards he held in his hand. It was all planned out by the unit psych and Colonel Webber. The protocol was simple: break detainees initially by having them reveal their affiliation with Delta Force, then turn to more personal issues to break their spirit.

The average time so far had been four and a half days in the box. Two of the male operators had actually held out for the duration, seven days and nights, before the exercise was called. The logic being that if you could hold out for a week in Black Ice, you stood a good chance of actually surviving a real hostile hostage situation. Hawk was just under the average.

The interrogator continued. "OK, OK, let's shift focus for a minute, Miss Bird. What about your dad?"

My Dad? Hawk was utterly surprised. *What the fuck do they know about my dad?*

"Your dad was a military man, right?"

"You figure that out all by yourself?" Bird asked. Beating on Hawk was one thing, but bringing up her dad was somewhere they better not go.

"Your dad liked to spend a lot of time alone with you, didn't he?"

Hawk started to shake. She couldn't believe the nerve of this asshole. Even if this was a training exercise, of which she wasn't entirely convinced yet, where in the hell did this dickhead come up with these questions?

"Your dad also was cited in a 2003 after-action report for cowardliness under fire during the initial invasion into Iraq," the cop said before quietly moving to the exit door. Before exiting, he turned back, raising his voice to ensure Cindy Bird could hear him. "That's a damn shame for a Special Forces man. Must be pretty embarrassing."

Colonel Webber motioned the interrogator to step out of the room. He had taken it all in. He was now alone with Hawk and her box.

"It's Colonel Webber, Sergeant Bird. It's time to go."

The voice was familiar to her. She couldn't be sure, but she thought it might be the Delta commander. She played coy, though. Even after three days—or maybe it had been four or five—of utter hell, her natural defenses kicked in. Who else could be standing outside her box? Without knowing for sure, though, she couldn't risk compromising herself to other folks not read on to Delta. Any more than she might already have.

Or maybe she was just so pissed off at the world right now that she wasn't in the mood to be cordial to anyone. No, not maybe. Cindy Bird was pissed. The comments about Troy were bad enough, but the comments about her dad were over the top. Hawk was so pissed that she had had enough of this army-game bullshit. In fact, now her toughest environmental engineering classes in college seemed like paradise, and Fort Riley, Kansas, didn't seem like such a bad place to be stationed after all.

Thirty more seconds of silence passed. She still hadn't responded to Webber.

Webber hadn't anticipated this. But the Delta psychs had. They warned Webber that a female would likely crack. They warned she would be a shell of the woman she was before she was scarfed up in a mall parking lot. Even after just a few days of no sleep, her mental capacity would be at its minimum. A few small cups of soup would ensure her survival, but little more. Even one of the first seven male operators had completely caved in by now, so why would it surprise anyone that a woman would break? Hawk would be at an all-time low.

But if Hawk was serious about what she had told the Delta Force psych Doc Johnson during her half-dozen assessment interviews two years earlier, then now was the time to prove it. The female pilot program had been briefed to the highest levels of the administration with mixed support along the way. Some were all for it, particularly the liberal left supporters of the president, but the more traditionally minded were dead set against using females in any capacity to protect a male operator on target.

If she came out of Black Ice, a culmination exercise of sorts, still committed to doing what was necessary for the security of her country, then Delta knew they had a winner. Moreover, Hawk's success would certainly create opportunities for other females to serve in the unit ranks.

That's what brought Colonel Webber all the way to Atlanta, immediately after he finished up the Commander's Board interviews at Delta tryouts. Where he should have been, however, was overseas in Afghanistan helping Kolt Raynor and the boys acquire launch authority from the JSOC commanding general to go after HVI number 2, Mohammad Ghafour, in the Goshai Valley. Not only was Hawk's success important to Webber, since he had been teammates with her father in Delta years ago, but the pilot program was his baby. He wanted her to succeed for herself as much as he did to validate the program, but even Webber wouldn't cut corners. It had to be done right. It had to be legit, which is why Webber approved the hot-button comments about his old boss, Lieutenant Colonel Michael Leland Bird. LTC Bird, or MLB, short for "major league ballplayer," was a legend in Delta. Anyone in the know knew this as fact. Doc Johnson insisted that if Webber wanted the pilot program to succeed and be recognized as not throwing softballs to the females, then MLB was fair game. Webber agreed. He didn't necessarily like it, but he knew the importance. And Webber knew that if the Delta psychs knew Cindy "Hawk" Bird's file, he knew the woman.

"Sergeant Bird, I'm here to take you home," Webber said with as much sincerity as he could muster. "It's over. We've seen enough," he added.

Moments passed where neither spoke a word. Hawk finally spoke.

"Fuck you, fuck this place, and fuck Delta!"

Webber ignored the profanity but couldn't hold back a slight grin. He didn't blame her for the intensity of her words. Hell, Webber knew he couldn't handle three hours in a place like Black Ice, much less three days. Still, for the pilot program to be fully accepted, the test parameters had to be more stringent on Hawk. If for no other reason than to quiet the critics of Webber's baby, many who had vehemently argued that women are shackled with emotional and psychological limits at birth.

Mohammad Ghafour Village, Goshai, Pakistan

Kolt squeezed the nylon fast rope as tight as he could to control his descent. He struggled to lock the insteps of his black and tan Salomon XA Pro assault boots onto the rope as gravity, coupled with the downward whipping of ice-cold rotor wash, propelled him to the snow-covered valley floor. Friction heat penetrated his thin Oakley assault gloves after only ten feet of descent.

The impact with the snow-covered ground knocked Kolt on his ass. The rope was pulled from his hands as the helo drifted forward and the tail rose, nosing down to gain speed from the two-minute hover. The fast rope still hung out the back like a giant thread whipping in the wind.

Instinctively, Kolt rolled out of the way. He knew better than to flounder on the ground after roping since the next operator would land on top of him. When that happened, things became a total clusterfuck.

But this time there were no other ropers.

Kolt stood to a crouch as the helo noise faded in the distance. Enemy gunfire, green tracers, and dozens of unseen 7.62 mm bullets chased the bird as it raced to escape the valley. Kolt wasn't sure where to start. Singleton missions weren't designed to come off the back of a MH-47G into the center of the enemy target. He'd have a chance if the rest of the troop was on the ground with him. They would methodically clear each building, killing every adult-aged male that stood in the way, until they found the precious cargo.

The assaulters would do the heavy lifting as per standard operating procedure. Kolt always made it a point to stay out of the way. If they needed him, or if it was time to flex off the original plan, then they would call. Normally, though, they just needed the troop commander to put his gun somewhere on the perimeter and stand by.

But now, as he crouched low in Ghafour's snow-covered backyard, he was not only unsure which building he was looking at but also had no idea where Shaft was. This was anything but normal. Time to develop the situation.

Snow completely engulfed Kolt's kneepads as he knelt behind the corner of a mud and stone building. He pressed the tiny button on his NavELite wrist compass to activate the blue Indiglo-type background. The pointed compass needle floated slightly, turning to true north and providing bearings. No time to be heading the wrong way out of the blocks. He peered through his NODs, searching for movement, searching for his man Shaft.

Kolt knew Admiral Mason wouldn't stop the helo from aborting the infil. He wouldn't risk everyone on board by turning it around to recover Kolt. Kolt figured he might not even know yet that he exited the back of the helicopter. Just in case, Kolt turned his radio knob two clicks clockwise to the Green SAT secure command frequency.

He feared more that maybe the admiral had watched him reach up and pull the cotter pin to release the fast rope. And maybe he watched as the nut-job Delta officer slid his HK416 assault rifle around to his left side before reaching for the near vertical rope with both gloved hands. And if he saw that, then he wouldn't dare take his eyes off Kolt. He had to have seen Major Kolt fucking Raynor step into the cold dark sky, short hop off the edge of the ramp, and in an instant, disappear below the bird's tail ramp.

But as much as Kolt wanted to say "eat it, sir!" he quickly turned his attention to his mission. One, safely recover Shaft. Two, get both of them out of the valley safe. And three, so the mission wouldn't be viewed as an entire failure by the naysayers back in the rear on the admiral's staff, secure the intel haul that most expected would lead to the al Qaeda leader Ayman al-Zawahiri or that might just foil a plot to attack America's commercial nuclear power industry. Kolt would settle for the first two, but he wanted it all.

Green tracers, fired from a distant rooftop, whizzed past Kolt's tan and black Opscor ballistic helmet. He needed to move. He slugged through the foot-deep fresh snow and found a short set of wood and mud stairs leading to the second floor of the building to his front. He reached up with his non-firing hand and dropped his NVGs to just in front of his eyes. A second later, he front-kicked the door open and entered, wondering if he should have led with a nine-banger first.

Kolt quickly cleared the doorway threshold. As he moved forward, he scanned left to right for immediate threats, and then turned hard left to continue deeper into the room.

Dry hole. What next?

Kolt stopped for a second to gain his bearings. Using the moonlight, he looked at the small GTG satellite map on his left forearm the same way a quarterback studies the next play in the huddle. Kolt's target picture had the buildings marked by numbers with a small passport-size photo of Ghafour's white-bearded face taped to the upper right corner.

Often it takes twenty to thirty minutes to locate the PC. But the averages were against success the longer the clock ticked, even for an entire assault troop. For a one-man show like Kolt, there was no empirical data.

An explosion grabbed Kolt's attention. He moved to a back patio on the second floor opposite the helo. His Peltor-radio headgear came alive.

"RPGs at nine o'clock!"

It was Smitty making a net call on the command radio channel. From the far edge of the patio, Kolt observed another rocket launched from the ridgeline at the departing and now out-of-range MH–47G.

Kolt peered through his night-vision goggles at two green halos created by the double-rotor blades' static electricity and panned to the north to the spot where he figured the rocket came from. Nothing. They couldn't afford to lose the last helo out there. Kolt didn't expect Admiral Mason to send Smitty back to get him and Shaft. No, that would be stupid. Moreover, Kolt didn't want to be responsible if the last airworthy helo was blown out of the sky.

He had no way to contact Shaft short of screaming out. He'd have to get lucky and run into him.

He left the patio and hit the internal stairs before descending to the bottom floor. He quickly cleared the room. Another dry hole. Kolt moved past livestock, chickens squawking and flailing up against the far living room wall, and paused at the open back door.

Through his night-vision goggles Kolt scanned the area. He hoped to see Shaft, but knew that was a long shot. But Kolt knew Shaft had brought a PVS-14 handheld NVG monocular. If Kolt activated his infrared laser on his HK416 and aimed it out into the snow-covered grounds between the mud homes and buildings in the valley, then maybe Shaft would see it. It was all he had at the moment.

Before he could get his rifle up to activate the infrared laser, Kolt's peripheral vision hit on movement out of the side of his goggles. He turned. Instinctively he raised his assault rifle chest high and thumbed the safety selector switch from safe to fire. His trigger finger was just about to begin the muscle-memory motor skills of engaging a hostile threat until something looked odd. Kolt hesitated. He quickly noticed Shaft's characteristic build. The narrow shoulders and five-foot-seven frame he had seen a thousand times before.

"Shaft?"

"Hey man, don't shoot!" he answered in his characteristically dry humor while shivering heavily. "Seen any bad guys around here?"

"You son of a bitch!" Kolt responded while slapping him on the shoulder, happy to see him again. "I almost stitched your ass. What happened to you? We lost your beacon."

Shaft was covered in snow. He quickly explained to Kolt how he accidentally shot his iPad 4 and then had held the green laser on the center of the landing zone until the prop blast from the hovering helo had knocked him down. Then, he said that he slipped trying to right himself and rolled about ten meters into a washbasin. As soon as he was able to right himself, the exploding rocket impacting the trail helo knocked him back into the basin.

Kolt could see Shaft's clothes were soaking wet. Kolt noticed Shaft's thick dark beard was covered with frozen snow and ice particles. His wool Afghan hat was iced over. He looked like the abominable snowman.

"You guys almost got stuck with an RPG before landing," Shaft said as he shivered in the dark.

"We didn't land," answered Kolt.

"What?" said Shaft, a little confused. "You guys roped?"

"Yes," said Kolt.

"I didn't think you guys were gonna make it."

"We didn't, Shaft," Kolt said.

"Come again, Racer?" Shaft asked.

"I'm it, brother," said Kolt. "I got out."

"You are it?" questioned Shaft. "You are alone?"

Kolt didn't have time to explain things to Shaft. He was also hoping he didn't ask. He knew Shaft would be pissed if he knew the details about Admiral Mason's abort call. Better to save those details for the hot wash.

Kolt just said, "Afraid so partner."

"Holy shit. We're screwed, boss."

"Not yet, brother. Let's get the PC and book it out of the valley."

"Book it?" asked Shaft. "Where's our exfil birds?"

"Admiral Mason was on my bird. Don't expect him to turn her around to get us. They're about out of gas."

Before Shaft could answer, the unmistakable sound of AK-47 fire interrupted the frigid air.

Kolt put his gloved index finger up in front of his lips to tell Shaft he was receiving a radio call. Kolt then motioned with his left hand for Shaft to take a knee. Kolt did the same, dropping his right Crye Precision kneepad into the soft snow.

"Major Raynor, situation report. Over!" It was Admiral Mason. Kolt was surprised Mason had thought he'd be able to reach Kolt directly on Green SAT. But more alarming, Kolt was aggravated to hear his true name over the joint-command radio net instead of his official designated alphanumeric Mike One-One call sign.

But this situation was anything but normal.

Kolt figured the commanding general was either so pissed that he ignored his abort call or, more likely, had no idea what Kolt's actual call sign was. Either way, given the current shit sandwich Kolt bit into, hearing the CG over any radio channel was actually good news.

Kolt couldn't hear the MH-47G engines or the distinctive-sounding rotor blades whipping in the distance anymore. He assumed Smitty and the rest of his Delta assault troop were either following the lame-duck 47 back to the border or, worse, were still in the area looking to execute a search and rescue mission.

Screw it. It was too late to change Mason's mind, anyway. The admiral wasn't going to reconsider aborting the mission. This Kolt was certain of. He was also certain that the bird was critically low on fuel, already likely flying on fumes, so even if Mason desired to turn the helo around to help Kolt, the gas gauge had a vote.

No, the helos weren't turning around. They would be focused solely on CSARing the downed helo and recovering all crew and operators. Kolt knew he and Shaft were on their own.

Kolt keyed his radio mike to transmit back to the admiral in the helo. He played it like it was any other op, ignoring the fact that he decided to rope on target all by himself. It would have been nice if some of his men thought to hit the rope behind Kolt and fast rope down to the target. But Kolt never really expected anyone to follow him. It was a split-second decision to help Shaft. He didn't have time to argue with Mason about it, or even let his men know what he was doing. With one helo struck by an RPG and limping out of the valley, he really couldn't blame Mason too much for making the call. It was just Mason. The risk-averse JSOC commanding general. Someone who had no business, at least in Kolt's mind, of even being on the helo. No, Kolt thought, the CG should be back in the JOC at J-bad, watching the mission on a flat screen, sipping coffee, and preparing to give a secure-victory call to the SECDEF about the successful cross-border mission and the capture of Mohammad Ghafour.

No, at the moment, Kolt knew the stark reality of things. There was nothing else to do but operate now. To do his thing. Turn a shit sandwich into a five hour meal at Gramercy Tavern. Recover Shaft first, yes. But somehow Kolt knew he wouldn't settle for just that. Ghafour was on the target list. Not only was the terrorist the golden nugget to finally finding the al Qaeda leader Ayman al-Zawahiri, but every Western intelligence agency was marking Ghafour as the mastermind behind attacks on America's critical infrastructure. The fact that POTUS wanted any attacks on the homeland stopped before it was too late wasn't lost on Kolt's decision-making process.

Kolt pressed the push-to-talk button, paused, and spoke into his mouthpiece very calmly, as if it was just another day on target. "This is Mike One-One. Negative PC. Still clearing the area. Over."

"We need to get out of here," Admiral Mason said with obvious urgency in his voice. "We are about out of fuel. Get you and your man out of there and over to the alternate pickup zone immediately. Over."

Kolt couldn't believe his ears. Well, he could a little, considering the circumstances, but what about the mission? What about capturing the guy who has vowed to attack America? What about the effort by everyone back at J-bad to develop this hit? What about the risk so many took to get all the way to the Goshai Valley? Are we really going to tell the president that we went into Pakistan and gave it the good ole college try but came up empty-handed? Sorry, Mr. President, but no word on Zawahiri or on the potential radiological sabotage that just might happen in the United States. Never mind the contingency of staying after the helos departed and walking out of the valley.

No. There would be no mission failure here. Not on Kolt's watch. There would be nobody moving to the alternative landing zone. Not yet, anyway. Not until they had what they came for in the first place.

All of it.

Kolt took his left hand from the push-to-talk button secured to the left breast area of his Crye body armor and reached down for the radio secured to his assault vest. He turned the multichannel radio knob one click counterclockwise to bring up Helo Common, the secure uplink to the helicopter pilots and air-mission commander Smitty, then regrabbed his push-to-talk.

"Smitty, how you guys doing with gas?" asked Kolt. "Can you give me a few more minutes. Over."

"We are currently in CSAR mode, downed helo. We need to be off the ground in ten minutes, or we won't make it all the way back to Afghanistan and the fuel blivets."

"Got it. Thanks, partner. Out."

Kolt turned the channel knob back to Green SAT. He could hear the admiral still on the frequency demanding the insubordinate troop commander come up on the net.

Kolt broke in. "Capital Zero-Six, we are headed for the old British fort—building six. All Eagles accounted for. Ghafour definitely went to the fort. I need five mikes."

"Negative, negative, negative!" The admiral was adamant. "Abort the mission. You will load immediately. Do you understand, Major? Over."

"Sir, we have enough fuel. I need five minutes," Kolt pleaded.

"Major, the precious cargo is long gone. It's a long shot that he is at the fort." The admiral was surprisingly at ease now—most likely because he finally realized that everyone and their brother were listening in to the command frequency—which pissed Kolt off even more. It almost sounded as if the commanding general was the calm and collected one out there.

"Fine, sir. Take the helos out of the valley and back to Afghanistan. We'll locate Ghafour and walk out as planned. Out."

Kolt sounded convincing. So convincing he almost thought the admiral would actually buy it. If Mason couldn't help him and Shaft, then Kolt wanted his space.

Kolt didn't have to wait long for the answer. "Load your man immediately," the admiral answered, a whole lot sterner than normal. "That's a direct order! Acknowledge!"

Kolt knew every operator still inside the helo was listening to his radio transmissions with the admiral. It would have been stupid to fall on his sword in the middle of Pakistan. For Osama bin Laden? Maybe. For Ayman al-Zawahiri? Maybe. For Haji Mohammad Ghafour, who only a couple of weeks ago was dubbed low-hanging fruit even by Delta's own intel analysts? No.

What about the good men who just went down in flames on the trail helo? Kolt didn't know if any of the men on the struck helo had even survived, but he did know his men wouldn't want to go home without this mission accomplished. Corralling Ghafour and dragging him home through the mountain pass certainly wouldn't make their deaths worth it. Not at all. Stopping a potential attack on a nuclear power plant inside the United States wouldn't bring his teammates back either.

Kolt felt even more strongly that he had to carry the mission through to the end. For it, a lot of men may very well have died, burning alive in a helo in a godforsaken valley. He was obligated to see this through. This was what Delta was all about.

Even if Delta was now only a pair.

NINE

Two miles south of Kolt Raynor, Smitty found a suitable landing spot to set the MH-47G down near the downed helo. He didn't like the spot. He wasn't even ordered to set her down, but he knew the game, and setting down to recover the crew and customers on a crashed helo was standard procedure. Smitty also knew the admiral and Kolt would be having words, some of which he was able to monitor over the radio, and even though it would be a tight fit with the addition of four 160th crew members and two dozen customers in the back of his heavy-lift Dark Horse, the little known nickname of the heavy-lift 47s, he wasn't leaving fellow warriors under fire of his own accord. No, Smitty was all in. Mason would have to make the call. He'd have to force him to leave Americans behind in Pakistan.

"We can't exfil. We have two men still out there. They need a few more minutes." An operator code-named Train calmly transmitted over the assault radio. Train had obviously been monitoring Helo Common and heard Kolt's radio transmissions.

"I know, Train," Smitty said.

"Negative, stand down, stand down," Mason said, cutting in. "We are RTB. I say again, we are returning to base."

It only took a few seconds for Shaft to point out the British fort to Kolt. Kolt quickly picked up Shaft's IR sparkle on the east side of the eighteenth-century fort's twelve-foot walls made of hard mud and a combination of silver fir and spruce logs. Sitting roughly seventy-five meters across the partially iced-over creek, built somewhat into the face of the valley's high western wall, it looked like a Hallmark Christmas card under the half-moon hovering above and well beyond the east ridge. But as pretty as the view was, Kolt was in no mood for caroling or eggnog.

"What do you recommend, Shaft?" Kolt asked as they remained on a knee in nearly a foot of fresh snow. "We gotta make it quick, though."

"Shit! No doubt. I'm freezing in these wet clothes," Shaft said. "I was inside the fort the other day giving out Ranger candy to the kids. There are at least two dozen women and children sleeping in there."

"I doubt they're sleeping now," Kolt said.

"No, but the noncombatants haven't gone anywhere. Makes sense that Ghafour would hide among the kids and women."

"Perfect sense," Kolt said.

"What are we looking at once inside?" Kolt asked if for no other reason than to confirm what he already believed after a week of studying two-dimensional imagery with the analysts at J-bad.

"Standard shit, really—green metal gate that locks with a fat stick, single story, rooms built into the outer wall, large well in the middle, goat and chicken shit everywhere," Shaft said.

"OK, frags are out, too many kids. How many FAMs?" Kolt asked, confirming to him and Shaft that they were only interested in hurting the fighting-age males, not the women and kids.

"Let's keep it simple," Shaft said. "Let's climb!"

"On point, you follow," Kolt said.

Kolt lowered his helmet-mounted NVGs and led the way toward the east side of the fort. Shaft, holding his monocular NVGs to his nonfiring eye and with an AK in his right hand and tucked under his right shoulder, followed at ten meters' distance.

After trudging through foot-deep snow that covered uneven and rocky terrain for thirty meters or so, they successfully negotiated the narrow fifteen-foot log bridge spanning the iced-over creek. Kolt was concerned about the double set of footprints they were leaving behind, but there wasn't much he could do about it. After slipping between a short fence made out of narrow tree branches and a short but thick mud wall, they reached the base of the fort before taking a breather and going to a knee. The windswept snowdrift had accumulated near the fort's outer walls, making them appear shorter than they really were. Kolt and Shaft, pushing their backs to the wall, faced out and scanned the area behind them, making sure they weren't being followed.

"What now?" Shaft asked.

"I thought you said we were climbing?" Kolt asked, taking his eyes away from the part of the village where all the commotion with the helicopters happened earlier to look at Shaft.

"Yeah, I guess. It's too damn quiet, though," Shaft said.

"They have no idea it's just the two of us. They probably think a hundred American commandos jumped out of the two helos," Kolt offered.

"Yeah, probably," Shaft said. "I'm sure they lock the gate at night, though."

"Standard," Kolt said. "Look, boost me over the wall. I'll see what's up."

"OK," Shaft said, as if to say, *And then what?*

"I'll take a look. If it is quiet, we'll both drop in and clear counter-clockwise until we find Ghafour."

"And if not?" Shaft asked.

"Well, if I see trouble, I'll take them with my suppressed HK416," Kolt said, not entirely sure of what he was saying.

"And?"

"And then we'll drop in," Kolt said.

"Dude, that's fucking suicide," Shaft said, trying to maintain a whisper. "Look, I know you came a long way for me, but is this ass clown worth it?" Shaft said.

Kolt could feel the apprehension in Shaft's voice. Hell, he wasn't so fired up anymore himself to hang it out in this godforsaken frozen shithole of a valley floor. No backup, no gunship support, and no armed Predator B's orbiting overhead. Nobody would blame them if they simply melted into the shadows and beat feet away from the village. Far enough away to mark a black landing zone and safely call in an exfil helo. And then, entirely unexplainably, his thoughts reverted back to his first tour in Afghanistan, weeks on the heels of 9/11.

"There is a lot at stake here, Shaft. This guy is tied to Z-man and planned attacks back home."

"Yeah, I know all that shit," Shaft said as he shivered underneath the wet clothing. "But screw that drop-in nonsense."

"I'm listening," Kolt said, happy that Shaft had agreed to complete the mission or go down trying.

"I'll boost you up the wall, but hold for a minute and let me get to the front gate. I'll bang on the door and fire off some AK rounds. They'll think I'm a tribesman, shooting at an American or something, and likely move all their guns inside to cover the gate as they open it to investigate the commotion."

"OK. I'll pop a red-pen gun flare when I'm in position and ready for you to bang on the gate," Kolt said. "I'll thin the herd of FAMs with my suppressor as they post on the inside of the gate. Watch the false cover with the gate; use the walls."

"Give me one of your door charges. I'll need to get in the gate if you can't get down there to unlock it," Shaft said.

"Rog."

After taking the tightly rolled eighty-four-inch-long linear-shaped charge and M60 fuse igniter from Kolt, Shaft crossed his fingers to cup Kolt's right combat boot and vigorously pulled upward to let Kolt reach up high enough to secure a fingertip hold on the lip of the high wall. Shaft then put a hand under each boot and stood up as tall as he could, maintaining upward pressure, to help Kolt scale the wall as quietly as possible. With Kolt now out of sight, he moved clockwise around the square fort to the front green metal gate.

Kolt slipped over the lip of the wall, keeping his silhouette as low as possible, and onto the roof of the corner room. A wooden ladder made of logs and twine was to his left, offering roof access from the ground. To his right, the roof continued to the far corner. Kolt picked up the smell of a woodburning stove and noticed smoke coming out of two of the three separate smokestacks protruding from the long dried-mud-covered L-shaped roof that hugged the inner side of the fort's wall. He lay down on his stomach and inched his body closer to the edge to look down into the compound.

Spotting the straight-edged top of the metal gate in the moonlight, Kolt leaned on his left side to reach his pen-gun flares with his gloved right hand. He pulled out the black thumb-spring device and screwed in a red flare the size of a Chapstick container. He rotated the toggle with his thumb, aimed the flare over the open courtyard of the fort and the front gate, and released the firing pin.

The red pen flare lit up the snowflake-filled sky as it sped high into the air, reaching about four hundred feet before impacting with the valley wall.

Kolt waited to hear Shaft fire off a few AK rounds and bang on the metal gate.

Right on time, AK-47 fire opened up. Kolt assumed it was from Shaft and fingered his IR laser and floodlight on top of his HK to steady on. He had a perfect position, easily the tactical advantage inside the fort, and a direct view of the front gate. The moon had settled behind the high ridge-line, protecting Kolt's silhouette from the danger of being backlit and thus easily discernible from the ground. Seconds later, he heard the banging on the gate.

Kolt's finger rested on the trigger. He had his NVGs down, holding his goggles just above his rifle so he could see the IR signature and engage at will. Nothing. Nobody moved.

Shit, what now?

Kolt was dumbfounded. He couldn't radio Shaft to execute the ruse a second time. Hell, if they didn't bite the first time, they surely wouldn't fall for it a second time.

Kolt startled at an abrupt noise twenty feet to his left. He turned quickly to see the ladder moving. Someone was climbing to the roof. Instinctively, he rolled to his back, brought his rifle to his chest, and aimed the IR laser and floodlight at the top of the ladder.

Fuck! I don't need company now.

It was a male. A fighting-age male, for sure. This much Kolt could easily tell. But he could also tell he wasn't your normal fighting-age jihadist. He was carrying something in his left hand, maybe a light of some sort or even a pistol. He also moved slowly, as if he either couldn't see where he was going in the darkness or was too frail or too injured to be negotiating obstacles.

Kolt studied the man closely, the large turban high on his forehead, the white dishdasha and dark-brown outer garment. The beard. Yes, the long, white, thick beard. He'd seen it before in a picture Shaft had sent the day before. It had to be him.

Fucking Ghafour!

The elderly man took two steps from the ladder and turned back around. He gingerly squatted into a ball, keeping his rear off the roof and wrapping his arms around his knees to keep warm, obviously unaware of his present company.

Kolt slowly stood to a low crouch. He delicately slid his HK around to his left side to free both hands and then raised his NVGs on his helmet. He pretty much knew this was going to be the easiest jackpot he ever participated in, but he needed every bit of stealth to prevent Ghafour from yelling out and alerting the others to his trouble. He couldn't believe his luck.

Kolt took three long steps to gain forward momentum and leaped toward the old man. He slapped a tight, rear, naked chokehold around the man's neck, cutting off Ghafour's carotid artery and instantly putting him to sleep. It was that simple. Not really a challenge. Certainly nothing to brag about given the skill and age difference between the two.

Then Kolt saw something drop from Ghafour's right hand. The familiar drab olive color was partially veiled by their huddled bodies' shadow as it rolled to the edge of the roof and stopped just a foot or so from the ladder. As it settled, Kolt could barely make out the square nipples protruding from the oval body. Kolt wasn't positive exactly what it was, but his spider senses told him it certainly could be a World War II–era Soviet F1 hand grenade.

Instinctively, Kolt yelled out, "Grenade!"

Kolt released his hold on the man's neck, grabbed Ghafour around the waist, arched his lower back, and pulled Ghafour up and away from the ensuing blast as if he was throwing an opponent in a Greco-Roman wrestling match.

The grenade detonated a moment later, rocketing blast fragments in all directions, tearing into whatever was in its way within fifteen feet.

Kolt's lower right leg took major frag. It was quick, the largest piece slicing through his calf muscle, and smaller shards tearing through the upper area of his tan combat boot and lodging somewhere under the skin.

Gritting his teeth to manage the pain, Kolt felt Ghafour's body go completely limp.

Shit! Don't tell me this guy already bought it.

Kolt felt the moisture on Ghafour's clothing and laid him on his back to check his wounds. The obvious smell of dehydrated urine mixed with the familiar smell of blood. Ghafour's pulse was still strong, telling Kolt the PC had obviously pissed his pants when Kolt grabbed him. His right arm was also bleeding heavily above the elbow, but he was just asleep.

Kolt pulled his Spyderco out and cut a long piece of cloth from Ghafour's shirt sleeve. He wrapped it tight around Ghafour's upper arm between the wound and the joint to control the bleeding before lowering his NVGs and turning back to the ladder.

So far, he was good. Kolt dragged Ghafour to the edge of the fort's tall wall and lowered him to roughly four feet off the ground before letting go of Ghafour's hand and letting the unconscious body drop into the snow, exactly where Kolt and Shaft had knelt earlier to develop their plan.

Kolt spider-dropped from the high wall, landing close to Ghafour. Moving quickly, he rolled Ghafour onto his back and reached down, grabbing his left arm. Kolt then placed his boots over the instep of both of Ghafour's leather loafers before pulling him up off the ground, naturally locking his knees. Kolt quickly ducked under to shoulder the precious cargo.

Kolt had his jackpot. Now, he just had to find Shaft and book it out of the valley.

Train knew his place. He wasn't used to debating these things with the CG. But the boys had always left that stuff to Colonel Webber or, at times, even Major Raynor. Train wasn't exactly sure what to make of Kolt Raynor just yet. He knew Kolt's reputation, but this was his first direct-action mission under Kolt's command. Either way, Kolt's questionable rep aside, Train wanted to make sure all his mates on the helo had heard his earlier transmission. He turned his radio to the troop internal frequency and keyed his push-to-talk.

"All stations, all stations, I say again. We have two Eagles still at the target," Train barked into his mouthpiece.

"Can't do it!" the monitoring 47G copilot responded. "We won't make it back to the gas station if we wait any longer. We're minutes from Bingo as it is."

Smitty broke squelch. "We needed to leave five minutes ago. Over." Smitty had pushed it as far as he could. Taking on the additional sixteen bodies was already pushing the aircraft's specs. He knew to trust his instruments, and he couldn't risk putting her down in Pakistan with two loads of troops.

Under nods Train could see Admiral Mason sitting just a few feet behind Smitty's center jump seat. He figured Mason was beside himself, seeing him fumbling with getting his headset plugged in properly to the console.

"BREAK, BREAK! This is Mike One-One in the blind. PC secure. EWIA. I have a wounded Eagle as well. Not critical. We can't make it back to the helicopters. We'll walk out of the valley as planned, out."

Under his tan Kevlar flight helmet and smoke-colored face piece, Smitty smiled. He was happy that the scumbag had been bagged but also that he could finally get his bird in the air. Having to scuttle a second now-overloaded multimillion-dollar Dark Horse inside the Goshai Valley was manageable, but having to abandon two Americans on target scared the shit out of him.

Smitty didn't need an order from Admiral Mason to get out of there. Kolt's call was enough. He also knew that as soon as they gassed up back at J-bad and off-loaded the injured men from the downed helo, they would be turning around to recover Kolt at some black unmarked landing zone. With or without the CG's blessing.

The burly MH-47G helicopter strained to lift her six balloon tires out of the snowdrift. The pilot turned the refuel probe off the nose slightly to the left. The whiteout created by the powerful twin-rotor blades was just as bad as it was during the aborted infil at the target. But this time, they weren't air-holding to fast-rope operators on target; they were getting the hell out of there with twenty-seven certainly frustrated but alive men on board.

The pilot pitched the helicopter's broad nose-refuel probe forward and began picking up speed. From his center seat, Smitty strained to look out the starboard side of the bird. He wondered exactly where that crazy-ass Kolt and Shaft were on that snow-covered Swiss cheese terrain. Smitty had known Kolt a long time, and even though he couldn't help but sit in awe of the Delta operator's personal courage, he figured Kolt Raynor's days in the special operations community were over.

And for the second time in just over four years.

* * *

Cherokee Power Plant, Gaffney, South Carolina

Nuclear Security Officer Timothy Reston hated his job, his superiors, and life in general. Everything he worked for, everything he dreamed of, and everything he was owed had been taken away from him. And none of it was his fault.

"Fuuuuuuuck!" Timothy shouted, slamming his fist against the arm of the La-Z-Boy chair. He dropped his game console in his lap and began slamming the palms of his fists against both arms. *It wasn't fair!*

He'd dedicated sixteen years to the Cherokee Power Plant and had been recognized on numerous occasions by the management team at EnergyFirst Corporation. His "I Love ME Wall" at home was adorned with the typical letters and cheap wooden plaques of adoration. Letters of appreciation, employee-of-the-year citations, and excellence in service—all adorned with the big gaudy red, white, and blue EnergyFirst logo. Below the dozen or so frames, his bookshelf was filled with various leadership and management books, all claiming to reveal the secrets to leading people successfully.

"Fuck, fuck, fuck, fuck, fuck!"

Timothy knew he'd done nothing wrong. He was a gamer, lots of people were. He shouldn't be punished for that. He lived alone and enjoyed connecting online with fellow gamers from around the world. He looked forward to the weekend and marathon sessions of HALO and Call of Duty. In those worlds, he was a rock star. He'd never said it directly, but he'd let enough slip that the rest of his teammates in the Brotherhood of Raging Dragons believed he was a Navy SEAL. Timothy didn't bother correcting them. He could have been a Navy SEAL. Hell, he *should* have been one. He was more gung-ho about protecting America than most soldiers in the army. He desperately wanted to be overseas fighting terrorists in Iraq or Afghanistan, or even Somalia or Syria, but his brilliant military career was cut short. It wasn't for lack of his desire to kick ass and take names; it was just that his addiction to a large Meat Monster pizza and a two-liter bottle of Coke for dinner most nights left him not quite the lean, mean fighting machine the navy needed him to be.

No matter how shitty life in the real world got, online Timothy was a god. ZooKeeper69 said as much. The kid idolized Timothy. They'd known each other for months and had become fast friends. They were even planning on booking a hotel room to share in San Diego for the next Comic Con. That would be awesome.

"Steel-Ninja, watch your left flank," Zoo typed. "I'll cover your right."

Timothy looked at the TV screen and realized he'd not been paying attention to the game. Leave it to Zoo to cover his ass. Zoo really was cool. He was forever amazed at Timothy's stories and always asking for more. They chatted for hours, texting and shooting enemy icons and having a great time. Zoo even asked about Timothy's "cover job" at the nuclear plant. It gave Timothy a chance to vent.

"You missed that guy with the RPG," Zoo texted, pausing the game.

Timothy banged his fists a couple more times and then picked up the console. He reached over the side of the chair and picked up his wireless keyboard, relieved it wasn't broken.

"Sorry, Zoo, fucking mad about work," he typed.

"More bullshit, Steel?"

"They took away my gun! Can you believe that? They're so jealous of my skills, they moved me out of my security shift and stuck me in badge processing!"

Timothy read his words on the TV screen and believed them, and why shouldn't he? What he said was true, anyway. They were jealous of him. They knew he was a warrior and so they punished him. All that bullshit about the psych wanting additional screening based on his sketchy "MMPI" test results and poor physical fitness was just garbage.

"That's crazy. You know more about security than all of them combined! You're the one that told me about the vulnerable access points and the lag in shift changes when the cameras weren't monitored."

"I know!" Timothy said, his hands flying over the keyboard. "I've spotted dozens of weak spots in the security at the plant, and this is the thanks I get. Fuck, if the plant were in Iran, I could take it down myself."

"You and whose army?"

"Fuck you, Zoo. You know I could. I know their moves, their timings, their procedures, everything! Taking it would be easier than this fucking game!"

"OK, let's do it," Zoo typed.

Timothy's stomach lurched. "What?"

"There's that big hydroelectric factory a kilometer ahead in the game. Let's pretend it's the nuclear plant and take it down. You lead, and I'll give you cover."

Timothy's entire body relaxed. *Right, the game.* "Fuck, yeah. It's on!"

TEN

Sana'a, Yemen

Sitting in the most secluded corner of the tiny Internet café on the corner of a frigid and dusty street in Sana'a, Yemen, thirty-two-year-old Omer Farooq smiled. It was the third time in as many weeks he'd got Steel-Ninja to walk him through an attack on the nuclear plant. Each time, he expected him to balk, but, if anything, Steel was becoming more emboldened. He'd even started naming enemy players after real men at the nuclear plant.

Farooq leaned back and stretched his neck. He hadn't anticipated playing online first-person shooter games as part of jihad, but he accepted this path. He longed for acceptance into al Qaeda. His constant ill health, something he shared with Steel-Ninja, a product of childhood asthma and the poor genes of his grandmother, kept him out of the fighting ranks. But Farooq had other skills. Skills any terrorist organization could use in the technologically advanced twenty-first century. He knew computers. So much so that he was suspected by U.S. intelligence as being one of the key authors of the "drone paper," al Qaeda's secret effort to find ways to shoot down, jam, or remotely hijack U.S. drones, hoping to exploit the technological vulnerabilities of a weapons system that had inflicted huge losses upon the terrorist network. And he liked to troll the net.

Finding Timothy Reston hadn't been difficult. Farooq easily searched the distinctive IP number through the Internet to locate the region Steel-Ninja surfed from. Once he knew what the man did for a living, it was simply a matter of stroking his American ego. He made Timothy feel important. He bought into his stories of imperial aggression as a Navy SEAL. He laughed at his jokes and sympathized with his plight at work.

The challenge had been getting specific information. Steel-Ninja was big on stories, but whenever they started talking about the small details of work, like addresses, number of guards, passwords, and the like, Steel would get vague. Coming up with the idea to attack the plant in the game was ingenious. Nothing was real in the game, after all. Farooq leaned forward and, as he promised, dutifully covered Steel-Ninja as he led their way into the nuclear plant.

Cindy "Hawk" Bird had known for a few days that Major Kolt Raynor was back in town. Word traveled fast around the Spine when a Unit member was wounded in action. Word was even faster when one was killed. Just the same, Hawk knew her place, and even though she had gotten to know Racer pretty well in her short time in the Unit, she figured she'd tend to her own business.

She planned to do just that. And she did, right up until the last three minutes and twenty-seven seconds of that morning's daily intelligence brief. It was groundbreaking news.

Haji Mohammad Ghafour, the middle-aged Pakistani that Racer took a frag for in the Goshai Valley and dragged fourteen miles to a black LZ for a helicopter ride back to Afghanistan, was talking. In fact, according to the CIA, the enhanced interrogation techniques were working so well that the analysts were beginning to second-guess the information Ghafour was providing. Which is exactly why the Unit intelligence officer giving the brief offered a caveat for every word.

And not only was Ghafour squealing like a pig, but the thumb drive Shaft secured from his minder, the same minder he smoked through his backpack the night Racer and the boys came to the rescue three and a half weeks earlier, contained some interesting and telling files.

But it wasn't necessarily the treasure trove of new intelligence that ultimately convinced Cindy Bird to risk being late for a dinner date with her

Green Beret boyfriend, Troy. No, that Troy stuff could wait. What was said in that meeting was something much more personal.

As Hawk turned her metallic-gray Beetle right off Morrison Bridge Road and onto the narrow dirt drive, she knew Kolt needed to be informed about it all. But as she slowed, moving past the first of four long, narrow, partially rusted tin chicken coups, the stench of chicken shit and dead fowl made her want to whip a U-turn.

She could make out a single and faint light barely shining through the vertical slats in the two center windows of the single-wide up ahead. She remembered the guys ribbing Racer about his accommodations while they were in Cairo looking for the missing SAM missiles. Truth be told, she had expected more, especially from a major in the Unit. But the boys were spot-on, down to the cinder-block foundation and heavily rusted, protruding trailer hookup. Then again, in their short acquaintance, she pretty much figured Kolt wasn't the courting type. She didn't think Kolt would be wining and dining any ladies at this dive of a place. He definitely wasn't the married type either, which for a special operator left only one type.

Cindy glanced at her cell, uncertain whether to call first. She didn't have Kolt's number, wasn't even sure if he carried a personal cell, but she could ring the staff duty officer and be patched through to his Unit-issued cell.

Deep down, Cindy Bird felt a crazy attraction to Kolt, and even though she hadn't seen him for the past three months, he was on her mind. So much so that she started seeing him less and less as a big-brother figure and more as a ruggedly attractive slightly older man, if thirteen or fourteen years' difference could be considered slight.

But Hawk wasn't visiting tonight to give Kolt a sympathy screw. Her Special Forces boyfriend wasn't necessarily the issue; one-night stands just weren't her style. Freaky attraction or crazy imagination—she wasn't about to be that third type. And besides, interunit relationships were entirely frowned upon and the quickest route to a swift reassignment.

No, what brought her to Kolt's trailer wasn't personal at all. It was professional. She believed in Kolt, had seen him operate up close, and knew he had his head and heart in the right place. So when she heard the unit intelligence officer tell the assembled group earlier that morning that Major Kolt

Raynor had been placed on "admin leave" indefinitely, she knew there was more to it than simply convalescing at home from his wounds.

Lost in thought, she rolled to a stop on the dead grass near Kolt's beat-up black pickup, too late for the courtesy call. Cindy tapped the horn once, then, considering, a second time. She was certain Kolt wouldn't recognize her vehicle and figured it was worth losing the cool points to keep her metallic-gray Beetle from eating some turkey shot from a drugged-up Kolt wielding an over-and-under shotgun.

She lifted the cellophane-covered ceramic plate of home-baked chocolate chip cookies off the passenger seat and stepped out onto the hard dirt and grass. *Yard work much?* she thought as she noticed the forgotten bushes and flower-bed and climbed the three wobbly aluminum steps to reach the doorbell.

The screen door was closed, but the wooden door behind it half open.

"Hold what you got!" Kolt yelled from somewhere inside. "Whattya need, partner?"

"Uh, Kolt, it's Cindy." *Dang, that sounded way too familiar. Maybe I should have used Sergeant Bird or even Hawk. Anything but my first name.*

"OK, again, whattya need?"

"Well, nothing really. Just thought I'd drop by and see how you were doing."

"Which asshole put you up to that? You lose a bet?"

Cindy laughed uncomfortably. She had almost forgotten how hard it was to read this man.

"No, just was baking cookies and had some extra. Figured you could use the calories."

"You bake? At twenty-three-thirty hours?" Kolt asked.

Cindy lied. "Well, I burned the first batch and then took in a movie with Troy."

She waited for a few uncomfortable seconds, but no response.

"I know it's late. I'll just come back another time," she said, looking for a natural but quick exit.

Cindy leaned over to set the plate of cookies on a small rusted coffee table and looked up.

Kolt startled her. He was standing in front of the screen door, shirtless and unshaven. As usual, his hair was a mess, hanging down one side in front of his left eye. She had never seen Kolt topless, but had to admit he looked pretty hot standing there in only a pair of black Mountain Hardware climbing pants, even for a forty-year-old. Cindy tried not to stare at the scars on his rib cage or even at his wide smile, and in doing so she couldn't help but notice the plastic bottles of prescription meds on the counter behind him. Painkillers for sure.

She followed his muscular right arm from his well-developed shoulder, past the bicep with the thick vein running the length, and to his rugged hand that grasped a bright orange Fat Albert Wiffle-ball bat.

She broke the ice. "Nice cane, Major!" she said, rolling her eyes. "That the best Womack can do for you?"

"Troy in the trunk?" Kolt said, ignoring her lame joke.

"Real funny."

"Social call, or is my beeper dead again?"

"Are you always such a jerk?" Cindy asked.

"Usually only when I'm doped up on meds after leaving some blood behind somewhere."

"I heard about the op in Pakistan. I heard it wasn't all your blood," Hawk said, uncertain if she was being too informal with classified Unit business.

"Look, I just paid for the UFC fight on HBO. Either join me or we'll catch up later. Cool?" Kolt said.

"Tap Out TV? I'm in. Besides, you'll probably need me to explain the more technical moves to you."

Kolt turned up the side of his mouth slightly for a second and narrowed his eyebrows at the comment before opening the door and shuffled backward to let her in.

Cindy stepped in and took a long look at the living room. "Love what you've done with the place!" she said. "Early American arms room?"

"What can I say?" he said. "TJ had poor taste in home décor."

Cindy took a seat on the worn leather couch. It was about the only spot not covered in clothes, magazines, or gun-cleaning rags. She didn't know how to respond about the TJ comment. It had been six or seven months since Josh Timble was killed. Only a week since his name had been added to the black granite wall at the compound. But she knew if anyone enjoyed the liberty to find humor with the deceased TJ, it was his former roommate Kolt. It wasn't tasteless; it was just Kolt.

"Looks like you haven't touched the place since Lieutenant Colonel Timble was here," she said, uncertain and trying not to reveal her discomfort with the subject.

"I haven't. Been a little busy," Kolt said, trying to lessen the harsh tone of his response.

Kolt lowered the volume with the remote and went for the fridge. He grabbed two bottled beers and twisted the caps off both before handing one to Hawk.

"Nice paracord wristband," Kolt said, eyeballing the pink and lime-green bracelet on her left wrist. "You make that yourself in the rigger shop?"

Hawk sensed a bit of sarcasm in Kolt's voice but let it slide.

"It's a monkey-fist survivalist bracelet. Troy made it for me. Twelve feet of cord if I ever need it. A magnesium fire starter and a pretty loud whistle weaved into it, too," she answered as she turned her wrist over to show the details. "You jealous?"

"Entirely!"

Cindy noticed the shoe box of medals on the coffee table. It was partially hidden under the gun-cleaning stuff, pistol magazines and holsters, and two-thirds of a Chinese-takeout box. She slid the box slightly out with two fingers. Cindy thought she counted five Bronze Stars with V devices on the ribbons, two or three Silver Stars. She was amazed in a way, but tried not to be too nosey. Also a Distinguished Service Cross, which she had never seen up close before. All those piled on another dozen, easily, of commendation medals, Purple Hearts, and the like.

She hadn't been around long enough to know where or what he did to earn the medals. She wasn't even sure she wanted to know.

"Admiring your hardware?" Cindy asked.

"Yeah, Webber's on my ass. Promotion-board time again. Some jackass in personnel told him I haven't had a Department of the Army official photo in over four years, hence the Brasso fragrance."

"Lieutenant Colonel Kolt Raynor," Cindy said as she lifted her bottle in a mock toast. "How does that sound to you?"

"Sounds like a kiss of death. Like the fast track to a staff job. Like too much rank to be operating on target anymore," Kolt said as he turned his beer up and eyed the cookies Hawk had brought.

Hawk noticed the power chug, prompting her to wonder how a recovering alcoholic was able to stay disciplined enough not to fall off the wagon again. "Everyone has to grow up someday, I guess," Cindy said. "You going all the way with the high and tight?"

She knew a guy like Kolt probably wasn't the lieutenant colonel type. She also knew he'd be comfortable getting busted back to captain if it would give him more time in a Delta troop and, of course, on target.

"I haven't decided to even get my dress uniform dry-cleaned yet. One thing at a time."

Hawk chuckled.

They spent a few minutes catching up and enjoying their beers. Kolt scarfed a few of the cookies. Cindy was enjoying the small talk, pleased he didn't turn his nose up at the baked goods, but knew the conversation would inevitably turn to shop talk. It had to. She knew Racer would want to know.

"Look, Kolt, I wanted to fill you in on some of the recent happenings at work." That was it; she crossed the line. She'd have to tell Kolt everything. He would know if she was holding back anything.

"Have you seen the news reports about a body washing up onshore on the west side of Manhattan?" she asked.

Kolt just shrugged.

"Well, that's all that is being reported. The administration is being pretty tight-lipped with the details, but there is a lot more to it," Cindy said.

"What's the big deal?" Kolt asked.

"There were actually two bodies. The other one surfaced farther north, on the Jersey side at Piermont."

"Boating accident? And?" Kolt didn't try to hide his sarcasm.

"Not exactly. Far from it, I'm afraid. Tied to one of the guys was a collapsible ladder, a five-ton bottle jack, and two four-by-four-inch-wide, four-foot-long sections of treated lumber. FBI suspects an attempt to infiltrate a storm-water drain line at the nuclear power plant up the Hudson River. Naturally, the authorities are tight-lipped about what the terrorist may have been doing."

"Interesting. Any nationality?" Kolt said, sipping his beer between thoughts. "Any link to Mohammad Ghafour?"

"Well, there is a possible link," Hawk said.

Cindy explained that JSOC was concerned about information found on a thumb drive taken off the target by Shaft and Kolt. On the USB drive, there were several pictures, mostly aerials pulled from Google Earth or Bing of Indian Point, San Onofre, and Cherokee power plants. The CIA and JSOC were convinced these were the mysterious X, Y, and Z targets embedded inside the MTSAK files pulled from the bin Laden bedroom porn stash. But only Indian Point had pictures that could be considered close target recce shots. And only the Indian Point power plant was up the Hudson from the washed-up body. The pictures were clearly taken with a zoom lens from across the river, and several were close-up shots of the plant's main parking area.

"Hawk, why the hell didn't you tell me about the thumb drive?"

"What? Call you in Ramstein while you were doped up?" answered Cindy. "I can hear it now: 'Umm, yes, this is Major John Doe's sister, can you please tell him that America is soon to be under attack?'"

"OK, OK," said Kolt as he raised his empty hand in surrender. "Point taken."

"Look, Kolt, Webber knows about it. Besides that, all I know is the analysts are running the numbers on the thumb drive's files, scrubbing the related message traffic again, and taking another look at the *empty sack* files," said Cindy.

Kolt listened but didn't respond.

"Besides, I knew you were bummed about so many teammates getting busted up in the downed helo," Hawk added.

"Got it. I appreciate that. But can you get me a copy of the drive?"

"I'm not sure I can do that, Kolt," Cindy said. "Things have changed. You'll probably have to visit the SCIF yourself."

"Webber has me on forced convalescent leave for another two weeks," Kolt answered. "He said he better not see me around the building at all."

Cindy figured Kolt wouldn't share the "admin leave" status with her. She had already heard rumors that he was potentially facing court-martial charges from Admiral Mason for insubordination and violating a direct order in combat. She wasn't sure he had heard that yet, and she wasn't going to spoil the UFC fight for him. And even though the thought of sharing this intel with Kolt is what really brought her out, she desperately wanted to spill about her time and performance in the Black Ice plywood box.

"The world won't end in two weeks, Kolt," Cindy said. "Besides, we're all safe with Gangster's squadron on alert status."

"No shit, that's not the point. The point is, if two guys have already been found washed up downriver from one of the power plants pictured on the thumb drive we pulled off target, it means they are into their target-reconnaissance phase. Possibly moving into their execution phase. Who knows?" Kolt said.

"My hands are tied, Kolt. You'll have to come up with a reason to get back to the Unit quicker than two weeks. Maybe get that photo taken?"

"Roger that," Kolt answered quickly as he reached for the box of medals and ribbons. "I've been meaning to get that DA photo taken ASAP anyway."

Kolt shook his head slightly as if the lights just came on. He looked back at Hawk, dead in the eye. "What did you mean by, 'Things have changed'?"

Cindy let out a sigh of relief, actually thankful that Kolt noticed and was giving her an opportunity to let out steam.

"I'm PCSing back to Fort Riley, Kolt."

"Bullshit!" Kolt said.

"I'm serious."

"What, you have an AD on the range or something?"

"No, it wasn't an accidental discharge," Hawk said. "I got rolled up, Kolt."

"What? When?"

"About the same time you and Shaft were dealing with the Goshai Valley."

"No shit!" Kolt answered with a surprised laugh. "You couldn't use your paracord-prepper monkey-fist bracelet to escape?"

"Yeah, I lived. But, to tell you the truth, I kinda wish I had an alibi fire."

"What happened?" Kolt asked.

"I lost it, Kolt."

"Couldn't have been that bad. You knew it was just training, didn't you?"

"I figured that out. But after three days of sitting in my own shit and piss, they broke me."

"Three days—that's messed up," Kolt said, surprised at the length of Hawk's stay in the box. But Kolt didn't know about Black Ice yet. He figured she went through the same twenty-four-hour program that he and the others often had to deal with unexpectedly during training exercises.

"Hey, full assault mode, right?" Kolt said, staying positive. "You stayed dialed in, right?"

"They said some pretty mean things to me, Kolt. I snapped. Colonel Webber's pilot program has been scuttled. I'm out of the training cell, been moved to the NBC shop and pending PCS orders."

Cindy looked away as Kolt was staring at her. She imagined he could see the pain and humiliation she felt.

"Well, that's bullshit, Hawk!" Kolt said. "You want me to talk to Colonel Webber?"

"No, Kolt," Hawk said as she abruptly stood and headed to the trailer's screen door. It was a nice gesture, but it would likely only irritate Webber. "I couldn't keep it together. I know Colonel Webber is only doing what he has to do for the good of the Unit. It's nothing personal."

"Our loss, Hawk."

ELEVEN

AQ safe house, Sana'a, Yemen

"Are you sure, brother Abdul?" Nadal asked. "You must be sure you have not created a circumstance for us."

"Yes, yes, I am certain," Abdul replied.

The tone of his voice made Nadal suspicious that he wasn't certain at all.

"How can you be so certain?" Nadal asked.

"Because it is the one our friend Timothy, I mean Patrick Henry, provided."

Nadal gritted his teeth. The fool had mentioned Timothy's real name instead of the code name they had given him.

Silence reigned on the phone. The connection was so clear that Nadal could hear Abdul breathing all the way in the United States.

"Did you learn the American mail system sufficiently? Did you execute the rehearsals as we discussed?" Nadal asked, ignoring Abdul's breach of security.

"I did," Abdul said.

"I want to go over this again," Nadal said, breaking down Abdul's part step by step.

Abdul confirmed every step of the procedure. Sulayk Nadal went over it twice, his faith in Abdul shaken. He had provided Abdul the address to mail the package to. It was the address obtained by Timothy Reston, the security trainer from the Cherokee plant in South Carolina. He'd also issued Abdul strict orders to mail half a dozen packages to him addressed to a post office box he was to have set up. The PO boxes were to have been established in three different post offices around the city.

"Confirm this, please," Nadal said. It was critical the markings were known and that the packages would be returned to sender so they could learn the process before sending the hunting phones to Timothy's plant.

"Yes, yes, brother Nadal," Abdul said. "Everything is in order. Allah has seen to it."

"Ma'aasalaama," Nadal said before killing the red CALL button.

Nadal sat back in his chair and said a silent prayer. The scrape of a stool made him turn. Omer Farooq slid his stool away from the small table and stood. He walked several steps over to the narrow freestanding space heater near the small kitchen and turned the temperature knob to the right.

"What are you doing, Farooq?" Nadal demanded.

"Relax, my friend, but we should not have to work in such frigid conditions," Farooq replied.

"It is important to maintain room temperature when shaping the plastique," Nadal said. "Do you not remember that from your studies?"

"I remember," Farooq said.

They had known each other for years and had become like blood brothers, but more like cats and dogs than the same species. Nadal knew that he could be curt, but no detail was too small in this war against the infidels. Friendship would always take second place.

Nadal had met Farooq at Balochistan University of Engineering and Technology in Quetta, Pakistan. Nadal, a foreigner from Romania, had been a fish out of water. Farooq, a far more gregarious and wild student, had gathered Nadal up into his small group, and their friendship blossomed. They hit it off early, confirming opposites do attract. Nadal was clearly more intelligent and religiously pious than Farooq, but Farooq was more radicalized and always spoke of becoming a mujahideen to defend Islam against the Western infidels.

Farooq had failed his final tests after his third year in the Engineering and Science Department and was forced to drop out. The university's vice chancellor scolded him in front of several students, accusing Farooq of substituting hard work and determination with complacency and lethargy, something that the competitive modern world frowned upon.

Nadal pitied Farooq and had taken him under his wing. He knew Farooq would go to the ends of the earth to redeem himself, and that was the kind of man Nadal needed. It helped that Farooq was also an artist. His skill was put to great use, first in learning to forge Pakistani bank notes and rupees, doctors' and marriage licenses, and later in undertaking far more challenging documents, including passports and entry/exit and tourist visas. Unlike the traditional cards and invitations, these documents demanded a heavier fee, tripling, even quadrupling, their income at times.

Their lives would have continued down the road of simple larceny except for the events of 2 May 2011 in Abbottabad, Pakistan. The shock, sorrow, and humiliation they felt when the greatest living Islamic hero, Osama bin Laden, had been killed, would quickly transform into abiding rage.

On that day, Nadal and Farooq vowed to give their knowledge to Islam and join the jihad.

"I know you do," Nadal said, offering his brother a small affection. "You were always a quick study. You were the first to master the RPG in the training camps."

"It is important to know which end to point toward the enemy," Farooq said, smiling.

Nadal didn't like to admit it, but Farooq had always been better with weapons. It was what had attracted the attention of those higher up in al Qaeda. Meeting Haji Mohammad Ghafour had been a dream come true for both of them. When he offered them the mission, it was a truly glorious day. And that was why Nadal strove for perfection. They would not get a second chance to strike the Western snake again. Not like this.

"I know, and it is also important to know the right address," Nadal said, unable to help himself from getting in a small admonition.

Farooq raised his hands and rolled his eyes. "I do know. You forget, but it was I that chose these targets. Who remembers the brave warriors who attacked the American embassies in Tanzania and Kenya in 1998? Or those that bombed the USS *Cole* or the nightclub in Bali?" Those brothers of jihad were celebrated for only a short time, their names not important enough to cling to the sturdy fabric of history. People forgot quickly.

Nadal bristled. "I do not seek fame for myself."

Farooq shook his head. "Fame is for the whores of Hollywood. I am talking about everlasting glory. Our nineteen brothers that attacked America on September eleventh are examples the world over. Their story is repeated in mosques everywhere. They are true martyrs and heroes of Islam. History has honored them with a glorious status. Do their names not reside now with those of the greatest Muslim heroes like Saladin?"

Nadal rolled his eyes. "We are no Saladins, my friend."

Farooq did not smile. "No, we are more, for we go into battle knowing of our martyrdom and embracing it. We take the battle to the enemy on his land, not ours. What we will achieve will rival the defeat of the crusaders!"

Nadal knew there was no reasoning with Farooq when he began speaking of Saladin and the crusades.

"Our plan is ambitious, my brother, of that I grant you," Nadal said. "But surely it is prudent to be . . . prudent. The American power plants are well guarded. We need far more than box cutters."

Farooq pointed to the array of explosives, chemicals, and model airplanes spread out on the living room carpet inside their nondescript two-story flat in northern Yemen.

"And so we have," Farooq said.

Nadal surveyed the disassembled microwaves, model airplane controllers, burlap straps, plastic ties, superglue, and other odds and ends that would be used to attach grenades to the bottom of the planes. Everything was neatly laid out to ensure accuracy and limit confusion.

"They are not full-size passenger jets, but these model planes will be like flying bombs," Nadal said, admiring his work. "They will never detect them until it is too late, as long as we are careful."

Farooq nodded. "You say so, brother, but I still believe your technique is too difficult, too many complicated steps, each strapping us with a vulnerability we may not be prepared for."

"Details, Farooq, details," Nadal said, putting on heavy-duty chemical-resistant gloves and picking up a cigar-sized test tube. He unstoppered it and began pouring the contents into a small glass beaker.

"But there can be too many details," Farooq said.

Nadal sighed. "Farooq, you will do well to allow me to handle the engineering and science of this matter," he said without looking up. "Please, put on your safety goggles."

Farooq reached down to the clear plastic goggles that hung from around his neck and raised them to his eyes, reaching back to settle the elastic band on the center of his head.

"The brothers that drowned near New York, yes, their plan was too difficult," Nadal said. "These flying bombs would have served them well, Inshallah."

Farooq watched in silence as Nadal finished wrapping the black electrical tape around the model plane's fuselage. It was clear to Nadal that Farooq still thought the planes were too difficult to use.

"To ease your mind, we will conduct a rehearsal," Nadal said. "A quarter of the plastique that I plan to use should more than suffice."

Farooq smiled. "I think that is wise."

Nadal pulled at the fingered ends of his gloves, removing them and putting them on the counter as he stood. Without removing his safety goggles, he walked over to the kitchen area to the large concrete block sitting on top of an old folded Aztec calendar blanket.

"We must discuss our security measures once more," Nadal said. "It is too important to preserving our mission and protecting ourselves and our tools."

"Nadal, we have gone over this a dozen times," Farooq said. "I am not dense, my brother. I do have some schooling, and I did help you build the device."

Four Soviet 152mm artillery shells were embedded upside down in the concrete block. Red wires, attached to the initiator assemblies, in the center of the flat tail ends of the four shells, snaked their way halfway down on all four sides of the concrete block. Black Thuraya cell phones, embedded in the concrete just past their tiny buttons, only the upper screen and top showing, identified the end of the red wires.

"Farooq, patience, please, my brother," Nadal said as he inspected the phones more closely, ensuring the red light on each was still active. "These are matters our brothers have sacrificed for in Iraq and Afghanistan."

Farooq knew he was referring to the lessons their al Qaeda brothers in Iraq learned the hard way. During the war in Iraq, U.S. Special Operations forces had expertly moved themselves inside the terrorists' decision-making process during the long hunt for Abu Musab al-Zarqawi. Zarqawi countered with setting traps for spec-ops troops that liked to pop in unexpectedly. They developed a standard procedure for all safe houses along the rat line from Syria to Ramadi, east toward Fallujah, and into Baghdad. Set a bomb in each house, one that ideally could be used to bait Americans inside and kill them. If not, a bomb that could at least make martyrs out of the brothers once Americans had stormed the house.

"Please, Nadal, I am skilled enough to make a cell phone call to activate the bomb receivers and detonate the artillery shells," Farooq said, motioning away from the concrete block and back toward the prepared model airplane. "Can we conduct our test now?

Nadal hesitated for a moment, ensuring he had positively checked all four sides of the concrete block, reassuring himself that all four shells would detonate with a single phone call and that everything in the safe house would be destroyed. An attack on their safe house by local security forces would set their plans back significantly, but the evidence of their ever being there or even of their methods would go up in flames.

Nadal moved back to the airplane on the floor and bent over. He gently picked the plane up with both hands, having forgotten to place his safety gloves back on. Nadal placed his right hand under the belly of the plane and reached for the plane's electric controller. With his left hand, he rotated his thumb to the top of the square black plastic control device and rested it on the red toggle switch that provided wireless power to the plane's toy engine.

Nadal turned toward Farooq and looked him in the eye from across the room. He smiled. This was what attention to details got you. They had a sophisticated weapon that would soon strike at the very heart of the Western beast by easily flying over the defenses of every power plant in America. "Brother Nadal, by the power of Allah, the most gracious and merciful, this test marks the beginning of our journey to strike fear and discontent into the hearts of the American pigs."

A millisecond after toggling the red switch, the plane in Nadal's right hand exploded, sending plastic and tiny shards of aluminum in every direction.

TWELVE

JSOC Headquarters, Fort Bragg, North Carolina

Making the early-morning drive from the Delta compound, east across Fort Bragg to the secure Joint Special Operations Command Headquarters that connected to Pope Army Airfield, Kolt wondered what the hell Admiral Mason wanted.

More like what the JSOC commander wanted to do to him.

Two days after Hawk's unannounced visit, Colonel Webber had sent word to Kolt that the JSOC commanding general wanted to see him. Admiral Mason had personally summoned Major Kolt Raynor for a 0900 hours meeting in his office, and at 0852 hours on a very sunny Monday morning, Kolt worried that he might be casually late.

Kolt knew it wasn't to pin a medal on him or even shake his hand for accomplishing the mission in the Goshai Valley three weeks ago. No. Kolt had blown off the admiral's order to abort that mission, and even though the admiral couldn't be one-hundred-percent certain that Kolt had heard the abort call before leaving the back of the hovering aircraft, he was certain of Kolt's refusal to move to the alternative landing zone to be picked up by the helicopter. All things considered, Kolt figured the meeting could go either way.

Kolt leaned over to check his hair in the rearview mirror, or what hair he still had. Even with a fresh high-and-tight cut yesterday for his DA photo, somehow he figured the commanding general wouldn't be all that impressed. Kolt also knew that leaving the goatee on his face until the last minute before his DA photo probably wouldn't impress the admiral either.

At the moment, he silently cursed his inherited thinning hair. For someone who was unflappable about the important things—things on the battlefield in particular—his internal vanity was a slow bleed that frustrated him. It was a bloodletting that he had no control over to stop. The hair in the shower every morning reminded him.

Delta operators have a certain look. At least Kolt thought they did. The image in his mind of the poster-boy operator was always of a lean but mus-cled warrior with thick flowing hair and the sort of good looks that were the envy of most of society. The kind of warrior typically found in ancient times that lived off meat and nuts and grain. The type of man ninety-five percent of the men in the world aspired to be. The type of operator Kolt had been before 9/11 and before the physical beating he had taken on the battlefield since the war on terror started.

Of course, if pressed, Kolt would argue that the best Delta operator was the guy who looked as normal as the next guy on the street corner. A guy that could blend in like a chameleon arguably could accomplish so much more in the realm of counterterrorism. Blending in, or hiding in plain sight, mitigated the risk of compromise significantly. Such an operator just wasn't as soothing to the eye.

But, privately, the receding hairline just sucked. The only thing that sucked more when it came to Kolt's appearance was the embarrassing love handles he carried. The same ones he struggled to reduce a little during his recent five-month deployment to Afghanistan. But whereas the male-pattern baldness was inherited, the love handles were courtesy of a few too many frozen yogurt stops in nearby Southern Pines.

With the irritating bright sun in his eyes blocking his vision, Kolt squinted as he pulled his black 1991 Chevy Silverado pickup through the heavily guarded checkpoint. He powered his window down, greeted the two patriotic Vietnam veterans proudly holding down a retirement gig as security guards, and flashed his unit-access picture badge. The guard checked his name against the visitors' roster, verified facial recognition in the database, and traded his Unit badge for a visitors' badge before raising the security barrier and waving him through.

The Joint Special Operations Command Headquarters was always a busy place. Like most compounds that spring up out of necessity, little attention was given to world events that might soon highlight the scarcity of parking spots. After a couple of trips around the main parking lot hoping for an open spot to appear, Kolt saw one in the next lane over. Out of pure habit, he *combat parked,* backing into the spot.

He thumbed his unit-issued Droid one more time before sticking it in the glove box and grabbed his tan beret. In Delta, berets were about as scarce as were dress uniforms, and very rarely required or worn within the compound. There were only two times when a Delta operator had to dig deep into his wall locker to locate his colored beret. Neither time was all that common, but in both instances it was typically a sign that something bad had just happened.

The most common time was when visiting higher headquarters. A tan beret marked a Delta operator as a former Ranger. Green, of course, let everyone know he was a product of the Special Forces A-Teams. Guys from Airborne outfits wore the maroon beret. Berets weren't necessarily a bad thing. They just weren't exactly the most appealing hat for operators with relaxed grooming standards and facial hair. The longer it remained atop long, thick hair, the more it seemed to rise on the head, giving you the feeling such operators were wearing the floppy hat favored by the eccentric Lady Gaga.

Besides visiting the head sheds at JSOC or the U.S. Army Special Operations Command, USASOC, a few miles south near main post, berets along with full dress uniforms went on after a teammate had fallen in training or battle. In those instances, which had been fairly often since the World Trade Center towers had collapsed in 2001, the fallen operator had plenty of teammates standing over him as he was lowered into the grave with dignity and full honors.

Kolt walked the hundred feet from his truck to the five-story command building. He passed several young troops that very smartly snapped a hand salute and offered the greeting of the day. It surprised him.

"Good Morning, sir!" they said in unison.

"Uh, morning, guys," Kolt responded as he tried to render a suitable hand salute in return. The Delta compound was a no-salute area just as any combat base overseas was. Kolt was out of practice.

Kolt approached the tinted double glass doors and reached for his visitors' badge. He flashed it in front of the proximity card reader and listened for the door lock to disengage.

He stepped inside and took an immediate right into the open elevator door. He pressed the number 3 button, and as the door closed he checked to ensure the buttons on his cargo pockets were still buttoned. He was inside the Joint Special Operations compound, and unlike the Delta compound, they still were sticklers for maintaining a sharp and properly worn uniform— even in a combat zone, a ridiculous and impractical standard Admiral Mason brought with him from the Pentagon. As the elevator came to a slow stop, Kolt looked down at his boots to check his spit-shine job.

Substandard. I'm out of practice with my boots, too.

The hallway leading to Admiral Mason's secret corner of the world was lined with framed posters of various motivational phrases. One in particular caught Kolt's eye. It read, PARARESCUE—BECAUSE EVEN SEALS, GREEN BERETS, AND RECON MARINES NEED TO CALL 911.

Kolt smiled slightly. *Yeah, Delta needs you guys too.*

"Hello, Major Raynor, great to see you," Mary said with a genuinely wide smile.

"Hey, Mary, how are you?" Kolt answered quickly. This wasn't the first time he had been called on the carpet in front of the JSOC commanding general, just the first time with Admiral Mason. Addressing the admiral's secretary by name was a pretty good indicator that he had spent way too much time at his higher command.

"That was a real nice article in *Newsweek* about the airplane rescue in India," Mary said with raised eyebrows and a slight tilt of her head. "The U.S. ambassador to India is one of the special operation community's biggest fans now."

"Really?" Kolt asked with interest. "Haven't seen it."

"Well, go on in Kolt. The admiral will be right with you," Mary said with a warm smile as she looked over her reading glasses and motioned to the office door.

Kolt marveled at the museumlike atmosphere inside the admiral's office. Covering the walls were framed photos in various sizes, sporadically separated by award certificates and other memorable correspondence. One was taken with the president in front of the White House. Another was with the Secretary of Defense, taken in front of the Tokyo Sky Tree, the 2,080-foot tower with bicyclists and a passing rickshaw in the background. Above and behind the large cherry desk, the most prominent item on display was the oversize and gaudy framed Naval Academy graduation certificate, made all the more ridiculous by the hand-rubbed antique-brass-finished vanity light hanging over it.

The admiral's entering the room startled Kolt. He turned abruptly to face him.

"Good morning, sir," Kolt offered, attempting his best impression of standing at a rigid position of attention with his beret gripped in his left hand. He expected the admiral to ask him to take a seat.

Sipping his coffee as he rounded the desk, the admiral nodded slightly in silence before taking a seat.

It was clear that Admiral Mason was in no mood for niceties. He reached into the top desk drawer and retrieved an unmarked manila envelope.

"Take a close look, Major," he said. He was very formal as he handed it to Kolt.

"Yes, sir!" Kolt answered as he opened the envelope. He pulled out a packet of paper, about twenty sheets in all, stapled together in the top left-hand corner. The cover page was military formal in every way. It was an army-regulation 15-6 investigation.

Raynor leafed through the pages, seeing numerous handwritten, sworn statements from individuals familiar with the raid into Pakistan that nabbed Mohammad Ghafour a few weeks earlier. One from Bill "Smitty" Smith, the air mission commander from 1/160th Special Ops Aviation Regiment. Another from Master Sergeants Jason "Slapshot" Holcomb and Peter "Digger" Chamblis.

"I'm under investigation, sir?" Kolt asked, somewhat surprised.

"Informally at this time, Major. Yes."

"May I ask why, sir?"

Mason paused before speaking.

"Major, I have initiated a 15-6 to determine the circumstances around the mission in the Goshai Valley to capture Mohammad Ghafour," Mason said. He was clearly trying to keep his emotions in check and not doing a great job at it.

"Sir, I was only doing my duty," Kolt said.

"Your duty, Major? More like your desire to do whatever the hell you want and ignore the chain of command."

Kolt understood now. Despite the success of the mission, Mason was pissed because he didn't get to control how it went down. "Sir, we had a compromised operator on the ground and the intel for capturing Ghafour was solid," Kolt answered. In fact, at the time he ignored the admiral's abort call and roped onto the target anyway, he hadn't known about Shaft's being compromised. He didn't learn that until they were back at J-bad during the hot wash.

Mason snapped. "Bullshit, Major! Your man could have walked out of that valley the same way he came in and never tipped his hat. You put two helicopters and close to thirty men in danger with your personal cowboy antics. You heard me abort the mission," Mason snapped.

Kolt placed the folder and packet back on Mason's desk. Then it hit him like a speeding freight train.

Kolt's body went numb. He felt an odd sensation of déjà vu. He had been here before. It was the exact same feeling he had experienced when he was first run out of the community for a different mission. Ironically, the earlier mission happened across the border in Pakistan, too.

"Sir, I did hear you say abort the op. I'm certainly not going to stand here and lie to you about it," Kolt answered.

"You son of a bitch! I knew it!" Mason replied, banging his fist on the desktop and standing up.

"Major, I specifically aborted that mission to protect the lives of everyone in both those helicopters. Your life, as well as mine, and dozens of others."

Kolt anticipated the walls crumbling around him or a pack of armed military police entering to whisk him away. He couldn't help notice the admiral's hair had fallen out of place when he banged his fist on his desk. Kolt didn't speak a word more than, "Yes, sir!" But he refused to whimper.

Kolt was human. Kolt was an American. He was devastated by his own revelation that he had intentionally ignored the admiral's order. Sure, it was hectic up there on that helo. Things were a bit confusing and uncertain. But that's the environment that Delta considers home-field advantage. Even so, blowing off the CG who sat only a few feet away from you was over the top. In fact, it was well over the top, but what was arguably cloudy inside the helicopter was crystal clear inside the admiral's office.

He knew the admiral was stating the facts and that they weren't open to interpretation, but he refused to give in. Kolt wasn't apologetic at all for executing that mission. He wasn't sorry for recovering his teammate, Shaft, and capturing Mohammad Ghafour. He didn't expect a medal. He didn't expect even simple thanks.

Kolt dug in.

"With all due respect, sir, the abort call you made was well outside standard operating procedure."

Admiral Mason slipped back into his leather chair, sipped his coffee, and laser-locked on Raynor's eyes.

"Explain yourself."

"Point of no return, Admiral. The specific location in time and space that an operation cannot be aborted, a point determined well before launch time by the planners at J-bad. Every mission has one. Our mission in the Goshai Valley had one, and that decision point was when we turned down the valley. At that point, sir, three minutes from being over the target area, the enemy could hear the helos approaching. At that point, we were committed."

"You can't kill anyone you want to, Raynor!" Mason said, obviously trying to change the topic of abort protocol. Details of the mission were well known at this point. Kolt and Shaft captured Ghafour and made it out of the old British fort. Kolt had been wounded in the leg, but five fighting-age males, all armed with AK-47s, were smoked as Kolt and Shaft dragged Ghafour out of the village.

"You aren't America's killer man, son," Mason said.

Kolt knew it was no use trying to match wits with the admiral. "Sir, I say again, we were hovering over the target. A single operator was on the ground. We were way past the time to abort that hit."

"That's bullshit, and you know it, Major!" Mason responded. "You have a reputation of doing what Kolt Raynor wants to do on target . . . chain of command be damned!"

Both men knew there was a secret investigation, apart from the 15-6 initiated on Kolt, into what happened during that mission. Kolt knew as well that Admiral Mason rightly feared being held personally responsible for the loss of an expensive special operations helicopter, particularly in Pakistan. First, a state-of-the-art stealth Black Hawk was left behind in Abbottabad after the SEALs smoked bin Laden. Now it had happened a second time. The one saving grace, well two, really, was that the trailing Dark Horse struck by an RPG on infil had successfully executed a controlled crash landing and that, besides some minor shrapnel wounds to one of the crew chiefs and a few broken bones and bruises suffered by the operators in the back, everyone survived. Everything made it out that night except the scuttled black MH-47G helo.

The second saving grace, of course, was that the assault force accomplished the mission. They had captured Mohammad Ghafour and successfully brought him into Afghanistan to interrogate. And that was the kind of stuff that made POTUS happy. Kolt would never point it out, but he knew that Mason knew Kolt was one of POTUS's favorites.

Admiral Mason swiveled his neck and tugged at the collar of his uniform. "Your pattern of insubordination, Major, in just the six months or so I have been in command has become intolerable."

Kolt stood rigid. He gripped his beret tight. He tried to process what was happening here, but it was happening too fast.

"Your episode of direct insubordination last month in the Goshai Valley is the final straw. Your continued inability to follow the rules and policies of this organization confirms to me your services are no longer needed by this command."

"Are you serious, sir?" Kolt asked, more smart-ass than sincere.

"Dead serious, Major!"

"Does Colonel Webber know about this?" Kolt asked.

Mason tried to set his coffee down delicately but spilled half the cup as he slammed his opposite fist on his desk.

"Damn it, Raynor!" Mason yelled. "I am the commanding general, not Webber, and not you. It is high time Delta realizes that. There will be a full investigation. Now, get the hell out of my office."

Only a moment after Kolt was dismissed, the phone on the admiral's desk rang. It was Mary from the outer room.

"Uh, sir, I hate to interrupt you, sir, but you have an important call on the secure line. It's from Washington . . . I think POTUS wants to talk to you."

POTUS! "Patch them through immediately."

Before Mary pressed the button on her end, the admiral overheard some small talk in the background. He tilted his head in curiosity and strained to hear what was being said outside his office.

"Great seeing you, Mary. Regards to your old man and tell your daughter to enjoy the prom . . . within reason," Kolt said. "Thanks for the *Newsweek*."

"Thanks, Kolt, I'll tell her," Mary whispered with her hand half over the mouthpiece, obviously not wanting to be heard over the phone.

Damn, is there anyone in the community that Delta major doesn't know?

THIRTEEN

Main access facility, Yellow Creek Nuclear Power Plant

The mail clerk always wondered why in the hell he had to deliver the mail to the main access facility at Yellow Creek station at the same time that the employees rotated shifts. Sure, he knew he didn't have to undergo such a detailed search as the others, simply because he had been making this same delivery, using this same green wheeled cart, for better than three years now.

But it was still a hassle, since the minimum staffing of security officers kept them busy as employees processed through the search trains, stepping first into the explosives detector as the robotic female voice announced "Enter," then remaining motionless for several seconds, and finally stepping out the other side upon hearing "Exit." Then they placed any metallic personal belongings—cell phones, vehicle keys, and so on—into the clear plastic bins on a conveyor belt to be X-rayed. It was similar to processing through a security checkpoint at an airport.

The employees took a few steps forward and walked through the metal detector before retrieving their belongings from the bins. Processing forty to fifty people stacked up in two lines took time, especially since they had to be absolutely sure their security protocols didn't allow any entry of firearms, long knives, or explosives.

The mail clerk was happy to see the first security officer available head

117

toward the glass handicapped door and unlock it. It was Officer Chad Simmons, a fellow Atlanta Braves fan.

"Morning, Mike," Simmons said.

"Morning, Chad. Appreciate you getting me in," Mike said. "Busy Monday morning as usual."

"You know how it is—never stops around here," Simmons said as he chalked open the wide glass door and pulled the Garrett SuperScanner metal detector from his hip.

Mike knew the routine all too well. Once the officer had the wand out and gave the head nod to Mike, he would push the mail cart another three and a half feet and stop the lead edge of the front tires on the bold white painted line.

"Go ahead," Simmons said, standing off to the side to make room for the wide cart. "A lot of mail today it looks like."

"Like the Pony Express," Mike said, shaking his head.

Officer Simmons slowly moved the wand over the top of the boxes, removing the first layer to check the bottom boxes.

"Braves are tearing it up this season," Simmons said. "A pennant year for sure."

"That would be nice—been several years now," Mike agreed. "We're due!"

Finishing the wand sweep, Officer Simmons replaced the metal detector on his hip and reached down to remove two square boxes and a circular tube mailer.

"Gotta run these, Mike," Simmons said. "Stand by for a second, will ya?"

"Yep, no worries," Mike said. Officer Simmons walked over to the explosive detectors carrying all three packages. He entered, waited the few seconds, and stepped out on the audible "Exit." Simmons placed the packages on the conveyor belt and watched as they moved into the X-ray shroud; then he stepped through the metal detector, ignoring the alarm because he was required to be armed.

Simmons stepped over to the X-ray imaging screen to confirm the contents were not contraband with the seated search-train officer.

"What we got?" Simmons asked.

"Looks like some gadget for maintenance and two boxes of cell phones," the seated officer said.

"Yeah, I heard we were looking at incorporating cell phones into our protective strategy. Must be vendor samples for the bosses to evaluate," Simmons said as he lifted the three packages from the belt and walked back over to the opened handicap door and the mail cart.

"Packaging looks legit. One from Sprint and one from AT&T," Simmons said as he placed them back on the mail cart. "Go ahead and process through the search trains, Mike. Your cart will be waiting on the other side."

Having processed into the plant, Mike pushed the cart into the mail room, which was near the security-officer ready room on the first floor. He logged each package and placed it in one of several large sheet-metal bins identified by the various departments that made up the organizational structure of the power plant. There was one for Operations, the high-paid prima donnas that ensured the profit margins were met; one for Maintenance, who ensured the three General Electric boiling-water reactors operated at one-hundred-percent power, generating the electricity that costs their two million clients a fair $0.077823 kilowatt-hour fee; and another bin for Security, the men and women that ensured no unauthorized access was granted to anyone without first undergoing an FBI background check, psychological evaluation, and fingerprint tests, run against the criminal and terrorism database.

Mike sorted the boxes, checking each addressees' name against the spreadsheet on the stand-alone screen to his front and placing them in their respective bins to be picked up by each department's designated representative before lunch.

Mike picked up one of the three boxes Officer Simmons's metal detector had pinged on and read the address label, recognizing the name as one of the older guys that worked in unit 2. He placed the box in the Maintenance bin, penciled the action on the paper log, and clicked the small box next to the word "delivered" on the screen.

Mike then lifted up a square box wrapped in white paper with heavy, clear packing tape. The address labels were typed neatly and had the yellow and black Sprint logo sticker and IPHONE5 FORWARD THINKING stamped prominently on three sides of the box. Mike recognized the professional packaging, but the name didn't check out on his paper log. This wasn't uncommon, and the protocol for such matters was simple. Mike turned to the computer, opened the employee database, and typed the name in the search line. The face of an elderly gentleman popped up on the screen, showing his status and previous positions at Yellow Creek.

Hmmm. Guy left the company months ago. Must have retired.

Mike secured the box and walked it over to the smaller bin on roller wheels near the door. The bin was marked RETURN TO SENDER.

Mike moved back to the cart and picked up the round circular mailer, roughly the size of a large coffee can, and rotated it to read the addressee and inspect the packaging. Again, the packaging from AT&T was professionally done and everything appeared in order. But, just as before, the addressee name was not on his paper log. Mike repeated the simple steps, but this time the database did not register the name. He tried again. No luck. No indication that the gentleman was ever an employee at the plant. Mike realized this wasn't as common as a former employee receiving mail after leaving the company, but it wasn't entirely out of the ordinary. No, the steps were the same, log it and place in the RTS bin. The rejected packages would sit there until the following Monday, at which time they would be removed before lunch.

It wasn't like the robust security process had been breached or anything.

As Mike finished up logging and delivering the mail, he closed the door behind him and began pushing the cart to the exit portals. Once outside, he would push the mail cart exactly 462 feet to reach the main warehouse and his own office. He'd make the trip again late that evening, twice a day on Mondays, Wednesdays, and Fridays, and he might not send another single package to the return-to-sender bin the entire week.

As Mike made the trip down the approved walkway, the freshly poured concrete sidewalk marked by yellow safety lines to identify uneven surfaces and trip hazards, the two packages in the return-to-sender bin chirped to life, having received an initiator code from overseas.

Immediately, the six iPhone 5s began hunting.

Within fifteen minutes, if all went as Nadal knew it would, the phones would remotely grab all seven CPUs inside the adjacent security center. It would kick out the stand-alone work computers and isolate the two connected to the internal local area network, where security-sensitive material is shared across departments and functionalities.

But Nadal wasn't just interested in security-sensitive information; he wanted the safeguards material, including target-set information, the plant's NRC-approved security strategy and implementing procedures. To do that, Nadal had to manipulate the phones' internal data and modify the encryption code so that when the phones received a specific signal, they would aggressively hunt, breaching firewalled systems and advanced security features like "air gaps." But to bounce undetected across the data diodes and compromise the unidirectional gateways, which provide the most important benefits of truly air-gapped control systems, Nadal figured a way to use the iPhone 5 as a transmitting appliance that would send a wireless sensor to a receiving appliance on the far side of the world. The hunting phones would acquire the light sensors located on the seven CPUs in the company's internal security network, but that was only half the performance. Nadal's game-changing breakthrough was figuring out how to hide the capture of secure data from an overseas Internet café from the NSA's supersecret Social Network Analysis Collaboration Knowledge Services, or SNACKS.

Yes, Nadal had done his technology homework at Balochistan University.

The iPhone 5 was more than an aggressive hunter, it was like a bloodthirsty wild animal that indiscriminately kills by nature. But in this case, it wasn't killing anything, just waiting on the correct initiating logic, a simple phone call, to prompt the hunt for the light sensors and begin capturing secure data.

Delta Force compound, Fort Bragg

Kolt rubbed his fingers along the side of his whitewall haircut, where the sides of the head were cut skin-close and the top of the head retained maybe an inch or two of hair. He stared into the reflective glass that covered an eight-by-ten black-and-white photo hanging on Colonel Webber's wall, a little perplexed by how young he looked without his typical long brown hair and salt-and-pepper goatee.

The photo, obviously aged with rippled fold marks from being handled roughly before finding the safety of a framed wall hanging, showed a group of grizzled men dressed in multicolored cold-weather clothing, rifles slung across their chests with the muzzles pointed downward. Behind them, in the gorgeous mountainous area near a village named Bujanovac at the base of the Vlasic Ski Resort of Bosnia and Herzegovina, a mix of snow-covered Scotch and European pines contrasted with the bright red and yellow North Face jackets. Kolt would come to know the place well years later, but this picture, circa 1995, marked the early days of the manhunt for Serbian war criminals indicted by The Hague.

Next to a thirtysomething Webber, then a junior captain, stood a taller man with a full dirty-blond beard and long locks kicking out of the edges of his dark green wool skull-cap. Kolt knew this to be the then major Michael L. Bird. Now, MLB—"major league ballplayer"—was one of the legends whose name is engraved on the triangle-shaped black marble memorial wall, the centerpiece of the Unit garden.

I wonder how much Hawk really knows about all the crazy shit her dad pulled off over the years?

Kolt heard Delta commander Colonel Webber greet his secretary in the outer entryway and turned quickly from the photo, not wanting to get busted appearing to be too much into the commander's past.

"Damn it, son," Webber said as he circled around to the back of his large desk and took a seat in the maroon leather high-back chair. "You're still fucking up by the numbers, aren't you?"

Kolt wasn't sure how to respond as he stood at the position of attention, arms tight to his sides, looking directly over Webber's head as he remained focused on an imaginary spot on the wall. He hesitated for a few seconds, searching for the right response, trying to gauge just how pissed off Webber was at him this time. Yes, this spot, on Webber's carpet, was very familiar to the wild-card Delta major over the years.

"Sit down, Major," Webber finally said, releasing Kolt from his motionless posture.

Kolt clasped the zipper on the front of his OD green jumpsuit and zipped it a little higher toward his neck. Sure, the uniform was standard-issue for all operators and worn probably eight to ten months out of the year by all operators, but Webber had stopped wearing one the day he became the commander just over two years ago. Kolt got it; he knew the colonel needed to be wearing a more formal military uniform in his current position. But he also figured he might be wise not to have the zipper too far down, showing the heavy soil and sweat on his light brown T-shirt from his having just tested his bum wheel by running the long obstacle course and the mile plus back to the compound for the surprise meeting in Webber's office.

Well, it wasn't entirely a surprise.

"Sir, about the meeting this morning with Admiral Mason," Kolt said—trying to get ahead of the curve and sensing Webber was eyeballing his fresh and goofy conventional army haircut—"I know I've got issues."

"Save it, Racer," Webber said, motioning with his right hand to stop him talking. "I'm not interested in your side of the story; it's already been beat to death at the hot wash. It's on file like the rest of them."

"Yes, sir," Kolt said, dropping his defense to what was certainly the tongue-lashing he was about to take.

"Look, Racer, no doubt the CG is still pissed about your Goshai Valley circus performance, and I wish we could handle it with some written counseling for your local performance file."

"Yes, sir," Kolt said again, letting him know he was listening but not wanting to take the floor from the commander yet.

"Personally, and I think you probably got this vibe from the hot wash, I think he ought to be pinning the DSC on your chest," Webber said, breaking a half smile as he talked. "That's off the record. But the CG wants your head, something I'm sure you picked up on this morning in his office."

"Yes, sir," Kolt said. "That message came through Lima Charlie."

"Well, here is something that isn't entirely loud and clear. Admiral Mason is stuck right now about what to do about you. He received a personal call from POTUS just after you left his office."

"Sir, why in the hell would the president be upset at the CG about Goshai?" Kolt asked. "Admiral Mason didn't have anything to do with my decision to rope, and we did capture the guy."

"Relax, Racer," Webber quickly said. "It wasn't to berate the admiral; it was to congratulate him on the Goshai mission."

"A little late, isn't it?" Kolt asked. "That op is old news." Well, not really that old, Kolt accepted. For the guys still in the sandbox it would be, but the fact that Kolt still had stitches in his lower leg from the pineapple-grenade blast at the British fort reminded him it hadn't been all that long—something readily apparent when he ran the O-course against his doctor's orders.

Webber continued. "Yeah, well, the CIA just cracked the encryption on several files on the thumb drive you guys pulled. Pretty big haul with some unique matches to the *empty sack* haul."

"Really?" Kolt answered, sitting up a little in the leather straight-back chair and leaning toward the commander a little more. "What's up, sir?"

"NSA SIGINT is pinging. Cell phone intercepts and Internet-café traffic confirm late planning stages of a hit on the Cernavoda nuclear plant in Romania."

Kolt knew SIGINT, or signals intelligence, was one of the Western world's most potent weapons against terrorists, who had to communicate somehow to plan, coordinate, and execute their attacks. If not, they would be no different than bin Laden, sidelined and in total blackout comms, hiding.

"Romania. What's al Qaeda's beef with them? Didn't they pull out of Iraq several years ago?" Kolt asked.

"Yes, but they did give basing and overflight permissions to U.S. and allied aircraft. They are still in Afghanistan, and their prime minister has been pretty open about continuing to support the Afghan army even after 2014," Webber said.

"But if the power plant is in Romania, why are the SEALs going to Yemen?" Kolt asked.

"We've narrowed the safe house of what we believe to be the planning cell down to somewhere in Sana'a," Webber said. "The agency also believes there is a connection to an employee of the Romanian power plant."

"A lone wolf?" Kolt asked.

"Close, but not exactly," Webber said. "More of a passive insider at this point, believed to be providing the terrorist cell with planning information and details about the security vulnerabilities of the plant."

"That's all good, sir, but why does all this preliminary, unvetted information stop the admiral from booting me from the command?" Kolt asked.

"Because word is the president asked about you personally and was tickled that you were on the Goshai operation," Webber said, trying to hold back a smile. "Guess the old man feels like he still owes you one for taking out al-Amriki before he knocked Marine One out of the sky."

"I'm touched, sir, but the president really needs to visit Section Sixty to thank the right person for saving his ass," Kolt said.

Webber got the inference. He knew Kolt was referring to Lieutenant Colonel Josh Timble's final resting place in Arlington National Cemetery.

"Either way, Racer, I'm not necessarily fond of losing you a second time. My time in command is coming to an end soon, and I figure I owe it to you, as well as the incoming Delta commander, to lower your profile a little in the near term," Webber stated.

"Sir, please don't offer to keep me around if you plan to take me off operational status," Kolt said, fidgeting in his seat. "I know what it does to guys to go to RDI. I'll just jack it in if it's just the same to you."

Kolt knew Webber understood his meaning. Research and Development Integration was a vital part of the unit's success over the years since its mission was to keep Delta on the cutting edge of everything. Locate or develop and then test the tools of the trade that gave Kolt Raynor and his mates, and all future operators, the best chance of survival. Kolt knew it was vital and that many a wounded operator migrated upstairs over the years to stay in the unit, and he hoped Webber wasn't offended by his last comment.

"Fat chance. You know we are short on healthy operators as it is. Even if I wanted to, that would be tough," Webber answered as he reclined a bit back into his leather chair. "Actually, I'm thinking something lower profile than that."

"Sir?"

"Yemen. With the SEALs," Webber answered.

"AFO, sir?" Kolt said, surprised. He hadn't heard about anything going down in Yemen since Gangster's squadron took down Amriki's staging area six months ago and didn't understand why the place warranted advance-force operations. Kolt even read the daily intel update before breakfast. Nothing about Yemen. Nothing until Webber mentioned the nuke plot a few moments ago. "Can't take my own guys, sir?"

"You won't be in charge of the operation, Major Raynor. The SEALs have the lead on the nuke plot. I'd never be able to keep that from Admiral Mason, anyway. You are just there as an LNO, liaison duty, nothing more, nothing less," Webber said.

"C'mon, sir, are you serious?" Kolt pleaded, forgetting Webber was actually looking out for him. "At least give me some decision-making authority over there with those guys."

"Well, the Six commander asked for you by name, but probably a stupid idea anyway, Raynor. On second thought, I already placed you on mandatory admin leave. I almost forgot. Go ahead and let personnel and finance know you are off operational status so they can dock your operator and hazardous-duty pay appropriately and update your records."

"OK, OK, sir. Point taken," Kolt said, quickly holding both hands up in surrender, seeing the colonel was dead serious. "It's ST6's show; I'm just a friendly straphanger."

"That's what I thought," Webber responded. "You leave tomorrow night for the beach."

"Sir, who is the target?" Kolt asked.

"The thumb drive included two martyr farewell videos," Webber said. "Some cat named Omer Farooq and another guy, a Romanian the agency says is named Sulayk Nadal."

"Farooq Nadal," Kolt said. "Sounds like a good Puerto Rican Christmas carol."

Webber didn't respond to the joke, remaining seated and staring at Kolt.

"What about my troop, sir?" Kolt asked, pushing it a little. "You replacing me?"

"No, Kolt. Your troop is fine. You guys aren't on alert status, and most of your assault teams are scattered to the four winds with training venues. They won't even know you are gone. Get your shit packed, update your power of attorney, and get your will posted in your locker."

"Will do, sir, and thanks!" Kolt said as he stood to walk out of the office and head back to the squadron bay to dig into the low-vis locker for Pakistani clothing and load out his kit.

"Major Raynor, slow down," Webber said, standing as well. "Don't even think about pulling any of your bullshit on this one. In Yemen, Six has the lead. I expect you—in fact, you can take this as a direct order—you will not, under any circumstances, do anything to draw attention to yourself. Got it?"

"Yes, sir," Kolt said. "No normal warrior shit from me. Understood!"

"I'm dead serious, Major." Webber continued. "I don't even expect you to pull out so much as a dull pocketknife the entire three-week deployment, because if you do, we'll both be receiving PCS orders."

"Yes, sir!" Kolt said, appreciative of Colonel Webber's hanging his neck out for him. "I'm just there to pull radio watch."

"Now, get over to the cover shop so they can get you off the books and backstopped," Webber said. "And Racer."

"Yes, sir," Kolt answered, pausing at the doorway.

"Make your own luck!"

FOURTEEN

JSOC safe house, Sana'a, Yemen

"Guys, I gotta tell ya. I'm not seeing this the same way you guys are," Kolt said, shaking his head. He stared at the large satellite map of built-up Sana'a on the wall just to the right of the beige refrigerator and wondered how they didn't see what he saw.

"What's your problem, Kolt?" the SEAL master chief, Rocco, asked. "You're seeing the same intel we are. The place isn't hard to find, man. It will be all over by midnight."

Kolt didn't disagree with Rocco. Farooq and Nadal's pad was easy to find. Looking at the map spread over the kitchen table, Kolt traced the yellow-highlighted bread-crumb route, which the SEALs had captured with a hidden Toughbook loaded with FalconView software while data-logging their driving route.

From the Saudi border entering Sana'a along a four-lane major highway known as Amran Road by the locals, the SEALs would pass by large marble and steel gates marking the entry to Al Thawra City. From there, the route was a series of turns that would take the team past the soccer stadium that masked the target house from the highway until they reached the immediate east-bearing road. In seven hundred feet, the two-story tan and sun-stained structure that was fronted by a rusting six-foot-high metal fence and gate, where Farooq and Nadal were believed to be staying at night, would be on the left. Kolt knew the SEALs couldn't mistake the soccer stadium, one of the most prominent icons in Sana'a, Yemen.

"It's not the intel I'm questioning; it's your guys' intended course of action tonight," Kolt said. "Your mission analysis is a little off, in my opinion."

"How the fuck so?" Rocco said.

It was clear the master chief didn't agree with Kolt's assessment.

"Well, for one—and you guys don't take this personally—you seem to want to take down the target before it's necessary, or even wise to do," Kolt said. He looked the seasoned, wide-shouldered and super-fit SEAL in the eye while trying to soften his obvious disdain for the groupthink that was going on. Maybe the fact that Admiral Mason was personally pushing this raid on the SEALs before it had been thought all the way through was the reason for this.

"That's bullshit!" Rocco said.

Kolt shrugged. "Look man, all I'm saying is maybe we should take the agency's recommendation on this one. The target house isn't going anywhere, but we have a chance here to get a whole lot more out of this if we execute a little operational patience and let it develop. Shit, we just got here. What's the hurry?"

Kolt knew it was typical shit from the SEALs. They were much less about patience and much more about action than the Unit. Sure, they would get at it about 2300 hours on a moonless night, kick a lot of ass in the heart of the Al Thawra neighborhood, and haul in some solid intel. That wasn't the issue. On this particular op, the collection resources were limited with the ongoing Syrian crisis and efforts in Somalia, which gave Kolt pause.

The SEALs were not given operational control of enough intelligence, surveillance, and reconnaissance, or ISR assets. It was a fancy term for all-seeing and orbiting drones that would watch the target house 24-7, and hitting the house without knowing that both their targets, Farooq and Nadal, or even one of them for that matter, were in deep sleep was pissing away an opportunity they might not get again.

"Look, Kolt, just because the CIA recommended a course of action doesn't mean we have to accept it," Rocco said. "This is our gig and the J-staff is expecting the hit to go down tonight. Besides, I'm not asking one of my guys to cross the border and look for a needle in a haystack."

Kolt looked passed Rocco, seated in a dated wooden dining room chair, to the two other SEALs at the far side of the room. Those two were lounged out on the sofa with PS3 controllers in both hands and Grand Theft Auto 5 on the flat screen sitting on the coffee table before them. They were both fairly similar to Rocco: minimum body fat, maximum facial hair, and much fonder of breaking shit than Kolt Raynor, who was currently serving up delicate stuff. Instead of turning a door handle to make entry, they preferred a mule kick.

"That's not what I'm saying," Kolt said. "The agency is still tracking Nadal from Mecca. When he reaches the Saudi-Yemeni border, we can track him from there. Follow him. See where he goes. Who knows? He might unravel some more threads for us."

"Sure, Kolt, we'll all just jump in the minivan and tool across the border, and when the superspies call us, we'll just sneak up from his blind spot and into the left lane and follow Nadal's bus to his hideout," Rocco said. "Is that it?"

Kolt realized he was clenching his right fist and forced it to relax. "Look man, I'm not here to make waves. But while you guys have been out and about gathering atmospherics, Scotty and I have been reading the cable traffic," he said. "Let's get someone on Nadal's bus when he reaches the border. You guys can still do the hit, just push it twenty-four hours to see what develops. Hell, we know Nadal won't be there tonight. How can we be sure Farooq will be?"

Rocco responded with a smirk as he turned around to make eye contact with the others on the sofa. From his seat at the kitchen table, Kolt could see they weren't impressed with the idea either. Both shook their heads at Kolt's suggestion without so much as taking their eyes off the screen.

"With all due respect, fuck that, Racer," Rocco said, loud enough for everyone to hear. "We hit the house tonight as planned, smoke Farooq in his bed, and grab what intel we can."

"Are you for real?" Kolt said, shocked at what he had just heard. Two thumbs-up from the couch potatoes offered support for Rocco's plan.

"Damn right I am. One terrorist asshole in the bag is better than a dry hole," Rocco said. "We can't stay here forever."

Scotty, the young Joint Communications Unit commo man, whose sole function was to keep the secure communication link working between JSOC headquarters at Fort Bragg and their safe house on Ali Abdul Moghri Street, about a quarter mile or so south of Tahrir Square, didn't move a muscle. He remained in the corner of the living room, acting as if he wasn't paying attention. Kolt knew Scotty would not want to get in the middle of a Delta-SEAL heated discussion. It was his job to support both equally, not break a tie.

Kolt knew he was pushing it. *Why can't I just let this go? Let the SEALs decide.*

Webber's direct orders were one thing, but fucking up an operation of this magnitude, of this importance to the nation, one that potentially could halt the Romanian cell in their tracks and stave off an attack on one of America's commercial nuclear power plants, was another. To Kolt, it was a simple matter of arithmetic. One highly irritated Delta commander *or* saving hundreds of thousands of Americans from radiological sabotage?

Raising his voice a little to ensure all four men in the room heard him, he said, "Guys, this Farooq character is a key leader in the Romanian cell. That much we know. But this is too important of an op for al Qaeda for only a couple of guys to be involved. Where's the support personnel, the cutouts, messengers, drivers, passport forgers, financiers, logisticians, and muscle men?"

"Kolt, OK, I see your point," Rocco said, somewhat admitting that Kolt wasn't a complete idiot. "Maybe we should let it develop a little longer since Nadal isn't due at the border till tomorrow morning. But I can't support having one of my guys get all muhjed up and get on that bus. That's fucking suicide."

Kolt was happy to hear Rocco give a little, but now he wanted to kick the master chief in the ass. He'd allowed his men to use the same operational vehicle for the past three days during their recces. Three different makes and colored vehicles, distinct in age and style, were available, parked in the outer courtyard, covered by tarps. Kolt bristled at what was obvious lazy field craft— the SEALs simply did not want to be hassled by changing cars twice a day. They had even forgotten to swap out license plates for two days straight now. That shit could compromise a team in a heartbeat, and you might not even know until it was too late.

Kolt and Rocco had known each other for years. They'd served in Iraq together on several tours and swapped out in Afghanistan more times than they could remember. Rocco was a badass—Kolt knew that much. And now was not the time to give Rocco and his SEALs a scolding about their tradecraft. Besides, even Kolt agreed that they had the correct target house identified. The J-staff was sure of the correct target house. The two trigger-happy SEALs on the sofa were sure as well and really somewhat amazed how easy the house was to find. And although Kolt couldn't put his finger on it, something about a terrorist safe house with no indicators worried him.

"Rocco, out of all of us, I'm probably the last guy to do this op," Kolt said, lowering his voice just enough for the SEAL leader to hear him across the table. "But my language skills are steady and I'm not near as swole as you guys. I don't have the hair these days either, so I'm probably the logical choice."

Kolt could see his logic had hit a button with Rocco. Even Rocco knew his guys had spent too much time in the gym, and their muscles, although highly valued in a direct-action door-kicking gig, were likely to get them compromised or, worse, killed on a crowded bus full of locals.

"Racer, I'm not so sure, man," Rocco said, matching the tone and volume to keep the one on one between the two of them. "I'm not interested in losing even you for this shit."

Kolt sensed Rocco's uneasiness and appreciated the concern for his health and welfare, but that was something Kolt knew had to be subordinate to the greater good. All the operators in the safe house were trained to operate as singletons; they all had language training—most, like Kolt, in multiple disciplines. Kolt also appreciated the fact that, even though the SEALs had been at war since 9/11 as well, JSOC had rarely required them to employ their low-visibility skills. AFO missions were typically sidelined by the SEALs, opting for more high-profile, aggressive assaults like killing bin Laden and smoking the Somali pirates in the Arabian Sea. As such, their James Bond skills suffered.

"We don't have a lot of time to debate it, Rocco. I can shave my head, leave the goatee, dig into the low-vis locker for plenty of Yemeni clothes, and be in a wadi at first light," Kolt said, trying to turn Rocco by downplaying the difficulty of what Kolt was proposing.

"Fuck, Racer," Rocco said under his breath. "You talking about inserting tonight?" Rocco knew Kolt had been to the border of Saudi Arabia and Yemen before on a different operation years earlier. It was one of the reasons the SEAL Team Six commander had requested him by name for this particular op. But inserting him tonight in an area unfamiliar to him and his fellow SEALs was pushing it.

"The intel is, Nadal returns tomorrow," Kolt said. "He is driving the timeline here."

CyberInternet Café, Hadda Hotel, Sana'a, Yemen

Farooq was running late this morning. At the end of the ninety-minute regulation play, the football game was tied. Farooq knew he needed to call it a night, get back to the safe house for a good night's sleep since he had an important task the following day.

A task Nadal had spent extra time explaining the importance of, how it actually worked, and what Farooq's responsibilities would be while Nadal was away. A task Nadal had trusted Farooq to undertake as he spent a few days visiting his father in Mecca.

A task Farooq had forgotten to do this morning. A fact that he could not share with Nadal.

Farooq wanted to get up from his seat and leave. The rain had been steady all night, slowing down the typically fast-paced game but having little impact on the excitement. But considering his excellent front-row seats at the midline were hard to come by, costing him a good amount of rupees, he remained seated. Besides, Nadal was not expected back from his Saudi trip until midday prayers the following day. Yes, he could enjoy the two fifteen-minute overtime periods—he had earned that much—and his required task from Nadal, to download the information, would still get done. But in the morning.

After the thirty-minute overtime, the game was still tied 0-0. The two opposing teams, their waterlogged and mud-stained uniforms untucked and sagging, trotted back onto the field like warriors. As they lined up near the twelve-yard line to begin their penalty kicks, hoping to outmatch their opponent and squeeze one kick, maybe two, past the opposing team's goalie, Farooq knew he had received his money's worth.

Now, as Farooq stood off the edge of bustling Hadda Street under the tiny awning that hung over the locked front door at a few minutes before 7 A.M., trying to shield himself from the sprinkling rain, he was hungry but content. The game had been worth it, his team winning 1-0 on a dramatic last kick attempt. Even though he failed to get much sleep and was unable to eat anything this morning, he was pleased he had arrived before the café doors opened. He would complete his task, Allah willing, and then move into the dining area for a bowl of *saltah*. Just the thought of the national dish of brown meat stew called *maraq*, a dollop of fenugreek froth, and *sahawiq*, a mixture of chili peppers, tomatoes, garlic, and herbs ground into a salsa, put him in a better mood. Maybe he would add some rice and vegetables to the *saltah*, which would not only improve the taste but make using the traditional flat bread to scoop up the food easier.

Farooq watched the young café attendant through the glass door unlock the door and open it. Relieved, Farooq nodded but didn't stop—he would pay him later—and moved directly to the back corner of the room. It was the most secluded of the fifteen desktop CPUs available to the public at the CyberInternet Café at the Hadda Hotel—well, number 15 to his left was the most secluded, but the prominent out-of-order sign taped to the screen forced him to settle for number 14.

Farooq slid the cracked plastic chair from the cubicle and sat down. He checked the battery life of his cell phone, logged in to the Internet, and unfolded a small piece of scrap paper he had pulled from his pocket.

Maintaining a watchful eye with his peripheral vision, Farooq accessed the browser and began reading a lengthy number-letter combination. As he did, he very carefully typed it in with his right forefinger. He waited for the underground Web site to fully load, frustrated by the slow Internet. After a few moments, happy with what he was seeing on the screen, he reached up and turned the screen a few inches away from any nosey bystanders.

Staying for the entire game was worth it, after all.

Farooq reached into the left breast pocket of his knee-length egg-white *salwar kameez* and pulled out a small yellow thumb drive. He rotated the protective cap to expose the male end and inserted it into the female end of the CPU's single USB port. He clicked the appropriate prompts, confirming the drive was accepted and reading fully.

Farooq turned back to his cell, tapped in the three-digit international dialing prefix, then the two-digit country code, then the ten-digit number, and pushed the green SEND CALL button. In a few seconds, the cell phone chirped, confirming a connection with the hunting cell phone packages inside the main access facility at Yellow Creek Nuclear Power Plant across the Atlantic Ocean.

Farooq dropped his shoulders, relieved that the cell phones in the package still had battery power. Nadal had estimated the window of access, based on Abdul's practice with dummy packages and rehearsing the U.S. mail system numerous times. Nadal was adamant that Farooq be at the café yesterday morning, when he believed the cell phones hidden inside the tubular containers would be in the middle of their internal battery's life of eighteen to twenty-four hours, their prime hunting time. At least that's what the vendor advertised. Farooq knew Nadal wasn't so ignorant to rely simply on the internal batteries. Not at all. Even at its best, even if the vendor was right that it would power the phone for a full twenty-four hours, it wasn't enough.

No, for this to work, for the cell packages to remotely pull the two dozen target sets, some 212 pages with colored photos and intricate details, from the secure LAN, the cell phones had to have much more power. Enough power to keep the cell alive, to support the attack vector, and to upload the sensitive data wirelessly, and Nadal's university education provided him the knowledge to understand all of this. He knew special lithium-foam-cell batteries were needed. The kind that powered the latest, most powerful, featherweight laptops. Actually, they weren't hard to find. Amazon shipped four directly to Abdul's apartment in North Carolina.

All those late nights of studying by Nadal to earn his engineering degree, while Farooq became lazy, ignored his responsibilities, followed foosball, and even chased women, were about to pay off.

Nadal understood that America had been slow to react to the imminent international cyberthreat, and worried more about domestic eavesdropping than about protecting its own systems. He'd talked to Farooq about it at length until Farooq thought his brains would run out of his ears. Major vendors were reluctant to share lessons learned in the cybersecurity software industry. The bottom line was what mattered, and as long as the Internet was powering the hopes and dreams of millions of businesses worldwide, software vendors would continue to protect their institutional knowledge base. If Farooq had heard Nadal say it once, he heard it a hundred times: *The hardware vendors are making the same mistakes that Microsoft made twenty-five years ago.*

Digital equipment, present in practically all of America's energy-related critical infrastructure and required to manage whatever the source of electricity is—coal, wind, solar, hydro, or nuclear—is highly vulnerable to cyberattacks. To protect safe shutdown systems from cyberthreats, a defense-in-depth strategy similar to the physical protection provided by armed guards and robust barriers is needed. The security basics are fundamentally equal and equally vulnerable. Something Nadal had capitalized on fully.

But the difference in protecting against cyberthreats is that you are not looking to stop a human body from attacking but, rather, are hunting for "data." Some of the critical systems involve digital components, which become attack vectors in cyberspace. Viruses can be carried in by a thumb drive or cell phone to infect systems. It's well documented that the United States government has been concerned with cyberattacks for close to a decade now, requiring commercial power plants to defend against them after adding to the Design Basis Threat shortly after 9/11. Nadal devoured this open-source information like a child mesmerized by the latest Harry Potter adventure.

It is much easier to overload a response system from a keyboard an ocean away than it is to physically attack a well-protected critical-infrastructure facility inside America. Yes, Farooq knew Nadal was very smart and very careful, even if he was very controlling and smothering of their sleeper brother Abdul in the United States. He would not want any more mistakes. Never mind that the model-airplane mistake that took his two fingers off was all Nadal's fault.

Knowing Nadal had everything covered, and seeing the information downloading to the yellow thumb drive presently, Farooq forgot all about neglecting his duties yesterday morning.

Yes, this is easy.

Farooq waited patiently as he watched the data download to the thumb drive. He was pleased with himself, knowing he was acquiring the most sensitive data on how nuclear power plants in the United States function and how they protect their assets. Another minute or so, tops, and he would be back at the safe house for a well-deserved nap before brother Nadal returned.

Nadal will be very pleased.

The download sequence on the computer screen suddenly ended. Farooq blinked and sat up straight. He leaned forward to grab the computer monitor and shook it vigorously. No luck.

He grabbed his cell phone off the table and checked to ensure the call was still active. It was. Farooq settled into the plastic chair, unsure what to do. He thought of calling Nadal but abandoned that idea for fear of his certain wrath. Yes, it was a simple task Nadal had entrusted him with. All he had to do was visit the CyberInternet Café, log into a single Web site, make an overseas call to the hunting phones, and plug in a thumb drive. A child could do that. Nadal and Abdul had seen about the difficult portion of the operation. Farooq didn't even have to hold a conversation with anyone. Yes, it was a simple but extremely important task that Nadal trusted him with, and had he visited the café yesterday, as Nadal directed, he might not be facing these troubles today.

Something has happened, something in America, not on my end.

FIFTEEN

Secret Compartmented Information Facility, Delta compound, Fort Bragg

In a small room deep in an obscure vault known as a SCIF, militaryspeak for Secret Compartmented Information Facility, the top-secret domain of Delta's intel and imagery analysts, the two enlisted operators sat in silence on the same side of a long gray table. Their sterile olive-colored full-body flight suits covered black nylon running shorts and tan T-shirts. Tan Oakley assault boats or Salomon mids covered their feet, and their Delta access badges hung from their necks. Their clean-cut color head shot adorned their badges, pictures that were taken when they first joined Delta. The passport-size mug shots looked very similar to a college yearbook picture. But only the troop sergeant major vaguely resembled his freshman-year photo.

Known as Slapshot inside the ranks of Delta Force, MSG Jason Holcomb appeared the most militarylike since he'd recently shaved his thick red beard. It had only been three days since, and, like Kolt Raynor, he was up for promotion. Slapshot was a shoo-in, of course, given his superlative track record in hostile-fire areas around the world. The photo was a simple requirement that even Delta operators were required to abide by. Even so, it seemed ridiculous to most of the guys since it took months to grow a beard that provided them a unique edge on the battlefield in Afghanistan. It was just one of the cultural barriers of the inflexible peacetime U.S. Army that had yet to be breached by the long war on terror.

The younger of the two sat on Slapshot's immediate left. At twenty-eight years old, MSG Peter "Digger" Chamblis was six years Slapshot's junior, one of the youngest master sergeants in the army and the guy that executed that hair-raising breach on top of the hijacked 767's fuselage over Indian soil about a year ago. He barely blinked as he sat as still as a statue. His ID photo seemed ridiculous now because his features were hidden by a brown full beard and long, dirty-blond California surfer hair.

Compared with Slapshot, Digger dressed a little more informally. As was common among operators, he had the top portion of his jumpsuit pulled down with the sleeves tied around his waist. A former accomplished triathlete, his tan T-shirt did little to conceal the lean muscles on his six-foot, nearly fat-free frame. And his titanium prosthetic lower leg, a product of an IED blast in Iraq years earlier, remained hidden under his flight suit.

It was obvious that the JSOC lawyer standing over them was an outsider. He just looked out of place. Lieutenant Colonel Seymour Spencer had never been inside the secret Delta compound before. He wasn't surprised that he required an escort wherever he went, even to the bathroom. Today's escort was the gray-headed longtime unit-command sergeant major, who stood conspicuously off to the side

In fact, LTC Spencer was a relative newcomer to the entire special operations community, hired to assist with the increased workload brought on by years and years of war. Spencer came with all the soft-skill attributes of a desk officer. Double chin, bulging belly testing the tensile strength of the lower two buttons of his fatigue top, and wired-rimmed glasses that sat atop a pointed nose with mismatched nostrils. If there ever was a fish out of water that didn't know it, it was Seymour Spencer.

Spencer figured this morning would be easy. After all, he directly represented Admiral Mason. In fact, Spencer's visit was driven by the general dissatisfaction with the two operators' sworn statements that were part of the written record in the AR 15-6 investigation. Mason sent Spencer across post to get it straightened out. Sure, Slapshot and Digger would treat him with the respect deserved by the rank on his collar. As long as the colonel reciprocated in kind, there would be no problems. But someone should really have briefed Spencer before he entered the Delta compound.

From the beginning, the balding and chubby army lawyer was all business. He pushed his glasses higher up the bridge of his nose and leaned forward on the table, still looking over his glasses and into Digger's eyes. He paused for effect and then shifted his attention to Slapshot. With straight arms, his hands covered two documents. He slid the papers forward on the table a foot or so until they rested in front of the two Delta operators.

With every bit of stereotypical sarcasm they expected from a non-special-ops staff officer, Spencer finally spoke. "So, it appears that the two statements you two submitted referencing one Major Kolt Raynor are severely inconsistent with what we believe to be true."

Slapshot and Digger looked down at the written statements. They took a few seconds to look them over to ensure they were authentic. When they were done, Slapshot looked at Digger. Digger nodded.

"No, sir!" answered Slapshot. "Our sworn statements look fine."

"Gentlemen, maybe we have a slight misunderstanding here." Spencer smiled as he lifted his arms from the table and straightened up, pushing his midsection a few inches over the edge of the table. "Look, you both are stellar soldiers with a lot to offer the army. I know that," he said with a sense of pleading. "But Admiral Mason has sent me here to give you men one more chance."

Spencer paused for a moment, then said, "Sergeant Holcomb, tell us what really happened on the helicopter in the Goshai Valley last month, and in your case, Sergeant Chamblis, on the highjacked Boeing 767 last year."

Slapshot sat up straight in his chair. Digger locked eyes with Spencer as the veins in the seasoned operator's neck stood out like thick climbing rope. Slapshot picked up both statements and held them out for Spencer to take back. "Sir, are you implying we fabricated these statements?"

"No, no, no." Spencer responded, shaking his head slowly but unconvincingly as he pushed his wire-rimmed glasses back up his nose. "I'm just saying that what you wrote and what we believe actually happened on those two missions isn't adding up."

Spencer continued. "We know you guys were just innocent bystanders to Major Raynor's insubordination and self-centered actions. I'm giving you soldiers an opportunity to save your careers." Spencer slid the statements back in front of Slapshot and Digger. "All you have to do is rewrite your sworn statements and everything will be fine."

Somewhat out of character for the quiet young operator, Digger exploded. "This is pure bullshit!" he barked as he hammered both fists onto the top of the table with every bit of force he could muster before standing straight up. His chair fell over as Spencer took two steps backward.

With a scowl that could kill, Digger laid into the army lawyer. "What the fuck is your problem, man?" he demanded. "You've got some brass balls to come in here accusing us of lying in our statements."

The unit sergeant major stepped forward. "Take it easy, Digger, the colonel is just doing his job."

Startled but holding his ground firmly as he sensed an ally in the sergeant major, Spencer came back at Digger. "We know what happened out there, Sergeant Chamblis," he said with conviction but in a whiny adolescent-like voice. "You men don't have to be party to a cover-up to protect Major Raynor."

A few seconds of uncomfortable pause followed Spencer's last comment, but the damage had been done. The temporary JSOC lawyer had pushed the wrong buttons. "This is your last chance!" he threatened.

Slapshot exploded straight up and lifted the table off its front two legs. The two statements and two ballpoint pens flew into the air as the table landed upside down. The lawyer frantically backed up to the wall and turned his body to the side as if to protect his vital organs. It was total fear. Almost as if their response was rehearsed, Slapshot and Digger closed on Spencer. He instinctively raised his hands to protect his face, yanking his glasses quickly off, fearing blows from the two operators.

"NO, NO! PLEASE DON'T," Lieutenant Colonel Spencer yelled out as he looked toward the sergeant major for help.

Slapshot spoke calmly. "Do you think we give a damn about your stupid-ass investigation? Do you think we give two shits about why you are here? You don't know who you are dealing with."

Trying to calm things down, the sergeant major jumped in front of Slapshot and Digger, placing his big opened hands on both of their chests to hold them at bay. "That's enough. Slapshot, at ease!" he said.

Slapshot ignored him.

"We have been teammates with Racer for a long time. He has earned our loyalty a dozen times over. I don't expect you to understand that, but don't ever try to come in here and get us to turn on a teammate again."

Slapshot turned to the unit sergeant major. "Sergeant Major, unless you have any objections, Digger and I have a date with the Gracie brothers now."

Not a word more was spoken as Slapshot and Digger headed for the SCIF door.

Lieutenant Colonel Spencer was just as surprised as the sergeant major that he didn't shit his pants.

They walked out the main double doors and headed for Spencer's black government-plated Crown Vic. As Spencer hugged the envelope marked CLASSIFIED under his right arm and awkwardly placed his black beret on his head, it was obvious that he was still shook up. He didn't even bother to stop by Colonel Webber's office to make a courtesy call on the way out. The sergeant major was glad he didn't.

The sergeant major could tell Spencer was just happy to be out of there with his skin. He was definitely in a foreign land at the Delta compound. It was a place where brilliance and innovation were typically championed by the Delta noncommissioned officer. It was a place where some things that could never be overlooked in a conventional setting could be ignored. A place where big-boy rules applied to all and the distinction between officer and noncommissioned officer could only truly be determined by scrutinizing monthly pay stubs.

As Spencer fumbled with the key fob to unlock his door, the sergeant major tried to gauge what might happen next after Slapshot's and Digger's uncharacteristic outburst.

"Well, sir, it was good to meet you. Don't let those guys get you down. They are a little wound up still from all the time down range. They have been at war a long time."

Spencer eased into the driver's seat and placed the envelope on the passenger's seat. He slid the key into the ignition and said, "Sergeant Major, those two soldiers were belligerent and absolutely insubordinate."

Trying to salvage the day, the sergeant major leaned down to nearly eye level with the distraught lawyer. " 'Sir, they were a little overboard, I'll give you that. But there are very few officers around here that would get that kind of respect from the assaulters in the building."

"A little overboard?" Spencer questioned in astonishment with his eyebrows raised.

"Sir, Major Raynor is a little eccentric and a bit extreme at times, no issues there," he answered. "But the boys know a great officer when they see one, and they are hard to come by in the army these days."

Spencer sat staring straight ahead. In his sixteen years of service, he had never experienced anything like what had just happened inside the SCIF. His left hand gripped the top of the steering wheel like a vice as he turned the ignition on with his right. "Is that the real story here, Sergeant Major?" he asked.

As he stepped back to close the driver's-side door, the sergeant major answered, "Yes, sir. After close to twelve years of war, that is the only story that matters around here."

Spencer backed out of the parking spot, ignoring the sergeant major's crisp salute, and maneuvered out of the crowded lot and toward the main gate. He didn't bother to return the wave of the security guards either, nor did he stop to turn in his temporary visitors' badge. His head was spinning. His thoughts were confused. It would be a miracle if he didn't wreck the car on the way back to JSOC headquarters.

Near the Saudi-Yemeni border

Kolt stood in his sandaled feet under his light blue, faded, and well-worn *thobes* as he watched the taillights of the Land Cruiser with the SEALs in it fade into the distance for the four-hour drive back to the safe house near Tahrir Square. The *thobes,* the traditional dress of Yemeni men, sported three simple buttons running down from the collarless neck to the top of the stomach. The baggy, long sleeves reached the edge of Kolt's wrist, and a small pocket was sewn on the left chest area. Considered by some to be a man's dress, a *thobes* drops naturally to just halfway between the ankles and kneecaps.

Kolt was comfortable enough in the getup. He knew it was a critical piece of his cover. He had no choice. A dark-brown twisted rope tied around his waist held a *jambiya,* a short dagger worn by Yemeni men from age fourteen until death, centered and vertical on his front.

Kolt wrapped the red and white kaffiyeh around his head. It wasn't as cold as Kolt expected it to be, but his shaved head released a lot of body heat, so the scarf provided more than just cover for action. Expecting forty-degree weather, at least that was the report he had received from the JSOC weather guys before they loaded the Land Cruiser to leave the safe house, was why he had brought a *zanna,* a traditional jacket. The faded black coat lined with aged and stained cotton would fit a larger man like Slapshot nicely, but it looked three sizes too big for Kolt—as it should be in a place like Yemen, where luxury items are hard to come by and even harder to keep from bandits.

He opened the light-brown sack he brought and pulled out a traditional one-gallon water blivet. He took a long swig and wiped his mouth with his baggy right coat sleeve. He capped the container and placed it back in the sack with a wad of Yemeni riyals and a worn copy of the Koran. Kolt traveled light and was unarmed by design.

He then walked due east for thirty meters before stopping.

Kolt sat down and leaned his head back against a small rock. He needed to let his night vision develop after having spent the majority of the longer, more circuitous five-hour drive in the back of the Land Cruiser studying the Raptor X satellite images on the SEALs' Toughbook. Now, out in the desert, he needed to see the dangers that might lurk ahead to keep from stepping on something or into something he shouldn't.

After a thirty-minute wait, Kolt's eyes had adjusted, and he moved out. He found the highway, but backtracked a few hundred meters to stay out of the peripheral footprint of any headlights from passing motorists.

Kolt laid low in a small erosion ditch and balled up to stay warm. He kept a keen eye on the highway off to the east that linked the Saudi village of Al Mubarakah and bisected the customs gateway, the centerpiece of the Jizan Province, serving both the Saudi and Yemeni side of the border. The sun hadn't broken the horizon yet, but it wouldn't be long. Things were lightening up, and Kolt edged a little deeper into the ditch. He wasn't interested in being spotted by a youngster pushing sheep around the area. In the distance, emanating from a large group of egg-white and cream-colored

UNHCR refugee tents struck no more than a few hundred feet from the highway, he heard the faint signal to move.

As the morning call to prayer reverberated from a distant loudspeaker atop a tan-and-white mosque, he took to his feet, shouldered his pack, and made his move.

Kolt knew the area from a previous visit, but not from this angle. He had traveled this same highway once before, balled up in the back of a private taxi during a classified op with indigenous CIA assets and Saudi security police who took him to the border checkpoint with Saudi Arabia. Kolt headed for the nearby bus stop.

After six buses passed, at roughly forty-five- to fifty-minute intervals— the time it took each to process through the customs gateway and enter Yemen—the bus described by the agency had yet to show. The last text he received from the agency assets that had been following Nadal put the terrorist positively in Al Mubarakah, though Kolt was unsure whether the agency had assets on the bus or was simply following the bus. Finally, he spotted the strange light-pink and yellow bus with the correct Arabic number-letter combination. He had been waiting for more than three hours and had finished off the water blivet thirty minutes earlier.

Stepping up into the bus with several other passengers, Kolt handed a wad of Yemeni riyals to the driver and made his way to the back, taking an empty window seat three seats from the rear of the bus.

The overcrowded bus ride really sucked. Before leaving Fort Bragg, Kolt knew that being the only Delta guy with a team of SEALs would ensure he drew the short straw every time. The shit missions. But this time he had only himself to blame. And even though they all knew the last guy that should have been doing this singleton op was Kolt Raynor, none of the SEALs ponied up to volunteer.

So far, the hour-long ride southeast over potholed or desert roads that bounced the passengers around like rag dolls had been every bit the shit mission. He wondered if Rocco and the other SEALs were right.

On the bright side, at least Kolt had been able to stall the overconfident trigger-happy SEALs long enough to let him build a little filler for the target folder. SEALs were great at finishing stuff but had little interest in the find-and-fix portion of operations. That was fine by Kolt. He'd let them save the world with their joysticks and then call them when their muscle was needed.

All things considered, things were actually kind of going Kolt's way. He was uncomfortably armed with a Galaxy II cell phone and three hundred riyals' worth of kat stimulant leaves to barter with. He had already sent a text message to the SEALs at the safe house letting them know he found the correct bus and was aboard. The next text, assuming things went as planned, even if it was a hasty plan, would be a confirmation text that Nadal was on the bus as well.

Kolt tried to keep from dozing off during the journey back across the Saudi-Yemeni border. But he also didn't want to engage in any conversation with fellow passengers if he didn't have to. It wasn't that he didn't trust his language skills. He wasn't concerned about his Arabic dialect since the hajj ensured this route was welcoming to all Muslim sects. But if it could be avoided, it wasn't smart to work a cover when exhausted. And Kolt was beat. The time change and jet lag, coupled with coming down off the two Ambien pills he popped before reaching Yemen airspace over a week ago, were still taking their toll. He craved shut-eye more than anything, though, and it wasn't long before he dozed off with his head leaning against the sun-warmed glass window.

Kolt woke up to the sound of rain pellets striking the top of the bus and a fellow passenger shaking his left shoulder. It was the young man sitting across the aisle from him. Kolt rubbed his eyes to clear his head. He could feel the bus had stopped and saw passengers filing down the aisle to exit. The sun was no longer visible since the dark rain clouds had moved in from the west off the Red Sea.

"We must get off," the young dark-skinned man said. "It is time to give glory to Allah."

Black, loose, curly hair sat atop the man's high forehead, crowned by a light-mauve Islamic knitted prayer cap. His nose had an unnatural-looking crook to the left and was split by a dimple, giving him the look of a Halloween witch. The man's left earlobe was noticeably missing, giving him an unbalanced appearance when viewed straight on. He wore a light-purple *salwar kameez* over a very narrow body, obviously soiled around the rim area from overuse. Kolt followed the oversize shirt down to the stranger's off-white baggy pants that rode high above his ankles. As the grip tightened on Kolt's shoulder, surprisingly firm, he picked up on the worn brown leather toeless sandals protecting the stranger's feet.

"Please, drink this," the stranger said as he placed a light-green container of water in front of Kolt's face. Kolt easily noticed something bizarre about the stranger's hand. There were five fingers grasping the container, but the end two seemed much smaller than the other fingers. They looked as if they belonged to a four-year-old child instead of a grown man.

After an uncomfortably long stare at the stranger's handicap, Kolt accepted. "*Shukran*—Thank you!" he said before pausing. "What is your name?"

"My name is Nadal. I am with my father, Malik Abu Nadal. It was his lifelong dream to visit Mecca," he answered proudly.

Fucking Nadal the Romanian? Kolt took a hard look at the stranger—he had to be sure this was his target. The facial features matched the CIA description sent to Rocco at the safe house, but Kolt was expecting someone much older. This Nadal seemed too young, too friendly, not much of a threat.

It's gotta be him.

"And your name?"

"Yasu," Kolt answered. Not entirely comfortable with the exchange, Kolt quickly added, "We better go," as he motioned to the other passengers already outside the bus. Kolt desperately wanted to text the safe house to confirm positive ID on Nadal, but it would have to wait.

A few seconds after prayer, the driver, a heavy balding man in his midthirties, raised the front engine hood. Another gentleman handed him a quart-size aluminum can filled with water collected from the heavy rain. The driver poured it into the radiator spout to cool the engine a bit. Steam rose a few feet above the engine and dissipated in the heavy, damp air.

Within five minutes the passengers had reloaded and the bus was on the move south, down the mud-scarred paved roadway. Kolt feigned sleeping for a few minutes, hoping his new acquaintance Nadal would take the hint. Kolt considered everyone on the bus the enemy, not just Nadal. He had no reason to feel otherwise. Years of combat action in Afghanistan and Iraq had convinced him of the absolute requirement to be wary of the Muslim mind. Sure, they weren't all Islamic extremists with a death wish for all infidels.

But without any obvious markings, who could tell the difference until it was too late?

Back on the bus and seated next to the window, Kolt held the Galaxy II, typing in "PC POS ID confirmed." But just as Kolt hit SEND, the connection to the satellites circling the Earth in a geosynchronous orbit dropped. His message to Rocco now hung in limbo, waiting for the storm clouds to clear out.

SIXTEEN

Northwest Yemen

The long ride took Kolt and the others southeast along Highway 5, which passed through the villages of Harad and Abs and eventually reached the hilly and rocky village of Al Ma'ras

It had been an entire day of wait-a-minute traffic along unmaintained asphalt and hard-packed dirt roads and thruways. Colorful single- and double-decker commuter buses, minivans jammed packed, pickup trucks with passengers in the bed barely hanging on, and motorcycles with two riders congested the highway to the point that the idea of being in a hurry was futile.

The sun hinted at reappearing through the dark ceiling as the bus crossed over the deep Wadi Maar. Likely the last chance before the cloud-hidden sun would finally set down in a few hours for the night. Another three miles beyond the wadi, and just a north of the village of Radmat Jubarra, the bus slowed to turn to the east, where it continued for another eighty miles, passing through the villages of Hajjah and Amran, before reaching the northern outskirts of Sana'a.

Kolt focused on the distant orange hue and the gorgeous naturally crusted and carved ridgelines and hilltops. The slow, bumpy ride tried to rock him back to sleep, but Kolt resisted, discreetly pinching his legs and

149

sides to stay awake. No. Kolt knew he slipped up earlier in the day. He was on target, even if it was moving. Sure, he had PIDed Nadal, accomplished his mission, and even though his Galaxy II was still not tracking satellites, he kept checking to see if his POS ID text message had left his outbox to alert the SEALs, but it remained stubbornly unsent. And so he wasn't about to doze off again.

A cell phone rang across the aisle. He didn't look over toward Nadal but heard him answer the call. He strained to listen as the bus driver traded honks with several white and yellow taxis that had turned onto Arman Road in front of the bus.

"What are you saying, brother Farooq?" Nadal demanded to know.

Bingo! Kolt tensed at hearing Nadal address his partner, Farooq. He had his man.

Kolt was able to make out a few words from the phone. The man on the other end sounded desperate. "Police!—shooting at us through the doors . . . Hassan is dead."

"That is impossible," Nadal answered. "I don't hear anything. Our security posture has been very well thought out. We have done well."

The unmistakable sound of an explosion sounded from the phone.

"Brother! Brother, are you there?" Nadal asked.

". . . is here. Your plan is not working. You should not have gone— what should we do?"

"It is not my fault," Nadal said. "Leave everything. The model planes, all of it. You must run, brother. But take the cell phone. Hurry, Farooq. Use the phone. Do not forget."

Kolt slowly turned to look at Nadal. Something was going wrong somewhere. He couldn't figure it out yet, and was careful not to stare. But he knew someone was calling from Nadal's safe house. He knew the SEALs weren't involved; they should still be at the safe house waiting for word from Kolt about Nadal's actions. They should be collecting spaceship parts and stunt jumping in Grand Theft Auto 5 about now, in for the night.

Kolt turned back toward Nadal and heard the terrorist say, "Inshallah, brothers," before thumbing the cell to kill the call.

Nadal stood up abruptly, looked over the heads of the other passengers for a moment, then walked briskly to the front of the bus and took an empty seat closer to the driver. Kolt looked up, seeing the back of Nadal's head. Something was definitely up. Nadal was straining to get a look at something out the front window. The sun had finally peeked through the thick cloud cover, signaling the weather around Sana'a was clearing up for the evening. Kolt tried to pinpoint where Nadal was looking. It was somewhere over the horizon, toward the leading edge of town and the first row of sprawling homes that pockmarked the sparse area.

A large fireball appeared against the bright blue sky ahead of the bus, maybe four miles distant. On the trail of the fireball was a massive smoke trail that billowed and spread out higher in the air, just beyond the soccer stadium and the tall high-mast stadium lights. A moment later, the sound of the explosion reached the bus, alerting everyone that something, maybe an accident, probably deadly, had occurred.

The bus driver pulled off the road, unsure of what was happening in the center of town. Kolt watched Nadal stand, speak to the driver for a moment, and head to the door. Others followed Nadal, giving Kolt sound cover to do likewise. He stowed his cell phone and left his seat. He put his foot down in the aisle and felt something below his foot.

Kolt looked down and saw a worn and yellowish notebook, the size of a small cell phone. He looked up. Nadal was gone. Kolt kneeled down, picked up the notebook, and quickly thumbed through it. It was written in a mix of Arabic and English. Phone numbers, e-mail addresses, and on a page somewhere in the middle, heavily scribed in all capital letters, the words PATRICK HENRY and another fifteen-digit phone number. A phone number with, as Kolt immediately recognized, a South Carolina area code.

Kolt stowed the notebook and moved forward down the aisle. He looked through the windshield as he headed for the door. He identified Nadal just ahead, walking with a sense of urgency in the direction of the blast. Kolt followed, but carefully, keeping as many others between him and Nadal.

And then Kolt's cell vibrated in his pocket.

Kolt dug it out and thumb swiped the screen. He typed in the four-letter password to clear the screen. The outbox cue had cleared, confirming the POS ID text had finally made it out and should be feeding into Rocco's cell phone back at the safe house. His in-box showed one message unread.

Kolt tapped his message icon. It was from the phone the SEALs had at the safe house.

Kolt looked up to ensure Nadal was still in sight. It looked like he was losing ground as Nadal quickened his pace. Kolt looked back at his cell to read the message as he continued to move forward.

"Racer, SEALs believed KIA. I watched it on ISR. Target SH exploded w all 4 inside. Fucked up shit. No survivors. Where r u?"

Kolt slowed his rate of travel to read the message again. Then, he stopped and replied to the text tapping the touch screen with both thumbs as he tried to reply as fast as he could.

"Who is this? R U POSITIVE? NO SURVIVORS????"

Kolt had seen the explosion himself. He had no idea it was Farooq and Nadal's safe house that had gone up in flames. He thought back to Nadal's phone conversation with a man named Farooq. He wasn't able to hear all of what Nadal had said, but he was sure about two things: Nadal told someone to get the hell out and to use the cell phone.

Kolt started to walk as he waited for a reply. He looked ahead to locate Nadal. Not a moment too soon, as he barely observed half of Nadal's body as it turned right and out of sight. Kolt started a slow jog, holding his cell in his hand, keeping his eyes on exactly where Nadal had turned. *How could the SEALs be involved?* Just last night, before they dropped off Kolt near the Saudi border, Rocco agreed to wait until Kolt reported in. Rocco agreed to push the hit twenty-four hours.

Besides, it's fucking daylight!

"It's Scotty . . . commo. No, no survivors. On phone w JSOC. They had feed up too. Ordered to exfil asap."

This made sense. Scotty was the JCU commo guy that accompanied the team to Yemen. He was top-notch and not one to freak out or get too excited about something if it wasn't true. It also made sense that if the SEALs were ordered to hit the safe house by higher, they would have the drone downlink pumped right into the command center back at Bragg.

Who the fuck ordered the hit?

"Why did they hit it?" Kolt texted as he desperately tried to stay on Nadal's tail. The streets were filling quickly with locals, all seemingly headed to the area of the loud explosion just east of TV Road in the Al Thawra City neighborhood.

Kolt continued following Nadal toward the leveled and still-smoldering safe house, wondering, what was the point? Scotty would have his hands full with multiple tasks right now. He'd need help responding to JSOC's million inquiries about what happened, closing up the safe house, sterilizing the area, and working the country exfil plan—which, Kolt assumed, was probably why he had yet to reply to his last text.

No, until Kolt had more to go on, it was futile to follow Nadal one more step. Even though he was unable to snap a picture of Nadal, simply identifying Nadal was mission success. As Kolt turned to cross back over to the west side of Amran Road, he knew the curly hair, high forehead, disfigured fingers, and dimpled nose would make it easy to find him a second time.

Who the fuck ordered the hit?

Delta Force compound, Fort Bragg

Two days after returning from Yemen, and his weapons and gear already turned in, Kolt felt like a fish out of water inside the unit compound. Nobody expected him to even come to work these days. Especially after he finished writing his statements about the SEAL disaster in Yemen and getting debriefed for the better part of six hours. He only had a few official days left, anyway. Everyone expected him to sign out on leave and take off without any fanfare. He still needed to see about the pistol a buddy from B squadron wanted to sell him, and to see the unit psychologist for his mandatory out brief.

Everyone sat through an out brief with the doc before walking away. His signature was required on everyone's clearing papers. Even though it was one of several formal requirements by the Unit before retiring, Kolt was actually looking forward to it.

Colonel Webber had covered for him as much as he could, but after the Yemen op, Admiral Mason was threatening to personally drive Kolt Raynor to the edge of Fort Bragg and boot him off the base. Kolt had his walking papers and his orders from Webber: attend mandatory schooling for a year or retire to the house. Kolt didn't have to decide on the spot, since Webber gave him thirty days of terminal leave to think it over. But he did have to decide.

Colonel Cedric Johnson had taken to Kolt over the years, and Kolt to the doc. Kolt had always been comfortable telling Doc Johnson exactly what was on his mind. He knew it would remain a matter of doctor-patient confidentiality. At least he assumed so, anyway. Besides, after twelve years of tending to the minds of Delta operators, it wasn't hard for Doc to notice when something was on Kolt's mind or was bothering him. Trying to hide it from him was futile. It was similar to hiding something from the same woman after thirty years of marriage. They just knew. Along with the unit chaplain, Doc was a tremendous stress reliever and invaluable to the operators in the building. Even more so in a war zone.

Doc Johnson stood quickly and walked from behind his desk. He wore a wide smile on his face. He extended his hand well before reaching Kolt. Doc always started things off with that patented, very relaxing, ear-to-ear smile. Kolt slipped into the comfortable brown leather chair that every operator for the last twelve years had used as Doc dropped back into his. They caught up quickly about Doc's kids. Doc had two boys, whom Kolt had taken to during a unit picnic six months or so ago.

Like every good psych, within a minute or two Doc eased delicately into business matters. To Kolt's surprise, Doc queried him about the mission in the Goshai Valley, where he ignored the abort call in the back of the helo.

"You still question many of our leaders' commitment in the war on terror?" Doc asked.

"Say again, sir," Kolt answered, trying to make sense of the question.

"It's a fair question, don't you think, Major?" Doc asked. "That night in the helo. You doubted the commanding generals' commitment and bravery to the war effort, right?"

Uncharacteristically, Kolt hesitated. Kolt knew the Doc was aware of the generalities. But he didn't know he was privy to the details. Kolt sensed his out brief would be a little more formal and extensive than he had expected.

"Uhh, well, no sir," Kolt answered, searching for the right words. "Not the CG's bravery, no, but I do question his commitment and his thought process at times."

"Is that off the record, Major?" Doc asked, raising his eyebrows toward Kolt.

"Only if you make it that way, Doc," Kolt said.

"Well, in light of your trip to Yemen, it seems you're not the only one questioning his decision-making skills," Doc said.

"Things getting a little uncomfortable for the CG?" Kolt asked.

"A little. Rumor has it POTUS is ticked off about him forcing the daylight hit and getting the SEALs killed," Doc said. "You were there. What's your opinion?"

News of the dead SEALs had traveled laser fast throughout the black operations community, with some high-level discussions that revealed that, even though POTUS had authorized the DEPORD, or deployment order, he was only signing up for advanced-force operations, not giving carte blanche executive authority to conduct direct action in a sovereign country where Americans are not welcome. With the Benghazi disaster still simmering and the Syrian chemical weapons still unresolved, POTUS could ill afford any more national security failures. And now, with this latest major international scene, POTUS and the State Department were forced to deny any American involvement.

"The SEALs should have never hit that place in the daylight. I had close follow on the Romanian target, and they agreed to wait until that cycle of darkness to hit the safe house," Kolt said. "Mason didn't have the situational understanding to force the SEALs to turn that target."

"Interesting perspective, Racer. I thought we learned those lessons years ago?" Doc said rhetorically.

"Several good men with names on the wall to remind us of that," Kolt said. "But I can also see how the CG must have been under a lot of pressure from POTUS to stop an attack on our soil."

"I certainly believe that," Doc said before changing the subject.

"How do you feel about the Unit's commitment these days, Kolt?" Colonel Johnson asked. "Still feel the same after, what, a dozen years of war?"

Kolt didn't hesitate for a second. He respected the doc, an African

American officer who happened to be the same guy that delved into Kolt's skeletons years earlier at Delta selection and assessment. Nobody cared that he had some; everyone does. What they cared about was whether he had recognized and learned from his mistakes. They didn't need operators with large financial debt or recurring drinking problems, guys who liked to rough up their old ladies, or anyone who may be slightly askew of a normal heterosexual.

"More so than ever, sir. But I realize now that we are weak sisters compared to our adversaries. We spend years in training, millions in funding, and still lack the key ingredients to be successful against these maniacs," Kolt said with a mix of frustration and excitement in his voice.

"Ingredients, Kolt?" Doc smiled with a raised eyebrow.

"Very simply, Doc, we are not willing to sacrifice ourselves even if it means victory for our nation, if victory is even definable," Kolt answered as he leaned forward and looked directly into Doc's eyes. "If you break it all down, we are inarguably an inferior and less-committed species than our terrorist enemies." Kolt caught himself talking too much and too fast, becoming a little too emotional and eased back in the leather seat a bit.

Doc's hesitation made Kolt a little uneasy. Flashing his big signature smile before speaking in very even tones, he said, "That's very interesting, Kolt. Is that an opinion formed from your numerous tours in the box or something you picked up since 9/11 watching Fox News?" Without waiting for an answer, Doc let him off the hook easy. "In any event, I see you feel stronger about it now than you did ten years ago."

Kolt knew it was a rhetorical statement, but he couldn't resist. "I do, sir!"

Doc shifted gears. He dropped the smile and jabbed back a bit. "What about you? Are you personally any more committed than your teammates?"

Kolt broke eye contact and thought about it for a moment. He looked toward the four framed eight-by-ten colored photos autographed by former Delta commanders hanging on Doc's wall—a clear sign of Doc's longevity inside the unit. They seemed to be staring directly at Kolt, pressing him for an answer, just like Doc was. He knew he wasn't *more* committed. He was just *as* committed, sure. Besides, Kolt realized that any comment would mark him as a self-centered arrogant asshole, certainly coming off as if he was more dedicated than the other operators. And since Kolt already knew he wasn't better than his teammates at anything and had no way to prove it if he was, it didn't make any difference.

Kolt sat up straight and looked at the doc. "No big deal, sir. What I say now doesn't matter, anyway. My time in the saddle is up. Besides, it's not like anyone has the balls to set something like that in motion, even if we had a dozen guys willing to sacrifice themselves."

Doc Johnson didn't say anything.

Kolt sighed. "Maybe we should have talked about this while I was still welcome around here."

"Again, Major Kolt Raynor, do you have the balls?" Doc asked. "You haven't been a super example of commitment within Delta."

"Sir?" Kolt responded, somewhat confused by the formality and serious tone of the question.

"How committed are you to winning the war against Islamic extremism?"

"Very committed, sir," Kolt said, leaning forward in the leather chair. "Hell, I counted it up the other day. I've spent forty-seven months in Afghanistan since 9/11. I speak Pashto better than I do English these days. But my time around here is over. It's time to go to school or go to the house."

Doc showed no emotion on his face. Kolt paused for a moment and, sensing the uneasiness, slid a few inches back into the chair and brought his fingertips together in front of him.

"Besides, it's not like I'm leaving the unit in a positive manner," Kolt said, referring to the 15-6 investigation. Doc didn't respond.

"Whatever happened with the removal of your tattoo?" Doc asked. "Why didn't you commit to completing that simple mission?"

Catching on quickly, Kolt resisted the urge to reply with something wiseass. He understood the seriousness of Doc's accusation. "Uh, fair enough, sir." Kolt sighed while nodding his head. "After 9/11, it didn't seem as important as it once was."

Kolt locked eyes for a second but then looked away toward the window.

"It's not a matter of importance over commitment, Major Raynor," Doc said, almost like a Little League coach during a pregame pep talk. "Quite the opposite. Seeing things through to the end is one of the most important characteristics of the men and women that walk these halls."

One of the traditional requirements in Delta was to have all identifying tattoos removed. It was necessary to protect their identity should they be rolled up by hostile security forces in some third world shithole. The tattoo removal process was lengthy, requiring a half-dozen laser procedures to literally suck the ink out of the body, allow the area to scab over, and then let the skin heal over with a new layer. It wasn't without a little pain, either. In the end, if done correctly, the procedure left no sign or scar.

However, like most everything else that required lengthy commitment, the events of 9/11 bumped many of those niceties down the priority list. So, when al Qaeda struck the World Trade Center, Kolt's aged and odd-shaped Black Panther was a procedure or two from disappearing entirely. A faint and forgotten jungle killer still ruled his right shoulder.

"I assume you are interested in being considered by the SMU board for squadron command selection? Doc asked.

"Yes, sir," Kolt said. "But I think that's probably unrealistic at this stage"

"Why is that?"

"Well, a second trip on the black Chinook for one, and schooling for two, sir," Kolt said, knowing Doc must know exactly what he meant already. "I can't see spending a year away from the Unit with all that is going on in Africa, Syria, and Afghanistan."

Doc reached down and opened a desk drawer, pulling out an unmarked manila folder. He removed three sheets of paper stapled together and slid it across the desk toward Kolt. Kolt turned the blank cover page out of the way to reveal the second page. In large, red, bold letters at the top and bottom, the typical classification—TOP SECRET/SCI—was stamped on the paper. Directly underneath it was an acronym Kolt was not familiar with: WHDP-TUNGSTEN.

"Take a few minutes to read this over, Kolt," Doc said as he pushed the paper across the desk and stood up. "I'm going to grab a cup of coffee from the chow hall. Can I bring you one?"

"No, sir, I'm good. Thanks."

* * *

Even though Nadal al-Romani's return to Sana'a was short-lived, Nadal having witnessed the rubble of what was, for lack of a better term, his personal bomb factory, he was happy to leave the rainy weather behind. And after a grueling four-hour-plus drive while cramped inside Farooq's second-hand '76 Datsun Bulletside pickup, one of over two million cars that had entered the country illegally in the past two years, it was nice to feel the salt-saturated breeze coming off the Red Sea comb through his curly hair and ride up his baggy *salwar kameez*.

They had topped off the hasty getaway car, grabbed what little they could recover from the smoldering safe house, squeezed three in the two-door cab, and easily negotiated the Soviet-funded switchback highway built in 1961 that changed elevations as often as Farooq changed the radio station. The road from Sana'a to Al Hudaydah covered just 143 miles, allowing them to make the final turn into Hodeida International Airport on fumes and four bald tires.

Men like Nadal and Farooq, and even their terrorist brother known as Joma, who had made the road trip as well—all duplicitous and foul Muslim men—were free to walk the dirty streets of the seaport village Al Hudaydah without a worry in the world.

Known for exporting coffee, cotton, dates, and hides, the seaport village of Al Hudaydah was developed in the mid–nineteenth century by the Ottoman Turks. After two and a half centuries, one would think Yemeni officials would have figured out how to turn the place into an extraordinary revenue-building resort town. However, anyone outside Nadal's ilk considering visiting Yemen would discover the place was a hive of terrorism, kidnappings, and bombings.

Yemen does have its booming industry; it's just mostly illegal.

Nadal remained behind in Yemen to tidy up their affairs and coordinate the final specifics for their spectacular attack on U.S. soil. An attack he put his full faith and confidence in Farooq and Joma to undertake. An attack he felt entirely confident in, even though their special equipment had gone up in smoke.

After he performed *Salatul Fajr,* the early morning prayer, Nadal took in a small meal of *ogdat,* a stew mixing small pieces of fish and vegetables, at a small waterfront walk-in before crossing the coastal highway, Route 60, and hoofing it to the Internet café near Al Tahreer Park. Very soon, his cell phone should be ringing, on schedule, as he had directed Farooq just before watching his brothers successfully clear customs inside the airport.

Until twenty-three minutes ago, he had been confident that all was in order. Short of the setback a few days ago when Yemeni security forces stormed their safe house, martyring themselves in the process and taking his masterpieces of body-cavity IEDs, model-airplane bombs, and makeshift microwave-denial systems up in smoke with them, by the grace of Allah, things were clicking along just fine.

Having recovered sufficiently from the shock of what he saw on the computer screen at the café, or what he didn't see, actually, he had retraced his steps back to the waterfront, crossing back over Route 60, and stood on the highway's western edge, looking down into the boat boneyard, where dozens of dilapidated rainbow-colored and sand-swept wooden fishing vessels rested in the flat dunes behind a manmade seawall at Le Port de Pêche, their masts having been confiscated, likely providing shade to places like where he ate breakfast that same morning.

"*Salam alaykum,*" Nadal said, after answering the phone on the first ring.

"*Wa alaykum salam,*" Farooq replied. "Brother Nadal, as I predicted, Joma and I arrived without incident. It was a long journey, but I was never worried, as Allah watched over us."

Nadal was not surprised that Farooq and Joma arrived safely, nor was he surprised that Farooq would be proud of his meticulous and professional work in forging the appropriate travel documents that allowed them to obviously breeze through U.S. customs at Dulles International Airport. Nadal understood that; they had been brothers for a long time.

"Yes, Farooq, your work was sufficient; you reached your destination without issue with the authorities," Nadal admitted. "But the thumb drive—it is practically empty!"

"That is impossible," Farooq said. "I watched the files download with my own eyes."

"There must have been a problem, Farooq," Nadal said. "Are you sure you followed my instructions exactly? Did you log in to the correct Web site and use the cell phone correctly?"

"I am not a child, Nadal," Farooq said. ""You should not treat me as such. With Allah as my witness, I did exactly as you described, exactly how we rehearsed many times."

"The important Scared Indian documents were not downloaded, Farooq," Nadal said. "Only basic floor plans and several underground-drainage engineering drawings, an outage schedule, and a shift schedule for a few days in March."

"I don't know what to say,' Farooq said. "I am under a lot of pressure here trying to coordinate the first attack, finding our friend Timothy, and avoiding the security police. But I cannot accept blame for the thumb drive in good conscience."

Having made his point with Farooq, reminding himself once again how easy it was for his old university roommate to become so easily distracted from the important and necessary things like his engineering studies and his faith, he backed off. After all, Farooq was now inside the enemy's borders, and Nadal knew his success during the first attack, no matter the fallout or death toll, was the diversion he needed to facilitate their overall strategy of striking the infidel in a manner that would make Black Tuesday look like a mile-long interstate pileup.

"What is done is done, Farooq. The seniors will not be pleased, as without benefit of a second Timothy, and without the secret target-set documents on the thumb drive, and with our special equipment destroyed, our chances have worsened a great deal."

"I understand, brother," Farooq said. "Allah shines on us still."

"Yes, the most graceful does, indeed, but I will take over the planning and coordination for Scared Indian. You will put all your efforts to Cherokee."

"Yes," Farooq said. "I am sorry, brother. I will make you proud with what we accomplish here."

"*Allah Hafiz,*" Nadal said before pressing the END CALL button.

SEVENTEEN

Tungsten headquarters, Atlanta, Georgia

Sixty-two-year-old Carlos Menendez II sat comfortably in his leather-bound rocker, his tough-to-find and thus very expensive Barker Black ostrich cap-toe dress shoes propped gently on the pillow-covered coffee table to his front.

In his left hand, a sterling silver coffee mug with the CIA logo perfectly engraved on one side, filled with Jacobs Kronung finest dark roast, the wrist surrounded by a platinum and ice-blue Cosmograph Daytona Rolex. The coffee mug was a gift from his former employer, the watch a gift to himself.

In all, the Tungsten handler Menendez probably left the house wearing more money than forty-seven percent of Americans bring home in a month. It was too bad he was stuck underground most days, running his assets, or "embeds" as Tungsten classified them, immediately available to backstop a distressed operative or activate a Priority One repatriation. Yes, it was a full-time job, not unlike his previous thirty-eight years of government service, but it would be nice to surface when the sun was still up and strut his stuff in action-packed downtown Atlanta, Georgia, from time to time.

It certainly paid well, though.

Carlos thumbed one more time through the file marked 0706 in the upper-right corner of the folder. He had gone through it in fine detail a week earlier, just twenty-four hours after it arrived by secure courier, prompted by a phone call from the Delta Force commander, Colonel Jeremy Webber. A few more times looking for specific indicators in the records that might highlight a personality vulnerability or innate characteristic that would automatically deselect an operative candidate for Tungsten. And now, with about eight more minutes before he would have to exit the secret headquarters, follow a long hallway, make two turns, grab the elevator to the upper floor, walk past the Braves rolling souvenir cart, past the escalators, and take his normal and private seat in the back of Footprints Jamaican Restaurant and Lounge to order the usual, oxtail stew and brown beans, he figured he owed it to Webber to give the guy one more look. It was an exercise in futility, for sure.

Maybe the Merc department can use this guy. But as an embed? No fuckin' way. This guy is a crackpot!

Carlos wanted to help Webber; they went way back, hustling the same women decades ago in the nation's capital, running the same camel caravans in the Middle East, and sharing the same sleeping quarters during Desert Storm. But that was years ago, a different time, and different place.

As Carlos sipped his Kronung, he wondered if Webber would be happy enough if he sent this kid's file straight to the guys that handle the Mercs. That's where the very-well-paid crackpots went, the guys with absolutely no conscience, the mercenary-minded that simply enjoyed killing other human beings. They wore no identifiable patches or markings, operated in the dark of night only, and generally were on call at Tungsten's discretion.

Both for pleasure and money, they did pretty much any off-the-books dirty work the U.S. government required of Tungsten.

The Mercs came from all walks of life but were mostly guys with a few years in the military who got out for one reason or another. A few former cops who happened to pull their issued piece one too many times, and a smattering of former agency independent contractors who tended to be a little more mature than the others. Carlos knew it was a good mix of shooters and helo pilots, and even though he often worried that the oversight was a little slack, so far they had remained under the radar and not a major ass wound to the president of the United States. Because if the lid ever blew off Tungsten's Department of Special Services, their politically supersensitive actions revealed, a lot of heads would roll, starting with POTUS himself.

If nothing else, Carlos knew, the Mercs sure could keep a secret.

But Carlos knew he couldn't let his personal feelings obscure his judgment. National security demanded his utmost honesty and expert intuitive ability to analyze the finer points of a potential embed's personality, past performance, and ability to make a decision for the president of the United States. A decision that, if bad shit went down, could create an international incident that the president would have to deftly defend on the world's stage with a teleprompter and that Carlos would have to answer for. No, it just wasn't the embed's reputation that was at stake, it was Carlos's, too.

Looking at his Rolex as the waitress set a large glass of sweet tea on a napkin, he took pleasure in the fact that he didn't have to give the bad news to his old buddy Webber; the decision had been made well above him. On this one, Carlos was in receive mode.

Carlos spotted a well-tanned man with a close-cropped haircut, maybe a quarter inch or so, and a thick salt-and-pepper goatee enter the restaurant from the courtyard. He watched him look left for a few moments, scanning the area beyond the bar, then back right until they made eye contact.

Carlos took a sip of his tea and, with two fingers, flipped the white cloth napkin into the air before placing it down on his lap. Within a few seconds, the stranger had taken the seat across the table, reaching immediately for the lunch menu, signaling to Carlos that the bona fides had been passed and that, for the first time, he was looking straight into the eyes of Tungsten's newest wannabe operative, Embed 0706.

"I thought you more of a ghost than reality," Kolt said. "But I can see now you are just threadbare and broke back."

"Come again?" Carlos said, straightening the napkin on his thighs.

"Sir, I'm sure you recognize Colonel Webber's humor," Kolt said, smiling. "He said he'd have my ass if I didn't say those exact words."

"Touché!" Carlos said, beginning to like this kid more than he thought he would.

"Yes, sir," Kolt said as he looked to the dark-haired, obviously very fit waitress. "I'll have what he is having, thanks." The waitress turned and walked away, her derriere still drawing both men's attention. "I see why this is your favorite truck stop."

"Please, son, call me Carlos." Carlos extended his right hand over the table to Kolt.

"It's not son, but Kolt. Kolt Raynor," Kolt said, firmly shaking Carlos's hand, ensuring his grip felt superior before releasing. "Pleasure to meet you."

Carlos smiled and nodded. He knew this guy had a chip on his shoulder at times, a fact that was very clear in his file, but he also knew Kolt Raynor to be a man of commitment and sacrifice. After just a minute or so, Carlos could see how this guy could be an unshakable leader in combat. He had balls, for sure, a file full of medals validated that.

Whether or not he thought Kolt Raynor would make a good drinking buddy at a Falcon's game, he had to be sure. Yes, the decision had been made above him, but Carlos had nearly forty years of clout. Even decisions by higher, given the correct data points, could be altered.

After reading Kolt's file, Carlos had wondered why he had been recruited in the program at all, given his obvious strong ties to his teammates and his long track record of insubordination—two key data points that could be a vulnerability should his covert adventures overseas be compromised. But what gave Carlos the most pause was Kolt's propensity to ignore traditional policies and play by his own rules. These flaws combined worried Carlos much more than they obviously worried his own leadership at Tungsten, or than could have ever worried his boss, Colonel Webber.

Carlos had questioned Webber as to why Kolt was sacrificing the potential for squadron command in a year. All he had to do was attend Command and General Staff College and suck it up in the classroom for a year, and then he would be back with the boys. Carlos realized Kolt felt enormously strong bonds with the men he was leaving behind. That's a hallmark trait of a good leader—Carlos got that completely. But Carlos's background didn't include the military, and nobody had ever expected him to understand the incredibly tight bonds warriors can experience and nurture over time. Throw in multiple combat tours together, and the relationship was carved in stone. Carlos knew Kolt was a single man like himself, after two failed marriages, but having not been there for Kolt's high-risk adventures across the globe, missions that good men were lost on while hundreds of bad men met their maker, he was beginning to feel a bit odd about trying to block Kolt Raynor's acceptance into Tungsten.

Who the hell am I to judge this fucking warrior?

"You up for this, Kolt?" Carlos asked, signaling the small talk was over and the interview was beginning.

"Willing to give it a shot, for sure," Kolt said, leaning back as the waitress set two plates of oxtail stew and beans down in front of them and topped off Carlos's sweet tea.

With the waitress gone and the other tables far enough away to ensure their conversation remained private, Carlos said, "Total compartmentalization."

"No problem," Kolt said.

Carlos knew he'd been operating inside the darkest reaches of one special-access program after another, crisscrossing the globe numerous times and, so far, had lived to speak of it only during the postmission hot washes.

No, Kolt didn't kill and tell.

"No nondisclosure agreements. No official 'read-ons' or 'read-offs.' No medals. In effect, no paper trail at all," Carlos said without emotion or expression while maintaining eye contact with Kolt.

Carlos wanted to make sure Kolt got the picture. Delta Force didn't exist to the world, which meant Tungsten didn't even exist to Delta. *Fuck this up, Raynor, and you'll be peddling sleeping bags and climbing gear in Southern Pines again.*

"You need something, you go through me. Me only," Carlos said. "All commo is secure. Encrypted e-mails, positive voice-activated caller authentication, weekly distress codes provided. When I call you, PRIVATE CALLER will display. Answer it. It will be me trying to sell you something as a persistent telemarketer. If alone and all is well, we'll talk. If busy, hang up. If you are in a tight, share the distress code."

"Sounds easy enough," Kolt said. "I assume creds and aliases?"

"Naturally. But I think we'll stick with your aliases from your former employer and nest the personal history into our database. Our analysts have reviewed their status and see no issues."

"Makes perfect sense," Kolt said. "Never know when some ass clown might yell out in a foreign airport at a chance contact."

"Exactly," Carlos said as he lifted his soup spoon and fork. "Dig in."

Carlos didn't want to waste time on the other details. Kolt would attend a full day of indoctrination briefs beginning in the morning at the Tungsten headquarters. His creds would be updated, driver's licenses issued, passports validated, and pocket litter—restaurant matchbooks, business cards, and so forth from around the world, which would strengthen his operational cover for status—would be added. Of course, none of these field-craft props would be kept at Kolt's apartment in the sock drawer, where they could easily be found.

These credentials would be passed back and forth by "dead drops" in and around the Atlanta, Georgia, area. Prior to arriving at the airport, a Tungsten representative, known as "saviors," would make a scheduled service based on encrypted, e-mailed instructions. It might be an upscale burger joint in Buckhead, where his creds would be taped to the underside of a certain table. Another time it might be the fifth-floor waiting room at Grady Memorial Hospital, where he could find his creds waiting under the center cushion of the plaid couch. Regardless of the dead-drop spot, Kolt would locate the goods, swap his true creds with his alias creds, and depart the area. Immediately after Kolt's departure, a savior would discreetly secure his true creds. Upon returning through Atlanta, he would hit another dead drop to swap his creds back before grabbing a cab to his apartment. Carlos knew none of this would be new to Kolt. These were skills he had learned well and used often in the Unit.

"So, how do you feel about operating on U.S. soil?" Carlos asked as he brought the cloth napkin from his lap to wipe the oxtail broth from his lips. "Any issues with that?"

"None," Kolt said as he took in another spoonful of brown beans.

Charlotte, North Carolina

Sitting rather uncomfortably on the hotel carpet, Kolt could sense that the two terrorists to his left, Joma and Farooq, were wondering how Kolt—rather, Kolt acting as Timothy Reston—knew so little about the security procedures at his workplace. How he seemed to know exactly how to slip the authorities, had all the answers about that, but little else. When questioned about it, Kolt credited a lifetime of shoplifting cigarettes from the local drugstores and slipping the law, but Cherokee Power Plant was obviously harder to handle.

They had been at it for five and a half hours by now. Empty pizza boxes were stacked by the front door and jugs of water were at each of their sides. It was almost 2 A.M., and it had been an exhausting night of planning in a local hooker hotel, the thick aroma of unbathed men stuffed in-between the two double beds making it that much worse.

Kolt did his best to answer the questions, trying to steer the plan to his liking, but it was increasingly difficult by not actually being Timothy the insider. Of the three, only the terrorist they called Abdul seemed to offer countersuggestions and engage often.

Carlos wasn't kidding that day at Footprints Jamaica in Restaurant when he asked Kolt if he was good with operating inside the homeland. That said, masquerading as one Timothy Reston, senior access officer for the nuclear power plant that was about thirty miles southwest of the hotel where the current planning session was under way, Kolt wasn't actually operating. If not for Kolt's dumb luck on the bus returning to Sana'a with Nadal the Romanian, no intelligence agency on earth would have a single lead on the nuke plot. The pocket-size notebook, accidentally dropped by Nadal as he made a hasty exit from the bus, was proving to be a treasure trove of intel.

Within six hours of the SEALs running into a trap, the CIA had run the ten-digit number handwritten inside the notebook through their database. They quickly determined that American citizen Timothy Reston had turned on his friends, coworkers, and country. And, even though he had taken the time to delete his Internet communication with Farooq, enough of it was recoverable to understand the link. The notebook also revealed several odd two-word phrases, what were assumed to be code words of some sort, that were screened through the CIA's historical cable traffic and then bounced against the National Security Agency's MAINWAY database of several trillion phone calls, as well as PRISM, its clandestine mass-electronic-surveillance data-mining program. And because the Romanian cell and the nuke plot were obviously major threats to the nation, they ran the code words through the X-keystroke software program. The software was able to analyze the myriad of data on the Internet and sift through it, picking out the bits regarding "persons of interest" under any number of parameters.

According to Carlos, all the suspected code words checked out, but one in particular didn't register under the NSA's DISHFIRE blanket analysis. Handwriting analysis was inconclusive, but the assumption was that Nadal had scribbled "Sacred Indian" several times in his notebook.

Yes, Kolt wasn't playing Kolt inside the hotel room that night, but he was trying to save the local population, and that clearly was the most important task. Kolt wanted to deal the cards his way, trying to drive the planning of an attack on an American power plant to where no innocent people got hurt. No, just the terrorists were to die.

But Carlos hadn't made it easy.

Tungsten was adamant that Kolt not roll up Farooq's cell—in good time, yes, but, for the time being, not until they were sure the cell was the only one in town. Terrorist chatter was heavy about a second cell, a fact the CIA and Tungsten actually agreed on. But this second cell was believed to be in Pakistan and had not yet reached the United States. It was a long shot, and certainly risky to Kolt's health, but planting Kolt as Timothy Reston, the terrorist's inside man at the power plant who had established a cordial yet cautious relationship online with the terrorist, was at the moment the only thread linked to parallel nuke plots and to Nadal the Romanian, whose trail had gone cold after he exited the bus in Sana'a.

If Kolt's planning skills were still as sharp as they were when he was a Delta operator, he just might be able to survive the attack without anyone the wiser. But Kolt wasn't sitting around the old Delta team room putting together a high-risk mission with the most professional and talented operators in the world. He was trying to shape an unprecedented mission to his liking. So far, with very little buy in.

Kolt leaned in with the others, three terrorist enemies of the state, and looked down on the spread of colored satellite photos of the Cherokee Power Plant pulled from Google Earth.

Joma and Farooq had become frustrated since it was becoming increasingly obvious that Timothy couldn't answer the specific questions they raised. Kolt felt they had already decided that Timothy was either stupid or a lying infidel pig.

"My friend Timothy, I fear you are not being honest with us," the smaller, narrow-shouldered terrorist wearing the green soccer jersey they called Farooq said.

"No, no, brother, I am just tired," Kolt said. "Some of your questions I just cannot answer."

"Why is that, Timothy?" Farooq asked. "Do you question our resolve in this matter?"

"Well, things in our strategy have changed since I left that department. They keep those things secret from everyone," Kolt said, trying to sound convincing and invoke some sympathy from the three terrorists. "I no longer have access to those items."

"OK, my friend. We have come a long way and have sacrificed much," Farooq said. "We do not have our special equipment anymore, but brother Abdul has secured enough Semtex explosives, a water vessel, and weapons to ensure our strike will be a glorious occasion. But we must have your expertise to be fully confident."

Before Kolt could reply, Joma threw the map he had in his hand in the air and jumped quickly to his feet. Kolt sensed his anger before he spoke a word and watched as the terrorist lifted his foot high in the air and stomped down hard on the Google Maps images.

"I am sorry, brother," Kolt said, hoping to calm him some. "Tomorrow I will do better. I promise I will."

"No, tomorrow is too late!" Joma said as he took the handle of a five-inch blade, seating his hand to the hilt and sliding it swiftly up and out of the leather sheath on his hip. With one continuous motion he jumped toward Kolt, raising his knife hand high in the air and striking down near Kolt's neck.

Kolt instinctively rolled to his rear, executing a somersault, but was stopped short when he impacted with the small refrigerator. Kolt sensed the downward knife motion and heard the knife blade impact the concrete flooring under the dirty carpet.

Kolt reached for Joma's right wrist, pulling him toward him as he rolled to his back to place him in his guard. The wrist control kept the blade at a safe distance, forcing Kolt to control Joma's body with only one arm. Kolt grabbed a deep handful of Joma's white T-shirt collar as he heard the other terrorist yelling to stop as they bounced off the beds.

I don't want to kill this guy—not yet, anyway!

Kolt quickly assessed the man's position, just as he had always done rolling with mates back at the Unit. He first thought arm bar, but gave that up because Joma still held the knife in his hand. Triangle choke was an option, but the setup was off and Joma's lower torso held tight to Kolt's right leg. But he didn't have time to run through the Gracie library searching for the perfect move in this particular situation; he needed something simple to stop the terrorist's aggression, but not so effective as to break a major bone or compromise the man's airway.

Screw it! Basics!

Kolt tightened his stomach muscles quickly and executed a sit-up, simultaneously pulling Joma's head toward his. He landed a head butt, impacting Joma just above the left eye, forcing him to release his hold on the knife. Kolt knew it was solid by the sound, the deep gash, and the fact that warm blood had spurted out of the wound and into Kolt's face.

Kolt allowed Joma to fall free from his grasp, toppling over the maps on the floor.

"I am sorry, brother Joma," Kolt said as he moved to a standing position to allow him some more flexibility should the other two pile on. "I did not mean to hurt you, but you had a knife."

Farooq stepped forward, kicking the knife away from both of them and putting himself in between the two combatants. He lifted his hands in the air to his chest to motion Kolt to keep his distance from Joma. The other terrorist, Abdul, had yanked a cover off a down pillow and quickly held pressure on Joma's left eye.

"Brothers, this is not Allah's way," Farooq said, rapidly looking back and forth at them. "We have much to do. This is too important for us to have such strong disagreements."

"I'm sorry, Farooq," Kolt said, now worried that he had just caused an unnecessary incident that could unravel the entire operation, his first under the Tungsten banner.

Then again, Joma had started it. And if he had any skills, he had equal chance to finish it. Had he not had his temper tantrum and pulled a knife, he wouldn't be bleeding all over his buddy Abdul and the bedsheets.

That motherfucker is lucky I didn't bust his larynx!

"All is well, brother Timothy," Farooq said, still trying to gain control of the situation and calm everyone's nerves. "It is best if you go now. We will contact you when we are ready to continue."

"Yes, yes, that would be best," Kolt said. "You have my cell number. Please call me soon."

"Yes, it will be soon," Farooq said. "But you must be ready next time. We must know these things to plan our attack. I trust you will be better prepared."

"Yes, I will be," Kolt said before heading to the door. "You can trust me."

"We must succeed in our mission. We have lost other brothers recently and even more are counting on us to execute our part of the larger plan," Farooq said as he opened the middle desk drawer and pulled something out.

Kolt tensed for a second, momentarily thinking Farooq was setting him up with the Mr. Nice Guy talk and was about to pull a gun on him. But when Farooq turned back around, Kolt saw he was removing a cell phone from a clear plastic bag.

"Brother Timothy, take this phone. This is how we will coordinate," Farooq said as he handed Kolt the phone. "It is safer this way."

Kolt knew that Tungsten was now playing interlude among all Internet traffic and cell phone calls between the terrorist cell and the real Timothy. Accepting the phone was no big deal and not entirely unexpected. Besides, it would be a simple matter to add the new phone's fifteen-digit IMEI number into the system. Kolt also assumed Farooq's previous comment was confirmation that the drowned swimmers that washed up on the shore of the Hudson River and the Romanian cell were all tied to the master nuke plot.

Yes, Kolt wanted to share the plant's security strategy, the nuances of the various security officers, the secret stopping places where external mobile-security patrols could remain off camera and unobserved by their meddling supervisors, and numerous other interesting points. Kolt couldn't afford to be Mr. Tough Guy here; he needed the terrorists more than they needed him. And, all things considered, even given the head butt, it had been a productive night.

Joma, rightly so, figured Timothy could answer all those questions. And if he was present in the hotel that night, he likely would have.

Tungsten had already determined that would not happen.

EIGHTEEN

Bruegger's Café, Raleigh, North Carolina

Cindy Bird strode up to the outdoor café's bronze-colored table wearing a knee-length lime-green skirt, four-button white blouse, and a pair of black two-inch heels. Kolt half stood up to greet her, keeping his head low enough to not hit it on the Dartmouth-green umbrella casting the square shadow ten feet away, and sort of reached over the small table to push her matching bronze chair out for her.

"I got it, thanks," Cindy said as she slid the chair back enough to sit down. She removed her pocketbook and hung it on the shoulder of the chair, reached down to grab both sides of the seat, dug her heels into the whitewashed concrete patio, and scooted close to the table.

"Come here often?" Cindy asked.

"Very rarely," Kolt answered as he handed Cindy a drink menu, trying not to eyeball her low-cut shirt and well-formed cleavage.

"Surprised, clientele doesn't seem rowdy enough for you."

"Stick around till after twenty-two hundred. You'd be surprised," Kolt replied.

"I'm sure I wouldn't be, but I'll pass. Thanks," Hawk said.

"I see Troy has upgraded your preppers' bracelet," Kolt said as he noticed the olive-green and tactical-tan military 550 cord around her wrist.

"Yeah, a double dragon knot this time, made with twenty feet of paracord," Cindy said as she held her wrist up and turned it side to side to show Kolt. "This one also has a buckle whistle and a magnesium fire starter weaved into the cord."

"Shit, they probably banned those things from tryouts, just like GPSs," Kolt said, smiling before taking a swallow of ice water.

"It doesn't really match the outfit, but Troy gives me shit if I don't wear it."

"Guess that telegraphs who you are seeing tonight," Kolt said.

"Look, Kolt, it's really good to see you, but I've only got a few minutes," Hawk said, wondering if Kolt would see through her bullshit. She missed Kolt and the Unit, for sure, just too proud to wear it on her shoulders.

"Yeah, no worries. Just wanted to pick your brain for a minute, Hawk."

"Kolt, as much as I want to, you know I can't tell you anything about the Unit. I'm on PCS leave right now, anyway."

"Guess Webber went through with it after all, huh?"

"Colonel Webber actually was willing to keep me," Hawk said. "But I had to move to the NBC shop."

"They spent a lot of money on you, Hawk. You kicked ass for over a year with several pretty hairy deployments under your belt. I'm sure they'd welcome you back in a year," Kolt said, trying to keep Hawk motivated.

"Maybe, heading to Fort Stewart, and, to be honest with you, I'm OK with it," Cindy said, making sure to maintain eye contact, lest she make it obvious that she was talking smack.

"Time heals all wounds, Hawk. They need you there."

"The Unit doesn't need anybody, Kolt. You know that better than most. But, we'll see," she said.

"What about you. What's up?"

"I'll cut to the chase, Hawk. It's about the Romanian cell," Kolt said. He didn't have time to get to Tungsten headquarters in Atlanta, and it would be a pain in the ass and too time-consuming to trade encrypted e-mails with Carlos and the analysts. He could probably hit the local library and do some open-source research on the Internet. But none of those options was as good as meeting with Hawk. He knew she'd know the answers to the terrorists' questions, at least fill in the major gaps, and was thrilled she agreed to meet him on such short notice.

"C'mon, Kolt, I don't know too much about that," Hawk said with as much sincerity as she could muster.

Kolt could see Cindy was uncomfortable with the topic. He realized now that it would be tough to get anything worthwhile from her. Kolt wished he could tell her he was working a SAP, working deep-cover ops for Tungsten, which might motivate her to help a little more. Reminding her of the threat to the homeland would certainly do that.

"I know, but I really just wanted to pick your brain about how a commercial nuclear plant works," Kolt said.

"Jesus, Kolt, we could be here for a week to get through that," Cindy said, grabbing a couple of white cocktail napkins and reaching back for a pen from her purse. She could see it in his eyes that he couldn't walk away from the Unit, the mission. She understood that.

"I just need the basics, Hawk," Kolt said. "What are the main buildings and what exactly does the nuke plant want to protect from sabotage?" Kolt figured if he knew at least this much, if he could gain a good appreciation for where and what he needed to keep Farooq and the gang away from, he would be in a better position to help manipulate a pseudo-false-flag attack that would minimize the number killed and maimed.

Cindy started to draw a series of rectangles in various sizes, a large circle in the middle, and smaller circles outside the rectangles.

"OK, nuke power one-oh-one. Don't blame me; you asked for it," Cindy said, pointing her pen at the large circle on her paper, seeming to get into it a little more.

"This large circle is known as the main reactor. It's where the nuclear fuel rods are stored. They are megahot, and when they come in contact with water, it produces a lot of steam. The steam is then pumped out to massive turbine generators, which in turn produce electricity. I recall some refer to the reactor as containment."

"OK, got that," Kolt said. "What next?"

Cindy continued. "One of these rectangular buildings could be the main control room. This is like a spaceship full of computers, sensors, buttons, and switches. The smart people that run the plant work in here. If you protect these two places, the reactor core and the control room, you are good to go."

"Basically the head shed, or even a joint operations center?" Kolt asked, wanting to understand the function of the control room a little more.

"Something like that," Cindy said.

"OK," Kolt said. "That's great information."

"Pretty simple, really. All these rectangles and the large circle are collectively known as the power block. It's controlled access."

Kolt thought he understood about the reactor core and control room. It seemed a lot easier than he had figured.

"So that's it. The armed security officers have to only be concerned with stopping anyone from messing with the main reactor or the control room?" Kolt asked.

Cindy looked at her napkin for a moment. Chewed on the back end of her pen. "Well, no. In fact, there is a third concern. The spent-fuel pool could be attractive to a terrorist, too."

"I got the control room. It runs the place. Whack a bunch of buttons and switches, and the plant can't properly cool the reactor fuel and it overheats. But what's the spent-fuel pool do?" Kolt asked.

She obliged Kolt. "It's where the old fuel is sent after it can no longer produce electricity."

"Why protect it if it is spent already?" Kolt asked.

Cindy sighed. She looked at Kolt. "Kolt, yes, it is spent, but it's still a major radiological hazard, and it's still hot as Hades for years and years. If that spent fuel isn't continually cooled, it would be a meltdown similar to the reactor core losing its coolant. Think Fukushima in Japan a couple of years ago. You'd have a major radiological release on your hands that could possibly kill hundreds of thousands of innocent Americans."

"OK, I got it, Hawk," Kolt said. "I see you really earned that university degree after all."

"University my ass, Kolt. Uncle Sam taught me all this in my NBC training," Hawk answered.

"Iranian DUGS, Syrian sarin attacks, and Russian HDBT target folders probably didn't hurt, huh?"

Kolt certainly was impressed with Hawk's knowledge about nuclear power plants. He knew she had been working the targets in Iran, where she studied all that nation's known deep-underground structures and hardened, deeply buried targets. But Kolt needed more. He really needed to know everything the intel shop at the Unit knew about the chatter of attacks on power plants in the United States. Kolt knew that knowledge base resided in the head of the lady he was dining with. He decided to go for it.

"These pools—is there any possible connection to the pools and those guys that washed up on the shore of the Hudson? Kolt asked, the comment by Farooq the night before in the hotel room still fresh in his mind.

"I don't think so," Hawk answered.

Kolt pressed it. "For example, is it possible that a diver could get to the spent-fuel pool from a large body of water like a river or reservoir?

"No, no chance," Hawk answered. "The pool water in a nuclear power plant is not connected to the cooling water drawn from a big body of water that is needed to cool the main reactor."

"No?" Kolt asked.

"Well, not directly, no. You can't swim to it through a long connection of pipes or anything like that. Too many twists and turns, cutoff valves, small pipes, and vertical turns to get a body through."

Kolt turned the napkin around a little so he could see it clearer. "The pool—it's inside what you said is the power block?"

Hawk's cell phone chirped. "Yes. Look, Kolt, hate to break up our date here, but I really gotta go."

"Really good to see you, Hawk," Kolt said, figuring it was Troy wondering where she was. "I appreciate your time."

"No problem, Kolt. Good luck at school—and please, please stay in touch. You've got my number, and I still have yours. Don't be a stranger," Cindy said as she stood, gave Kolt a short hug, and wheeled around on her high heels.

When Cindy Bird drove up looking for the Brueggers Café sign, she wasn't the only one interested in where Kolt Rayor was. No, Farooq had handed him the new cell phone last night not simply to make it easier to communicate between the two parties. Yes, that was certainly part of it, but the phone's tracking ability through GPS technology was the real motive.

It worked.

Abdul had made several passes driving the three of them around in his used blue Honda Civic as Farooq, sitting in the passenger's seat, corrected him at every turn, constantly shifting his eyes from the phone to the direction of the convenient outdoor tables at Brueggers Café.

Within the last five minutes, Abdul had erratically crossed from one lane to the next, practically rear-ended an elderly infidel, and banged a U-turn within hearing distance of Brueggers. Farooq was not impressed—in fact, he was losing patience with Abdul, now understanding why Nadal the Romanian had micromanaged him from Sana'a.

"Stop the vehicle over there," Farooq said to Abdul, after deciding they would attract less attention from the authorities if their vehicle was not moving.

Abdul pulled the Honda into an empty spot in a fairly sparse parking lot for a lunchtime crowd. The shadows of the trees reached just past the vehicle trunk, offering them a comfortable hiding place.

Farooq turned around and looked past the bandaged Joma in the backseat and through the rear window, ensuring he still had line of sight on the couple at the outdoor table. Several waist-high bushes masked part of the view, but they had a decent picture of everything from the green umbrella down to the man's and woman's shoulder blades.

It had been a long day already for the three terrorists.

They had decided late last night, soon after stopping the bleeding above Joma's eye, that Timothy was not being forthright and magnanimous. They felt he was wavering, likely changing his mind, and, worse, possibly considering going to the authorities. Farooq reminded them all that if that happened, they would all be at risk on foreign soil, and, if caught—and Farooq certainly believed they would be caught—they faced incarceration at Gitmo, where they would waste away like the rest of the mujahideen.

Farooq wasn't about to let history get away with that. No, his dreams of supermartyrdom were stronger than ever. Nothing would stop him from *his* mission. And, as much as Farooq didn't care to admit it, he needed Timothy Reston much more than Timothy needed them.

Earlier that morning, they had driven to Timothy's house, but with nowhere to park to discreetly observe when Timothy came and went, and no sign of his vehicle, they decided to locate him through the cell phone they gave him.

"That was not that difficult, brothers," Joma said from the backseat.

"No," Farooq agreed.

"They must be holding hands," Abdul said, viewing the couple at the table through his rearview mirror. "Most assured that is Timothy's wife."

"I didn't know he was married," Joma said. "A girlfriend, perhaps?"

"Whoever she is, we should detain her. That will make Timothy talk, provide us what we need to plan a suitable attack," Farooq said. "If we have his wife, Allah willing, he will not be so openmouthed with the authorities."

"Are you sure, Farooq?" Abdul said. "That can be very dangerous."

"We take her, or we must kill Timothy," Farooq said.

"Yes, we must be careful," Joma added. "But Farooq speaks the truth. We must have some leverage on Timothy, or we will not succeed."

Farooq, sensing an immediate ally in Joma, pounced on the opportunity. "It is decided, brothers."

Just then, Joma spoke up. "The woman has left. She must be walking to her car."

"Don't lose her. Keep an eye on her," Farooq demanded.

They watched as the woman walked from the outdoor tables, around the corner of the building, crossed several lanes of parked vehicles, and reached a metallic-gray Volkswagen Beetle.

"What should we do?" Abdul asked.

They hadn't planned to roll up a woman today, or any day for that matter. That was never part of the plan. But Murphy, being an indiscriminate problem maker, reared his ugly head equally for the good as well as for the bad guys. Farooq bounced in his seat slightly, trying to maintain a visual on the woman. She had yet to enter the car, was still standing outside, talking on her cell phone.

"We must act!" Farooq said.

"How so, brother?"

"Abdul, drive over there, slowly," Farooq said, trying to develop a high-risk plan on the fly. "And Joma, when we get there, you will step out and grab her, put your knife to her throat, but keep her quiet."

Abdul turned the key and backed out as Farooq had ordered. Farooq could see he was extremely nervous by the death grip on the steering wheel, his rocking back and forth, and his low voice, reciting a passage from the Koran.

"Relax, my brother. Allah is with us."

The last time Kolt Raynor had talked to Cindy Bird, he had called her from the table at Brueggers to tell her she had left her purse. Kolt knew she wouldn't get far, as he assumed the purse she had left hanging on the chair contained all her identification, her money, her makeup, and the keys to her Beetle. She had thanked him, apologized for being such an airhead, and, chalking it up to a busy week, was on her way back to retrieve it.

But after waiting for another ten minutes, Kolt called her back.

This time it wasn't Hawk that answered, and what they were demanding shocked the shit out of him.

"OK, OK, brother Farooq," Kolt said, trying to remain calm as he paced the sidewalk outside the café. "I understand. But, please, don't hurt her." Even though Kolt was calm, he was extremely nervous and felt guilty as hell for getting Hawk involved in this operation. It wasn't supposed to go down that way.

Just a quick drink and some face time. That's it.

"Do not underestimate our faith, brother Timothy," Farooq said. "I assure you, we will not hesitate to sacrifice the female's head in the name of Allah the merciful."

"She has nothing to do with this," Kolt said. "She knows nothing of my problems. Knows nothing about my relationship to you or our plans."

Kolt was torn between spilling the beans and confessing that he wasn't the real Timothy and pleading to release his wife. How could he admit to the deception? Even if they believed him, they certainly wouldn't just drop Cindy Bird off at the next bus station and wish her well on her way. No, they would kill her, likely videotaping it for the world stage while they lobbed her head clean off.

Moreover, killing Hawk wouldn't help stop Nadal the Romanian, who everyone believed was in the final stages of an attack on another commercial power plant. Most believed the Cernavoda nuclear plant in Romania, his hometown, but others, including Kolt, believed that chatter was more a diversion than reality. They believed Romania was not the target but that another, undisclosed plant in the United States was.

"That is unfortunate, Timothy," Farooq replied. "If she holds no value to you, than we can rid you of your problem in short order."

"No, no, Farooq. That is not what I am saying," Kolt said, raising his voice. "I love her, OK. I love her a lot. All I am saying is, I need time. Time to research the answers to your questions. Please, you have to trust me."

Kolt waited for a response. Nothing. He wondered if he had dropped the call, maybe not noticing as motorists sped by him on the sidewalk. He looked at the phone's face, palming one hand over the phone's screen to shield the sun. It appeared OK.

"Farooq, Farooq," Kolt said. "I just need time, maybe a week, and we will have what we need."

Farooq spoke calmly, pronouncing each word with clarity and emphasis. "You have seventy-two hours, or we will slaughter your infidel woman like the dirty swine she is."

Immediately, Kolt heard the call drop.

With those last words, Kolt knew he had few options and very little time.

He ran the numbers quickly as he headed for his truck. He knew he couldn't alert the FBI, even though that just might put a stop to the Cherokee attack. But if he did that, he would certainly compromise Tungsten and doom Hawk to a violent death, Farooq's cell might go to ground, and the Romanian cell would likely never be located.

Kolt knew there was at least one other cell planning an attack and that Nadal the Romanian was still out there, possibly planning a simultaneous hit on a different power plant. With Hawk's nuke lesson at the outdoor café, he figured he had enough information on how a power plant operates to come up with a suitable plan that Farooq and the others could live with. But that was before the threatening phone conversation with Farooq.

Now that Hawk's ass was seriously on the line, Kolt realized he didn't know shit about the finer details about how a commercial nuclear power plant operates. To request an immediate meeting with Farooq now would be useless at best and would get him and Hawk killed at worst.

Those motherfuckers!

Even with his initial success infiltrating the terror cell as Timothy, Kolt wasn't entirely sure about Tungsten. After he read about the general concept back in Doc Johnson's just a few weeks ago, it took him some time to think it over. He didn't know anyone who had actually gone into the program, so he couldn't get the scoop on the deal before he signed on. He assumed there were others, though. He was torn between retiring and taking on the Tungsten gig. Attending advanced military schooling was out.

Tungsten wasn't Delta, but it was close, which made his mind up. Leaving the ranks of Delta is always one of the toughest choices a Delta operator has to make, but one every operator must face eventually. At least this time he wasn't getting the boot, he wasn't PNGed, persona non grata, and, who knows, he figured there might be room in Delta once Admiral Mason moved on.

Above all, though, after over a decade in Delta, what made Kolt most attractive to the secret brain trusts behind Tungsten was his natural impetuousness. Kolt took risks—a character trait Doc Johnson witnessed for so long—all but ensuring his future in Tungsten. Kolt Raynor was hardwired for Tungsten. He couldn't say no. And they knew it.

But right now he needed something quick. He needed information. Something he could give Farooq to ease the terrorists' suspicions that he wasn't dedicated, that he wasn't a truly violent insider with a major axe to grind. Cindy Bird had been helpful, but it was limited. She could only speak in general terms about commercial nuclear plants. It was better than nothing, for sure, but Kolt needed details about Cherokee, or Cindy Bird was soon to be headless. And only one person could provide that information. The real Timothy.

NINETEEN

Cherokee Power Plant, Gaffney, South Carolina

Kolt arrived at 0900 hours sharp, amazed that Carlos was able to pull it off in less than two days' time. Tomorrow, Kolt would be meeting Farooq and his brothers again. Seventy-two hours would be up, and Kolt would provide the information they demanded or he would never see Hawk alive again.

Carlos had used every bit of access he had developed over the past thirty-eight years to work the particulars to get Embed 0706 access to Timothy Reston at Cherokee. Masquerading as a weapons dealer who wanted to provide the plant a great deal on the latest .50 caliber Barrett rifles was the perfect pull-out-of-your-ass cover for action. It was the kind of challenge tailor-made for Carlos Menendez II, and even though he and Kolt both knew it wasn't perfect, it was certainly doable.

Cherokee's senior access officer, Mr. Timothy Reston, was waiting for him at the main checkpoint, a small whitewashed building with a baby-blue awning that marked the boundary of the plant's property line, where employees and visitors were required to present their picture ID. Kolt's first impression of Reston wasn't a good one. The man was easily forty pounds overweight and wheezed as he walked up to Kolt and shook his hand through the open car window.

"Were you in the service?" Reston asked. His smile was big and bright.

Kolt played it low-key. "First Gulf War. I was a weapons tech working mostly on small arms. Closest I got to combat was when a Scud missile landed seven miles away from us. Scared the hell out of me."

Reston's chubby face lost its smile. "Oh. I thought maybe you were a sniper or something."

"I knew some," Kolt said, realizing he'd better not play it too low-key. "Did a lot of work on their rifles. Talk about your anal-retentive types."

Reston's smile returned. "I'd love to hear about it."

Kolt and Timothy spent the next few hours talking about various sniper rifles and long-distance shooting. Kolt was surprised at how much the man knew, although it was clear he'd never been in the field. As they talked and walked, Kolt noticed that Reston's coworkers seemed to be going out of their way to avoid him.

During their conversation, Kolt got his eyes on the target. The doctrinal military term for his visit this morning, if anybody believed Unit members followed any specific doctrine, was that Kolt was conducting a leader's reconnaissance. Kolt wanted to see for himself what the target looked like before he committed his men to action. In this case, Farooq's men. Though it felt wrong in so many ways, Kolt needed the reconnaissance even though it was for a terrorist attack he was going to be part of. It was a simple pet peeve of his and one he rarely felt comfortable doing without.

Enjoying their first cup of coffee together inside Timothy's cramped office, Kolt noticed a picture on the desk near Timothy's computer. Kolt pounced on the opportunity to break the ice a little and move away from sniping. Kolt commented on how gorgeous the snow was, actually more impressed by the beautiful brunette in the yellow North Face jacket and Oakley goggles.

"Who are the two happy skiers?" Kolt asked. "They look like they were having a lot of fun. Where is that?"

Timothy's answer shocked him.

"That's my third cousin, Darren Smith, with my sister," he said proudly. "We were at Lake Tahoe back in two thousand."

"Darren Smith?" Kolt asked curiously. It was a fairly common name. There had to be a million Darren Smith's in the world. "He ever serve in the military?" Kolt asked, certain it was just a crazy coincidence.

"As a matter of fact, he did," Timothy said as he stood up and walked to pick up the picture. "He was a hero, they said."

"Really?" Kolt asked, trying not to seem too excited or interested. "How so?"

"Well, I don't know any details, really, as it's all top-secret."

"Why?" asked Kolt.

"He was in a special unit," Timothy answered as he handed the picture to Kolt.

Kolt was speechless as he stared at the photo. He focused in on the face of the man wearing the red hat.

"I'm sorry for your loss," Kolt said as he set the picture back down in its original spot and tried not to seem too enthused.

Kolt immediately assumed Timothy knew all about his cousin's service with Special Forces and his death in the Middle East. He didn't want to push it; Kolt was concerned about upsetting Timothy and quickly changed the subject. He needed info about the plant, not about the cousin.

Part of Timothy's problem was the feeling of always having to live up to his cousin's success in the army. That was obvious to Kolt now. It drove his affection for commando and SWAT stuff since it got him as close to his cousin's special operations lifestyle as he could ever hope to get. One could argue that his deeply felt jealousy contributed to Timothy's disgruntled status at Cherokee Power Plant. Kolt wondered if Timothy's supervisors had any idea.

Timothy obviously wanted to talk about his cousin a little longer. "We don't know any details about how it happened. Just somewhere over there."

Timothy spent the next two hours briefing Kolt on the licensee's protective strategy, discussing their implementing procedures, and going over what Timothy referred to as security issues still open with the corrective action process, all in an effort to determine how the bargain-priced .50 caliber rifles could improve their overall security posture.

After a quick lunch at the plant's cafeteria, Timothy easily secured Kolt a visitors' badge and escorted him around the protected area, pointing out the microwave-volumetric security zone and alarms, the electric-field taut wire zones and functions, and how visiting vehicles are processed through the sally port. Kolt was impressed with Timothy's knowledge and energy. Timothy seemed to get stronger as the day passed by and enjoyed talking tactics and how best the plant might use a bunch of new .50s.

After walking down the protected area, Timothy took Kolt into the power block and helped him process in to the radiological controlled area, where a special radiation monitor had to be worn on the chest and proximity key cards were required to gain access and move through the area. Timothy showed Kolt the main control room first, which prompted Kolt to recall what Hawk had said the other day. Hawk had told him that the MCR is the specific area that keeps the reactors operating safely and that it serves as the nerve center.

Leaving the control room, Timothy escorted Kolt through the auxiliary building en route to the main reactor building, passing through a series of heavy flood doors and fire doors that required entrants to have special access, which was activated by the tiny microchip embedded in one's photo ID.

As Kolt moved closer, Timothy pointed out the features of the card reader. "Simply swipe your badge down through the thin slot, watch a little light change from red to green, wait for the distinct audible of balance-magnetic locks to release, and then open the heavy door to enter," Timothy said. "Pretty simple but secure."

After moving through the door, Timothy pointed out the large circular door of the tubular entrance point to the reactor's core. The personnel access hatch was the primary point of entry to the main reactor, where the nuclear fuel rods were kept.

"If the uranium fuel inside that thing explodes, would it be like a nuclear bomb going off?" Kolt asked.

"Ha. No. That's a common misconception, for sure, though," Timothy said, clearly enjoying his role as escort and educator. "It's physically impossible for the nuclear fuel to explode like that. The fuel is only about three- to five-percent fissionable uranium."

"Hmmm," Kolt said. "So what is the percent for a nuclear bomb?"

"Geez. Nuclear weapons have in excess of ninety-percent fissionable uranium," Timothy said.

"So what exactly is the threat?" Kolt asked. "Why so much security and all those barriers outside and elevated ballistic towers with armed officers?"

"Good question. Well, the threat is release of radiation to the general public. Ever heard of Chernobyl, or more recently Fukushima, where scores died from acute exposure to radiation? If the core is breached, or even if the used fuel we store in the spent-fuel pool can't be continuously cooled, this place will melt down in hours, releasing a godawful amount of deadly radiation into the atmosphere."

"What's the risk to the public?" Kolt asked, noticing that sweat beads had formed on Timothy's nose and chubby pink cheeks.

"Well, opinions vary," Timothy answered. "Some so-called experts say upwards of two hundred thousand people will die, others disagree. If nothing else the genetic and financial fallout would be extraordinary."

After a few minutes of answering Kolt's general questions, they left the reactor building and retraced their steps back through the auxiliary building. From there it was a quick climb of the three levels of the turbine grating stairs with their bright yellow handrails, until they reached the locked heavy door controlling access to the fuel-handling building.

"The blue number painted on the wall. Six hundred and forty-five? You have that many doors around here?" Kolt asked as they processed through another key-card-access door.

Timothy laughed and shook his head. "No, this floor is supposed to be six hundred and forty-five feet above sea level, give or take a few feet, I imagine."

Kolt shook his head, acknowledging the response while reaching up to tighten the plastic knob on the back of his white hard hat. Sweat had formed around his head, too, causing his hard hat to slip down close to his eyes. Close enough to see the large sweat spot on Timothy's lower back, Kolt followed his escort toward the large body of water the size of two dozen vehicles parked in a Wal-Mart parking lot.

"We can't go past the yellow handrail due to radiation-dose limits and FME," Timothy said.

"Foreign-material exclusion," Kolt said. "They use that term in the air force on runways, I heard."

"This is what we call the fuel floor, or fuel deck. Inside this large pool are the spent fuel rods."

Timothy walked Kolt to the edge of the massive pool and stopped at the yellow handrails. Kolt held on to the waist-high railing as Timothy pointed out the tops of the fuel rods that could barely be seen through the twenty-three feet of glowing and glimmering water.

Kolt shook his head, amazed at the simple but ingenious idea that nuclear energy was being used to produce the electricity that powers billions of cell phones, laptops, and flat-screen TVs every single day.

"So they are moved to here from the main reactor core?" Kolt asked, understanding the process a little better now.

"Yes, the fuel is replaced about every eighteen months," Timothy said.

"Wow, pretty amazing!" Kolt said. "So we can go swimming in the pool if we wanted to with no issues?" Kolt asked.

"Uh, you can, not me," Timothy said, chuckling a little while lifting his hard hat higher on his forehead. "The radiation still in the fuel rods keeps that water hot as hell, about one hundred to one ten degrees Fahrenheit. Even hotter the closer you get to the silver-colored assemblies."

"I guess that would be slightly uncomfortable, kind of like a high-end hot tub where the temperature gauge failed miserably," Kolt said.

"The water temp isn't your biggest problem. It's the lethal dose of radiation you most likely will take swimming in that pretty pool," Timothy said.

"Kill ya, huh?" Kolt asked, almost assured already Timothy would answer in the affirmative.

"Only one hundred and fifty thousand Rem per hour if the fuel is fresh from the reactor core," Timothy sarcastically said. "But it dissipates over time."

"I take it that is a lot," Kolt said. "So if someone falls in there accidentally, he will die of a lethal dose of radiation?" Kolt asked.

"Immediately, no. Over time, it's certain death," Timothy answered. "It all depends on the total dose your organs take from the radiation still emanating from the spent-fuel assemblies."

"Sounds tricky," Kolt said.

Charlotte, North Carolina

In the last few hours talking with the terrorists, Kolt hadn't heard anything from them that really sparked his interest. Nothing the terrorists said presented a true opportunity for him to actually control the outcome of their impending attack on Cherokee. After talking to Timothy yesterday at Cherokee, Kolt knew he needed something to exploit, just not in a way that would kill a lot of innocent people. Kolt didn't want anyone dead except the terrorists. All of them but one, anyway. He would have to keep one of them alive to lead him to Cindy and, he hoped, to Nadal the Romanian.

During a pause in the discussion, out of nowhere, Kolt recalled something Timothy had mentioned to him during Kolt's visit with him yesterday.

"Those ops guys," Kolt said with an obvious tone of disgust, "they think they are above the law."

Farooq bit. "What are you saying, Timothy?"

"Once every twelve-hour shift, an ops guy has to make checks of critical equipment off-site."

"What is an ops guy? When do the shifts start?" Farooq questioned.

"Oh, sorry, ops is slang for operations. They run the plant. There are two shifts. One day and one night that run from seven to seven."

"Where do these ops guys go?" Joma asked, pulling the larger street map in front of him and placing the Google overhead of Cherokee adjacent to it.

"They have four checks to make each time they leave the site," Kolt explained while pointing to the street map on the table. "They make a radio call back to the main control room after each one."

Kolt pointed confidently to four different locations with obvious road access as Abdul circled each with a red marker. Kolt wasn't entirely sure about any of the stops except the corner gas station.

"Then, they always go by the 105 Auto Shop before they come back to the plant," Kolt added. "Even though they aren't supposed to."

"What, a whorehouse?" Farooq said in astonishment "You are serious, no?"

"No, a convenience store. They grab donuts and coffee. Security would never get away with that. We don't leave the plant for anything during our shifts. Typical ops jackasses!" Kolt snorted.

"Do you know who is going to be on each shift?" Joma asked.

"Yea, I can check the schedule. It's published a month out," Kolt offered.

"Then you should be able to get a picture of the guy, or woman, on each shift, right?" asked Abdul.

"Uh, yeah, I should be able to go into the security database and get a picture off their identification badge."

"Would you be able to get into his personal office before he arrives to work or after he leaves for the day? Maybe at lunchtime when he is in the cafeteria?" Farooq asked.

"Probably. Why?"

"Good," Farooq said. "Take a family photo off his desk and Xerox a copy for us. Don't forget to put the photo back in the same place. Do you think you can do that?"

"Sure, but I don't understand why," Kolt said.

"Just do it," Farooq said.

"It's settled, then," Kolt said, trying to assert some authority over the operational planning. "I'll be on duty at the plant's main checkpoint when you guys attack. I'll make sure I'm out of the booth and conducting random checks away from the action."

They looked at Timothy, each making eye contact and silently wondering if Timothy actually had the balls to see this thing through. Kolt understood the gravity of what was transpiring. He knew the American culture. He had seen nothing the day before to confirm the real Timothy was a traitor to his country. Sure, he despised his supervisors and coworkers, that much was clear. But that was a far cry from becoming a modern-day Benedict Arnold.

Kolt knew Carlos's call to insert him as Timothy was incredibly risky, but at least it took Timothy out of the picture. Timothy Reston wouldn't have to pull the trigger against his own country.

"Are you worried, Timothy?" Farooq asked softly.

Kolt didn't answer right away. He struggled for the appropriate response and slightly shrugged his shoulders.

"It's OK to be nervous a little," Farooq offered. "It helps you concentrate and ease the soul a bit. We feel the same way."

Farooq looked around the small room at the other jihadists.

"But, my new friend, we must have assurances that you are truly with us in our mission."

"I said I am OK," Kolt answered, unsure exactly what Farooq was getting at.

"Timothy. You will not be at work on twenty-one April," Farooq said.

"Why is that?" Kolt asked.

"Because on that night you will be with us. You will carry a weapon and attack with us. You will obtain revenge from all those that have admonished you over the years," Farooq explained. "And, if you desire to ever see your wife again, you will show your faith to our operation."

"Attack with you? No way, I can't," Kolt said, not having to manufacture surprise. He hadn't expected them to force him along at the last minute.

"You must, brother Timothy. We cannot be successful without you."

Kolt thought it over for a few seconds. He knew he would go on the attack with them, if for no other reason than to ensure the least amount of injured Americans as possible. And, of course, he desperately wanted to rescue Hawk. But he wasn't even sure they still had her in the area, and he didn't have so much as a single starting point.

"Farooq, please do not doubt my desire to help. But I must see my wife, for the last time of my life, before I commit to accompanying you brothers on the attack," Kolt said, seeking some sympathy.

"That is impossible," Farooq said. "Your wife is OK, but she is not near us."

"Farooq, would you deny me a simple phone call? A chance to hear her voice and provide me peace of mind before I embark on our path to martyrdom with you?"

Farooq thought about it for several seconds. He looked at the other brothers and obtained nods of approval from Joma and Abdul.

"Very well," Farooq said as he picked up his cell phone and dialed a number.

Kolt waited as Farooq spoke Arabic with an unseen person on the other end of the phone. He understood the words "wife" and "Timothy" and the phrase *athbatta* and *haajam,* Arabic words for "prove" and "attack." And then Farooq handed the phone to Kolt.

Kolt had his proof of life.

•   •   •

Cherokee Nuclear Power Plant

The night of 21 April was a moonless one. Farooq and Joma were just about complete with the installation, and even though Kolt wanted to be in on the job, he figured he better sit this one out. He sat in the van down the street at the all-night gas station on the corner. Timothy's house sat only a few miles away to the east. And as the sky filled with stars over the midsize suburb, Kolt figured that very soon Timothy would wish he had taken the night off to take in some Xbox.

Kolt's mind drifted to thoughts of Shaft standing in the snow in Pakistan. He wondered where he would be right now had he not ignored Mason's order to abort.

He had a load on his shoulders—his primary services to Tungsten, his orders to stop the nuke plot and prevent a devastating attack on the Cherokee power station, and his most pressing operation, to rescue Cindy Bird from these asshole terrorists—and he could feel the pressure. Kolt couldn't predict the future, but after hearing Hawk's faint voice over Farooq's cell for a few seconds, he was certain she had been beaten severely. All this combined to stretch his core to the absolute outer limits.

The loud honk of a passing motorist brought Kolt back to the present. He looked at the time on his cell phone and wondered how the others were doing. He hoped they would cross the wrong wires and blow themselves into kingdom come, but that wouldn't help him find Hawk. But, all things being equal, Kolt needed the attack on Cherokee to happen.

How hard can it be to open a vehicle trunk, remove the spare tire from the wheel well, and replace it with fifty pounds of Semtex bulk explosives?

A verse of "Back in Black" by the eighties heavy metal band AC/DC started playing as his cell phone rang. That song always took Kolt back to his carefree high school days. But carefree was exactly what he didn't need now. He needed to be switched on.

Kolt fingered the answer button. "Yeah?"

"We are ready, Timothy," Joma whispered. "Pick us up immediately."

"Are you sure everything is ready. Do we need to wait for another night?"

"Yes, yes . . . come get us. We must get to the water."

"Did you activate the detonator? See a red light come on?" Kolt continued, practically ignoring Joma's requests for pickup.

"Yes, yes, just as we rehearsed. Allah saw to it that we were successful."

"Yes, yes, brother, I knew Allah was with you. *Allah u Akbar!*" he answered, changing tones slightly. "Be there in five minutes."

Kolt was oddly pleased to be teamed with Abdul tonight. Not that he trusted the son of a bitch necessarily. He was still a terrorist, and Kolt would just as soon choke him out right there, but he had seemed to take to Kolt the most. Abdul had been the least aggressive toward him in the seedy hotel room during planning. And at the moment, he was Kolt's teammate and needed to be treated accordingly. More importantly, in the 105 Auto Shop gas station parking lot just off the eastern edge of Wilkinsville Highway, Abdul was currently Kolt's only link to Cindy Bird.

The two of them had not been alone at all since they met. As they waited on the others to finish up loading the explosives, Kolt knew another opportunity might not present itself. He decided to throw the Hail Mary.

"Abdul, do you miss your family?"

"They are in good hands," Abdul responded stoically but clearly startled by the question. He didn't make eye contact. He remained nervously alert, looking out the rain-spattered window for any signs of trouble.

"You are a lucky man," Kolt said as he looked toward Abdul. "I envy you."

Neither of them spoke for several moments. Kolt thought twice about continuing on with the same conversation. Speaking of family with a fellow Delta operator was usually a great way to break the ice and lower the tensions when on a high-risk mission. Kolt assumed it was a sure-bet acceptable topic with a terrorist as well.

To Kolt's surprise, Abdul spoke next. "You don't speak much of your wife," he said. "Have you forgotten her?"

Kolt stared straight ahead, out the driver's-side window. He had to be careful. "My wife would not be proud of me," he whispered.

"No?"

"Her and her family believe in defensive jihad only," Kolt said with a tone of empathy in his voice. "They desire peace in the world."

"I see."

It was now or never. Kolt knew he wouldn't have another chance. If things developed the way he had secretly shaped during the hotel planning, then Abdul was only an hour or so away from martyrdom. He needed information on Cindy's location.

"Abdul, my biggest fear is being captured by these infidel dogs, yes?" Kolt said.

Abdul turned to look at Kolt. "God willing, we will be heroes to all Islam. Allah will accept us tonight."

"Yes, that is a wonderful feeling," Kolt answered as he placed his right hand on Abdul's left shoulder gently. "But I fear the harsh treatment my wife is enduring for so long in captivity. I'm afraid I would not be able to endure days and days of isolation as she has."

Startled a second time, Abdul hesitated. "Your wife is being treated fairly. But she is stubborn."

"No, no, I could not survive a day in captivity."

"You could, Timothy," Abdul responded, looking at Kolt reassuringly, "just as your wife is."

"So my wife is still alive?" Kolt said in amazement.

"But she is." Abdul answered confidently. "I am certain of it."

Kolt paused for a moment to let it all sink in. "How so, brother?"

Before Abdul could answer, a white Ford King Cab F-150 turned into the convenience store parking lot. On the driver's-side door, a red, white, and blue EnergyFirst logo confirmed the occupant.

Just as Timothy said he would, the ops engineer stepped out of the truck as he had done every weekday night for the past two years and lifted his light Windbreaker over his head to block the rain as he quickly headed for the front door. Kolt exited the van, slipped his T-shirt over the handle to the .38 Abdul had provided, and followed the man into the store. Abdul pulled out a black balaclava hood and quickly slipped it over his head to expose only his eyes and lips. Thin rubber surgeon's gloves followed before he slipped out into the parking lot.

Kolt overheard the cashier as the man approached the counter. He was recognized by all the store cashiers. This wasn't a surprise. Kolt figured they routinely rang up the same amount each night.

"The usual tonight, Warren?" asked the thirtysomething woman two-fingering a half-burnt cigarette behind the counter.

"Yep, Deborah, nothing new at the power plant," answered Warren.

"Alright, then, four cups of house-blend coffee, a cherry pie, and three honey buns comes exactly to . . ."

Warren interrupted and finished her sentence while smiling. "Six dollars and sixty-six cents."

"You got it, Warren," answered Deborah as she took his money and opened the cash register. "But that number always spooks me."

"What a bargain!" he said, smiling.

Warren pocketed his change and gently picked up the four-section cardboard coffee holder and the plastic bag.

"Careful with the coffee. It's really hot," Deborah said.

With his arms full, Warren backed gently into the glass door and pushed it open. He spun around and took a few short steps before stepping lightly off the wet curb. His worn leather boots splashed dirty puddle water on top of his boot toes as he fumbled for his truck keys.

Warren opened the driver's door and gingerly placed the small bag of snacks on the plastic leather front seat. He pushed the four cup holder around the seat-belt buckle and rested it against the back of the passenger's seat to ensure it wouldn't spill. He turned the key, and the engine roared. Warren placed the truck in reverse and backed out of the parking lot.

Kolt walked out of the storefront, pulled his black balaclava over his head, and took the wheel gun from his pants as he moved briskly to the F-150.

As Warren eased onto the empty asphalt road, he reached to the radio and turned it on. A second later, the fifty-two-year-old chain smoker was having a hard time breathing. His most immediate concern was the force of Abdul's left forearm pressing against his larynx.

Warren's inherent survival instincts kicked in immediately. He grabbed Abdul's forearm with both hands to relieve the pressure even a little. His right foot instinctively hit the brakes, and the momentum threw them both forward slightly. Kolt threw open the passenger's door and slipped into the front seat next to Warren, sliding the coffee and sweets over.

"Don't panic, Warren," Kolt said as calmly as possible. "Follow instructions and save your own ass." Abdul eased off Warren's larynx enough to allow him to talk.

"What, what do you want?" Warren struggled to say. "I don't have any money."

"Your money is safe, Warren," Kolt answered. "It's your family you should be concerned with."

"Pull into that church parking lot ahead and drive around to the back."

Warren regained the wheel and eased into the parking lot. He drove toward the back, past the side doors, and stopped near the edge of the old graveyard and behind the white sided Mount Ararat Baptist Church.

"Kill the engine," Kolt ordered.

"OK, Mr. Warren Samperson," Kolt began. "Father of a beautiful daughter living at home as she attends the local Spartanburg Community College and happily married for thirty-three years to the lovely Eleanor."

"What in the world . . ." Warren barked before Abdul reapplied the neck pressure to cut him off.

"You are a family man, right Warren?" Kolt asked. "We know everything about you and your family," Kolt assured him and then placed the colored photocopy of his family in front of his face.

"Basically, Warren, you have two choices here," Kolt continued. "And your decision will directly impact on whether or not your daughter is around long enough to graduate.

"Now, all you need to do is drive this truck back to Cherokee. Proceed through the checkpoint, hold your badge up to the window like you always do, and continue to the parking lot in front of the main access facility.

"If you do this, Warren, act as if nothing is amiss, then your family lives," Kolt offered, before giving him a few seconds to think it over. Kolt could see the rapid pulse from Warren's neck as it pressed against the skin of Abdul's forearm.

Kolt whispered into Warren's right ear. "If you don't, Warren, with Allah as my witness, your family will be videotaped being raped, tortured, and murdered just as the American pigs are doing to our women on Muslim holy land."

"OK, OK, please don't hurt my family," Warren begged. "They haven't hurt anyone."

"I know, Warren. I know," Kolt quickly answered. "Head back to the plant and don't let the muzzle of this .38 Special against your funny bone bother you."

For the first time since the night began, Kolt allowed his emotions to power down a bit. Even though he was able to maintain his composure while talking to Warren, his adrenaline had kicked in overdrive as they neared the plant. Sure, it was exciting, but Kolt wondered at what loss of life and psychological cost? At the moment, there was no telling.

So far, so good. The mission was going according to plan. Warren seemed assured of being on board, albeit reluctantly, and the other pieces were falling into place. But on this mission, Kolt was still troubled by one thing.

How can I pull this mission off and still not harm any of the good guys? Abdul might have decided that Warren needed to die, but to Kolt the ops engineer's future certainly hadn't been decided.

TWENTY

Floating offshore on the calm lake water less than two miles from the amber glow of Cherokee Power Plant's towering high-mast light poles, Joma and Farooq huddled close aboard a red and white Sea Doo 1250 Jet Ski. Highlighted by the half-moon glare off the still water, a few feet behind the impeller boot and exhaust sat two large tractor-trailer inner tubes carefully rigged with a mix of nearly three hundred pounds of fertilizer and Semtex explosives.

Farooq's cell phone rang, and he reached into his shirt pocket carefully so as not to upset the delicate balance of two adult males on a single Jet Ski.

"Hello?"

"Brother Farooq, peace be upon you, we are ready, my brother," Abdul said enthusiastically into the phone. "We are almost to the checkpoint; execute your mission, brother. May Allah be with you both."

Shaking his head vigorously, Farooq answered. "Yes, yes, yes, *Allah u Akbar!*"

"Allah u Akbar!"

It had been just under an hour since Farooq and Joma had pulled off McKowns Mountain Road, cut the chain lock on the simple cable barrier, and taken a narrow north-south dirt road for half a mile to the public boat ramp on the southwest edge of a no-name reservoir. Farooq easily backed the trailer wheels three feet into the water and waited for Joma to unhook the Jet Ski and let it float off the trailer in the calm, frigid water.

After pulling the vehicle and trailer into the tree line, Farooq and Joma slowly slipped their way northeast up the reservoir, hugging the west-side shore as much as possible as they maintained course toward the ambient artificial light surrounding the power plant. They had remained under the overhanging tree limbs until they reached the left turn that would be their last hiding place as they awaited the phone call from Abdul. Now, only a thousand feet from their target, Cherokee's large concrete intake structure, everything was in place.

Joma reached for the limb of a tree, maintaining a shaky balance, and stepped off the ski with his rifle bag slung over his right shoulder. He nervously turned to Farooq. The men didn't expect to survive this mission. In fact, if they did survive, then something would have gone terribly wrong. For their own honor, for the honor of their families, both needed to martyr themselves on the soil of their enemy. They were the vanguard cell, with a lot expected of them this night.

Allah willing, brother Nadal and the others would follow their success a month later.

"May Allah be with you, brother," Joma said, before turning to disappear into the darkness. From the detailed planning with Timothy in the hotel room, Joma knew he needed about eleven minutes to reach a sniper position that overlooked two very intimidating bulletproof towers. His dark-skinned partner, Farooq, had only to wait for his phone call before he would maneuver the bomb under the lackadaisical eyes of the infidel and enter the gates of martyrdom.

Joma still marveled at how bitter Timothy was. He spoke long and angrily about the lapses in security at the plant. How he had pushed for thermal camera installations to protect the plant from this very thing—foot intruders with long-range weapons. Without thermal cameras to pick up heat signatures deep in the tree line, or out into the murky reservoir, the security officers in the towers had to rely on the naked eye or what they could detect from the standard monochrome security cameras. The decision makers at "higher"—the same term for upper-management personnel was used by civilians and by the military—disapproved the security department's last three requests for advanced thermal cameras.

Joma smiled in the dark. Arrogance would be America's undoing.

•   •   •   •

Timothy didn't mind working the graveyard shift, especially since he was recently given back his officer quals and carrying a sidearm again. It was peaceful but boring duty. Almost four hours into his eight-hour shift, the light impact of raindrops on the roof of the checkpoint building reminded him of a tin-roofed cabin in the mountains. All he had to do was get through the next ten minutes or so and his shift relief would arrive, allowing him to move inside the plant and throw down the leftover slices of cold pizza he had with him that day.

Checkpoint duty was the post that everyone on the security force understood as the least defendable. There were no bullet-resistant enclosures to jump into in an emergency, as there were surrounding the actual reactor building and other vital areas. The building's tempered glass was merely tinted and vinyl covered for safety, not bulletproof to save an officer's life. Another example of a simple business decision by the guys with the advanced diplomas on the office walls.

It was understood that if a security officer drew checkpoint duty and a real terrorist attack happened, then they were expendable. Cannon fodder.

Two years had passed since Timothy submitted a conditions report to his superiors. He pushed for upgrades to the checkpoint position. It was the farthest armed-security-officer spot from the actual reactor fuel. It was also the most vulnerable. Only the width of two lanes of blacktop road separated thick, beautiful pine trees and intermittent oak trees. This always bothered him. Yes, they were gorgeous and kept Cherokee from looking too much like Fort Knox, but the fact that terrorists could slip through the trees and thick brush under the cover of darkness made the four cameras on the roof obsolete.

Timothy had pressed for installing thermal cameras that would pick up the body heat of a terrorist lurking in the tree line. Early detection was the key, and for a mere sixty thousand dollars, the guy or gal tabbed with checkpoint duty might just have a fighting chance.

At the moment, though, he wondered if his relief was going to be a little late. He had monitored the radio calls of his coworker, Officer Collins, and knew he was on the other side of the plant taking care of the hourly security checks. The clock had just struck 11 P.M., so no worries just yet.

Collins would certainly be back soon enough, and cold pizza was cold pizza.

Sure, Timothy was a disgruntled employee. He wasn't the only one. Cherokee had four hundred employees, so he wouldn't be the last. They had gripes. They had issues they wanted addressed. Some legitimate, others ridiculous.

Timothy Reston hadn't gone full traitor on his country. He may have if Nadal hadn't dropped his notebook on the bus. And who knows? A few more gaming hours with ZooKeeper69 and things may have taken a turn for the worst. Maybe Timothy would have taken the next step. Eventually, he might have shared more than some basic blueprints about what each structure was called, maybe even the code words the security force used. If given enough time, and enough positive praise from ZooKeeper69 about his gaming skills, maybe he would have given some information on the critical-safety-shutdown equipment.

Having a target set to a commercial plant was like having the blueprints to the White House. Target sets are classified safeguards, translated in military terms as "top secret," and for good reason. These documents outline the specific pieces of safety equipment that, if destroyed or rendered inoperable, would cause a release of a deadly radiation plume into the atmosphere that would kill every living thing in its path. And even Timothy knew that if they fell into the wrong hands, it could be catastrophic.

No, Timothy, from his perspective, was simply a disgruntled employee, not a traitor to his country. Yes, he wanted to see some heads roll at his workplace, but he wasn't necessarily interested in a lot of innocent people buying the farm.

But the moment Timothy Reston shared the plant's blueprints with a faceless new friend over an underground bulletin board and online gaming channels, he became much more than a simple pissed-off employee. On that day, some two or even three months ago, he became a traitor to his country.

His fellow employees had no idea. Timothy gave no indication that he was willing or capable of committing an act of terrorism. They never guessed that his selling out his coworkers, the general public, and even himself had been snowballing. Cherokee's long-touted Behavior Observation Program missed the signals.

Timothy was now what government intelligence analysts and officials feared most from nuclear power plant employees. He had become an "insider." And not just any insider. He was an insider who possessed an extensive knowledge of Cherokee's protective strategy, had access to every key at the plant, and was willing to sell his soul to the devil, all because he didn't like the way his supervisors treated him. It was really a shame.

Yes, Timothy was extremely disgruntled. Timothy had willingly conspired with al Qaeda terrorists, and although he had never laid eyes on them or even talked with them over the phone, he had crossed the line. And had Kolt and Tungsten not entered the picture, tonight might be his last day on earth. If things had been different, the world would soon know that Benedict Arnold's treason would be a footnote in history compared with Timothy Reston's complicit support in engineering radiological sabotage on Cherokee Power Plant—an act of terrorism unequaled on United States soil.

The radio on Timothy's hip startled him. "Checkpoint, this is Central. Radio check. Over."

Timothy turned to look at the clock on the wall. Where had the last hour gone since the previous hourly radio check with the Central Alarm Station?

"Central, this is Checkpoint. All clear," he responded while eyeballing the suite of four monochrome flat screens on the wall above his head, almost as if he was worried the boogeyman was about to attack. Timothy's post was protected with 360-degree camera coverage. Mounted on the four corners of the stone white checkpoint building, the cameras monitored each cardinal direction from within the building. Inside the protected area of the power plant, both the Central Alarm Station and the Secondary Alarm Station received the same feed that Timothy saw at the checkpoint.

The radio squawked to life again.

"Central, this is Collins. Over." Timothy's eyebrows rose quickly. He looked down at his hip to see the red light flashing on his radio. Why in the world is Collins calling Central right now?"

"This is Central. Send your traffic. Over."

"Uh, yeah, Central, seems I have flat tire out here behind the cooling towers," Collins said.

"Do you need assistance?"

Collins was quick to respond. "Well, I wouldn't need any if the tire jack was where it is supposed to be. But since it is missing, I guess I need some help."

"Understand. Stand by for assistance."

Timothy shook his head in disgust. *Shitty evening all around, I guess.*

Timothy was feeling the hunger pains, but he was a professional first. He didn't sweat it and sat back down for some more time-killing gaming on his cell. As Timothy tapped through the selections, he noticed the head-lights of an approaching vehicle. He leaned up to see just over the bottom edge of the window and around the flat screen on the corner table, hoping it wasn't a delivery vehicle that would require him to exit the booth to search it for contraband and explosives.

It's just Warren.

From twenty feet away, Timothy recognized the company truck and the face of Warren Samperson, the longtime plant engineer, in the driver's seat. He wouldn't need to step out into the rain to check his vehicle. Timothy knew the only thing he was bringing back to the plant that he hadn't left with twenty minutes earlier when making his rounds were his coworkers' donuts and coffee.

Officer Reston opened the door to the security booth to wave Warren Samperson through as he activated the button to raise the yellow drop-arm barrier but remained in the doorway to stay out of the rain.

The vehicle barely came to a stop before the first round was fired. From the backseat directly behind the driver's seat, Abdul ripped the balaclava off his head as he raised his H&K .40 caliber auto pistol, leveled it at Timothy's chest, and fired two rapid shots that blew the safety glass out of the left rear window. Abdul didn't even bother to roll the tinted window down. Timothy never saw it coming, and it shocked Kolt almost as much. That wasn't the plan.

That son of a bitch! I knew it!

Immediately after both shots were fired, Warren ducked into a ball on the floorboard. He didn't think to place the vehicle in park first and acciden-tally pressed the gas pedal with his knee. The vehicle lurched forward and rammed directly into the metal barrier twenty feet ahead before it stopped cold in its tracks. Both passenger air bags deployed, one engulfing Warren and the other slamming into Kolt's head like a sledgehammer, knocking the revolver from his firing hand.

Bleeding badly and quickly heading into shock, Timothy struggled to crawl away from the truck. Abdul's marksmanship was effective, but off the mark. Timothy was bleeding from his left hip as the first round grazed the holder of his Mace can and entered just under his gun belt. The second copper round had pierced his left palm since he had instinctively raised his hand as if he could stop a bullet.

Lying in his own blood, he didn't think to make a radio call to Central. He didn't have time to sound the general duress alarm. He was too busy scrambling to survive. At that moment, every bit of tactical training Timothy ever received rushed back to him.

He had been training for this moment his entire life. All the preparation over the past sixteen years was for the moment when he would have to deploy his weapon for real. For when he would have to actually use deadly force against an armed intruder. For when he would have to do his duty, his duty to protect the American people. The moment when he would quite possibly live up to the extraordinary standards of professionalism and dedication to a cause that everyone in his extended family colored his cousin Darren with.

Timothy didn't have time to go into shock. No, Timothy knew exactly what he had to do.

He drew his semiautomatic sidearm and power stroked the slide to make his weapon hot.

But Timothy's body wasn't keeping pace with his survival instincts. Inside the truck, Abdul swapped his pistol for his AK–47 rifle. He placed the backs of his upper arms on the door, ignoring the small pebble-size glass pieces still present, balanced himself, and stuck the rifle out the window.

"Allah u Akbar! Allah u Akbar!"

Kolt turned from the front passenger seat toward Abdul. "NOOOOO!" he yelled. It was too late.

Lying on his back and panicking now, Timothy pleaded, "Don't do it. Don't do it." He nervously raised his pistol, fighting the wobble nerves, and broke the hammer three times rapidly. Three 9mm rounds tore into the side of the vehicle, failing to penetrate the truck's door.

Timothy missed, but Abdul didn't. He struck Timothy once in his bulletproof plate and twice in his upper chest area, closer to his shoulder.

Timothy's grip released his sidearm, dropping it to the tarmac just outside the doorway. It bounced three feet away before coming to rest near the truck's left rear whitewall.

Kolt quickly reached toward the coffee holder, picking up two Styrofoam cups and flipping the plastic tops off with his thumbs. He lifted them out and, in one smooth motion, reached over the seat and threw the scalding hot coffee in Abdul's face. Abdul let out a painful scream, dropped his rifle, closed his eyes, and, naturally, brought his hands to his face.

Kolt reached over and turned the ignition off. He barely noticed Warren, still huddled on the floorboard. Warren's hands were over his head, as if to protect himself from falling objects. The deflated air bag rested on his shoulders.

Kolt frantically searched for his dropped revolver, ripping the air bags out of the way. No luck.

Kolt bailed.

Abdul should have bailed, too, but he didn't.

Kolt moved quickly to Timothy's side and took a knee. He didn't have time to unclip Timothy's rifle sling from the lower receiver and pull the rifle away from his body. Instead, Kolt leaned down and placed his right eye behind the Trijicon day sight and raised the muzzle to place the red dot near the back window. He steadied it at the head propped back on the headrest.

Abdul had already shaken off the sting of the hot coffee and had recovered his rifle, now aiming it out the window at Kolt and Timothy. He fired a burst that ran high and left, barely missing Kolt's hooded head.

Kolt steadied his aim before breaking the trigger of Timothy's AR-15. Two well-aimed shots pierced Abdul's burned face. His body slumped forward, now lifeless, as his head and one arm remained outside the window.

Kolt set the rifle gently on the wounded officer's chest. He checked his vitals by placing two fingers on his carotid artery. Kolt felt a heartbeat, but it was weak and labored. He reached under the small area of Timothy's back, feeling for the telltale sign of an exit wound. He found a large amount of blood and what he was sure were bone fragments from high-powered and heavy 7.62 rounds. He knew he couldn't do anything to help him. He wasn't prepared to deal with a sunken chest wound.

Timothy opened his eyes slightly. It surprised Kolt. Tears mixed with sweat rolled off the side of his face. For the first time, Kolt realized he had never told Timothy his true name. Kolt's face was still concealed behind the black balaclava.

"You are a hero, Timothy. You did fine," Kolt said with as much enthusiasm as he could muster given the situation. "You stopped a terrorist attack on Cherokee station and saved thousands of lives. Congratulations!"

Barely audible to Kolt, Timothy struggled to speak, but Kolt knew there wasn't anything he could do for him. The golden hour was ticking away fast.

Kolt reached over to Timothy's neck to check his pulse again. It was a ridiculous gesture; he knew he wasn't staying around to administer CPR until the paramedics arrived. It was just simple reflexes from a lifetime of training. It was just experience kicking in, mixed with a lot of adrenaline. Everything seemed in slow motion to Kolt. It was a familiarity he had felt many times in the past. Operators called it vapor lock.

Kolt shook off the elastic moment in a life-and-death struggle where a human's fight-or-flight instincts kick in. Firefights and casualties seemed to make the world go silent for about thirty seconds or so. In life-and-death situations, everyone goes one of two ways. And in this instance, Kolt didn't have thirty seconds to spare.

Kolt quickly moved back around the Ford truck and opened the door opposite the dead Abdul. He reached for the AK-47 and leaned back out of the truck. He dropped to a knee behind the right side of the truck, steadied his aim, and neutralized both cameras on top of the checkpoint building. Until then, everything was on camera, captured on video via closed-circuit cameras and assessed in real time by the two command centers inside the plant. Had Timothy had his way years earlier, the entire incident would have been caught on thermal-analytic cameras, too. Nevertheless, in this situation, the CCTV cameras, coupled with the standard pan, tilt, zoom cameras, were good enough to capture the incident for eternity.

Certain the cameras were out, Kolt threw the rifle back into the truck near Abdul.

Although he could easily hear the humming of Cherokee's twin power reactors in the distance, things seemed eerily silent. He wondered if Farooq had been successful with the Jet Ski bomb. Had he successfully martyred himself according to the plan and his promise to Allah? In all the excitement at the checkpoint, he hadn't heard any distant explosions.

What about Joma?

Then Kolt heard the monotone emergency announcement in the distance. "Code Red, Code Red. Halt! Deadly force is authorized!"

Within seconds, he heard an explosion from a half mile away, coming from behind him, toward the main parking lot at the power plant. Kolt knew this to be the VBIED Farooq and Joma had positioned earlier that evening using a side road that bypassed Timothy and the Cherokee checkpoint.

Kolt stood and sprinted for the wood line. He headed straight back to the planned linkup spot. He had only been moving for a few minutes when he heard another explosion coming from the plant behind him.

Farooq and the Jet Ski. Damn.

Without explanation, Kolt's conscience stopped him in his tracks. He wanted to stop running away from the danger. He instinctively wanted to run toward the danger. To help fellow Americans under attack.

The fact that Warren Samperson had lived certainly wasn't predetermined. Kolt knew it would be tough to conduct the attack without any innocent security officers or other plant employees being harmed. In fact, Kolt deliberately but very discreetly manipulated the tactical planning to prevent as much American bloodshed as possible. But once the team had agreed on the concept of the operation, the plan of attack, whoever happened to get coffee duty on the night of 21 April was predoomed from the start. Nevertheless, his former Delta teammates would never give Kolt a pass on this one.

But this wasn't Delta; it was Tungsten.

Kolt's natural urge to assist Americans in harm's way tugged hard at his heart. With each step he took moving away from the besieged Cherokee station, his desperate desire to go back and help Americans hardened. Kolt had never run from a firefight before; he always headed toward the sound of the guns. But he had to remember that tonight he was a terrorist. He had to remember that he was on the other team. He had to remember that he wasn't an American that evening. That was the toughest, most distasteful part about being a Tungsten operative.

As for killing Abdul, it was necessary and just. In fact, that kill was payback on several levels. It was payback for rolling up Cindy Bird and for murdering Timothy in cold blood. It was payback for 9/11. It was forward payment from America for the terrorist attacks Abdul would certainly take part in had he survived this one.

Even before the mission, Kolt knew both he and Abdul couldn't survive the attack. But after Kolt turned on him, he obviously would never be able to return to the terrorist hotel room. Kolt had to remember that the Cherokee attack was an end to a means. It was not just the first necessary step to unraveling the nuke plot but to rescuing Cindy as well. And if he was somehow able to repatriate his old teammate then as an encore performance, he would get back to Tungsten's primary business: that of giving his own life to neutralize Ayman al-Zawahiri.

Fuck, Abdul! Kill them all and let Allah sort it out.

TWENTY-ONE

The checkpoint fiasco was over within two minutes. Kolt was so focused on his piece of the fight that he failed to hear the sniper peppering the bullet-resistant towers that housed one of Timothy's fellow security officers. From the other side of the plant on a grassy hilltop, Joma settled the crosshairs and sent a dozen rounds of 7.62 armor-piercing ammo to the tower's windows from his hilltop position. Armed responders from two adjacent guard towers returned fire through their small gun ports. Joma shifted his position farther behind a tree, giving him a better angle to answer the fire.

Within seconds, and exactly according to plan, the Jet Ski–driving terrorist, Farooq, came out of the darkness and into the ambient light that bled off the hundred lights that made Cherokee visible from outer space. Joma and Kolt had kept the armed responders busy. So much so that the simultaneous attacks by the sniper Joma and by Abdul at the checkpoint allowed them to completely miss Farooq, approaching on the Jet Ski under the protection of the long shadows.

Approaching from the west, Farooq had both of his hands cuffed to the watercraft's handlebars. The Jet Ski didn't take a single round as he headed for the intake structure at thirty-five miles an hour. He squeezed the hand lever and accelerated.

"Allah u Akbar! Allah u Akbar!"

The watercraft and towed explosives plowed right into the large metal trash screen before detonating. The explosion was magnificent, sending water and debris over one hundred feet in the air. Kolt was already running from the mess when he heard Farooq complete his mission.

On the hill, Joma, feeling awfully alone now, strained his neck to locate Timothy and his brother Abdul. He had heard the gunfire and explosions near the checkpoint as he crawled into position. *They should be driving up soon, he thought.*

After firing roughly three magazines' worth of ammunition, roughly thirty rounds, Joma became nervous. *Where are Timothy and Abdul?* he wondered. *They should already have passed the checkpoint.* Joma rolled down the back side of the hill slightly and pulled out his cell phone. He called Abdul. No answer. He quickly speed-dialed Timothy's number.

Kolt felt his cell phone vibrate and immediately removed his black balaclava. He answered the phone.

"Joma, is that you? Listen to me, brother. You must escape immediately," he pleaded. "Meet me at the linkup point as planned."

Joma didn't bite. "No, no, Timothy, that is impossible. This was supposed to be a suicide operation. In the name of Allah. Farooq completed his mission. He is in paradise now. The sheikh won't be pleased if we do not carry out our mission."

"No, you are wrong," Kolt pleaded. "I'll explain everything later."

Joma began praying vigorously into the phone. Up on his knees, he rocked back and forth rapidly while reciting phrases from the Koran, oblivious to everything going on around him.

Kolt abruptly interrupted. "Listen to me, Joma. Abdul and I killed two infidels and blew up the checkpoint."

"Why are you still alive?" Joma demanded.

"They surprised us. We had no choice. Brother Abdul is a martyr, just like Farooq. Allah knows and will welcome them. We have been successful here. You and I are alive by Allah's will and are more prepared to participate in another operation for the jihad . . . and in his name. It is your duty to survive. Meet me as soon as possible."

Kolt was growing frustrated at the situation. He knew he needed to put a lot of distance between him and the power plant, and fast. Bickering with

Joma was only slowing him down. But Kolt knew he would need Joma to rescue Cindy Bird and to uncover the other cell in the nuke plot.

Joma debated it for a few long seconds before he started taking heavy fire from his right side and below him. That made up his mind very quickly. He dropped the rifle and all his gear and took off back down the hill and through the trees.

Minutes passed, still with no sign of Joma. Kolt wondered if Joma was caught or killed, since the last thing he heard over his cell phone before it went dead was gunfire in the distance. Kolt needed him alive. He needed the company.

A few hundred yards from the checkpoint, Kolt found the dam that spanned the Broad River. Ignoring the no trespassing sign, he easily negotiated the fence obstacle, then carefully stepped into the inch-deep water spilling over the round edge of upper basin. Balancing under the moonlight like a circus tightrope performer every step was a risk. One slip and he'd fall seventy feet into the rocky lower basin. After moving cautiously for several hundred feet he finally reached the safety of the weathered brick control building on the far side.

Joma finally showed up and was soaking wet from having to swim across the shallow water of the Broad River, which was just south of the man-made dam.

Kolt summed up the damage with Joma. It was a dramatic and brazen attack in the heartland of America. And even though Kolt knew Timothy Reston was likely the only American killed, the American liberal news media would have a hard time labeling this as anything other than a major victory for al Qaeda.

Certainly, al Qaeda's senior leadership had hoped to surpass the damage done on 9/11. And they certainly would have had the nuclear-reactor core been breached as planned. But Kolt knew there was zero possibility of that happening. He saw to it in the planning that the attack would fall well short. Even though the attack didn't technically result in radiological sabotage, a core meltdown, or a hazardous release of deadly radiation, it was still a stunning success. Al Qaeda terrorists had infiltrated America and attacked a commercial nuclear power plant in the heartland.

They detonated a simple car bomb in the parking lot, blew up the intake structure with a Jet Ski bomb, gave the guard towers hell with dozens of bullets, and claimed an American life during Timothy's last stand at the botched checkpoint entry. All in all, it was enough for even the most inexperienced terrorist organization to claim victory.

Sure, a couple dozen expensive SUVs, pickup trucks, and sleek midsize cars went up in smoke with the car bomb, but in the big scheme of things, the only thing hurt was America's pride. Kolt wasn't entirely pleased with that, but, all things considered, he knew it was well worth the national embarrassment. Timothy had sold out his country and paid for it. Thousands of others had been saved. Kolt was in a good position to locate Cindy Bird and the other nuke-plot cell.

He also knew the way Timothy expired was the best possible outcome. As soon as the investigation was complete and the forensic evidence proved the bullets in the head of the terrorist Abdul were fired from Timothy's weapon, he would be remembered as a national hero. Timothy couldn't have survived, and Kolt knew it, but he was proud that Timothy went down fighting.

In the end, Kolt had saved the plant and prevented tens of thousands of civilian casualties in the area. But Kolt's undivided attention remained directed toward saving his teammate Cindy.

Lewisburg, West Virginia

It had been two days since Joma and Kolt had fled the scene at Cherokee, two days of convenience store food and leftover delivered pizza, and two days of listening to Joma recite what had to be all 6,236 verses of the Koran, several times. The only quiet Kolt got was when Joma was on his knees praying.

Truth be told, Kolt needed the time to think as well. He had removed his cell battery prior to the attack to prevent the authorities from finding him, and the fact that the local and state cops were going pretty much door to door within a hundred-and-fifty-mile radius of the Cherokee plant looking for the terrorist, maybe two, that got away made the fleabag motel in Lewisburg, West Virginia, all the more suitable.

There was no point stopping to try and reason with Joma during the five-hour drive. He was in major vapor lock, and his clothes were still wet from swimming the Broad River. Worse, he kept asking the same question over and over—*Why am I still alive when brothers Abdul and Farooq martyred themselves?*

Kolt gave up trying to answer that hours ago and let Joma tire himself out. He had enough to worry about. Kolt had never planned on martyring himself and so had kept an eye out for transportation. He spotted the ride underneath a tin shelter north of the narrow gravel that topped Old Seine Road. Kolt yanked off the blue tarp and dropped it behind the red Massey Ferguson farm tractor. Kolt and Joma had only moved maybe a mile and a half southeast of the plant.

It didn't really matter that Joma was frantic, since Kolt could barely hear him. What pissed Kolt off more was the fact that the soaking-wet asshole was squeezing the shit out of him. Kolt wasn't interested in commuter-friendly gossip, anyway; he was just interested in putting distance between the 2006 Kawasaki Ninja 650R they were straddling and the smoking problem area, and very thankful the bike came with matching helmets.

Kolt had broached the subject of his hostage wife several times with Joma. But Joma didn't know where Cindy Bird was, at least that was his story. Actually, Kolt played the role of a grief-stricken and heartbroken husband, even whipping up a few crocodile tears, but still nothing. Kolt wasn't even convinced Joma was lying, because he had a hard time understanding just what the motivation would be for Joma to keep that information close.

Which told Kolt one very important but disturbing thing.

Either Hawk is already dead, or there are other al Qaeda sleepers in town holding her still.

Awake before sunrise, and not looking forward to hearing Joma recite his early-morning prayers, Kolt jotted a quick note on the hotel stationery letting Joma know he was bringing breakfast back, quietly opened and closed the door, and walked down the dead street to the twenty-four-hour convenience store on the corner. He welcomed the short stroll, breathing in the clean West Virginia air, redolent with the aroma of local mineral springs mixing perfectly with the tang of thuja "Green Giant" evergreens and the natural fragrance of oak-hickory forests descending from the high peaks of the Blue Ridge Mountains. Turning the corner past the fire hydrant, Kolt practically forgot what brought him to this ghost town in the first place.

Inside the store, Kolt grabbed a half-folded newspaper from the wire bin, recognizing the major story, ARE WE WINNING? NUCLEAR ATTACK MAY BE JUST THE BEGINNING. He put it under his arm to fix two cups of black coffee before pulling two egg-white croissants from the warmer and grabbing a pouch of Red Man from near the counter. After paying with a ten spot and pulling his change from the autodispenser, Kolt went back outside and began reading the article as he walked back to the hotel. Besides the fact that some undisclosed U.S. official had leaked the possibility of another imminent terrorist attack on U.S. soil, he found what he was really after halfway down the last column. In bold black letters larger than the details, the citation read, *"American Hero Timothy Allen Reston, Nuclear Security Officer, Cherokee Power Plant, Badge #568, died 21 April 2013. Rest in Peace."*

Kolt continued to read through the generalities of his death, his hometown, where he went to high school, and what jobs he held before putting the paper in the hotel's outside trash can. Kolt stood there for a few moments, debating what the hell his next step should be. He couldn't remain on the run forever, another couple of days, three tops, and the gig would likely be up. He knew he really didn't care to spend another day with Joma, sleeping with one eye open for fear he might go ape shit again and whip out a steak knife from the kitchenette. He'd had about enough of the Koran lesson, too, and Joma wasn't willing, or was unable, to help him rescue Hawk.

Fuck it, time to get Carlos earning those top-shelf designer clothes he wears.

Kolt reached into his front pocket and pulled his cell battery out. He unclipped his phone, removed the cover, and mated the two properly. He watched as the phone powered on, searching and locating dozens of satellites and cell towers. Once it had fully synched, Kolt punched in the distress code for Tungsten and waited.

In less than two minutes, his cell rang.

"Hello," Kolt said.

"Hello sir, my name is Ronald Epps, senior sales associate for the Best Buy Visa card. I was hoping"—

Kolt cut him off. He knew the protocol but was really in no mood to play spy games at the moment, nor had he had time to visit his secure e-mail account and acquire the password of the week.

"Carlos, I don't have time to explain. I'll leave the battery in the phone. We are in room fourteen," Kolt said, mentally checking off the minimum amount of information Carlos would need to find him and knowing they could geolocate his position as long as the phone remained powered on.

"Authenticate zero-seven-zero-six," Carlos demanded.

Holy fuck! This guy really is from central casting.

"I'm not alone," Kolt said, ignoring the request for a code word.

"Get rid of her," Carlos said.

Kolt was impressed how professionally astute Carlos was, realizing that if he was in a situation where he couldn't talk, he wouldn't have spilled what he had already. Kolt didn't pick up any positive vibes, though, or for that matter any indication whether Carlos thought his embed's brain housing group was entirely fucked.

"Not a broad, one of the terrorists from the attack," Kolt said, keeping his voice as low as he could outside the room.

"You are shitting me!" Carlos said. "And he's still breathing."

Kolt picked up on the sarcasm right away. He couldn't blame him for the response, since Kolt knew Carlos hadn't agreed to handle him thinking he would get weak-kneed when the chips were down. Kolt could also see how it would sound odd, especially to someone of Carlos Menendez II's storied past, without the proper context to hear that he is shacked up with an enemy of the state.

"Look, long story. But I need this guy alive," Kolt said. "We are not armed, so don't send the gorillas in, guns-a-blazin'."

Carlos couldn't let it go. "OK, Kolt, tell me why this terrorist is not dead yet?"

Just then, the dark green door to room 14 flew open. Kolt turned to see Joma standing in the doorway, a soiled wifebeater snug to his soft chest and belly above his pair of oversize camouflage pants, which Abdul had purchased from the army-navy surplus store in north Charlotte for them.

"Please, please answer, Mary." Kolt pleaded into the phone as he bent over to allow Joma to observe his suffering. "I can't live without "—

Joma interrupted him. "Timothy, what are you doing?" Joma demanded. "No phone calls. The authorities will find us."

Kolt walked toward Joma with the natural urge to slap a flying-triangle choke on him right there in the parking lot. Just get it over with, do what Carlos expected him to have done already, pay back the faggot-ass in front of him for trying to break bad in the last hotel they were in together.

But as Kolt closed the distance, he remembered that Joma was still the only link to Hawk. He had to know something, and in time—if Hawk didn't die in captivity first—he would come around. More than Hawk, or less, depending on who was asked, Joma would be the key figure on Tungsten's colorful and confusing link-analysis chart, used to unravel the next phase of the nuke plot and eventually kill Nadal the Romanian. Waterboarding will be a whole lot more painful than the chilly ride on the back of the motorcycle.

"I bought you an egg sandwich. Your coffee is on the window sill behind you," Kolt said.

"Yes, yes, *shockran,*" Joma said. "But, please, you must turn off your phone. No more calls to your wife."

"It's off," Kolt said as he held it up to Joma and tapped the screen with his thumb a few times to convince him.

"No more phone calls," Joma demanded. "Agreed?"

Agreed, motherfucker!

Tungsten headquarters, underground, Atlanta, Georgia

"That concludes my briefing gentlemen," the analyst said as she wirelessly flipped to the last slide, titled "Questions?" and motioned to the gentleman-statue to bring the lights up a little.

Kolt set his borrowed pen down, sat back in the firm black leather mid-back chair, interlocked his fingers behind his close-cropped head, elbows winged to the sides, and smiled at the petite Peabody-looking analyst in the khaki pencil skirt and black sleeveless scoop-neck with matching two-inch heels.

She knew her shit, that much Kolt was certain of.

Without as much as a single stutter or misstep, she spoke about decisive point, synergistic execution, momentum shift, kinetic solution, and competent authority. Yes, in the last forty-two minutes this four-eyed bookworm must have hit on pretty much every commando buzzword in the book.

"Operation Shadow Blink, is it?" Kolt asked the briefer before raising a white Styrofoam cup to his lips and depositing a long stream of tobacco juice.

"Yes, sir," she said. "That's correct."

"Well, I must have blinked one too many times, because you people are certifiable," Kolt said with an even voice. "You are fucking nuts!"

"Excuse me, sir?" the analyst said, obviously taken aback by Kolt's choice of words.

Carlos jumped in. "Ma'am, gentlemen: Can I have a moment alone with the embed?"

Kolt watched Carlos stand up as the others headed for one of two doors. Carlos nervously checked the gold cuff links on his Rolex-wrapped wrist and then straightened his plum-colored half Windsor before buttoning the top button on his Armani pinstripe, which had to have taken, easy, forty thousand silkworms to make.

After the last of the four left, two exiting through each door, Carlos stepped from in front of his leather chair and walked upright, chin high and confident, to the short end of the conference table, stopping toward the center of the room. At home inside Tungsten's secure briefing room, Carlos knew to edge a foot or two to the left, toward the door, to stay out from the ceiling-mounted projector's cone-shaped beam of light that was still throwing the "Questions?" slide on the large white drop-down screen.

"Look, Kolt, she couldn't say it, but the president is pissed," Carlos said calmly.

"He's pissed? Hell, I'm pissed. We don't kill innocent Americans. We got lucky at Cherokee—a lot of good people could have died. You guys knew that, and you let it go on," Kolt said, standing up in anticipation of their confidential face-to-face getting a little heated.

"You knew what you were doing, Kolt. The trade-off—one American dead, a traitor at that—is potentially worth it."

"Bullshit, Carlos!" Kolt shot back. "You were willing to trade a lot more innocent Americans if it led you to the bigger fish, willing to"—

Carlos cut him off. "Yes, Kolt, the president had a tough choice to make. He let the Cherokee attack happen, knowing it likely would result in innocent people dying and possibly get him raked over the coals about another failure by his intelligence community to connect the dots of an imminent attack, and his domestic law enforcement unable to stop . . . Yes, it took presidential-size balls."

"I get that. Damn it!" Kolt said as he leaned at the waist and placed both palms flat on the glass-covered mahogany conference table. "I got it!"

"Then what exactly is the problem, Kolt?" Carlos asked.

Kolt felt a bit patronized, and was becoming a little irritated that the gray-haired Carlos was maintaining his cool while Kolt felt like breaking shit.

"Because POTUS is pissed off, and made a promise years ago about releasing the detainees at Gitmo, some thousand-pound brain gets a wild hair and thinks it's a good idea for me and that shit bag Joma, wherever the hell he is now, to spend some quality time getting to know each other at, of all places, sunny Guántanamo Bay, Cuba," Kolt said, now pacing back and forth down one of the long walls, waving his hands like a big-city defense lawyer while he talked. "But wait for it . . . it gets better."

"Calm down, Kolt," Carlos said as still as a molded-hair men's mannequin at Jos. A. Bank. "Why don't you take your seat?"

Ignoring Carlos, Kolt kicked it into high gear. "Let's drop embed zero-seven-zero-six and Joma the boy wonder into the middle of the badlands with a dozen freshly released and highly pissed-off terrorists on a sliver of hope that they somehow lead me to Nadal the Romanian or Z-man himself. C'mon, Carlos, I think I've seen that movie."

Not backing down for a second, Carlos said, "Yes, that's the plan, Kolt, with some minor differences from your colorful explanation."

"I didn't know I was signing up for this kind of shit. Who else is involved at this level?"

"You are it, Kolt. Nobody else ever screened for Tungsten has demonstrated the consistent potential"—

"To what, take an ass whooping over and over, too dumb to tap out?" Kolt said.

"Close, but before you interrupted me, I was going to say the consistent potential to both piss off everyone in command while at the same time demonstrating the courage of a god damned lion. Oh, and all with the personal backing of the president of the United States," Carlos said. "And with that comes the blessing of your entire nation. Certainly not something given in haste."

"Humping me won't cut it, Carlos," Kolt said.

"The White House is trying to prevent mass public panic after the Cherokee attack. Nut-job conspiracy theorists are not buying that there was no release of radiation."

"There wasn't, Carlos," Kolt said. "I planned it that way."

"We figured that, Kolt, but that's not the issue," Carlos said. "With lack of corroborating intel, POTUS just can't activate a single state's local law, and he is being pressured by the right to activate the National Guard and send them to every piece of critical infrastructure or large gathering of civilians possible."

"That might slow them down, but it won't stop an attack that is most likely in its final planning stages," Kolt said, moving back to his rolling chair and sitting down.

"The media would have a heyday with the unprecedented move to activate the nation's entire Army National Guard," Carlos said.

"I can imagine. But Carlos, Gitmo? Pakistan?" Kolt asked, turning his palms up out in front of him.

"Look, son, if I was thirty years younger—hell, twenty years younger—and given what I know now about this jacked-up world, I would jump at the chance to be in your shoes today."

"Well, grab your kit, big boy," Kolt said, daring Carlos to join him on the mission and knowing that was impossible.

"If we weren't perfectly clear on the operational warts when you signed on, that's on me. Colonel Webber said you were a good man—in fact, the best man—to do the things our nation needed doing when the line was zero people deep," Carlos said.

Kolt thought about it. He thought about Hawk, possibly sacrificing herself for something she had nothing to do with. The guys from Six, ordered to hit the safe house in Sana'a and not as much as a dog tag to ship home. And Timothy, a down-on-his-luck, average guy who took a raw deal and turned it into a nightmare.

Then it hit Kolt. Carlos was not giving him an out at all. No opportunity to bow out.

Why the hell would somebody want to live forever, anyway?

"Are you the thousand-pound brain?" Kolt asked.

"Indeed, I am," Carlos replied, adjusting his handmade jacket by the two dark gray lapels but remaining poker-faced.

"How is the deal with the Gitmo detainees supposed to work again?" Kolt asked. "Another POTUS issue?"

"Pretty much. You recall when the president tapped the attorney general to head up the Guantanamo Review Task Force a few years ago?" Carlos asked.

"Vaguely," Kolt said.

"Well, that task force determined they had forty-eight problem children, detainees determined 'too dangerous to transfer but not feasible for prosecution.'"

"And Shadow Blink is going to take care of this without the American Civil Liberties Union the wiser," Kolt said with a hint of sarcasm.

"We are thinking a dozen," Carlos said.

"Fuck me, Carlos. You want me to smoke a dozen rag heads while Joma watches and then play all-American homeboy turned terrorist to locate Z-man and Nadal the Romanian?"

"You won't be doing the killing, son," Carlos said. "The Mercs will be."

Kolt looked up from his notepad, where he had scribbled the letters "WTF" and "48" and raised his eyebrows before locking eyes with Carlos. He thought back to that first lunch date with Carlos in the Jamaican restaurant. He recalled what Carlos had said about the uber-unique personnel assigned to Tungsten's Department of Special Services.

The Mercs?

Yeah, those jacked-up, high-priced off-the-books killers on beeper.

"Damn it, Carlos. I'll go, but you have to promise me one thing."

"If it's reasonable, it's done," Carlos said.

"I need you to find Hawk's body, get her into Arlington," Kolt said. "Section sixty, near her father. She earned it."

"We'll do our best, Kolt," Carlos said.

"Well, if that's the acceptable standard, then I'll do my best at staying alive long enough so I can off myself in some shithole halfway around the world."

"I've got your six, Kolt," Carlos said.

"You strap-hanging on the infil aircraft?" Kolt asked, already knowing the answer.

"Just into Gitmo," Carlos said. "But you never know."

TWENTY-TWO

Guantanamo Bay, Cuba

Kolt was still awake when the white, freshly painted Gulfstream G650 with a nose-to-tail red and blue pinstripe had gone wheels up from Dobbins Air Reserve Base in Marietta, Georgia, watching the terrorist known as Joma freaking the hell out. Strapped to a jump seat near the rear of the twenty-five-seat passenger jet, Joma, with his hands flex-tied in front of him and wearing a double black hood over a bright orange jumpsuit, was rocking back and forth like a German cuckoo-clock pendulum. Around his boney, seemingly hairless ankles, two adjustable leather ankle bracelets connected by grade-70 heavy chains had tangled with his stockinged feet.

As Kolt had watched him oscillate, he knew the only reason he couldn't hear the relentless reciting of the Koran was because someone had jammed a kid's sock in his mouth and wrapped his head with gray duct tape in case he decided the taste wasn't to his liking.

Sucks to be you, man.

Besides Kolt and Joma, Carlos and the petite brunette Tungsten analyst, both having dressed down for the trip, had made the great circle distance of 1,117 miles flying a fast cruise speed of 595 miles per hour before touching down at the U.S. naval base in Guantanamo Bay, Cuba. All in less time than it takes to see a flick on the silver screen.

Once at cruising altitude, Miss Peabody had sat down close to Kolt and Carlos at the front of the cabin with a sterile manila folder. Kolt vividly recalled her reaching up and pulling the ballpoint pen from the crease between the side of her head and the top of her right ear before opening the folder and retrieving a long checklist.

Kolt was briefed on his soon-to-be neighbors first. The list included Khalid Sheikh Mohammed, the admitted mastermind behind the planes operation of 9/11. It also included several other high-level AQ operatives like Abd al-Rahim al-Nashiri, the Saudi-born mastermind of the bombing of the USS *Cole* and other terrorist attacks. And Yemen-born Ramzi bin al-Shibh, the so-called twentieth hijacker and key facilitator for the 9/11 attacks.

These were al Qaeda's heavy hitters for sure, which was exactly why the secret maximum-security isolation cells, known collectively as camp 7, were not disclosed to the Red Cross or ACLU. The eight-by-twelve-foot box waiting for Kolt was just one of a dozen or so "heavy cells," the nickname the original Camp X-Ray guards dubbed them years ago, on what was internally known as the "black mile corridor" that sat beneath dark sniper meshing that camouflages the walkway. It was a play on the actual people that resided there, HVIs, high-value individuals, a place reserved exclusively for detainees suspected of being inside the now fish food Osama bin Laden's inner circle.

Kolt was to be registered as a former al Qaeda facilitator. A title, had it had any stretch of truth to it, would get a guy on the unit's kill list if he was in Afghanistan. But Kolt was reminded that masquerading as one and being one could be equally dangerous. Not that he needed that reminder, of course, but it was important to keep the camp guards and officials from asking a lot of questions. More importantly, because the other detainees in "heavy cell" would likely know if Kolt was actually a card-carrying member of AQ or not, he would have to be isolated from the other prisoners, his interactions entirely controlled, entirely scripted.

About fifteen minutes out from landing, Kolt was required to change into his own orange jumpsuit, hood, flex ties, and shackles. After touching down, four uniformed military policemen assigned to Joint Task Force–GITMO boarded the jet and escorted the two new arrivals down the eight-step drop-down stairs to the tarmac. Kolt couldn't see their faces, but he was able to see their boots and the bottom of their fatigues from under the hood.

Kolt and Joma, still hooded and baby-stepping in their shackles, were steered by the guards to two OD green canvas litters mounted above two bicycle tires to form a makeshift gurney. And after a very short helo flight, where they remained on the gurney, they landed not far from Windmill Beach, not far from camp 7. As they wheeled the two new interns through the high-security fence lines and gates and into the black mile corridor, Kolt had felt a strong tail wind off the beach. The military personnel watching had no idea that the taller of the two was actually a pure red, white, and blue American. The other detainees didn't know either, except for Joma, of course.

"Most men don't come out of heavy cell," Kolt recalled Carlos saying during the flight down the east coast of Florida.

Fortunately for Kolt, he would just be faking it.

Now, though, after two days of solitary, forced to shit and piss on himself like everyone else in heavy cell, he began to wonder if Carlos had forgotten about him. He appreciated Carlos's comments; men don't come out of that place, at least not with the same mental state as when they entered. The place could wear on a man, any man. And inside his box, Kolt realized he was just as human as the rest of them. Like Cindy Bird learned from her visit to Black Ice a couple of months ago, heavy cell wasn't picky about who it broke. It wasn't specific about religion or nationality. No, the high-value-individual cell was an equal opportunity torture chamber.

To say Kolt might be having second thoughts was an understatement. It was something he was careful not to reveal to Carlos, though, as his handler stood outside his box early in the morning. Carlos knew full well Kolt had only undergone mock interrogations, big shows with fake blood and pulled punches, but Joma's responses confirmed he thought Kolt was being tortured as he was.

"You're taking the pills, aren't you?" Carlos asked.

The pills, actually they were liquid drops, had been part of the twenty-thousand-feet brief as well. Kolt's meals were to be laced with an odorless liquid, in slight doses, as the super-extra-strength tanning chemicals developed by DARPA were rumored to have turned a white rat into a black rap artist in a week. The liquid was intended to rapidly darken his skin to prevent him from severe sunburn in Pakistan and give him a slight edge in helping him look more like the people he would certainly come in contact with. It wasn't much, but Kolt was taking everything he could get at the moment.

"It tastes like shit," Kolt said, sensing Carlos smile. "You alone?"

"Yes," Carlos said. "Look, Kolt, things have turned for the worst for the president in the last twenty-four hours. He is getting hammered by Congress, both the House and Senate, and most of the public opinion polls."

"OK, so what's that do to Shadow Blink?" Kolt asked, unable to see Carlos's face from inside the box. "Mission abort?"

"No. Accelerates the timeline," Carlos said. "We launch tonight."

"Are you kidding?" Kolt said. "I've only done four interrogations with Joma. That's insufficient by a mile. Hell, Carlos, I haven't even been toured around the place so the dirty dozen we are vacationing with can get an eyeful."

"We've adjusted the Mercs' task and purpose," Carlos said, trying to reassure Kolt that kicking off Shadow Blink and entering Pakistan two weeks earlier than planned would be OK. "They won't let you down."

"I have no doubt," Kolt said.

"But that's only half the problem, Kolt," Carlos said. "NSA has been running the numbers and e-mail accounts that were penciled in the notebook you lifted from the bus through DISHFIRE and POLARBREEZE. Last night, one of the numbers hit, and the NSA intercepted traffic between Nadal and an unidentified male in the middle of Quetta. We are banking that Nadal is currently located in the North-West Frontier Province at a suspected terror-training camp."

"That is a significant update, Carlos," Kolt said. "Any details on their conversation?"

"The analysts couldn't be positive, but they believe the guy Nadal was talking to may have been a nuke-plot player, likely one of the muscle men planning to infiltrate the U.S. to attack another nuke plant."

"Any mention of the odd code word?" Kolt asked. "Sacred Indian."

"In fact, NSA did mention that, but no further info yet," Carlos said. "Good question."

"We better roll then," Kolt said.

"Exactly," Carlos said. "But Kolt, just as a reminder to ensure we are clear on your tasks."

"They were pretty clear back at Tungsten headquarters," Kolt said. "Locate and neutralize Nadal the Romanian or Z-man."

"Just so we are clear, and the president supports this decision, you are to go for Z-man first. POTUS is willing to play the odds of no second attack. If you get close enough, take him. If not, Nadal is a close second as HVIs go."

"You guys don't ask for much," Kolt said before shifting gears. "Any word on Cindy Bird yet?"

"None."

Kolt always believed that assassination was dirty—physically, mentally, and spiritually. Within months after 9/11, Kolt knew the CIA was prepared to cycle their Ground Branch shooters through structured debriefs and endless counseling once the assassins returned home. This requirement of the Western mind-set, that psychs be standing by at Langley, essentially doomed the program before it ever got out of the blocks. Even though Kolt recognized his own profession as the cog in the assassin wheel, he also clearly saw the problem with the conventional military. He believed strongly that some people just needed to be killed in cold blood. He also knew firsthand that a lot of guys talk a good game, but when it comes down to it, when it's time to make the decision to kill another human being in cold blood, inside a restaurant bathroom, a seedy hotel room, or even as the target sits relatively peacefully at a traffic light, the human capacity to break the trigger rests with a very finite number of human beings.

On any given military raid or assault, safely getting the troops off the target and back home is a critical phase. If things go right, getting in, getting out, and lounging back at the tents is fairly routine. But these operations are typically handled by platoon- or company-size units, where forty to seventy guys keep each other company. Besides the element of surprise, they usually have a great advantage in numbers. The CIA assassin who is within striking distance of his prey, knows he would be well short of teammates on his right and left.

Ultimately, the only chance the secret CIA program had was if that exfil was never called for. For the deed—the lethal hit—to have been successfully executed, the best option would be to do as our adversaries did. Target neutralized. No exfil logistics needed. No further American lives put at risk during a daring black helicopter extraction. No Doc Johnson or CIA psychs needed.

Essentially, Kolt had to establish a firewall for his native emotions, knowing full well he might be sacrificing himself in the process.

Western Pakistan

Flying nap-of-the-earth, adjusting elevation according to the folds in the terrain below, the three black MH-47G twin-rotor-blade helicopters came in low over the rocky ridgeline. Almost entirely invisible to the naked eye, two of the large beasts banked south and entered into a short orbit to await call-in. The lead 47G descended the last hundred feet, lowered its six rubber balloon tires into the sandy soil, and dropped the tail ramp onto the black landing zone. Ten minutes earlier, Kolt had placed a black hood over his head. Kolt knew the drill. He knew it was coming.

The former Guantanamo inmates cross loaded on the other two helicopters had been hooded for the entire flight. Including Joma, who twenty minutes into the flight was administered .08 cc's of zolpidem, a sleep medicine to treat severe insomnia, to put him completely out. They sat strapped to the cold metal floor along the outer skin of the aircraft. A Toyota pickup sat centered in each helicopter, tethered with heavy chains and j-hooked to the recessed metal O-rings in the floor.

Kolt certainly didn't like it, though. After his temporary stay in Guantanamo, his fun meter was just about pegged. The terrorists about to be repatriated onto Muslim soil weren't the only ones with their heads covered, though. The twenty or so uniformed guys making the trip with him wore tan face masks. The kind of tight Spiderman-like full head covering that offered small holes for the eyes and mouth.

Before being hooded ten minutes out, Kolt had sized them up during the hour-plus-long flight. Their MultiCam uniforms were sterile. None showed any identifying name tapes or patches. No rank insignia. No call-sign patches. No identifying marks on their helmets. All signs of a uniquely disciplined unit. Telltale signs of a *black* unit. All were heavily armed. An M240B general-purpose machine gun stood on its butt plate, held between the legs of one of the mystery soldiers. Another held a smaller 5.56mm light machine gun, muzzle up toward the roof of the helo, between his legs. The only thing that stood out as odd, even though Kolt understood the thought process, was the dingy, naturally aged, blue-dot special tennis shoes each of them wore and the half-dozen household brooms lying on the aircraft's metal floor.

Carlos was right; the Mercs had skills, that much was obvious.

A heavy hand prompted Kolt to stand and nudged him to the edge of the rear ramp. A slight push, and Kolt skipped off the edge and dropped a foot or so to the sandy soil of Pakistan. The powerful rotor blades kicked the fine dust up into a massive sand plume. Without any goggles to protect his eyes from the blistering particles, maybe the bag on the head wasn't that bad after all.

Kolt was led up a rocky ridgeline along a small animal path. Still hooded, his view was limited to the area around his feet, but with about ten-percent illumination he really couldn't see much. His night vision had yet to adjust, tripping a few times along the way. He knew the landing zone was supposed to be in Pakistan, but the place smelled no different than Afghanistan. A light musky aroma hung in the air. It was the kind of raw, fresh air not infected by mass industry and man-made machinery.

The Mercs moved in a line, roughly arm's length apart and spanning the highest point of the rocky hillock. They lay down on their bellies and settled in behind their weapons, the 240B on the east side, the LMG on the west end. The Mercs were all business. They wore the oddball-looking four-monocular night-vision goggles famously worn by SEAL Team Six when bin Laden was smoked in Abbottabad. White-light discipline was observed.

A few minutes after reaching higher ground, Kolt heard the approach of the two follow on helos from the direction of what he assumed was west, coming from Afghanistan. Kolt knew these helos would be carrying the terrorists. The same terrorists critical to Kolt's success in the next few days. As the helos positioned to touch down, Kolt tilted his head back just enough to observe touchdown.

Kolt watched the terrorists file off the tail ramp single file. They were a strange mix of Guantanamo detainees collected over time during the war on terror. Kolt noticed all had both arms secured behind their lower backs, certain a set of black plastic flex ties secured their wrists. A long light-colored rope, tied around each terrorist's waist, linked them like ducks in a row. Each wore a black hood similar to Kolt's, and he knew, under the hood, they would also have a white rag tied around their eyes and one in their mouth to keep them quiet. It was impossible for them to make a break for it. No, for the time being, falsely assuming they had just exited the freedom bird, they would remain as compliant as lambs.

A half minute later, the pair of two-door 1980s-era lemons appeared, un-assing the tail of the helos. A dark blue Toyota and a white one expertly maneuvered down the slightly angled tail ramp, gained the soil surface, and then drove across the sandy dirt to the main road. Choreographed perfectly, the three black MH-47Gs powered up, lifted off the sand, went nose down, and gained speed, heading west.

About twenty meters separated the white Toyota from the dark-blue one. Most of the terrorists were placed inside the trucks. A driver in both. A right-seater as well. Some in the bed of the trucks. A few were escorted by the arm and positioned in random areas around the vehicles, placed as if they had been thrown from a speeding train. Or maybe they had been able to get out once the shooting started? They might have been the brothers who tried to make a break for it. Allah would be proud.

Kolt noticed some of the Mercs scatter pocket litter on the ground in various spots before climbing the hill to link up with the others and lay down in position, where they could find a clear spot with good fields of fire down toward the Toyotas and bounded terrorists. He knew the litter would be doctored credentials, dated passports, worn pocket Korans, some black-and-white family photos, and documents confirming a recent stay at Hotel Gitmo. The drops would support the ruse, for sure. It was a mock-ambush scene that would have made a Hollywood stage manager pump his fist in triumph.

Obviously pleased with the setup, several of the stage hands carrying corn-bristle brooms moved to the helo touchdown points, careful to place the soles of their tennis shoes within the impressed sand lines that were left by the tires of the pickups. They delicately swept the helo tires' impressions, leveling the sand to remove any evidence of its presence. Continuing backward, they were careful to remove the tire-tread imprints as well as their own tennis-shoe prints until they reached the hard dirt road again. Within fifteen minutes or so, the three Mercs had reached the hilltop and the ambush line.

The scene in the shallow valley floor roughly thirty-five meters to Kolt's front and about fifteen meters below was incredible eerie. A dozen bound and hooded men, still in their prison whites, some likely relaxing, excited about the impending prisoner release, seeing their families again after years in captivity, hopeful of a productive future. Others, equally ecstatic about the surprise-release announcement by the president of the United States weeks earlier, maybe considering a little time off, just enough to catch up with family and friends, before rejoining the jihad and plotting to pay back the arrogant infidels as soon as possible.

Kolt overheard the Merc kneeling three meters to his front right and just behind the linear-arrayed, prone operators whisper into his helmeted mouthpiece.

"Blaster, check, check, check," the obvious leader said.

Kolt tensed up, shaking his head quickly in an effort to lift the black hood a little higher on his forehead to improve his vision of the ambush area. He was fairly confident Joma couldn't see him even if he was unhooded and awake inside the kill zone.

"Stand by, five, four, three, two, one, execute, execute, execute." *Not much of a warning,* Kolt thought. But he knew the language. He figured he was the only one without ear protection and quickly raised his hands to cover his ears while holding the hood above his eyes. An operator squeezed the clacker three times, initiating the textbook ambush with the most casualty-producing weapon first—an M18 antipersonnel Claymore mine. Seven hundred steel balls traveling at just a hair under four thousand feet per second shredded the terrorists lying in the sand, peppered the thin skin doors and rear beds of the two Toyotas, and shattered the tempered-glass windows. The elevated ambush line of prone marksmen and machine gunners opened up simultaneously in classic high-noon ambush fashion. Thirty seconds of cyclic-rated machine guns, simultaneous with nearly two dozen personal M4 rifles, cut the convoy to pieces. Then, talking in sequence, first the heavier 7.62 mm M240B and then the lighter 5.56 mm LMG swapped back and forth, sending red tracers and ball ammo into the X with resulting ricochets careening into the distance until they reached tracer burnout. One operator popped up to a kneeling position, yanked both ends of a five-and-a-half-pound M72A3 antitank launcher to fully extend the weapon, and rotated it to his right shoulder. He steadied the rocket, aiming through the pop-up peep site, and slightly tilted his head to the left.

"Back-blast area clear!" he barked before pressing the DETENT button and sending the internal 66 mm warhead to the engine-block area of the dark-blue Toyota.

Except for the massive loss of life, it was really no different than training on a static ambush range back at Bragg, using wooden vehicle facsimiles and paper e-type silhouettes. In about sixty seconds, it was all over and Kolt removed his fingers from his ears.

"Cease fire, cease fire!" the leader yelled.

The operators stood very professionally, dropping their spent mags and inserting fresh ones. They began moving back down the goat path the same way they came. They deliberately left the spent brass and metal machine-gun links where they landed on the hilltop. It was just another piece of the intricate puzzle set up to alleviate any doubt in the Taliban's eyes.

Once at the bottom of the hill, the still-hooded Kolt was moved into the kill zone and placed near the back of the white Toyota. He watched the ambush force systematically remove the flex ties and hoods from the dead former Gitmo detainees. They moved deliberately, half starting from the right, the other half from behind Kolt and to the left. They met in the center and then continued on through the other team's sector to ensure they didn't miss anything that would compromise the insertion.

The blue truck's back leather seats were engulfed in flames. A thick black smog snaked out of the shattered windows and high into the air. The engine hood, thrown from the vehicle when the warhead impacted, lay mangled and pockmarked roughly forty feet off the road. The smell of leaking gasoline and engine oil hung in the air.

The mystery operators moved around the kill zone with a sense of urgency. Some opened large black trash bags as others removed the hoods from the dead and cut the plastic flex ties from their wrists. Within a couple of minutes, the kill zone was sterile.

A few seconds later, three helmeted and masked commandos approached Kolt. Two were carrying a hooded man, who Kolt figured was Joma. They set him down on the desert floor next to the lead shot-up and burning vehicle. Two operators flex-tied Joma's ankles together and wrists behind his back before rolling him on his side. One of the operators pulled out a Glock 19 9mm while the other two positioned his leg away from his body. He aimed it at Joma's outer leg, depressed the trigger safety, and broke the four-pound trigger. A single shot at close range gave Joma a clean, flesh wound on his thigh and a mean powder burn. It looked worse than it really was, and Joma didn't feel a thing.

"What the fuck are you guys doing?" Kolt growled as several of the Mercs suddenly corralled him to the ground. They didn't answer him. Instead, they flexed Kolt just as they did with Joma, wrapped a rope around his mouth to keep him quiet, and laid him on his back. They then dragged him away from Joma, back around the rear shot-up pickup truck, and placed him on the other side, opposite Joma. Kolt struggled only slightly, worried that if Joma was watching all this somehow through his black hood, then the mission was compromised already and he wouldn't see the sun come up.

With the two guys still holding him on the ground, the gunman holstered his pistol and unsheathed his fixed blade knife. With a quick swipe, he delivered an unexpected quarter-inch gash on the back of Kolt's head, cutting a three-inch hole in the black hood.

"Motherfuckers!" Kolt screamed as much for the pain as for the surprise. Instinctively, he turned around and lunged for the knife man, grabbing his assault vest and finding his M4 hung in front of his chest. Blind to his surroundings, Kolt maintained his grip on the operator's vest, just below the armpit, and delivered a palm strike to the chin, but he couldn't shake the right hand grip on his own collar.

In an instant, Kolt grabbed a handful of his opponent's right sleeve to control his elbow while punching in a high grip with his right hand to control the left shoulder. Using both tight grips, Kolt pulled himself up and into his opponent as he planted his left foot on the operator's right hip. Kolt launched into the air, thinking standard arm lock by simply falling backward to the ground while controlling an arm. Kolt sensed the operator was skilled in jiujitsu, feeling him crouch to counter the attack. This keyed Kolt to remain high, rotate his body counterclockwise around the man's head, and push hard off the man's right hip. Now practically sitting on top of the man's shoulders, from behind Kolt leaned forward and locked in a triangle with his legs around the man's upper body. Kolt and his opponent were locked now together, where Kolt goes, so goes his adversary.

Kolt let his body weight carry him forward, dropping his head between his opponent's legs. With Kolt now upside down but facing his opponent, he executed a forward roll while reaching back to grab the man's right ankle. Kolt now could control the roll as they both tumbled, executing a complete forward roll locked in unison. The flying reverse triangle is a risky move, particularly when you are hooded and in the dark. Kolt was about to stick it, but, to lock in the submission, he tightened the crook of his right leg over his left foot, pulled the operator's leg into his body, and arched his hips forward.

It was tight—Kolt could feel it—and he could feel the man tense up and struggle. Kolt felt the operator tap his hands frantically against Kolt's leg, which, if they were simply rolling in the dojo, Kolt would release the hold . He was going to put him to sleep, no matter how many times he tapped. Kolt was pissed.

Thinking ahead, as soon as the operator went limp, Kolt would reach up and remove the rope from his neck and tear the hood off. But the surprise impact of a rifle butt on top of his head kept him on his back, causing him to release the triangle and open the man's airway again. Kolt felt the hands of several operators pouncing on him before being rolled over to his stomach. He felt at least three knees in his back and a foot or two on his legs, pressing him to hard dirt road.

"Relax, man," a deep authoritative voice whispered in his ear.

Kolt started to struggle again as soon as he felt the muzzle of a firearm against the fleshy part of his rear right hip. Unable to free himself to do a damn thing about it, Kolt heard the shot and felt the excruciating pain simultaneously.

Lying facedown, now under an operator's dingy tennis shoe pressing on his upper back, he applied direct pressure with his right hand to his wounded hip. Kolt wanted to go ballistic, he wanted to roll over and snap the asshole's leg in half, he wanted to get up and beat the shit out of every one of those jackasses. The knife wound was bad enough, but a bullet to the ass was way over the top.

He knew that would end the mission to locate Nadal the Romanian; find the terrorist cell before it attacked the United States; maybe locate Ayman al-Zawahiri; and, just as important as the first three combined, rescue Cindy Bird, or, find her body.

Kolt stopped resisting, letting the operators understand he probably had figured out on his own what he was up against and what he was about to blow.

His wounds, like Joma's, were effective, not deadly. Kolt realized they were part of the plan all along to protect their true identities and provided legitimacy to the mock ambush. Nobody in the North-West Frontier Province would believe only an American and one Muslim would have miraculously survived a near ambush like that one. No, nobody would buy that. They'd be tagged as spies right away, beheaded in short order. The plan to wound them hadn't been briefed back at Tungsten headquarters in Atlanta, but at least the wounds wouldn't keep them from walking.

"God bless you, man," the same voice whispered in Kolt's ear as he maintained pressure on his hip wound.

"*Allah u Akbar! Allah u Akbar!*" Kolt yelled, overtly signaling to the operators from the Department of Special Services that he was good to go and they could initiate their exfil plan.

Eight minutes later, the ambushers were lifting off in two black helicopters and heading west. The only witness to the anarchic carnage, Kolt Raynor—Embed 0706—was bleeding out all over his white Gitmo prison uniform from two flesh wounds among a dozen or so martyred brothers.

Kolt's insertion operation had begun. He was pissed that, without warning or explanation, they wounded him and Joma on purpose. At least Joma was unconscious when he was shot. That certainly wasn't briefed in any of the numerous mission briefs he attended. But, as he lay in the sand listening to the sound of whipping helo blades fade away, he realized that even though the wounds were painful, and a pain in the ass, they just might let him keep his head.

Kolt understood it wasn't something that he could really plan for or rehearse. He figured Carlos, the Mercs, and everyone else in Tungsten read on to the operation knew that as well. And reading Kolt's file, they knew there was high risk that Kolt would be pissed enough to abort the mission himself.

Fucking Carlos!

Besides the hip wound, Kolt reasoned the cut on the back of his head held merit. It was a real bleeder, but it didn't affect his vision. Blood wouldn't run into his eyes. Moreover, it kept his mind off the pain of his leg and required him to hold a dirty rag over the wound to control the bleeding. If there was early doubt about Kolt's legitimacy by his finders, the blood might be necessary.

Alone with the dead, Kolt caught himself cussing not only Carlos but also Colonel Webber a little. Moreover, he realized that he was in a strange situation. He had been on dozens of raids where the blood and guts and aroma of death were part of the landscape. This time was different. He wasn't accustomed to being left behind in rubble. That part of the raid was usually passed to the conventional army unit that owned the battle space. Those guys usually showed up an hour or two after Delta had serviced the target to conduct what some referred to as "sloppy seconds." The military, though, in its typical acronym-rigid fashion, prefers the term SSE—sensitive-site exploitation. Essentially, anything of potential intelligence value was rounded up and bagged, itemized, and photographed. Large caches of money, pictures, cell phones, computer hard drives, weapons, ammunition, explosives, and various IED-producing parts like boxes of old wind-up clocks, key fobs, garage door openers, and toy-car remote controls topped the list. The SSE force would question the family members left behind, women and children really. All fighting-age males were either smoked immediately or, if of potential intelligence value, marked as PUCs—person under custody—ostensibly to appease the political winds and the picky lawyers. PUCs would have been removed already by Delta and delivered elsewhere for questioning.

Kolt's thoughts wandered back to the guys responsible for all the destruction. Who were those guys? The tan masks didn't hide all the gray hair and salt-and-pepper goatees. Besides the leader giving the commands on the hilltop and the whisperer behind the truck, they didn't talk at all. They were synchronized, efficient, focused, and certainly moved with the purpose and precision characteristic of America's most elite Tier One commandos.

They weren't Delta, though, since he didn't recognize any of their body styles or their movements in the darkness. Delta operators move on target in a very distinct way, and these weren't Unit guys. He also wondered how in the world a guy comes by a slot on their team. He also figured they wondered who in the hell Kolt was and how he worked himself into such a unique gig. A gig they most likely weren't too jealous of after seeing him wounded and left behind as they flew away. To Kolt, though, whether they knew the details about Embed 0706's mission wasn't anything to waste time worrying about now. What was important was that the mysterious operators were willing to kill men in cold blood and face the demons later. Just like Carlos said they would.

Operation Shadow Blink had survived the first phase.

TWENTY-THREE

Tungsten headquarters, Underground, Atlanta, Georiga

Several thousand miles away in the Atlanta underground headquarters of Tungsten, a half-dozen eyes were glued to the plasma screen. The persistent eye in the sky turning circles at twenty-five thousand feet above ground level, the Predator RQ-1 reconnaissance drone, provided real-time video downlink to Carlos and the other senior leaders of Tungsten. Even during inclement weather, or haze, clouds, or smoke, its onboard synthetic-aperture radar still communicated via satellite thousands of miles away.

"Three hours and counting," Carlos said to the group seated around the large oval mahogany table. "Forty-six minutes and negative movement."

"Are you sure he isn't dead?" the attractive female intel analyst who had accompanied Carlos and Kolt to Gitmo asked the group. "Could his wounds be so bad that he would have bled out?"

The ones who remained seated and standing nearby and who were still focused on the three large plasma screens secured to the wall wondered how long it can take to respond to a torrent of gunfire and a dozen dead guys. Surely someone heard something. The locals always did.

The others, busy working other future or ongoing Tungsten ops in other parts of the world, had migrated back to their cubicles.

"Wait a second. One of them is moving," Carlos stated excitedly before turning around to one of the analysts working the current operation. "Chat the drone operator and direct them to zoom in."

"That's gotta be 0706 or Joma; everyone else is confirmed dead by the insert force."

Western Pakistan

Kolt startled awake to complete silence, his body responding to the trauma and loss of blood. He wasn't sure how long he had been asleep. An hour? Maybe two? After at least a couple of hours waiting for a passing vehicle to discover the ambush and having gone through his story a hundred times in his head, Kolt had fallen into deep sleep.

Now awake, he pushed to a knee, gained his balance, and stood up straight. He repositioned the makeshift tan head bandage he had stripped from one of the dead terrorist's clothing and positioned it correctly. A second bandage, taken from a pant leg of the same terrorist and torn in two using the sharp edge of some broken glass still in the window, was tied around his right leg, deep in his crotch and routed around his lower right buttocks.

Walking with a limp, he did a complete 360 around the ambush site. Nothing looked different or combed over from earlier. There was nothing that the Mercs might have overlooked earlier that might compromise him or raise undue suspicions by the Taliban once they arrived.

A stream of warm blood ran down Kolt's neck just as he heard a blood-curdling gargling sound. He quickly dropped to a knee, assessing whether an animal or human was responsible for the noise, and tied a second knot on the head bandage to help stop the bleeding.

"Shit!"

Kolt couldn't tell if the ambush had been discovered by a local or if one of the terrorists from Gitmo wasn't actually dead yet. Anyone alive certainly risked compromising the mission. He figured the operators responsible for the bloody mess would have ensured everyone was dead before they hastily departed. Had something gone terribly wrong? Only Kolt and Joma were to *survive* the ambush. Joma was still out of it, the drugs not having worn off yet.

Allah was expecting everyone else.

Staying on his knees, Kolt crawled closer to the white pickup. Who knows what the mysterious operators of the insert force might have left behind. Kolt vectored in on the stifled gurgling. Only a few shards of glass were still present in the back window. The claymore mine and subsequent gunfire had taken care of the rest.

Kolt tried to peak over the two dead terrorists from driver's seat. He didn't want to be seen first by whomever it was that was still alive. It was tomblike dark. Too dark to actually make out with any certainty what he was seeing. He eased closer to the window.

"Brother," the stranger laying back in the passenger seat said with labored breath.

"What the fuck?" Kolt whispered.

"Brother, please, please help me."

Kolt moved closer. He opened the driver's-side door, yanking several times to free it, and leaned into the cab. As he closed the distance, the image of the third survivor became clear.

"Help me!" the dying brother pleaded.

Kolt snapped out of his trance. *Help you?* Kolt asked himself. *That will be impossible. You are the enemy. I know this seems a little strange to you, but we are not brothers. I am an American. You are a terrorist.* Reality hit Kolt like a freight train. He knew he couldn't allow this man to survive. But, without knowing his exact injuries, who could say if he would expire soon or not? Hell, he might still be alive when whoever it is that is going to discover this goat fuck gets around to it. That is unacceptable. Kolt knew what had to be done. And it had to be done fast.

Kolt slid into the driver's seat and up close to the dying man. He studied him for a few long seconds, sizing him up.

"Please, help me," the man pleaded again, barely audible.

Speaking in English, Kolt whispered back. "I don't fucking know you pal." The dying man's eyes widened in amazement at Kolt's English tongue. He shook his head slightly, signaling his inability to understand English slang.

Kolt hadn't expected an answer. He was focused on his own actions. The man was obviously in a great deal of pain. *Heck, he might not survive another minute in this condition, Kolt thought. Maybe I can just let this guy expire on his own? Let God's will take over from here.*

Underground in Atlanta, Georgia—Tungsten ops center

"Good to meet you, sir," Carlos commented while delicately switching his coffee from his right to left hand. Carlos thought the man's grip was surprisingly limp for such a large man with a long military service record.

"Likewise, young man!" Bill Mason responded louder than necessary. "But cut the 'sir' crap. It's been Bill for fifty-two years, admiral for the last eight, and now ambassador. Take your choice."

Carlos hesitated for a moment. He certainly didn't like the patronizing "young man" comment, considering he was at least ten years Mason's senior, and he felt himself resisting the urge to roll his eyes. He had first heard the rumors weeks ago about tapping a retired military man as the new director of Tungsten but hadn't met him since his presidential appointment a week or so earlier. And even though Bill Mason was a stranger to him, the admiral's reputation had preceded him. Carlos specifically recalled that Admiral Bill Mason was referenced exactly forty-seven times in Kolt's secret file. It wasn't all flattering, confirming Carlos's first impression of Ambassador Mason.

The retired three-star vice admiral Bill Mason never imagined his post-military career would bring him to Atlanta, Georgia. He had hoped for, even politicked for, a cushy, high-paying, high-visibility job inside an influential Washington, D.C., think tank. Or maybe he would land an ambassadorial appointment to some stress-free overseas post like Switzerland or Amsterdam. The president granted half his wish, but the post location was a little less spectacular than he had hoped for.

Before retiring, as the Joint Special Operations commanding general, he was one of the select few military men to be read on to Tungsten. But that's where it ended. Basically, he knew of its existence but nothing more. He knew of the program's ultra-top-secret classification. He knew its status within the highest chambers of the United States government. Tungsten was a top priority. No other *black* unit came close, not even Mason's Delta Force or SEAL Team Six. And that fact really crawled under his skin. Worst of all, the Tungsten director's post was the nation's most covert appointment. The White House didn't share the name of the program's boss. For a flashy guy like Bill Mason, the idea of plugging away day to day without fanfare or public recognition ate at him tremendously.

"What do we have here today, Carlos?" the new ambassador growled, alerting everyone in the small soundproof conference room that calling the new director Bill wasn't going to cut it. Not if they valued their jobs. It was also obvious to everyone in the room that Bill Mason probably would still prefer the title admiral over ambassador.

Carlos figured someone above his pay grade had already briefed the ambassador on the ongoing mission. Or maybe the ambassador was just looking to hear it all again from Carlos. *Typical military officer,* he thought.

"We are handling zero-seven-zero-six currently. Operation Shadow Blink kicked off about five hours ago with a covert embed. The insertion of zero-seven-zero-six was spot-on. Besides a momentary Predator glitch, no issues yet. We anticipate linkup in a couple of hours, once the sun comes up."

"Is that it up on screen number three?" Mason asked as he pointed with all five fingers.

"All three screens are dedicated to the operation currently, sir," Carlos informed him. An operation of this importance required it. At any time, the reconnaissance Predators could blink or go tits up for maintenance. It was a lesson learned the hard way over the years. Things materialized in an instant on the other end of the downlink. Not having backup cameras could prove disastrous. It had before.

"Screens one and three are currently covering key intersections approximately three to four miles north and south of what you see on center screen two," Carlos said. "That's the infiltration point."

Carlos noticed Mason shift his eyes from screen 3, lock eyes with him for a few seconds, and then turn to stare at screen 2. He wore a high-end white button-down, collared shirt tucked into a pair of tan slacks that rode slightly high around the ankles, exposing his dark blue socks as he walked. The waist line on his britches rode equally high, giving the navy man the makeup of a 1960s university professor. The striped tie was noticeably uncomfortable for the former military man, appearing to restrict his air intake and shade his face perpetually red. With his hands on his hips, Mason focused on the movement of the hot spot in the middle of screen 3.

"Who is moving down there?" he asked with great curiosity, stepping a few feet closer to the screen.

Anticipating the question, Carlos quickly answered. "Not exactly sure, sir, but we believe that is either Embed Asset zero-seven-zero-six or his shadow moving down there. The insert team confirmed all other props neutralized prior to their exfil." Carlos wondered if he would have to explain what the slang term "props" meant or who the insert team was.

Mason's eyebrows narrowed and his lips tightened. "Shadow?"

"Uh, yes, sir, operationally we simply refer to the other man, Joma, as the embed's shadow," Carlos answered, trying to anticipate the admiral's next question and wondering if he had listened to anything the intel analysts had told him during his initial in-brief and read-on to current operations.

"Also, sir, it is standard operating procedure to establish a specific support group for each of our embeds. I'm zero-seven-zero-six's handler, and two other assets, people we refer to as saviors, actually, are in Afghanistan now, briefing the chief of station and the ambassador to Afghanistan on Shadow Blink."

"Yes, I've been briefed, young man," Mason answered, without taking his eyes off the plasma screens.

Carlos decided to test the waters a bit. "Sir, we call him 'shadow' because the success of this mission hinges on zero-seven-zero-six's ability to stay with Joma. As you know, Joma is the link to the other nuke-plot cell we are looking for in the North-West Frontier Province."

Admiral Mason didn't respond as he accepted a ceramic mug of coffee from an observant office assistant. Carlos wondered if it was because he either was entirely on board with the operation or if he had severe reservations.

Carlos thumbed a laser pointer and tried to hold the red dot steady on the moving individual on screen 2. "That guy there, he moved to the back of the truck here and got in for a few seconds." Carlos added, "Now he is back out."

The ambassador listened intently as he stared at the large plasma screen on the wall. He was very comfortable with viewing scenes like this, black-

and-white video footage from twenty-five thousand feet over some obscure and far-off worthless piece of land on the other side of the world.

Deep down, these types of scenes and actions had a way of stirring a great deal of patriotism in the former admiral. He knew it took guts to do what special operations soldiers did. As he grew older and wiser, he wondered if he could have ever measured up had he been selected in his prime.

"This embed asset zero-seven-zero-six fella, former military?" the ambassador asked, as if to let Carlos know to use the full official term for the company's human assets.

"Army, sir," Carlos said. "He's relatively new to the program. This is his first major embed operation. He is a special case that acquired some, well, let's just say unique preparation."

"Green Beret?" the ambassador asked with an equal amount of enthusiasm and assumption. Mason was a longtime Special Forces fan and always had a soft spot in his heart for Green Berets. "What special training could a Green Beret need?" he asked with a condescending and questioning tone.

"No, Mr. Ambassador, former Special Missions Unit operator, DSC and triple Silver Star winner, and a boatload of other valor awards," Carlos answered, ignoring the question and now knowing the ambassador hadn't been briefed yet on the details of Shadow Blink. Carlos decided he didn't need to make it that easy for the new director. The ambassador was retired now, and everyone had to earn their pay in Tungsten. Carlos did, as Kolt was now.

"A SMU?" the ambassador asked, using the slang acronym pronounced as "smew." "Army? Delta?" the ambassador quickly said after swallowing a mouthful of coffee and turning his head with an eyebrow raised toward Carlos.

Western Pakistan

While Carlos and Ambassador Mason were getting to know each other, two thousand miles away their little project in Central Asia had taken care of his first problem. Kolt not only had a stranger alive that could potentially compromise his identity but also had seen headlights in the distance. He knew he needed to take action immediately. The stranger had to die.

Kolt leaned toward the terrorist, who was gasping for air. Their eyes locked on each other. The terrorist's eyes willed with hope that Kolt would save him. That Kolt would at least offer him assistance and make his pain more manageable.

But if the dying man's eyes begged for mercy, Kolt's eyes signaled cold-blooded death. Kolt reached up with both dirty hands and wrapped them around the stranger's light brown neck. His eyes widened and stayed glued on Kolt's. He didn't blink. Kolt positioned his thumbs directly on the front of the stranger's neck. In an instant, he pressed his thumbs, still covered in his own dried blood, against the stranger's larynx with every intention of killing the man quickly.

The stranger reacted with more strength than Kolt imagined possible given the man's condition. As asphyxiation kicked in, the natural instinct to survive accelerated. Kolt maintained the pressure as the stranger jumped out of reflex. He sensed death. He didn't like it at all.

His right hand reached for Kolt's face. Kolt turned away but kept him in his peripheral vision. The hand grabbed Kolt's left wrist. Kolt concentrated on maintaining full pressure with his thumbs. Kolt stared at the stranger as he strangled him. Fifteen seconds later, the stranger went limp. His eyes locked open, still staring directly at Kolt.

Even though the man was now dead, Kolt noticed the grip on his left wrist was still tight. Kolt turned his eyes from the stranger's and looked at the hand. In a second or two, the grip released and the hand fell to the cloth seat.

Kolt slowly climbed out of the driver's seat and moved around to the lead truck to find Joma. Joma appeared to be coming out of the drug comma, but the effects hadn't worn off entirely. Kolt knew it would be any minute now and suddenly noticed the ties on his ankles and wrists.

Shit!

Kolt had forgotten about his responsibility to remove Joma's restraints before he woke up. If he woke, still flex-tied, it would be one more piece of the puzzle that Kolt would have to somehow smooth over at best, and at worst it could be a potential showstopper. He reached for a shard of tempered glass from the vehicle windows, but the piece crumbled in his fingers to pea-size pellets. Kolt picked up a piece of sharp metal from the warhead that had impacted the dark blue Toyota's front end and started to cut away at the wrist tie.

Joma's sudden struggling startled Kolt. Joma obviously didn't know who was behind him.

"It's me, Joma—Timothy!" Kolt whispered, trying to calm him down while flinging the flex ties into the darkness.

"Praise be to Allah, praise be to Allah," Joma repeated.

"You are hurt. Your leg," Kolt said, pulling the soiled cloth of Joma's pants away from the wound to inspect it.

Joma rolled over and looked at Kolt.

"You are injured, too, no?"

"Yes, Joma, but we are so fortunate," Kolt said, trying to add a sense of amazement to his comment. "I think we are the only survivors."

"Where are we?" Joma asked.

"I overheard one of the Americans soldiers say we were in Gulistan," Kolt said, turning his palms upward as if he was unsure of where that was.

That startled Joma. "Gulistan?" Are you sure?"

"I can't be sure, Joma, but I think that is what I heard," Kolt answered convincingly. "Are you familiar with that place?"

"Yes, yes, Timothy. Praise be to Allah. We are in Pakistan. The hills, the stars, the wonderful aroma. I am certain of it," Joma answered.

"What should we do?" Kolt asked.

"Nothing," Joma answered.

"Nothing?" Kolt asked

"Timothy, it is best that we preserve our strength. We are both injured. We won't make it far, and I'm uncertain which way to go until morning. Someone will come. It's Allah's will," Joma said.

"But are you sure, Joma?" Kolt replied. "Will we be OK staying here?"

"Yes. Yes we will. Someone will find us in the morning. This I am certain of."

"OK, Joma. I trust you," Kolt replied.

"Yes, Timothy, we are no longer in your country. Pakistan is my birthplace. We are in the heart of my people, the Zarranis. We will be OK here. But now we must rest to preserve our strength."

•   •   •

Kolt awoke to bells ringing as he laid motionless on the desert floor. He was lying in a drying pool of his own blood, and only his blinking eyes showed any life as the goat licked his cheeks. The soft ringing of the bell wrapped around the lead goat's neck confused him slightly. If the bell ringing wasn't enough to assure him he was still alive, the colorful camels loaded down with family belongings sure did.

The stench of death lingered in the air. It seemed to hold to the tiny ambush area sitting in the middle of nowhere. An old man with a long cane poked at the dead. Once certain of their death, he reached down and pulled off their shoes and dropped them into a yellow cloth bag being held by a boy no more than six or seven years old. To a family of nomads making their way to cooler climates for the summer, shoes were more valuable than money.

Another little boy, who was no older than Kolt had been when he stalked deer as a kid behind his grandma's house, squatted in front of Kolt with the barrel end of his AK-47 less than a foot from Kolt's head.

The boy yelled out, "He lives! He lives!"

He didn't see the person that grabbed his left foot and pulled him away from the truck. But he definitely felt the excruciating pain.

Kolt spoke first, *"Assalam ahkam."*

"Where are you from?" a middle-aged man asked.

Kolt paused for a moment. He wasn't exactly sure how to respond to this. He wasn't trying to hide the fact that he was an American. But that was something better left to Joma to explain. Something to be eased into carefully.

"Joma, where is my friend Joma?" Kolt responded as he wondered how long he had been out.

"Who are the others?"

"Brothers," he answered, pausing to gauge their reaction. The nomad tribesman whispered among themselves as a little boy offered him a cup of water.

Kolt didn't know who might find him half-dead in the desert. He hoped it wouldn't be a coalition patrol that might have accidentally strayed across the unmarked border with Afghanistan. After all, he was there to access al Qaeda, not to spend valuable time at a U.S. interrogation facility like those in Bagram and Kandahar. He rolled the dice.

"We came to join the struggle against the occupiers," he said with as much conviction as he could muster. "We are heroes from the infidel prison in Cuba."

Sensing the tribesmen were less than convinced, Kolt added, "Look, my friends, we are all still dressed in our white prison garments. The infidel dogs refused to return our belongings."

One of the marvels of the eighteenth-century backdrop of vast wasteland and uninhabited valleys is the speed of the word of mouth. Even without a landline phone system, news travels fast. It wasn't long after Kolt took a shot with the nomads that his wish was answered.

Within earshot, somebody yelled out, "This one is alive as well."

Kolt knew it must be Joma. Joma would vouch for him. Joma was his cover. Without Joma, Kolt would have little chance of surviving alone in the lawless land of the Federally Administered Tribal Areas. A place where the Pakistani military had no control over the populace or the Taliban.

Another tribesman, younger and clean-shaven, wearing a short, rounded chartreuse and lime-green cap known as a *taqiyah,* came around from the left. He stopped to talk to the bearded man with the black turban who had been questioning Kolt. They spoke in a Pashto dialect prevalent to the area near Quetta. They motioned toward Kolt several times. The conversation was heated, and Kolt strained to hear what they were saying. Kolt wondered if Joma had turned on him.

Then, as if someone pulled the power from their conversation, they both smiled widely and reached down to help Kolt to his feet.

TWENTY-FOUR

It had reached the hotter part of the day with the sun directly above their heads by the time they finished digging the twelve shallow graves for the dead terrorists. Kolt and Joma knelt in prayer with the nomads as the caravan's elder recited several verses from the Koran. They had tried without luck to repair the white pickup after pulling the dead brothers from the front seat and the man Kolt had strangled to death the night before from the backseat.

Kolt did his best not to watch. He'd smeared blood all over the man's neck to hide the bruising from being strangled, but he was still worried.

"Praise Allah, we are blessed to be alive, my brother," Joma said, patting Kolt on the shoulder.

"He is to be praised," Kolt said, nodding sadly toward the graves of the others. Kolt knew he was being watched and did his best to play the role of grieving jihadist.

"And now we must go," Joma said. "Mercifully, our journey is not yet over."

After several hours of walking the road, Kolt wondered if Joma still felt that way. They were heading northeast, but it could have been straight up. Every muscle in Kolt's body was in agony. His head pounded and his thigh burned. When the caravan was intercepted by a convoy of jingle trucks and several yellow and white taxi cabs, Kolt found himself muttering a small prayer of thanks to Allah. The occupants of the vehicles weren't militants but businessmen running supplies across the region. They agreed to take control of Kolt and Joma and, after another hour or so, had brought them to a joint Taliban–al Qaeda training camp several miles northeast of Quetta.

Kolt knew this was where the shit would hit the fan. He was in the heart of the enemy, and there weren't any U.S. Marines to guard him now.

"Will they kill me, brother?" Kolt asked.

Joma shook his head. "I will not let them. You are a true jihadi. You have fought the enemy well and on his own land. I will make sure they understand."

Kolt wanted to be reassured, but putting his life in Joma's hands was harrowing. "Will they understand, these brave mujahideen?"

Joma smiled at Kolt. "I will make them. They are like us, warriors. Many fought at Tora Bora, others at Shahi Khot. One of gray-bearded elders had fought the Soviets. But only you and I can claim to have hurt the Western beast where he lives."

Surprisingly, Kolt felt better. "You are a true friend."

"As are you," Joma said.

The next two days were a series of interrogations by ever more senior al Qaeda leaders. Kolt found himself retelling the events of the night at Chero-kee station so many times he began to believe the lies he'd inserted as part of his cover. Even then, Kolt was certain he would have been executed if not for the widespread media coverage of the attack.

Explaining Gitmo was harder, but luckily he and Joma weren't the first returnees from Cuba. Their disorientation was believable and their wounds, while not life threatening, were serious enough to sell the story. Kolt's desire to seek revenge against the Mercs that cut his head and shot him faded away. Still, if he was fortunate enough to run into them again one day, he'd haul off and break their noses before apologizing and then buying them a beer.

It was early afternoon in the foothills of Balochistan Province and Kolt had just completed midday prayers with the others. He stretched his back and rolled his head. The sun was still bright, high in the sky, and keeping the temperature a comfortable seventy-eight degrees. He rocked back on his knees and labored to his feet. He bent over and picked his prayer blanket up by the two closest corners before folding it delicately and placing it under his arm. He slipped his bare feet into his worn, toeless sandals and started to feel a few hunger pains.

It had been just under two weeks since he and Joma had been delivered to the training camp, and as far as Kolt could tell, the camp cadre was still uncertain whether they were Western spies. Yes, they had been as convincing as they could, at least enough for them to be placed into the ranks of terrorist trainees, but their fate was far from certain.

As he walked with Joma and a few others to the washbasin to clean his hands and feet before the midday meal, Kolt thought about Carlos and the folks back at Tungsten. Still nursing his ass wound, cleaning it with fresh water each day, he wondered if they had forgotten about him entirely by now. After all, it seemed like a lifetime had passed since his insertion. Had they moved on to another mission? Is Carlos handling another embed by now? Kolt suddenly felt very lonely.

Suddenly, the distinct sound of AK-47 gunfire was heard from the high ridgeline. Kolt looked skyward and observed the green tracers arcing toward the sky, cutting center mass through the sun before tracer burnout. It was the standard signal, as they had been briefed, that important visitors were approaching the camp.

"Hurry, hurry, line up, line up!" the cadre yelled.

That's a little uncommon, Kolt thought. Since he had been at the camp, they had only lined up for instruction but not for a visitor yet.

"What's going on?" Kolt whispered to the cadre member nearby, named Qatir.

"I don't know," whispered Qatir slowly. "We've only lined up for one visitor in the past. For Amir al-Mu'minin Mullah Muhammad Omar."

"Must be someone important," Kolt replied a little too loud as he turned his head to see a single white late-model SUV come into the area. Gone were the days when al Qaeda leaders traveled in large convoys with truckloads of armed fighters. That signature always attracted the attention of the seemingly persistent eye in the sky, the Predator drones that patrolled the skies above eastern Afghanistan and western Pakistan. And if the drone was armed, Hellfire rockets soon followed. If not, the convoy had about thirty minutes before a pair of American fighter jets would be overhead stalking their prey.

"Silent!" the cadre member yelled toward the ranks as the visitors started exiting the SUV.

Kolt stood tall in the afternoon sun. He squinted to get a close look at the visitors as they stepped from the vehicle out onto Pakistani soil. Then he recognized him. Everyone recognized him. He contrasted greatly with the camouflage-clad security detail that surrounded him as he slowly approached. The large white turban propped high on his forehead seemed noticeably too big for the man's small head. It was the Egyptian doctor. It was Kolt's primary Tungsten target. He couldn't believe his eyes. He felt like he had just won the lottery. He never expected it to be this easy.

Ayman al-Zawahiri stood only a few feet in front of the first rank of trainees. From roughly the center of the third rank, Kolt shifted his weight slightly to see around the others. Kolt squinted as he watched the doctor pontificate while waving his arms in wide circles and injecting lengthy Koranic phrases. Kolt was surprisingly awestruck.

Few Americans had ever been this close to Ayman al-Zawahiri. Certainly nobody harboring an intent to cut his throat. Certainly no American special operator. But as the al Qaeda leader spoke, Kolt felt himself just as attentive as any of the other trainees. Kolt was amazed at how well-spoken the doctor was and how distinguished he looked, even though Kolt only understood a few of the Arabic words the top terrorist spoke.

Several times, Kolt raised his left hand to wipe the sweat out of his eyes as he strained to look Zawahiri in the eye. And although his adrenaline pumped through his heart like a locomotive, he knew it was time to act. It was hard to restrain himself; he knew this might be his only chance. Not jumping on this opportunity would be a failure of epic proportions. Yet, deep down, the natural instinct to survive, to live, quickly crept into his consciousness while he assessed his chances. Kolt hadn't anticipated the feeling, but he couldn't ignore its powerful hold. But before he could right his thought process and make his move, the move Carlos and the rest of Tungsten expected him to make, the doctor's next comment dropped Kolt's jaw to the hard-packed sand.

"Mujahid Joma, Mujahid Timothy, peace be upon you."

Kolt was stunned. Did Zawahiri just say my name? Did he just single me out from the two dozen terrorists in these ranks?

"Please, little brothers," Zawahiri continued, "join me here."

Nobody moved in the ranks. Certainly not Kolt, since he was stunned by the personal attention. Kolt didn't sense Joma stirring either.

Two camp cadre quickly moved into the ranks and grabbed them both by the arm.

"Come with me, brother; it is an honor," the cadre member whispered to Kolt as he escorted him to the front of the formation and directly in front of Zawahiri.

Kolt and Joma greeted Zawahiri with a soft bow and placed their right hands over their chests momentarily. Kolt adjusted his AK-47 sling slightly as he stared through the Egyptian's wire-rimmed glasses and deep into his dark brown, deep-seated eyes, all the while wondering if he should be taking a knee in front of the al Qaeda leader. Kolt hesitated, deciding it would be better if he just took his cues from Joma.

Zawahiri stepped closer to Joma and Kolt. Kolt realized the AQ leader's beard had completely grayed, practically matching the shade of his white turban and long *kameez* over matching white *salwar*. The beard was much lighter than the most recent CIA targeting pictures he was shown at Tungsten. But if he harbored any doubts that the man in front of him could be anyone but the most wanted man in the world, the large birthmark splotch over his left eye put that to rest.

I'll be damned!

"With Allah as my witness, the crusaders will reap the wrath again," he said with an odd mix of humility and vigor. "The planes operation of September will be but an afterthought soon."

Kolt was stunned. He tried to listen while resisting the urge to quickly remove his AK-47 from his shoulder and kill the doctor.

Too many people here. I'll never get a shot off before they are all over me.

Kolt changed gears. Maybe he could simply jump him and strangle him to death, similar to the man in the white pickup truck. Or simply break his neck. Did he have time to even do that?

Before Kolt could decide, Zawahiri shared the important details with the group.

"The American infidels will experience the same pain and anguish as our sons and daughters across the Middle East," he said. "Your brothers here, Joma and Timothy, made the initial blow against our enemies. Several others martyred themselves in an attack on a nuclear building in America. Brothers Farooq and Abdul, peace be upon them. The details are complete. Praise be to Allah!"

Kolt ignored the thought of not being able to complete his mission, quickly putting it in the back of his mind as he tried to absorb Zawahiri's every word. But the thought of failure, the thought of not executing, was still clinging to Kolt's conscience, no matter how much he tried to suppress it.

Kolt had already come to grips with his decision to sacrifice himself in order to neutralize the most wanted man in the world. That's what the Tungsten program required, and Kolt certainly hadn't forgotten that part. But this golden opportunity just wasn't clean enough. Too many things could go wrong. Kolt wasn't scared. He was just too professional to blow it. And the fucking doctor had thrown him a definite curveball.

"We have brothers in place across the ocean. Brother Nadal al-Romani has departed as well. They are readying to strike another blow into the hearts of the American dogs. Allah willing, we shall receive good news shortly," Zawahiri said as he turned from the two and walked back toward his vehicle, surrounded by a half dozen camouflaged and armed mujahideen.

"Peace be upon you, brothers."

Kolt couldn't believe it. He was there to complete a mission, and before he could carry it out, he was given a different mission. Not by his handler, Carlos, of Tungsten, but, amazingly, by the same man he was sent to neutralize.

First, Joma revealed the second nuke-plot mission, the one to be carried out by Nadal the Romanian, the same Nadal that Kolt had ridden the bus with in Yemen before the three SEALs had walked into a trap. Now, the leader of al Qaeda all but confirmed exactly what Joma had said. Nadal al-Romani was en route to America, and there would be a second attack on a nuclear power plant.

Kolt knew that passing on the opportunity to kill Zawahiri on that hot late-spring afternoon would raise a stink about his commitment. It was only natural of an organization like Tungsten. They demanded results and frowned on gut-feeling hesitation or outright changes. But in Kolt's book it wasn't a question about commitment. It was a matter of sizing up the situation and executing tactical patience.

Kolt had no choice. He had to get out of the camp and back to the United States.

"Wake up, brother Timothy," Joma said as he shook Kolt awake. "You were having a bad dream."

"I was?" Kolt asked, still half asleep and covered in sweat.

"You'll wake the others," he said. "Who is Hawk?"

Kolt froze. His heart pounded. Sweat poured from his forehead. His nightmare came rushing back to him. He saw it as vividly as if it were yesterday. The sound of a dying man's last breath. The sound of a man pleading for help from a fellow man in the middle of nowhere. The feeling of pressing his two thumbs forcefully on his larynx until he stopped breathing. The cold-blooded killing of another man who had asked for his help. Kolt could describe these events in detail to Joma simply from his nightmares, but he couldn't explain why he was dreaming of Hawk.

"My wife, Joma." Kolt lied—as Timothy, but as Kolt, he wondered if it was more than a slip of the tongue. "I call her Hawk. She loves birds."

"I see, brother Timothy. I understand. I'm sure Nadal will let her go free as a payment for your help with the attack," Joma said, reassuring Kolt.

"I pray she is OK, brother Joma," Kolt said before he turned over to return to sleep.

Kolt knew he was about to leave soon. He kicked himself for falling asleep in the first place and having the nightmare. Maybe it only woke Joma and not the others. His escape from the camp would require everyone to be sound asleep. If one person questioned him, he would have trouble leaving tonight.

Kolt knew the pressure was starting to cloud his thinking and he took a few breaths. He needed to retrieve his materials first, stash them outside the camp, then consider how best to make his escape.

Kolt waited at least forty-five minutes, to be absolutely sure that Joma was in deep REM sleep. The terrorist had stopped tossing and turning and had rolled onto his right side, facing away from Kolt. Kolt quietly reached for his AK-47 next to his bedding and slowly slipped out through the tent flap. It was wicked dark, since the moon had not yet risen, giving Kolt the concealment he needed to move away from the tent area. He held his rifle low and waited a few minutes to allow his night vision to adjust before moving around the side of their canvas tent. Hugging the tall wall until he reached several pickup trucks parked in the corner of the compound, Kolt gently laid his rifle on the ground before quietly lifting a two-gallon container of gasoline from the middle truck bed. He secured his rifle and, with both hands full, left the cover of the vehicles and hugged the wall again until he reached the back gate. Kolt took a knee, set the jug down, and carefully checked the gate latch and chain to make sure he could open it quickly but, more importantly, quietly. Kolt knew he had two more important things to take care of before he bolted. First, he needed to grab his water canister, knowing dehydration would set in quickly as he moved across the desert, irritated that he forgot it when he first left the tent. Second, he needed to make a decision about Joma.

Leaving his rifle with the jug, Kolt backtracked to his tent at a crouch, keeping the tent between the sentry sitting in the corner guard tower and him. Only a few yards from the tent flap, Kolt froze. He had picked up on a second sentry patrolling the inner compound at thirty meters' distance. Kolt slowly slipped closer to the side of the tent and took a knee in the shadow. He quickly assessed the situation, running the two options through his brain housing group while keeping an eye on both camp sentries.

Joma was an enemy of the state, for sure, and he certainly needed to be terminated with prejudice. Hell, that went for every terrorist in the camp. Kolt weighed the pros and cons, and, given the circumstances, he realized he had no good options. He knew that if Mujahid Timothy left without anyone's knowledge and left a bigger-than-shit dead Joma behind, then the chance of locating Nadal the Romanian or interdicting the second nuke-plot cell inside the United States was shot. Even if he made it a clean kill, one with no blood, no sounds, no struggle, the larger, more important mission would be compromised. With only one of them gone, however, the mission for Joma still might go. Especially if they thought Timothy had simply gotten cold feet.

Yes, Joma had to live for the time being.

For the second time in a day, Kolt gave up the chance to kill an enemy of America. It was starting to piss him off, but he knew in each case it was the right thing to do.

It pained Kolt to leave Joma alive, but he didn't see a way around it. Accepting it, he turned to penning a quick suicide note. He kept it short, but made it emotional and referenced Allah a few times for good measure. The crowning touch was his regret that he was too weak to see the great missions of the mujahideen fulfilled.

Kolt placed his note on his bed and slipped out of the tent. He paused and looked around the camp. He knew the senior leadership was in the collection of three small houses in the compound to the east. He desperately wanted to call in an air strike and take the whole place out, but, again, the risk was too great that it would tip off the terrorists that their nuke plot had been discovered.

"Fuck it, time to go," Kolt whispered, setting off into the dark.

The night was cool and the sky clear. He'd have no trouble orienting himself by the stars. Kolt retraced his steps to the gas jug and the back gate. He slowly lifted the chain and eased the gate open just enough to squeeze through. He looked up to get his bearing and eased away from the compound walls, heading west toward Afghanistan.

Kolt figured he had been walking for at least three hours, skirting the dirt road that meandered generally west, careful to stay twenty to thirty meters off the edge of the road. It was mostly rolling desert terrain covered by small rocks and knee-high scrub with intermittent stretches of rough terrain, rocky outcrops that sapped his strength and tested his endurance.

Reaching a dense tree line high in the hills, he set the gas jug down before easing down on his left butt cheek to keep from opening his wound again and leaned against a large rock, wishing now he would have carried a jug of water instead of gasoline. Happy for the rest, Kolt looked up at the moon, sitting nearly directly above him, contemplating the time of night.

Kolt knew he could never make it to a friendly coalition or U.S. base in Afghanistan without food and water, without a more precise form of navigation than the stars, or without finding a vehicle to steel. The cards would be stacked against him—he understood that, which is why he had humped the gas jug for the last three hours.

Kolt stood up and looked around the area. He lifted the gas jug to the top of the highest rock to serve as a point of reference as he moved away to find enough deadfall and brush to erect an aerial distress signal. Using the moonlight to carefully step around the basketball-size rocks lying sporadically on the hillside, he collected what he could carry and returned each time to the gas jug. Within a half hour, he had collected what he needed to erect the Delta Force in extremis distress signal. All he needed to do now was set it on fire.

The fire, and thus the distress signal, would be picked up by a Predator RQ-1 that Kolt hoped would be circling overhead. The drone would in turn bounce its image to whichever tactical operations center happened to see the signal—it would be so strange and out of place that they would be alerted that something was up. The unique design of the burning signal should, Kolt hoped, kick the signal all the way up to the JSOC center in Jalalabad. If . . . no, when that happened, the chances were extremely high that a Delta or SEAL Team Six assault force, or even a platoon of Army Rangers, would be sent to the border area to recover whoever had set the signal. Kolt was banking that it was just too unique of a signal to ignore.

Fire! Shit!

Kolt certainly knew it was a long shot. Erecting the distress signal wasn't anywhere in Tungsten's plan for Kolt. And now, as much as he knew it was entirely sketchy that it would, he realized that water wasn't the only crucial item he left behind in the tent.

Without matches, Kolt's inability to start a fire was now his biggest showstopper. He thought it over for a moment, searching for a solution. He needed something to start a fire, something to at least create a spark over a handful of dried brush, which he could massage with the right amount of man-made power while blowing to produce flame.

That damn prepper bracelet!

Kolt's thoughts turned to Hawk and the prepper bracelets her Special Forces boyfriend, Troy, had made for her. She had shown him both of them, and they both had small whistles and fire-starting flint sticks woven into the paracord. Kolt realized Troy might not be the whacked-out end-of-the-world survivalist he thought he was.

But a spark couldn't be that hard to create. Kolt looked around for a piece of metal that he could use to strike a hard rock. He felt the thirty-round magazine of the AK-47 that was slung over his shoulder sticking into his lower back and slipped the rifle over his head. He dropped the magazine and studied it in his hand.

Kolt realized that next to fire, maintaining noise discipline to prevent compromise was a close second. Banging a metal magazine against a rock was risky. Sound carries forever at night in the desert, and even though he had been careful on his march and was sure nobody was within striking distance of him, he couldn't be sure at all that a small village was not hidden behind the hills, or even that a small camel caravan wasn't bedded down nearby. The last thing he needed was a group of locals surrounding him. He had his night vision adjusted, but he would certainly be flock shooting with his AK-47's iron sights. If it came to that, his mission was dead in its tracks.

Screw it! I can't debate this all night.

Kolt moved to the distress signal he had laid out in the desert floor and doused it with the gasoline, thoroughly soaking it from center to end and on each leg. He emptied the jug and discarded it before gathering a handful of brush nearby. He balled the brush up in his fist, setting it gently on the dead fall. He reached for a rock, felt its strength, and dropped it. He reached for a second rock—it was heavier, more solid—and he banged it against another rock to test its strength.

Kolt cringed as the noise definitely carried across the vast desert floor.

Kolt grabbed the AK magazine, lined it up over the rock, and began striking downward just above the ball of scrub. The sound was even stronger, louder than the impact of just two rocks. After a dozen or so powerful strikes, Kolt saw a spark and dropped the magazine. He leaned over and cupped the scrub, protecting it from the wind, and began blowing vigorously.

After several quick breaths, the smoke flashed, and a small flame grew from the edge of scrub. Kolt blew a few more times, giving the flame the oxygen it needed to take, allowing the fire to grow and spread before setting it delicately on a larger portion of brush and the deadfall.

Within a few minutes, with the help of the doused deadfall, the fire successfully spread across the entire signal.

With signal burning, Kolt began a slow walk around the fire. He cradled his AK-47 as he walked. He wanted the Predator to see him. As he walked, a thought occurred to him. As far as the SEALs and Delta were concerned, no one from their command was missing. So who the hell would have set the distress signal?

"Come and find out," Kolt whispered to the stars, hoping someone somewhere was curious.

TWENTY-FIVE

"What do we have, Sergeant Major?" General Allen asked after having been summoned from his personal quarters minutes earlier. He had hastily thrown on his fatigue pants and brown cold-weather top but didn't bother with his fatigue top.

"Well, sir, I know what we have here, but I can't explain why we have it," said JSOC Sergeant Major Castor as he pointed to the plasma screen from the center of a standing-room-only crowd of night shifters, all inquisitively staring at the odd thermal image in white-hot mode.

"What's the source?" Allen asked, not taking his eyes off the screen.

"The 25th ID in Kandahar. Their Predator picked up a strange fire near the border, about fifteen miles west of Gulistan," Castor said. "They didn't know what it meant, if anything, so they asked around."

The new JSOC commander, Lieutenant General Seth Allen, having replace Admiral Mason just a few weeks prior, wasn't too keen on launching aircraft for something that could be a Taliban trap. General Allen was a longtime Special Forces man, for sure, well known throughout the community, but he wasn't stupid. He motioned for Castor to step away from the crowd and led him over to the coffee table near the tent's front entrance.

"What's your take on this?" Allen asked in a low tone, wary of anyone that might invade their space.

"Well, sir," Castor said, "it is unmistakably the correct ground-distress signal we teach our Tier One operators. Nobody can dispute that."

"Are we missing anyone?"

He shook his head no. "Every team is accounted for. All radio checks have come back solid. We don't know who that is."

"So it could be a Taliban- or AQ-baited trap," Allen said.

The comment wasn't lost on Castor. He knew very well the pain of losing the SEALs and others, thirty-eight in all, when the National Guard CH-47, call sign Extortion 17, was shot out of the sky by Taliban rocketeers just a couple of years earlier—a tragedy that is still considered the worst loss of U.S. military life in the entire twelve-year campaign.

"It may not be an active SMU operator," Castor said. "We have a lot of former guys doing independent contract work for the agency."

Allen knew this to be true. Ever since 9/11, JSOC personnel were highly recruited by the CIA, which meant the signal could be from a former JSOC operator. The CIA had numerous former operators on their rolls now as ICs. They had been supporting CIA covert operations around the globe, operating all over the Middle East, Central Asia, and Africa. Yes, they were active and very discreet in the war on terror, and the one country that could boast having the most covert American operators on their soil was without question the Islamic Republic of Pakistan.

"Do they have their personnel accounted for?" Allen said.

"Chief of station in Kabul already called, sir; they are one-hundred-percent sure they are good to go," Castor said.

"Damn it!"

"Sir, do you see the man in the image walking around the burning signal in a large circle?" Castor said.

"Sure, why?" Allen said, not sure where his sergeant major was going with the question.

"That's the signal that the man is compromised but his location is secure," Castor said. "In other words, sir, if the guy felt threatened, he wouldn't be near the fire at night because it's a bullet magnet."

Allen nodded, confirming he understood the significance of what Castor was saying. The general thought about it for a few seconds, beginning to feel the enemy threat may be low.

"Sir, it is a tough decision for you. But I have been in this business as long as you, fourteen years in the Unit. I wish I could explain it, but in my opinion there is a friendly out there that needs help."

"I agree, Sergeant Major," Allen said without hesitation. "Let's spin up the JOC. Wake up the key leaders and let's assemble in the war room in ten mikes. We gotta get this done in this cycle of darkness, or we'll have to push twenty-four hours."

The wheels of war were spinning up quick.

Afghanistan–Pakistan border

Just after 0400 hours, three MH-60M Stealth Black Hawks lifted off from Kandahar Airfield, having stopped en route from J-bad to top off from the fuel trucks. They executed a sharp turn to the east and headed toward the Afghan-Paki boarder, south of the faint lights pockmarking the village of Spin Boldak.

General Allen didn't have to tell the professionals from the 1/160th that this wasn't the ideal time to be executing this kind of mission profile. They knew too well about the early birds in that area, the goons that kept rocket-propelled grenades on the roofs of their homes covered by blankets, ensuring they remained at the ready for coalition aircraft executing flybys in the middle of the night. But the risk was certainly mitigated by the type of aerial chariots pushing the border carrying twenty-two grizzled and seasoned special operators.

These were the same type of state-of-the-art helicopters with the outerspace–looking tail rotor that put the SEALs into Osama bin Laden's compound in May 2011. They were outfitted with the latest avionics and positioning systems, refuel probes, and advanced engineering that made them the quietest, most stealthy assault helos in history.

"Captial Zero-Six, this is Comet Four-Seven, Green SAT. Over," CW4 Bill "Smitty" Smith calmly said into his mouthpiece from under his night-vision goggles. He scanned the horizon through the cockpit's bubble nose, turning his head slowly and deliberately. "Checkpoint seven, we are committed."

"This is Capital Zero-Six. Roger, we copy checkpoint seven," General

Allen answered. He remained several hundred miles away at the JOC in J-bad, acknowledging the helos had reached the point of no return, where the only thing that would stop them from continuing to the target area was an act of God or an enemy vote.

After hearing the JOC's confirmation, and without receiving the code word to abort the mission, Smitty turned the black knob on his communication suite above his head to the troop internal frequency the customers in the back were monitoring.

"One minute, one minute," Smitty calmly transmitted.

"Roger, one minute. Any sign of the package?" the Delta troop sergeant major code-named Slapshot asked from the rear, feeling the helo slow down as it approached the distress signal. Slapshot, along with eleven other operators, were squeezed in tight in the back of the bird. On either side, three operators sat with their legs hanging out both sides of the helo's open doors, the NVGs attached to their helmets allowing them to scan the ground below them for any threats.

"Negative on PID. Fire is out as well. We are going to do a wide flyby and circle back," Smitty said.

"Roger," Slapshot said.

Smitty adjusted his approach, moving slightly south but remaining at one hundred feet above the ground to lower their profile and allow him to sweep in quickly if necessary to pick up the package.

"Shit! Contact front, ten o'clock, heavy tracers," Smitty transmitted.

"Put us down," Slapshot said.

"Negative. I can't do that just yet. Landing zone is too hot. I need to back off into orbit and gain some altitude until we figure this out."

Slapshot didn't blame Smitty. He knew he was calling the shots on this one, especially while they were still airborne. It would be stupid to set down in the middle of a shit storm not knowing who was fighting whom down there.

As the two helos banked off the approach and climbed, Slapshot and the others jockeyed for firing positions in the back of the helos. The ones in the center took knees facing out, while the ones in the doorways settled their arms on the safety straps and activated the infrared lasers on their HK416 rifles.

"I've got movement!" the operator name Shaft announced as he tried to hold his laser steady on the figure below.

"I've got him," Slapshot said, confirming the mark by his mate Shaft. "Looks like one body. Weapons hold on that guy."

Smitty understood the weapons-hold call from Slapshot and relayed it across his helo internal net to his door gunners to hold their fire on the single figure until they could PID that it was friendly or not.

"Whoever that guy is, he sure seems like he is on the wrong side of things," Digger said over the troop net.

The single figure below was running at full sprint as he came over the small ridgeline from where they expected the distress signal to be. He stopped, took a tactical position behind a group of rocks, and shouldered his rifle, firing three rounds in the direction he had just come.

Slapshot studied his movements and took note of the clothing. "No military uniform, looks local dress," Slapshot said. "Guy seems to know his shit, though."

Smitty powered the helo into a tight circular orbit, forcing the operators in the back to scramble to the opposite door to observe the single figure on the ground.

The shooter again stood and moved backward, meticulously watching where he was stepping. But then he did something incredibly stupid that the operators on the port side of the helos had a first-class view of. It was hard to believe what they were seeing, but it was happening right in front of their eyes in full lime-green color.

"Is he flanking?" Digger asked.

"Looks like it. Looks like he is tired of running," Slapshot said.

The figure below jumped two large rocks, sliding down the opposite side of each, while holding on to his rifle. He stepped behind a third rock, appeared to lift up on the balls of his feet to fire over something, and unloaded with several bursts of his rifle.

"Green tracers!" Shaft said. He didn't have to say it—they all could see it—but he was reminding everyone that enemy tracers are green, whereas coalition troops' are red. It was a simple note to remain alert that the guy performing below them might not be friendly.

The figure moved farther from the helo, lower down the ridge, now out of sight of the operators in the helo.

Slapshot yanked the helo's customer headset off the hook and put one earmuff to his right ear and pulled the voice piece in front of his mouth. "Comet Four-Seven, we've lost visibility of the guy we were scoping. Can you get closer?"

"Negative. I can't risk that. The JOC has spun up a fresh drone from Kandahar. We need to sit down somewhere and give it time to get in the airspace," Smitty said.

"Wait, wait, wait!" Slapshot said. "We've got him again. He is walking with his hands up. I think he is waving at us."

The two-and-a-half-hour helo ride from the pickup point roughly two miles into Pakistan back to Jalalabad Airfield seemed more like ten minutes to Kolt. His heart raced as he shivered underneath the two green wool blankets the loadmaster had wrapped around his shoulders. It was uncomfortably cold at the altitude they burned through the sky at as they pushed 120 knots and skirted jagged mountain ranges by just a few yards. Kolt wondered why the hell they didn't close the doors for the trip home.

Kolt was strapped into a jump seat near the cockpit. It was crowded, but the troop medic on board gave him a thorough check, hastily cleaning and dressing his wounds and inserting an IV in his arm to replenish his loss of fluids. Even if Kolt needed more advanced medical care, the Delta aid man could practically operate on him in the back of the helo.

But besides the cold, Kolt was fine. He was a little startled that the recovery force actually arrived. Amazed that a Predator drone actually picked up on his distress signal. He had only enough gasoline to set the distress signal once before he'd have had to take his chances moving toward the border and dodging Talban patrols, lookouts, or even goatherders and bedouins. After getting compromised by a small group of locals, most likely because he was forced to violate noise discipline to start the signal fire, continuing to run away was a nonstarter.

But what shocked Kolt the most was that someone had enough authority, or the balls, to order a Joint Task Force launch, an incredibly risky mission based on sketchy information. Cross-border ops, even in extremis, took SECDEF-level approval. Kolt shook his head, a little amazed, really. *Tungsten really does have some juice,* he thought.

"Dude, what the fuck is going on?"

Startled after having dozed off sitting, just barely hearing the question over the booming helo static, Kolt sat straight up. Wrapped tightly in the blankets, he looked up directly into the menacing eyes of a helmeted, short-bearded operator.

Kolt recognized him immediately but wasn't really ready for any friendly interrogation. Who could blame the guy, though? Any Delta operator putting himself and his mates in harm's way on a short-string mission would demand answers. Kolt was just happy his first interrogator was his old teammate Slapshot.

Kolt knew his cover was blown. At least the identity part. It would be ridiculous to act as if he didn't know his rescuers or as if he was anyone other than Kolt Raynor. Sure, he may be able to preserve his true Tungsten mission for a while, and he wasn't about to offer more than required, but for the immediate time being he was just another old teammate who was still contributing to the war on terror. Timothy wouldn't work with this audience. It might be in an unconventional manner, which hadn't been uncommon for former unit members in the past few years, but his identity had to revert back to his given name at birth.

"Good to see you, Slapshot," Kolt yelled over the low roar of the helo's Sikorsky engine. The helo was nicknamed the Silent Hawk, but it wasn't entirely silent.

Slapshot wasn't about to settle for small talk. He took the customer headset by both earmuffs and placed it on Kolt's head, moving the voice piece in front of his mouth and handing Kolt the push-to-talk.

Slapshot keyed the mike, sending his comments across the troop internal net for all the operators to hear. "Kolt, first, you look like shit. Second, why are we even on the same helicopter again flying over this shithole country?"

Kolt smiled and reached up to shake his hand like two very close old buddies.

"Are you with the agency?" Slapshot said.

Kolt noticed every operator's helmeted head swivel toward the cockpit, probably amazed at what they had just heard over the troop net. Kolt keyed the mike. "No, no, I'm not, Slap," he said as he shook his head side to side quickly.

"State Department shit? Contractor? Pissed-off private citizen?" Slapshot asked, still confused and somewhat in shock to see his old troop commander under these circumstances.

"Look, Slap, I know you can appreciate that it's best for both of us if don't say anything just yet. All I can tell you is, I'm not a shit bag; I'm not a traitor to my country or anything crazy like that."

Kolt had no idea what may have been said of Kolt around the building after he left for the Tungsten program, but after the Cherokee attack, it was certainly plausible that in certain circles, Kolt Raynor might be considered a damn traitor.

"Dude, I know you aren't a traitor," Slapshot came back quickly as he grabbed Kolt's shoulder and shook him as if he was ecstatic to see him again. "But you are one crazy bastard."

Kolt chuckled.

"We'll catch up on the ground," Kolt said, nodding up and down.

Slapshot just looked at Kolt. He knew very well the guy sitting in front of him. At least he used to. Only a few months or so had passed since they had seen each other, and every operator would tell you that Kolt Raynor seemed to fall off the face of the earth. That wasn't entirely odd—most guys moved on without much fanfare, especially if an officer was heading to school for a year before coming back. Webber had told the command that very cover story to explain Kolt's absence. The fact that Kolt had vanished without even saying goodbye was a bit hurtful, but then officers did what officers did. But what Slapshot did know was obvious.

He knew Kolt's every habit, good and bad. He knew his character, good and bad. He knew his commitment to his nation. And most important, he knew, as he pondered Kolt's last comments, that if Kolt needed help, he would move mountains, ignore regulations, and risk it all to help him. After all, Slapshot knew damn well Kolt would do the same.

"OK, Kolt," Slapshot said. "I'll find you at J-bad." He removed the customer headset from Kolt's head and hooked it back to the communications suite behind the jump seat.

Almost having forgotten about the cold, the starboard-side-door gunner shifted in his seat and moved his machine gun slightly aft. The blistering wind blast smacked Kolt dead in the face.

"Thanks, Slap," Kolt yelled as he pulled the blankets up to his chin. "And thanks for understanding."

Slapshot turned and scooted on his kneepads back into the darkness, toward the aft of the helicopter, eased his ass down on the cold metal floor between several other jam-packed operators, and hooked his safety line back into the floor.

Having landed at J-bad only an hour earlier, Kolt now felt like a caged animal. Even worse, he felt like any other prisoner scarfed up on the battlefield. He wondered who was behind his status of PUC—person under custody. Kolt found himself in some type of isolation. Most likely while the new Joint Special Operations commanding general was trying to wrap his hands around just what the hell was going on.

Obviously, someone had gone to great lengths to preserve his status and his identity. It was no secret, though, and Kolt knew it. Half the guys on the helo that picked him up in Pakistan recognized him before he was helped onto the Black Hawk, as soon as the red light was flashed in his face. Now, sitting in the small and slightly damp room, he wondered how long his cover status would hold up.

Kolt knew people wanted answers. Phone calls would be made. Folks would be whispering among themselves around the camp about the mysterious guy the world stopped for last night to fly into Pakistan and recover. *Things are about to get interesting,* he thought. But at least he was warm. Interesting or not, Kolt's most pressing matter now was getting back to the States to stop Nadal the Romanian.

Tungsten headquarters—Atlanta, Georgia

Carlos could tell right away Admiral Mason was in no mood for any grab-assing inside the situation room of the secret Tungsten headquarters. Everyone else in the secure room sized up the situation pretty much the same way. Nobody dared open the discussion before the director.

"Alright, listen up, all of you," Mason barked, as if he was still in the military talking to a formation of young privates and sergeants. "As you know, this Raynor fella, I mean embed asset zero-seven-zero-six, set a top-secret distress signal in Pakistan. I just got off the phone with the special ops commander in Afghanistan, who has him in custody."

Carlos perked up immediately. More than anyone else in the organization, he had the most riding on Kolt. Everyone knew Carlos was Kolt's handler. They also knew that if a handler's asset completed an unprecedented mission like taking out Zawahiri, then the handler was looking at a quick promotion and a healthy bonus.

But Carlos wasn't thinking that pettily at the moment. Sure, he was concerned about whether Kolt had accomplished his mission, but he was also concerned about Kolt's personal health. Everyone knew that 0706 was to locate Nadal the Romanian and, hopefully, to blend into his cell enough to learn the nuke plot. He was also under orders from Tungsten to take appropriate action should he come across Zawahiri; that was his first priority. That action being to terminate in cold blood. Then, and only then, was 0706 to seek extraction. Assuming he was even still alive.

Carlos couldn't help himself.

"Sir, given the extraction protocol, has anyone confirmed if zero-seven-zero-six completed his mission?" Carlos asked as everyone looked toward him as if he was crazy for interrupting the director's train of thought. Carlos figured that since Kolt was exfilling after less than two weeks in Pakistan, he had quite possibly located Zawahiri. And maybe, just maybe, he took the terrorist leader out.

Pushing his luck a bit, Carlos quickly said, "And which mission did he complete?"

Admiral Mason didn't turn his head but cut his eyes toward Carlos in the back corner of the room. He wanted to respond with the guy's name first, but he couldn't remember if it was Carl or Carlton.

"Negative. I mean, no. I have no confirmed information that he completed his mission."

Carlos continued as if the two of them were the only two people in the room.

"So zero-seven-zero-six didn't locate Nadal the Romanian and didn't locate al-Zawahiri?" Carlos asked. "Why would he exfil, then, sir?"

Director Mason ignored the question and looked toward the small seated audience of Tungsten's top deputies. These were the same guys, and a couple of ladies, who had appreciated Kolt's thought process and efforts to accomplish his mission at Cherokee. They seemed to be fully seated in Kolt's corner. Carlos knew it. Mason sensed it.

"Our assets in Kabul to brief the chief of station are en route to Jalalabad," Mason said. "We'll know for sure in a few hours, tops."

Jalalabad, Afghanistan

Lieutenant General Seth Allen, the current JSOC commanding general, wasn't impressed. The barrel-chested West Point grad and army three-star knew he wasn't getting the full story. Not from the guy for whom he risked sending a force of very scarce helicopters and elite troops to recover across the border in Pakistan earlier that morning. Not from the mystery men dressed in part–Afghan slum, part–5.11 Tactical who had arrived a few hours ago from Kabul.

Like his predecessor, Admiral Bill Mason, Lieutenant General Allen had been read on to Tungsten's existence. But that's where it ended. Allen knew nothing of the program's details, who pulled its strings, or who padded its pockets. Sure, he had his assumptions, but now his smooth-running, war-fighting operations tempo had been interrupted, and he wanted answers.

As General Allen sat uncomfortably inside his large tent-and-plywood command center, he evil-eyed the secret squirrel strangers. They had to be twenty years his junior and almost certainly CIA. In Tungsten circles, their official title was that of savior. The two, who were also strangers to Kolt Raynor, had deployed to Kabul to secretly brief the CIA's chief of station about the potential to kill or capture Zawahiri.

The general squirmed in the brown folding chair, trying to find comfort. To his guests from Kabul, he seemed almost bored by the details.

"Say that again one more time," General Allen said as he leaned forward on his elbows and pushed his coffee mug slightly to the side.

"General Allen, sir, you fully understand this is a top-secret special-access program," the stranger in the long dark coat and 5.11 khaki britches said in a slightly demeaning tone. "We are not authorized to divulge any more than is absolutely necessary to get the job done."

"Let me get this straight." The general leaned back in his chair and clasped his fingers together as he placed them on the top of his head. "You wanted me to stop what this task force was doing and spin up a fixed-wing cross-border air-assault raid into Pakistani airspace to roll up a man whose name you aren't even going to tell me? No pictures? No habits? Not even his favorite color or flavor of ice cream?"

"Your point is well taken, General," the shorter of the two visitors replied.

"You're damned right the point is taken!" General Allen barked as he leaned forward in his chair.

The general lazily pointed toward Kolt. "Before we even break for breakfast, gentlemen, I want to know what the fuck is going on with Major Raynor here."

Taken back by the general's reference to Kolt's true name, the taller Tungsten official spoke up. "General, I know this must seem a little unorthodox to you."

"A little?" The general huffed. "This is a fucking circus."

"Sir, I am not at liberty to divulge this gentleman's exact mission. Suffice to say, he is on an executive-level, priority, singleton mission for the United States of America," the taller savior said with as much conviction as he could muster and using as many high-level buzzwords as he could spit out without compromising Kolt's mission.

General Allen was a seasoned operator. He knew as well as anyone how things worked in Washington, and he certainly understood and respected established protocol. "OK, fella, what's his target? What's his mission?"

"His target is the senior leadership of AQ," the Tungsten savior replied.

"Bullshit!" the general bellowed. "How can this guy find the needle in the haystack that this very task force and the world's entire intelligence apparatus combined haven't been able to locate in the last twelve, thirteen years?"

Kolt knew the general's reputation. Special operations was a very small community. He figured it was no surprise they knew of his mission. After all, word travels fast when a former unit member is plucked out of Pakistan by a bunch of his former coworkers.

Kolt stood up, more for effect than anything else, and walked over to the general's table. He leaned on the front edge and looked the general in the eye and smiled slightly. "Sir, it's no longer Major Raynor, but I'm humbled by the reference."

Kolt continued. "A few days ago I stood within an arm's reach of Ayman al-Zawahiri."

"Where?" the general quickly asked. "Near Quetta?"

"Yes, sir," Kolt answered calmly, almost surprised that the general didn't call him a flat-out liar. "A small village in Gulistan, west of Quetta."

"Gulistan?" The general was astonished. "Where is the intel? What proof do you have?"

Here it comes, Kolt thought. Before he could answer, one of the saviors stepped forward and interrupted them.

"General, you can appreciate the fact that we can't discuss any further details," he said very formally. "We don't have the authority, and frankly, sir, you don't have a need to know just yet."

The general stood immediately. "What kind of candy-ass game do you guys think you are playing here?"

His face turned red, and his eyebrows narrowed to a point above his nose. "Is this some kind of State Department dick dance or something?"

The savior answered professionally. "Sir, you know that is not the case." He continued. "I think it is best if you speak directly to our director. I can arrange a secure line through to Ambassador Mason."

"Mason?" the general asked, obviously shocked by the news. "Retired Vice Admiral Bill Mason?"

If there was anyone in the room more shocked than the general by what the savior had just revealed, it was easily Kolt. *Did he just say Bill Mason?*

Kolt turned his head quickly toward the savior sitting down. The savior looked back, somewhat startled by Kolt's look. He had no idea Kolt didn't know who the director of Tungsten was. Moreover, he had no knowledge of Kolt's checkered past with Bill Mason.

Kolt turned back toward the general but didn't respond. The savior still seated nodded in the affirmative as the speaking savior verbally confirmed Kolt's worst nightmare.

"Yes, sir!"

"Well, I'll be damned," the general said as he leaned back in his seat and looked toward Kolt. "That's where that son of a bitch went to."

It didn't take long to arrange for the secure phone call between the current JSOC commander, General Seth Allen, and his predecessor in that same billet, the retired vice admiral Bill Mason, who sat comfortably at his desk in the Five Points neighborhood in downtown Atlanta. The JSOC commander's last comments about Mason made Kolt wonder. He wasn't sure if the general thought Mason was a jackass or if the two men were longtime buddies.

After a little catching up on the phone, Ambassador Mason and the general got down to business. In about ten minutes, Mason was ready to blow his stack. He had kind of hoped the general would provide a clue that Kolt had completed his mission of neutralizing Zawahiri. Instead, he only learned that Kolt had aborted his opportunity to do just that.

Admiral Mason had had about enough of Kolt Raynor for one career, but it seemed to the retired navy man that a change in uniform wasn't enough to escape the escapades and shenanigans of the former maverick Delta troop commander.

"Raynor says he knows where HVI number one is," General Allen said. "In a remote village west of Quetta, Pakistan, but he can't provide any more details—rather, he won't provide any more details."

The general continued. "He says, and two of your central casting goons are saying, I need to launch into this village and kill or capture Zawahiri."

Admiral Mason had to be careful. Notwithstanding their longtime friendship, he knew he couldn't bullshit the general. Holding all the cards close to his chest was his only option. Besides, just as the savior told the general earlier, he didn't have a need to know.

"Look, Seth, I need your help here. Raynor works for me, and that's about all I can tell you. You'll have to speak to the secretary of defense if you need to know anything else."

"Yeah, Bill, I kinda got that feeling from your two henchmen who showed up from Kabul," the general remarked. "Where did you get those characters, anyway?"

"Just go easy on those guys, will ya?" Mason asked. "And hold on to Raynor for me. I'll get back to you within the hour."

"Alright, Bill, but I'm going back to normal business around here in the meantime," the general answered. "I'll try to keep the circus your man has brought to town under control."

My man? Mason thought. *I guess he is.* "Thanks, Seth, I'll be in touch."

The National Command Authority wasn't too happy with Tungsten's report from Embed Asset 0706. Kolt's revelation to the JSOC commander, Lieutenant General Seth Allen, that he had positively identified Zawahiri from as close as two feet away met with exasperation and discontent at the highest levels. At Tungsten's Atlanta, Georgia, headquarters, Bill Mason took it as a personal embarrassment. For the second time in his life, he took an ass chewing over a secure line from the vice president. Both times, he had Kolt Raynor to thank for it.

Kolt's decision to temporarily divert from his primary mission to some half-baked United States–based terrorist attack was pretty Delta-like. More specifically, it was very much Kolt-like. His file was full of actions like this. Robin Hood–like acts where the decision of right and wrong, good versus evil, execute or abort was saved solely for him.

Ambassador Bill Mason, lacking any further details, considered these acts nothing more than fuel for the arrogant personal self-interest of Kolt Raynor. But, as usual, Kolt saw things differently. According to him, he was acting exactly how a warrior should. And to Kolt, if you didn't carry warrior creds yourself, you should not be second-guessing someone who does.

Around a beautiful mahogany table, in the same boardroom in which Carlos talked Kolt into taking on Shadow Blink, Tungsten's senior staff— not a warrior in the bunch—openly questioned Kolt's actions. The room was full of slightly overweight coffee drinkers trading snide comments and cries of failure. What was he thinking? Why didn't he execute the mission? Carlos and the psychs at Tungsten, though, were less worried. They knew Kolt's file best. After all, it was their job to *handle* him.

The Tungsten psych reminded the group of this type of consistent behavior in Kolt's profile. He wasn't surprised that Kolt would make a decision like this and openly questioned why anyone would expect otherwise. To hold off on his priority mission in order to save the lives of others was characteristic of Kolt according to the records kept by the Delta psych Doc Johnson for many years. The problem now was that the Tungsten psych actually read the entire inch-thick file. He wondered if anyone else had and pondered, Who could question a man in Kolt's position?

Ambassador Mason could. He had been surprised that Kolt was recruited into Tungsten in the first place. But he wasn't surprised that Kolt chose what rules to follow and which ones to ignore. Deep down, Mason blamed Kolt for his early retirement from the navy. He also blamed Kolt for his not being named Vice Chairman of the Joint Chiefs of Staff—a position Mason had politicked for years for and one that came with a fourth shiny star. Mason was fully willing to grind the axe into the Kolt voodoo doll some more.

"This guy has always been a maverick of sorts. He likes to march to his own drummer," the ambassador stated to the small crowd, obviously trying to impress everyone present that he didn't need to read the file. He already knew all about Embed Asset 0706's history and capability.

"How in the world did he ever get in this program?" he questioned pointedly. "Didn't you guys read his performance file?" he demanded as he looked slowly around the room before locking eyes on the psychologist.

"Yes, sir, we did. Extensively so." The Tungsten psych respectfully answered Bill Mason's obviously rhetorical question. "That's exactly why we recruited him. However, sir, with all due respect, zero-seven-zero-six is in seminal space here."

"How so?" Mason blurted out with a dismissive hand wave.

"Well, sir, he is the first Tungsten operative to accept a singleton mission on this level. We are asking him to sacrifice himself for a problem his country, and might I specifically add the CIA, couldn't solve in the last fifteen years."

Admiral Mason fidgeted in his seat as he struggled to find something authoritative to say.

The psych continued with a leveled voice. "I'm just saying, sir, maybe we owe the gentleman the benefit of the doubt here. His service record seems to have earned him at least that much."

As the debate continued, Carlos was sure of one thing. If Kolt ever got wind that Mason was running Tungsten, they'd lose him. Carlos couldn't imagine a scenario where the hard charging operator would stay under Mason's command, but then again, miracles did happen.

TWENTY-SIX

As one of the company's black Crown Vics tooled south down busy Interstate 75 and into the heart of Atlanta, Kolt Raynor stared out the the passenger window, at nothing in particular, feeling like a high school kid on his first date and afraid he would say something stupid. Because if his handler Carlos wasn't going to be cordial, not even engage in small talk, he figured he would match the attitude.

What's with the cold shoulder?

In fact, since Kolt stepped off the back of the C–5M Super Galaxy at Dobbins Air Reserve base only forty-five minutes ago, met the Crown Vic, and jumped in the passenger seat, Carlos hadn't said a word. Kolt knew it was overkill to catch a ride on one of the largest military aircraft in the world; he would have been just as happy spread out in the back of a C130 cargo plane—he was going to rack out the entire way, anyway. Tungsten must have pulled a puppet playhouse's worth of strings to borrow the only military aircraft that could make it from the 'Stan, taking the Arctic Circle route, and land on the East Coast without hitting a single strategic tanker. All that for one man could mean only one thing.

Mason must want a major piece of my ass!

After pulling into the covered three-story parking garage and finding a spot near the center elevator, Kolt and Carlos stepped out of the car. Kolt followed Carlos, not surprised by the way his tweed jacket had been tailored perfectly to fit snug to his upper body. He had to give it to the old man, he was obviously passing on home-cooked seconds and doing his crunches.

After taking the elevator to the basement level, they walked a good ways down a damp, narrow hallway that obviously hadn't been swept in years given the dirt buildup on the edges and the musty smell. Kolt watched Carlos slide a key in the shoulder-high dead-bolt lock and a different one in the dead bolt just above the door. Carlos led the way into a small white-walled anteroom with several leak-stained egg-white ceiling tiles on either side of the fluorescent light above them, stepped in front of what looked like a proximity biometric scanner on the wall near the steel door, and placed his access badge near the IR light module.

Once the light flashed green, Carlos placed his feet on the two green-painted shoe prints near the iris scanner and leaned forward to center his eyes. Kolt heard the lock disengage and tailgated Carlos into the headquarters. Kolt was impressed by the discreetness of Tungsten headquarters, but was too jet-lagged and too lucky to be alive to put up with the silent treatment for another moment.

"Alright, Carlos, are we secure enough to talk now?" Kolt said, not trying to hide the sarcasm from Carlos.

"Let's get inside the briefing room first, Kolt," Carlos said, turning to walk away.

"No fucking way, Carlos, you tell me what the hell is going on, or I'm walking back out that door and you guys can have this shit," Kolt said.

"Look, Kolt, there is something you need to know."

"You found Cindy Bird?" Kolt asked. "Is she alive?"

"No, Kolt. I wish I could say we did find Bird, but this is something else," Carlos said.

"What, someone have their panties in a wad over me not killing my-self?" Kolt said. "Screw them! I've had enough of this Mickey Mouse second-guessing."

"Take it easy, Kolt," Carlos said. "Nobody is pissed at you. We are happy to see you, in fact."

"Then what's with the kids' games?"

"William Mason ring a bell to you?" Carlos asked.

Kolt looked at Carlos, wondering why he would ask that since he knew Mason was the major reason he was no longer in the Unit.

"Of course. Why?" Kolt asked.

"He is the new director of Tungsten," Carlos said, looking behind him to ensure nobody was in hearing distance. "He is waiting for us in the conference room."

"Yeah, I know that, Carlos," Kolt said. "Who gives a shit? Let's get on with it."

As Kolt and Carlos entered the back door to the darkened conference room, Kolt wasn't surprised to see Miss Peabody again, front and center, like a fine-haired, poised cat. Kolt remained in the back of the room, not wanting to interrupt the briefing, and listened to her spit out buzzword after buzzword for thirty seconds or so while her pink form-fitting skin-tight tank tempted every man in the room. Obviously, it was a good bit nippier in the room than it really felt.

Off to her left, Kolt noticed one of the plasma screens was on. A bespectacled middle-aged man, his wire-rimmed glasses slipped to the edge of his pointed nose and his high hairline running away from his white collared shirt, sat fairly motionless at a table in a nondescript room. Behind him and above his head, several large digital clocks with red font hung on the wall. Focused on the papers neatly stacked in front of him, Kolt hadn't noticed the stranger look up at the camera a single time yet.

"Excuse me, sir," Carlos interrupted, "I believe you have met our newest embed before?"

Kolt watched Bill Mason at the head of the conference table reach up and push the mute button on the video-teleconference speaker, barely acknowledging Carlos's comment. Kolt stepped up, barely making eye contact with Mason, took a seat at the table, and cracked the half-liter Niagara bottled water to his front.

"Continue, please," Mason said to the briefer in pink as he tapped the button again.

"Well, yes, sir," she said. "Our recommendation is, we stand down from the nuke plot and refocus our assets on finding, fixing, and finishing HVI number one."

"Agreed!" Mason blurted. "Effective immediately, in fact."

Kolt cut his long swallow of water off abruptly at hearing Mason's reply, spilling spring water down the front of his shirt.

What the fuck?

Kolt quickly looked at Carlos, trying to make sense of what he had just heard. Carlos didn't move a muscle or say a word, allowing Kolt to assume he agreed with Miss Peabody's recommendation and with Mason's decision.

"Sir, if I may," Kolt said, turning toward Mason. "I respectfully disagree with that course of action."

Mason reached for the VTC mute button again.

"Is that so, young man?" Mason said as he set his pen down.

The elephant in the room was just too intense to ignore, and although Mason so far seemed to be maintaining his professionalism, not letting on to the others that he had any history with 0706, Kolt could see the hate in his eyes.

"Look, sir, Director, Admiral," Kolt said. "Hell, I'm not even sure how to address you these days."

"It's still Admiral," Mason shot back.

"Look, Admiral, I obviously didn't get a chance to hear the analyst's brief, so I'm not sure exactly why we would be standing down. I assume Nadal the Romanian has been picked up by somebody or was struck by a drone somewhere?"

"That assumption is incorrect," Mason said. "But it is no assumption that your efforts, to date, are the reason we are sitting here tonight."

What? That son of a bitch! Kolt wanted to detonate, but took a deep breath and gave way to Mason after getting the vibe from Carlos to settle down. Going ballistic now wasn't going to do anybody any good, especially Kolt. In fact, it would probably be the quickest way to unemployment.

"Sir, with all due respect," Kolt said. "I have about gotten my ass shot off at least three times, from Yemen to South Carolina to Pakistan, hunting for Nadal. In my humble opinion, *that's* the reason we are here tonight."

"God damn it, Raynor!" Mason barked, slamming his fist against the conference table. "That's enough insubordination from you. My decision is final: You will stand down Raynor, or"—

"Or what, sir?" Kolt said. "You'll court-martial me like you tried to a few months ago?"

"Enough!" Mason barked.

"Kolt, take it easy," Carlos said. "We can handle this like adults."

"I'm good, Carlos," Kolt said, looking at his handler and then back to Mason. "Just having a professional conversation among two adults that seems to confirm we have differing professional opinions."

"Ladies and gentlemen, I've made my decision," Mason said as he gathered his files and stood to leave. "I will call the SECDEF immediately to inform him. We are late as it is."

Kolt stood as well, not because he had much respect for Mason, but because Carlos and the others did. Kolt watched Mason and another gentleman exit the room by the front door before he heard Carlos speak.

"I'm not sure what just happened here," Carlos said. "But everyone please take your seat."

Kolt wasn't in the mood to keep the games going and was actually debating whether to just throw in the towel, put Tungsten and Mason as far behind him as possible.

Screw that!

"Can somebody turn the damn lights on?" Kolt said, looking around the room.

Miss Peabody stepped quickly to the light knob, bringing the lights up before killing the laptop on the podium and the projection on the screen.

"Kolt, I'm pretty certain Director Mason will not budge on this," Carlos said.

"Damn it, Carlos, that makes no sense," Kolt said, turning to Peabody.

"Ma'am, I'm sorry. I should know your name by now," Kolt said.

"Alexandria," she said. "Alex for short."

"OK, I'm Kolt. Pleased to meet you again," Kolt said, knowing she had briefed him twice before but never letting it get too relaxed. "Let's go over what we know. Would you mind doing that for me?"

"Umm, no, I guess not," Alex said.

"Nadal al-Romani. Any update on his location?" Kolt asked.

"Not exactly. Some say still in Pakistan; some say he has already entered the U.S."

"OK. Any new SIGINT?"

"Well, the same day you fled the training camp, NSA intercepted a phone call between what they believe to be two terrorists associated with Nadal," Alex said.

"Anything?" Kolt asked.

"The translation was inconclusive, but most opinions are that they were coordinating picking up somebody important today or tomorrow," Alex said.

"What about Sacred Indian?" Kolt asked. "I won't hold you to it, but what is your best guess on that?"

"Well, we ran it through the nation's critical-energy-infrastructure database, including all electricity, petroleum, and natural gas plants. The words 'Sacred Indian' didn't hit—no matches, or even the slightest indicator of any connection."

"That's crazy," Kolt said, looking at Carlos simply to not make it so obvious his eyes were drifting down Alex's pink tank. "We're missing something. I feel it. These bastards are not satisfied with just Cherokee."

"Some of our analysts believe 'Sacred Indian' is not really a code at all but interpret it as any large public gathering, like a large festival or even po-litical rally. The ethnic inference to places like Indian Point Power Plant, near where the bodies washed up, or the Cherokee plant near Gaffney, South Carolina, is a no-brainer. But we think those two targets are off the table now. Some are even wondering if the phrase was recorded correctly by Nadal, believing the word 'sacred' might really be the word 'scared.' They're running that weak thread through the databases now," Carlos said, seemingly trying to give Alex an assist as she collected her thoughts.

Kolt thought about it, running everything through his head one more time. The capture of Ghafour, the washed-up swimmers on the shore of the Hudson, the bus ride with Nadal in Yemen, the attack with Farooq, his and Joma's surprise meeting with Ayman al-Zawahiri. There was just too much to point to a second nuke plot, this one not yet uncovered.

"There is one thing interesting we learned the other day," Alex said, breaking Kolt's train of thought. "Probably nothing, though."

"Nothing too small at the moment," Kolt said.

"Well, the FBI sent us some fuzzy images of a hooded man pumping gas in Shiloh, Tennessee, just this morning," Alex said. "Possibly a match on Joma."

"My Joma?" Kolt said, jumping out of his seat. "Joma from the Cherokee attack?"

"We think so," Carlos said.

"That's something to work with, then," Kolt said. "I'm telling you guys, an attack on U.S. soil is imminent." Kolt saw Joma clear as day, sleeping beside him in the tent in the training camp in Pakistan. Kolt had made the call to not kill Z-man or Joma, but to instead make it back to the U.S. to disrupt the nuclear attack. He was still certain it had been the right call, although he couldn't say 100 percent.

"Kolt, look, maybe you are just too close this whole thing," Carlos said, trying to keep things in perspective.

"Bullshit, Carlos!" Kolt said, turning back to Alex. "Besides the Civil War monuments and a few hundred tourists on a holiday weekend, what the hell is near Shiloh that a terrorist would be interested in?"

"An energy plant," Alex said. "Yellow Creek nuclear power station."

"No shit?" Kolt said, fist pumping for a second.

"But it's not in Tennessee," Alex said. "It's about ten miles south of Shiloh, just across the Mississippi border."

"That's it. That's gotta be the explanation for Sacred Indian."

"I don't know, Kolt," Carlos said, not sold just yet.

"Carlos, it fits. The other terrorist, Abdul, must have already built the target folder on the plant, doing the reconnaissance piece for the attack cell months ago before he was killed," Kolt said, entirely confident in what he was saying and knowing they had nothing better at the moment. "Maybe Abdul couldn't read English or Nadal couldn't understand him?"

"Well, maybe," Carlos said.

"I can see that," Alex said. "Nadal must have misspelled the first word of the code phrase when he scribbled it in the notebook. He meant to write the word 'scared' instead of the word 'sacred.'"

"Scared Indian!" Kolt said. "Kindergarten code for 'yellow creek.'"

"Come again, Kolt?" Carlos said. "Nadal wrote it three times."

"I agree." Alex stepped in. "'Yellow' is to 'scared' as 'creek' is to 'Indian.'"

Kolt chugged the rest of the water and headed for the door. "I need a car, a cell phone loaded with Raptor X and those relevant phone numbers, and some alias-backstopped government creds. Carlos, get me into Yellow Creek tomorrow morning. Tell them the president wants a vulnerability assessment done or something. Whatever. Please, just make it happen."

As Kolt exited the room, looking for the men's bathroom, he heard Alex over his shoulder.

"What do I tell Director Mason?"

Yellow Creek Nuclear Power Plant, near Luka, Mississippi

Nadal crouched low in the passenger seat of the black Dodge Durango, silently celebrating the months of detailed research and planning. He was uncomfortable, but he didn't want to be silhouetted by the parking-lot lights and reveal himself to the armed officers in the tall towers surrounding the plant. He motioned with his cell phone for Saquib and Hasan to stay low as well.

It wasn't happenstance that brought Nadal to the main parking lot of Yellow Creek Nuclear Power Plant. No, there were many choices—dozens and dozens, in fact. There wasn't much special or unique about the reactor design or the structure of the power block at Yellow Creek from a vulnerability perspective. Like many others in the United States, it produced electricity using decades-old technology. No, Yellow Creek wasn't much different than, say, Cherokee nuclear plant, except for the business decision made just over three years ago by the corporation's board of directors.

Nobody could argue that it wasn't a smart business choice—after all, everyone knew security at a nuclear power plant was a financial drain on the plant's profits and affected the shareholders dividends. By abandoning Yellow Creek's outer checkpoint, shuttering its ballistic structure, removing the security cameras, and dropping the heavy metal-plate barriers, they had saved hundreds of thousands of dollars and offered a friendlier, welcoming image to the surrounding public. The decision also made life easier for terrorists driving truck bombs to get much closer to the main reactor.

Nadal brought his cell phone up to his mouth.

"Yes, brother Joma, we are in position and our entry point is clear as well," he said.

"Should I wait for you?" Joma asked.

"No, insert the battery and activate your device," Nadal said. "Once the red light flashes, drive immediately to your target."

"I cannot lie, brother Nadal. I am nervous in Allah's eyes," Joma said. "I seek courage and your blessing."

"It is OK to be of a solemn mind, my friend. You must use the chains to defeat a weak mind."

"Yes, brother, I will use the chains."

"Good, brother Joma. You have done well. Allah is all-knowing and shines upon his newest martyrs."

"Yes, Allah is merciful and compassionate. Peace be upon Him," Joma said. "Inshallah."

Nadal ended the call and crawled into the backseat with Hasan. Nadal looked past him to the two large packages in the rear of the van. They took up the positions of the two back jump seats, which had been removed to make room. The vehicle's rear shocks had held up well under the additional weight of explosives, well enough to successfully pass the abandoned checkpoint and reach the parking lot only twenty meters or so outside the main access facility. It wasn't necessarily the parking lot that was important to Nadal's meticulous planning, but one parking stall in particular.

"It is time," Nadal said, reaching over and ripping the blood-soiled pillowcase off Cindy Bird's head. Gagged and blindfolded after a month's worth of isolation and intermittent beatings, the woman looked dazed and gaunt.

"Your suffering is almost over," Nadal said. "Mujahid Timothy made his choice. He is a traitor to both America and Islam. I know you longed for his return, but he chose to abandon you. Allah will not judge him kindly."

The woman said nothing, but that was as expected. Nadal was amazed at her resistance, even when all hope was clearly lost. She had resisted violently when she was first rolled up at Brueggers Café in Raleigh.

Nadal tugged gently on the chain strapped around Bird's waist before slipping the blindfold off her eyes and over her head.

"You should be comfortable," Nadal said. "Would you like to convert before you face Allah's judgment?"

Bird tilted her head toward the window and away from Nadal at the sound of his voice. Nadal followed her gaze. He saw the round dome of the nuclear reactor in the distance, noticed steam coming from the top of the turbine building, and, in the distance, easily identified the thick wall of evaporating water gushing the from the top of the six-hundred-foot-tall hyperboloid-shaped cooling tower.

"Even now I offer you the mercy of accepting Allah."

Bird looked at Nadal, her eyes flashing a hint of the anger she had displayed throughout her captivity.

"Very well," Nadal said. He looked away and bent down, pulling away the floor carpeting and lifting up a piece of sheet metal covering a hole cut into the floor of the Durango. He eased his feet through the hole and then slowly lowered himself down to the asphalt. The dull sheen of the manhole cover confirmed they were in position.

Saquib handed Nadal the crowbar. It took a minute to get the right angle, but Nadal finally lifted the cover and slid it off to the side. The scrapping sound echoed from under the Durango, and Nadal gritted his teeth.

Saquib now passed Nadal several thick plastic bags, accidentally banging the contents of one on the asphalt below.

"Be careful with the scuba tanks, brother!" Nadal said. He climbed down the concrete shaft until his head was below ground level and then powered on his Petzl headlamp to illuminate the way down.

"What do you see?" Hasan whispered.

Nadal did not answer right away. It occurred to him that this was a moment when he should utter something profound as the Prophet would, but as Nadal stared at the graffiti of a cock and balls sprayed there by a worker, words escaped him.

Kolt did his best to keep his temper in check but knew he couldn't win the battle much longer. With lives at stake and time running out, he was once again dealing with people who did not understand the urgency. In addition, he had taken on yet another identity and was growing tired of being someone other than who he was.

"Look, Mr. Jones, we appreciate you coming on such short notice, but we've been at this all day," the chief nuclear officer of Yellow Creek Nuclear Power Plant said. My folks are exhausted, and I need to send them home. We will reconvene in the morning."

Kolt let his breath out slowly. "I understand, ma'am. I think we can wrap this review of your protective strategy up in another hour or so," he said. He looked out the large fourth-floor window that overlooked the Tennessee River as two Coast Guard cutters sailed by on patrol.

"Mr. Jones, I'm sorry, but we really need to call it a night right now," the CNO said. "I just received a call from the governor. At the president's directive, he has activated the Army National Guard."

It's about fucking time!

"That's great news, ma'am. They arriving tonight?"

"No, they haven't been alerted yet, but we expect the advance element to be here in the morning to coordinate the overall security plan."

Kolt kept his smile to himself, but he was pleased the president had taken this unprecedented step. Kolt didn't see how he could have avoided it much longer. The intelligence was just too telling, too frightening, and after Cherokee the continued fallout of negative opinion polls and congressional squabbling about becoming a police state made the callout inevitable.

Kolt turned to the plant manager. If there ever was a time that he needed to work his cover and masquerade as Mr. Jones, this was it.

"Bob, has anyone shown signs of nervousness lately? Over the past week? Since the attack on Cherokee?"

Kolt was convinced there had to be a Timothy at Yellow Creek station. There must be an insider. After spending the day with the real Timothy at Cherokee and after Hawk's cocktail-napkin Nuke 101 lesson at Brueggers, he realized how excruciatingly painful and difficult it was to understand the inner workings of a nuclear power plant. He now knew that the terrorists would be hard-pressed to successfully reach the reactor or the main control room without the required detailed knowledge that was only obtainable from someone who had worked there for many years—or, short of that, without three rifle companies of United States Marines.

"Who is the smartest guy here on these engineer drawings?" Kolt asked. "Who knows the most about the underground pathways?"

"That would be Samuel Price. He works in my office," one of the engineers in the room announced.

"Where is he now?" Kolt asked.

"Well, good question," the engineer said.

"What's up?" Kolt asked.

"We were having breakfast in our cafeteria when the Cherokee attack hit the news that next morning," he said. "Sam said he didn't feel well and went home for the day."

"Happens, I'm sure," Kolt said. "So where is he tonight? We need him in here to help us fully assess our vulnerabilities with undergrounds."

"Can't do that, sir," the engineer said to Kolt. "Before coming back to work, Sam decided to take two weeks of vacation."

"Vacation?" Kolt asked.

"A cruise to the Bahamas, I believe," the engineer said. "We haven't heard from him since he left over a month ago."

"Call him!" Kolt said.

"Why?"

"Just do it. Just check on him," Kolt demanded as he noticed the business-suited CNO raise her right hand in the air as if to signal *stop*.

"Don't call him, Bob," the CNO said, interrupting. "Mr. Jones, I am not bothering one of my most trusted employees at this hour. Mr. Price is on extended leave for an illness that is confidential. I'm sure you can appreciate that. Please, I have to put my foot down here. We are going home."

"OK," Kolt said. Nothing he could do to change the CNO's mind, that much was obvious. Besides, after the late night drive from Atlanta, he realized he needed some eyelid maintenance as well.

"If we are the terrorists' target of choice, and God help us if we are, I am confident that our security professionals can defend this plant," the CNO said.

You'd better hope they don't have to prove it.

Joma eased the Durango into a long shadowed area created by the two-story building on his right. He reached back with his left hand, turning his body in the driver's seat awkwardly because of the uncomfortable bulletproof vest, and activated a small red toggle switch embedded in a small black box connected to the wooden crates. Turning back around to face the looming nuclear plant to his front, he removed the iPhone 5 battery cover, reached to open the ashtray in the dash, and pulled out the lone lithium-ion battery. Joma inserted the battery, delicately seated the battery cable, and replaced the cover without bothering with the tiny screws. After powering on the cell phone, he waited a few seconds for it to run through its activation sequence, registering itself with cell towers in range. Joma fingered several numbers into his cell and watched as the phone connection was made on the screen, before looking in the rearview mirror to check his work. The LED counter activated and flashed triple zeros for a few seconds before flashing to 2:00 minutes.

1:59

1:58

1:57

As Kolt and the plant's staff headed down the marbled circular stairwell like a herd of stampeding cattle, he knew he was the only person concerned about being attacked by terrorists. His cell phone chirped three times. He froze in midstride, slowing the crowd and forcing them to move around him. A few threw him dirty glares as they passed, then quickly went back to their small talk about how early the morning would come and what they still needed to pick up from the store before getting home. Others were more cordial.

"Have a good night, Mr. Jones."

"Get some sleep. We'll get back at it tomorrow."

Kolt nodded and quickly waved as he ripped his cell from its carrier above his right hip. He swiped in an L shape with his forefinger, providing the correct password to unlock the phone. On the screen, Raptor X had pinged on Hawk's iPhone 5.

That can't be right.

Kolt stared at the number in disbelief, trying to understand how Hawk's cell number had been entered into the Raptor X hunt on the phone Tungsten gave him last night.

Carlos!

Unbeknownst to Kolt, Raptor X had been hunting remotely for Hawk's phone, the distinct fifteen-digit identifier just as it hunted for the terrorist-related numbers since he left Atlanta. Kolt was shocked, though; he refused to believe it. Now alone, he sat down on the stairs to steady his nerves and take a closer look.

Kolt knew it was a shot in the dark. Alex had told him before he left last night that his cell could only run a lite version of Raptor X and offered a quick analogy of the differences. She told Kolt to think of it like hunting a running deer but only being able to open your eyes every other minute. With your eyes open for one minute, you can see the deer, but it keeps running. But you'll have to close your eyes for another minute. You have an idea of where you last saw it but are hoping for another sighting when you reopen your eyes. If you are lucky, the deer will stop running and try to hide for a few minutes so you can hone in on its position.

Kolt got enough out of Alex's lesson to understand that it wasn't simple, that it wasn't a procedure: it was a hunt.

He decided to tap the geolocate button, which, if it worked, would bounce off the local cell towers and tell him exactly where Hawk's cell phone was. But, unlike the more robust Raptor X that used satellites to quickly track Shaft when he was on a singleton mission in the Goshai Valley, Kolt's iPhone could only task Raptor X Lite to remotely hunt for a device by connecting to an Amazon server in Seattle.

Kolt stared at the screen as it gathered cell towers to provide a location of the phone down to a hundred meters. He thought about how quickly he could finish up in the morning with the Yellow Creek staff. How soon after breakfast he could leave the CNO and her colleagues alone and get back in his rental car to focus his attention on Cindy Bird.

The shadowlike blue line crawled slowly from left to right, signaling the phone was still searching.

"Holy shit!" Kolt said. "It's here!"

TWENTY-SEVEN

Joma delicately placed the iPhone 5 on the passenger seat. He ensured the phone line was still open, still transmitting to the receiving timer in the rear seat. This was the exact spot where a simple Google Earth photo showed ample shadow in which to hide, as well as the ability to hold an open call with the help of the 432 registered antennas in the tripoint area of Mississippi, Alabama, and Tennessee. It was the spot where the device in the backseat should be activated. After he activated it, what stood in the way of his achieving the objective of melting the infidel's nuclear plant to the ground and hopefully killing hundreds of thousands of people was very little: just two twelve-foot-high chain-link security fences set roughly twenty-five feet apart and the horizontal fishing-line-size taut wire that would trip an alarm, letting everyone in the plant know that something, or someone, had breached security zone 18.

Joma had faith that he could easily overcome the fences. As vile as the infidels were, they built strong vehicles, and the SUV would easily smash through the shiny, razor-sharp, circular wire attached to the inside of the fences. Once through, it was imperative that he keep his speed so that he could get past the tall, ugly guard towers, where men with machine guns stood watch. Speed was the key. Despite his bulletproof vest, Joma had no other protection. He had to get past the guard towers quickly.

If only, he started to think, then stopped himself. Joma missed Timothy.

Why had he run away? Joma refused to believe Timothy had betrayed them. While the others were certain that was the case, Joma could not accept it. They had been through too much together. If Timothy were here now, he could have set up a sniper position, as Joma had during their last attack. His supporting fire could occupy the guards in the towers and give Joma that extra bit of time he needed.

Joma shook his head. He was on his own, and, as he told brother Nadal al-Romani, he had accepted his fate.

With nothing left to consider, Joma put the Durango in drive, eased out of the shadows, and turned the wheels slightly to the right, aligning himself perfectly with the fences and the large silver makeup tanks a couple of hundred yards in the distance. He looked at the cell in the passenger seat one more time. The phone line was still open. He then looked in his rearview mirror to ensure the green LED numbers were descending in order.

1:32, 1:31, 1:30, 1:29 . . .

Satisfied all was in order, Joma pressed hard on the gas pedal, flooring it with a loud squeal of the tires as they grabbed the asphalt surface and increased speed.

"*Allah u Akbar, Allah u Akbar!*"

The large volume of gunfire gave Cindy Bird the cover and diversion she needed. Opening the paracord bracelet with her picture-perfect white teeth, she quickly unwound it. She wrapped the ends around each of her hands several times to ensure she had a solid grip and reached over the driver's head, rapidly dropping the paracord in front of his face. She yanked it backward, bringing the back of his head around the side of the driver's-seat headrest. Bird leaned back, raised her strong leg, the one she used to punt footballs with as a kid, and brought her three-inch stiletto heels toward the lower right part of his head, as if she was trying to bust out a windshield or kick in a locked door.

The heel found the fleshy part to the right of the brain stem and below the base of the skull. She maintained violent pressure on the paracord, slowly tearing away the skin below it. She pushed with all her quad strength, jamming the designer heel an easy two inches into the base of the terrorist's skull. She heard the terrorist stop in midscream, certain she had compromised his central nervous system. Certain she had killed the asshole, the son of a bitch that had beaten her silly, she relaxed and waited for his body to go limp as a rag doll.

But Hawk wasn't a born killer like she thought Kolt was. The last time she killed another human being—no, the first time she killed another human being—was during the hit on the office building in Cairo last year. That time, she had little time to react. It was all muscle memory, just like her Delta-operator-training cadre told her it needed to be. And that time, Kolt depended on her tremendously. She couldn't let him down. This time, she had a little more time to first think it over, over a month, in fact. She also had no idea where Kolt was at the moment. So Bird knew this killing was all about her and much more personal. No excuses.

Oh, my!

But the driver, more powerful than she expected him to be at this moment, suddenly shuddered. She knew he certainly was stunned by the penetration into his upper neck. It had taken a full two inches of her heel, this she was certain of.

It obviously wasn't enough to put an end to Hawk's misery.

Holding on as tight as she could to both ends of the paracord, she pulled with all her remaining strength, pushing the heel end of her stiletto deeper.

She felt the man fall forward toward the steering wheel, pulling Hawk's foot from her heel while leaving the heel embedded. Regardless of what had penetrated his upper neck, the terrorist obviously recovered from the initial shock quickly, and he certainly wasn't dead yet.

"NO!" Hawk screamed as she looked directly at the business end of a stainless steel semiauto pistol held high over the terrorist's head. It was wobbling, showing the terrorist was having trouble blindly aiming at the psycho bitch in the backseat.

Two shots rang out.

Hawk slid the olive-green and tactical-tan military-grade paracord back to her from around the terrorist's neck, leaving the heel embedded several inches inside the man's brain.

She then pulled one of the running ends to her until she felt the plastic end. She moved it toward her lips, took a deep breath, and started to blow.

•   •   •

The Yellow Creek security officers in elevated, ballistically protected positions opened fire after seeing the Durango crash through several layers of protective fencing and razor wire. Small arms fire, all .223 caliber bullets fired from Colt-model assault rifles, entered the front fenders and hood, tearing small holes into sections of the heavy-laden SUV engine. The shooters were nervous, but the advanced thermal sights mounted on the top of the rifles' upper receivers ensured they didn't miss often.

Three rounds tore into Joma's 7.62-level IV-rated body armor protecting his vital area. The armor did its job, stopping penetration, but leaving severe blunt trauma on his chest cavity. He had expected this and was well prepared. But the round he couldn't defend against was the one that found his left upper thigh muscle. Barely slowed by the Durango's thin steel doors, the copper bullet sliced his femoral artery in half and exited the underside of his leg. A two-inch-diameter exit wound ensured he began losing blood fast.

But he had already succeeded. He didn't have to ram the truck into the large tanks. He didn't even have to get within a vehicle's distance. One hundred feet was close enough. Farooq had told him more than a month ago that the TNT-packed, vehicle-borne IED would leave a large blast hole in the asphalt drive, but that wouldn't cause a meltdown. What would be critical, and a done deal, is if the blast overpressure buckled the three-eighth-inch-thin metal circular makeup tanks' walls nearby. Once disfigured, gravity and the sheer force of the thousands of gallons of makeup water inside the tanks would buckle the rivets. The tanks would rupture, and water would flow out at 650 gallons a minute. Without the water, in less than an hour, the aluminum fuel assemblies holding the nuclear fuel rods deep inside the reactor's core would overheat. Eventually, melt the container rods. Eventually, create a radiological catastrophe that would impact hundreds of thousands for generations to come.

If the officers had only spotted the vehicle earlier. Maybe taken some shots to flatten the tires, slow it enough to allow others' overlapping cross-fire to finish the job. Or maybe taken out the driver. Anything to prevent the truck from coming within a hundred feet of the large tanks.

Cheers went up inside the command center as the DI 5000 thermal-analytic security cameras slewed to cue, remaining fixed on the smoking Durango.

Officials threw their hands in the air, ecstatic to see the red box locked on the display screen and the heat of their officers' bullets tearing into the vehicle's engine block. Certainly happy at what had just been done there were high fives for everyone. To them, the protective strategy had worked. It was sound. Its effectiveness was something they always argued about but that was difficult to prove short of an actual attack. The truck bomb was stopped; the terrorists had failed.

Kolt knew it was too close, though. He looked at the camera screen closely, then back to the large overhead photo on the wall. Then he looked at the close-to-scale terrain model off to the side. Too close. The VBIED was still too close. If not too close to the tanks, then possibly to everyone in this building.

Kolt bolted through the crash-barred door and exited the central alarm station without saying a word. There was no time to discuss it. No time to evacuate plant employees, or even to make a plant announcement over the PA system to move away from the northeast corner of the protected area and the imminent blast.

Kolt ran past post 7, who was located in a ballistic-steel, V-angled defensive position with his protective mask already donned. Kolt gained the covered stairwell, descended two flights of stairs, and exited, turning down a hallway near the cafeteria. He hadn't passed anyone else by the time he exited the administration building into the courtyard at full gait.

He sprinted toward a thirty-foot-high ballistic enclosure, passing directly underneath, yelling as he ran.

"Cease fire! Cease fire!"

An armed officer inside a ballistic tower at three hundred yards' distance, the one on the northwest corner of the plant, opened up. It was impossible for him to discriminate between friend or foe. Kolt was wearing civilian clothing. He obviously wasn't a security guard. The shooter could at least determine that. All plant employees were drilled in what to do when under attack. They knew to take cover and stay there, something they demonstrated numerous times during their own mock exercise attacks. So, to the armed responder a few football fields away, a man running at full speed across the opened protected area could be nothing but a terrorist.

Bullets kicked up the ground around Kolt's boots as they slapped the asphalt with each long stride. He reached the Durango and grabbed the driver's-side door, yanking it open. The terrorist was still alive. His gray pants were puddled in blood from the exit wound on his left leg. The black body armor was shredded in three different spots, two in the chest and one over the upper belly. His right shoulder was covered in blood. His breathing labored.

What the hell!

"Joma?" Kolt said as soon as he looked at the driver's face.

Kolt reached for the back passenger door and yanked it open. There it was. Where the backseats were before, three simple wooden crates filled the area, each the size of an average microwave oven. Wires protruded from the top of each box and met in the middle. Red duct tape held the wires together as they snaked into a black plastic box. The green LED readout was obvious. The numbers showed 14—fourteen seconds.

Kolt couldn't believe his luck. It had been several seconds since he looked at the timer. The number wasn't changing; it seemed stuck on 14. For some unexplained reason, the VBIED counter had stopped before detonating.

Euphoric about his good luck, Kolt turned his attention to Joma. Kolt knew better than to leave the bomb where it was. Anything could trigger it. He had to move it. Get it out of the protected area. If it ultimately exploded, preventing any negative effects on any safety-shutdown equipment was critical. Besides, Kolt knew that for EOD techs to be successful in disarming the bomb, they would need it much farther away from the nuclear fuel rods inside the reactor and the spent-fuel rods in the spent-fuel pool.

No, the VBIED had to go.

Kolt grabbed Joma by the chest armor with his right hand and pulled the terrorist slightly toward him, leaning over and unbuckling the seat belt. With both hands, Kolt tugged until Joma lost his grip on the steering wheel. Kolt hadn't seen the handcuffs securing his right wrist to the steering column. He grabbed the cuffs and shook them, tugging vigorously, trying to pull them loose. No luck.

Kolt thought about asking Joma for the key. Or even digging into his pockets for them. He quickly figured that wouldn't work. He had one option left.

Kolt grabbed Joma's left arm and left pant leg. He pulled Joma off his seat and let his body collapse to the ground next to driver's-side foot step.

Joma's right arm was still tethered to the steering column, the only part of his body still inside the Durango.

Kolt started to step into the vehicle. He sat in the bloodstained driver's seat and heard a tone of three beeps. Instinctively, he looked into the rearview mirror. The green LED clock now read 13. Somehow, the bomb had reactivated and the timer was ticking down.

"Shit! Shit! Shit!" said Kolt.

Kolt instantly knew he blew it. He was unaware of the dead-man's switch Joma was likely connected to. It must have been inside the seat, the weight of a human controlling the firing sequence. He was severely aggravated at himself for being so sloppy. Nothing he could do but to get the VBIED as far from the tanks as possible.

Kolt turned the key. Nothing. The engine refused to turn over. The smell of radiator fluid mixed with the acrid smell of fresh blood. Kolt threw it in neutral. He stepped out of the Durango and turned to face the front of the vehicle, reaching back in to place his right hand on the wheel. He braced his left hand against the door jam. And he pushed. And pushed. The flat front tires gave Kolt trouble. As did Joma's pooling blood on the street. Kolt's boot treads had no luck in gaining purchase.

The flat tires inched forward slowly. Kolt's leg and back muscles gave every full measure. The vehicle had only moved one, maybe two feet. He looked back at the green LED. He watched it tick through the final seconds. *Five, four, three . . .*

Kolt knew he was finished. Sweat beads dripped from his forehead. But he was surprisingly calm. There was no need to run. Nor was there any point, really. In two seconds, the VBIED would detonate, sending vehicle debris and body parts sky-high and scattering them for a thousand feet in all directions. Worse than Kolt's death would be the destruction of the makeup-water tanks and the hundreds of thousands of deaths that would come from the nuclear meltdown.

Two, one. Kolt gripped the steering wheel tighter. He pushed harder, trying to gain some rolling momentum. Even another foot or two might protect the tanks from the blast. He knew he was still too close. But it was hopeless. He was out of options. The VBIED would detonate, killing dozens at the plant, eventually killing hundreds of thousands.

Kolt closed his eyes. He thought of TJ, his best friend and teammate who had died six months earlier as they wrestled with Amriki outside Andrews Air Force Base as the president approached in Marine One. A flash of Cindy's face came over him. He was clearly disappointed that he was unable to save her. She would certainly be killed now. Kolt said his good-byes in an instant, knowing Joma was heading for hell and wondering if he wasn't himself.

Zero.

Kolt tensed up. He waited another second, certain the bomb was just a moment or two late. Maybe a faulty wire or some other unseen problem that would fix itself momentarily. He was happy for the delay. He thought of heaven and Jesus before the faces of so many teammates killed in action flashed before his eyes.

But still nothing. No massive explosion. And no obvious explanation.

Five seconds, then ten, then fifteen seconds passed. Kolt opened his eyes.

What the fuck?

A dud. It must be. Or had Kolt been had. Not just him, but all the armed security officers at the plant had been duped. This Dodge Durango was a rabbit VBIED. A fake. A similar vehicle to the real one used to draw attention away from the actual bomb.

Kolt reached down to Joma, who was still chained to the steering column. A long shot, but it was all he had now to connect him to Cindy.

He pulled Joma's clean-shaven face close to his.

"Open your eyes!" demanded Kolt.

No response. Joma was barely breathing. He had lost a lot of blood.

Kolt shook him violently. "Wake the fuck up, you son of a bitch!" screamed Kolt. "Where the hell is she? Where is the real bomb?"

A faint grin came over Joma's ashen face. Both eyes opened slightly. Joma coughed. Blood seeped out of the corner of his mouth—he was struggling to stay alive. The emergency sirens began wailing, loud enough to reach five separate counties in a ten-mile radius.

"What's so funny?" demanded Kolt, straining to hear under the booming sirens.

"Brother Timothy, you are here," Joma said. "I knew you would not desert me."

"Joma, where is the bomb?" Kolt said again.

"We tricked them," Joma said. "Nadal put the real bomb with your wife. Allah willing, she will make the sacrifice for all of us."

Kolt heard about every other word, but he had heard enough to snap. He back-fisted Joma across his boney face with his right hand. Shook him hard with his left. Strangely, for a moment Kolt wasn't sure if he was more worried about finding Cindy or about finding the real VBIED.

"Where is the real bomb?"

"It is over," Joma whispered. "Allah has decided."

"Allah don't decide shit, asshole!" Kolt said as he watched what was obviously the final breath exhale from Joma's lungs. Kolt let go. Joma dropped limply back to the ground, half his body still in the driver's doorway.

Kolt froze. His mind raced. Think Kolt. Think. He knew he had been tricked. So far, he'd only stopped the fake bomb. The real one was still out there. Somewhere. Maybe it was about to blow. Kolt needed to find it.

That's it! A second black Dodge Durango. It must be. Joma likely didn't know which of the two was the real bomb or which one was the rabbit. Either would require full commitment to Allah to attack the plant.

Kolt bolted toward the main access facility, darting in and out of the long shadows. Minimal safety lighting was starting to come on as the backup generators kicked in. High mast lights, sixty feet in the air, slowly powered up.

Running left toward the gravel roadway, Kolt hit the paved walkway at full stride. He passed the plant's lighted and flashing LED TARGET ZERO and SAFETY-CONSCIOUS WORK ENVIRONMENT signs on his left. According to the flashing red block numbers, the plant hadn't had a lost-time accident in six years.

Kolt entered the double glass doors, stepped forward to the card swipe, and fumbled with his badge around his neck. C'mon, c'mon.

"Cease fire! Cease fire!" Kolt yelled, to ensure he wasn't fired upon by the security officers in the building.

Kolt swiped his magnetic badge from left to right. It seemed like a lifetime before the audible click was heard, unlocking the turnstiles. Kolt stepped in and pushed the horizontal steel bars forward, baby-stepping along with the turnstile as it opened.

Kolt blew right through the portal monitor that tested for radiation contamination and hit the crash bar on the tinted glass door at full stride.

Seconds later, he was outside the building standing on the edge of the parking lot, near a long line of four-foot-tall, poured concrete blocks that served as security barriers.

Kolt's head quickly swiveled from side to side.

A large crowd full of commotion had gathered. Kolt figured it had to be the standard rallying point for the employees in the event of an on-site emergency. A place to account for everyone. To get a head count and determine who was missing. Kolt figured that at least forty or fifty plant employees were already gathered there.

As Kolt approached the crowd, he saw uniformed men in distinctive tan over tan. He heard them tell everyone to sit down and not move.

It has to be close. Kolt quickly realized that during an attack, this area quickly became the most active and populated spot on the entire property. Moreover, every employee or visitor had to pass this spot coming or going. Where else would the terrorist park a vehicle bomb? This was the perfect place. Kolt jumped on the engine hood of a nearby Ford F-150 and stood to scan the area, searching for the other black Durango. He started on the left, panning to the right, hoping to get lucky and spot the right vehicle.

From only twenty feet away, Kolt noticed a second black Dodge Durango idling quietly in a handicap parking spot. The vehicle running lights were on. Its back windows were tinted dark. But Kolt couldn't make out anyone in the driver's seat through the windshield.

But more obvious was the wheel jam pressed down to just above the tire tread. The fender covered several inches of the tire tread. Kolt looked at the front-end fender gap. It was twice the size. That's it. Had to be. The heavy weight of the bomb in the back of the Durango served to lift the front nose of the vehicle while depressing the rear of the vehicle uncharacteristically low. He couldn't believe his luck.

Kolt sprinted toward the vehicle, entirely oblivious to the danger ahead. If it was the real bomb, they were all dead.

Kolt stopped at the left rear window. He heard an odd whistling sound, sporadic and uneven. It seemed like it was coming from behind the vehicle, or even from inside. He put his hands up to cover the streetlights as he peered through the tinted window and into the backseat.

He saw the same three wooden boxes, the same wires, the same small box with green LED readout. This one was also steadily counting down.

Kolt tried the back door, but it was locked. He turned his back toward the vehicle, raised his right elbow, and crashed it against the window. Safety glass shattered but remained attached to the polymer-tinted laminate. Kolt elbowed it again, and again, the third time resulting in the window's falling into the Durango itself.

As Kolt reached into the window and lifted the door lock, the unmistakable odor of death coupled with filthy body odor exited the now-open window. Kolt winced at the smell as he lifted the door handle. He leaned into the backseat and reached over the wooden crates. He made for the bomb timer and turned it around to read it.

2:47, 2:46, 2:45 . . .

"Shit, shit shit!"

Kolt saw Cindy lying on the floorboard behind the driver's seat. Her wrists were secure with silver-colored handcuffs. The lime-green skirt she was wearing when they met over a month earlier at the coffee shop had ridden up high on her thighs. Her panty hose were torn in several spots, the skirt and her white blouse heavily soiled in blood. Both feet were bare, the left leg still lifted over the back of the driver's bucket seat.

"Hawk!" Kolt yelled.

No answer.

Kolt reached for his former teammate. He pulled. Cindy barely moved. Kolt looked closer. She was strapped to the floorboard. Chains ran under the two front seats. Her scrunched-up skirt and soiled blouse, along with some crimson-colored blood, hid the chrome chains wrapped around her torso to anchor points just under the front seats

"Racer. Please, go. You can't stop it. It's going to blow," Hawk faintly said.

Kolt looked Cindy in the eyes. "I'm not leaving you, Hawk."

Kolt placed his fingers on her neck, feeling for a pulse through her carotid artery. She was barely alive.

"Keep talking, Hawk, keep talking," Kolt said. He looked over the front seats in hopes he might spot a half-empty water bottle or anything he could give the obviously dehydrated Hawk. An aluminum can of Pepsi was in the passenger's-side cup holder. Kolt leaned over and grabbed it.

Kolt caught a glimpse of another body. The driver was lying motionless, leaning over into the passenger seat. Kolt looked more closely. The man's right ear was half gone and bleeding. A skinny heel was jammed into the back of the man's head, just to the right of his brain stem. There was a black and silver Ruger SR9 9mm still in the man's right hand, turned backward, with his thumb, oddly, still inside the trigger well of the two-stage trigger.

Just then, Kolt picked up the smell of gunpowder, turning back to Hawk. He could easily see the blunt trauma on her forehead as he poured a little bit of Pepsi onto her lips. Her left eye was swollen shut. Kolt wiped away the blood running down the side of her face. The hair on the side of her head was moist and matted. It wouldn't be long before she went into shock.

Too much blood in this vehicle. Has to be something more. *Look for the bleeder.*

Kolt ripped Hawk's button-down shirt wide open. The buttons flew. Her left pink bra cup was covered in blood. Blood had run down her stomach, seeping over the angles and into the depressions made by her seven-percent body fat and well-developed ab muscles.

Kolt noticed the bullet hole just above her right breast. It was a classic sunken chest wound. Air oozed in and out with the rhythm of her heart. Kolt knew she was lucky—still only alive because the bullet found her right breast and not her heart. Kolt slapped the palm of his right hand against the wound in a feeble attempt to seal the hole. Her skin was cold, but her blood warm. Kolt could feel the air from Hawk's body continued to seep out in synch with the faint beat of her heart.

Kolt continued to look Cindy over. His eyes locked down on her right upper thigh. More blood. A lot of blood. Kolt made a fist with his left hand and pressed it, knuckle-down, against the entry wound.

Hold pressure. Control the bleeder, or she is done.

Arterial blood squirted upward, past Kolt's fist, spraying him in the mouth and neck.

Kolt spit over the driver's seat.

He looked back toward the bomb's timer.

2:28, 2:27, 2:26 . . .

"Move the bomb away from the plant, Kolt!" pleaded Cindy, whispering in her final woes.

"It's OK. It's too far from the makeup tanks to cause a meltdown," answered Kolt.

"I don't know Kolt," said Cindy. "Are you sure?"

Kolt turned back to Hawk to tell her to shut the hell up. To stop questioning him like a mother hen. But then Hawk stopped blinking. Her eyes had locked open. Her mouth as well. It was the face of death that Kolt was all too familiar with.

"Hang on, Hawk!" yelled Kolt."Hang the fuck on!"

He wanted to give her CPR. He wanted to tear his own shirt off. Rip it into thin strips and stuff it in her chest wound to stop the bleeding. He knew he could help her if he could just get her out of the vehicle and lay her on the ground. He'd have more room to work with. To stop the bleeding and dress her wounds. But the chains prevented that. And they weren't coming off. They had done their job. When Cindy Bird's captors had secured the Master combination lock to the eyebolt in the floorboard, they had wanted her to remain with the vehicle. The chains worked.

The plant's loud public-address system grabbed his attention. It droned out instructions on where to go and listed a set of designated locations. Kolt glanced behind him to yell for help. But he stopped. He saw the plant employees, some local police, and the flashing red and blue lights of what he figured was an ambulance bouncing off the other vehicles in the parking lot. They were mustered only about forty-five feet from him. They were too close. And there were more now than when he first arrived on the scene. At least a hundred or so. Kolt couldn't be sure.

"Open your eyes, Hawk," Kolt said, trying to maintain his composure as much as possible. "Stay with me, Hawk!"

Kolt did know that when the bomb blew, Kolt and Hawk wouldn't be the only two victims of the enormous blast. He had seen enough bomb craters and carnage left behind after al Qaeda vehicle bombs were detonated in Iraq.

And then, what might have been Cindy Bird's last breath provided the key piece of information that just might save two hundred thousand innocent Americans.

"Kolt, air bottles. Small ones," Hawk said as she closed her eyes, falling into unconsciousness.

TWENTY-EIGHT

Kolt thought about it. Hawk was definitely implying that the terrorists went into the storm drain. *Why?* There was no water in those drains this time of year. Moreover, they wouldn't need supplemental oxygen tanks like scuba gear—self-contained breathing apparatuses. So why lug around scuba gear if there was no water in the underground storm drains? Were they being overly cautious? Kolt dismissed that at once. They weren't worried about surviving the attack. He thought about it some more. Hawk had said that the waterways and the spent-fuel pools in a power plant were not connected.

No, a terrorist wouldn't need underwater breathing support to melt-down the land-locked Yellow Creek from the parking lot. Some other power plants or critical infrastructure in the United States, maybe. Hydro-electric dams, for sure—even some chemical plants located on major water-ways. But scuba at Yellow Creek?

Kolt recalled the conversation with Cindy at the café and the napkin she doodled on. She was giving him a crash course in the operation of a pressurized water reactor. Could that be it? Cindy mentioned that all plants have large pools of water that store the spent nuclear fuel. Fuel that has al-ready been used inside the main reactor and can no longer create electricity efficiently. She said this large pool holds the spent fuel rods for years to allow them to cool over time.

Think, Kolt, think! You gotta decide!

It was the hardest decision of his life. He knew it, and he had less than a minute to make it. Likely not enough time.

Hawk or the nuke cell? Save a Delta mate or save tens of thousands of innocent Americans sleeping in their homes tonight, unaware that al Qaeda has struck again on U.S. soil.

"Damn it, Racer!" Kolt barked. "Think, you son of a bitch. Think!"

Then Kolt remembered the turned-over Pepsi can, most of its contents spilled on the floorboard.

That's it; that's my out.

The aluminum can wasn't the entire solution, but it was a good first step. Kolt knew that if he released the pressure from Hawk's major arterial bleeder, she was a goner. But he had to do something, or the bomb would take a lot more people out than just the two of them.

Kolt noticed the paracord and whistle in Hawk's right hand. He pulled it from her and quickly wrapped it around her upper right leg, pushing it as high as he could toward her blood-soiled crotch to get the pressure between the bleeder and her heart.

Kolt noticed Hawk barely flinched. *She's alive, but definitely going into shock!*

Satisfied he had the paracord as high on her thigh as possible, Kolt tied an overhand knot, cinching it down as hard as he could, holding one running end in his teeth to maintain tension while routing the other end to finish the square knot.

Kolt didn't waste time assessing if it worked or not. He reached for the Pepsi can with his left hand and set it on the cloth seat. He wiped Cindy's blood from his hands on the seat before continuing. Yanking his pocket-knife out and thumbing the blade open, he jammed it into the can. Forced to use both hands, he cut an odd rectangle and triangular shape in the side of the can, wiggling and pulling at the edges to free it from the can. With the small piece in his hand now, he folded two edges over, then one more fold, leaving him with a narrow piece of aluminum with a point end about a quarter inch wide.

Kolt dropped his knees onto the floorboard and found the Master combination lock under the driver's seat. Holding the lock in his left hand, he inserted the folded piece of aluminum into the narrow space where the

U-shaped steel shackle enters the stainless steel outer case of the lock. He pushed down with the aluminum pick slightly and tugged on the shackle. No luck. His fingers were still sticky with Hawk's blood and were making it difficult for him to manipulate his field-expedient lock pick. He needed a light but solid touch.

Kolt wiped his hands vigorously on his pant legs, ensuring he had found a dry spot to clean the blood from his fingers. Satisfied, he went back to the lock and tried a second time.

This time it worked. The shackle released from the case, and Kolt frantically pulled the chain from the eyebolt secured to the floor. He pulled it from around Hawk's handcuffed wrists, finally freeing her from her certain tomb. He looked at the LED timer attached to the bomb.

00:56, 00:55, 00:54 . . .

Kolt reached under both of Hawk's arms, secured a good hold on her armpits, and pulled her from her seat and out into the parking lot. He lifted her up just as a new groom carries his bride. He turned, spotted the source of red and blue lights, and took off for the ambulance.

Weaving through several parked cars, Kolt moved toward the first two paramedics he could see.

"Medic! Medic!" Kolt yelled.

The two paramedics turned to see Kolt carrying Hawk. Their eyes went wide, and they came over to help right away. Kolt laid Hawk on the hard asphalt.

"She is critical," Kolt said calmly. "Sunken chest wound, right side, major arterial bleeder, right leg."

The paramedics called for another medic to bring the oxygen and stretcher from the ambulance.

Kolt kneeled down next to Hawk, placing his hand over her chest to control the air escaping from the wound. He knew he couldn't stay long, but something was freezing him in place. Something personal, for sure. He vapor-locked for a moment, experienced vivid visions of TJ lying in the parking lot behind the long tractor-trailer near Andrews Air Force Base, and shivered at the thought of his longtime buddy Josh Timble dying in his arms.

"Sir, we'll take her from here," the paramedic said. "Are you hurt, sir?"

"No, no, I'm fine. Do what you can for her," Kolt said. "She's a Delta operator . . . a true hero," he said, his voice catching.

The paramedics looked at him as if he had a head wound.

Kolt turned his attention back to the black Durango sitting ominously only four or five car lengths away. He jumped to his feet and sprinted for the Durango, weaving back through the cars in the way.

Kolt opened the driver's-side door and pulled the terrorist's body from the car. The Ruger fell out and bounced off the asphalt. Kolt picked up the pistol and slid it into his waistband near his appendix. He bent over and patted the terrorist's two front pant pockets, looking for the keys. He jumped in the driver's seat and frantically reached for the ignition area on the dash, praying his hands would find the keys still in the ignition. They were.

The Durango turned over easily, providing a short moment of relief to Kolt. Kolt placed the gearshift in reverse and turned around to see through the back window to ensure he had a clear path of travel. Just as he stepped on the gas, he looked at the LED counter.

00:32, 00:31, 00:30 . . .

Steering with his left hand and still turned to navigate through the back window, Kolt gunned it, burning rubber and letting everyone in the area know that there was something seriously wrong. Kolt was headed directly for the intake canal, the long, narrow body of water that pulls fresh water into the power plant to cool the reactor fuel and to produce steam to turn the turbine generators.

Kolt dodged a few cars, having to touch the brakes twice, before he was about two hundred and fifty yards away, at the back end of the main parking lot. He noticed a long row of poured concrete blocks that were four feet high and five feet wide and maneuvered the Durango twenty yards behind them.

He threw it in park, opened the driver's-side door, and jumped out of the Durango. He didn't look back as he ran for the protection of the concrete blocks. He knew he was inside the kill zone of the imminent blast, and that he would certainly suffer major eardrum damage from the overpressure of the massive explosion. But if he survived this mission, he could get a hearing aide. What he desperately wanted to avoid was eating frag from the Durango.

Kolt reached the blocks at a dead sprint and, without breaking stride, jumped on top, took two steps, and leaped off the other side, rolling his body forward in a somersault before coming to a stop on his back and looking into the star-filled night sky. If nothing else, he may just be able to see a flying engine block soaring toward him.

This won't hurt. This won't hurt. Fuck m—

Kolt's body first sank, then rose from the ground as the force of the pressure wave from the explosion passed by. His chest cavity vibrated with such force that he wondered if every rib was broken. He pulled his shirt up to cover his mouth, but it wasn't enough to filter the thick mix of smoke and flying dirt that made up the massive smoke plume. Unable to see if any major pieces of debris were heading his way, he rolled over to his belly and tried to cough his lungs clean.

Kolt blinked several times and shook his head. His ears were ringing, and every nerve in his body was crying for attention. It took another minute before he was able to get back to his feet. He stood, looked down, and inventoried his body from his chest down to his boots. He ran his hand over his shaved head, feeling the layer of dirt that had settled. No blood. He ran his hands down the front of his chest, feeling the semiauto pistol he had taken from the dead driver, then bent over to continue down his pants. Still no blood. He felt for his wallet—creds were still with him.

Holy crap, I'm frickin' good to go!

The blast was violent and had created a wicked-looking mess of metal shards. Still, given that he survived this close to ground zero, he was pretty confident everyone else had. If anything, Kolt had hoped the blast would quiet the loud emergency siren.

The plant's standard taped PA announcement pulled him back to what he knew needed to be done.

"CODE RED, CODE RED. INTRUDERS HALT. DEADLY FORCE AUTHORIZED."

The fight wasn't over. Kolt knew it, and he knew the terrorists knew it. First, he had identified the rabbit VBIED in the Durango Joma was driving, then the real vehicle bomb had safely been detonated away from the vital plant equipment. But Kolt knew the rest of the terrorists were still unaccounted for. Two were dead, but there had to be more. He knew they would have planned something more complex than simply one vehicle bomb and a diversion bomb.

And then he remembered the hole in the bottom of the Durango, just behind Hawk's rear seat.

"Shit!" Kolt said. "The underground pathways."

Kolt took off at a dead sprint back to the second black Durango's original parking spot. Well, he meant to. His first few steps were more like a drunk exiting a bar at closing time. He slowed his pace and focused on the mechanics of putting one foot in front of the other. The blast might have ruptured an eardrum and fucked up his balance. As he ran, he hoped like hell that the vehicles were the sum total of the terrorists' plan, that the nuke plot had been thwarted. That there was no penetration of Yellow Creek's protected area or, worse, the vital area where the nuclear fuel was located.

Kolt picked up speed, regaining his sense of balance. *This is more like it.* He closed the distance at a rapid pace, spying several squad cars parked near the main access facility. Their blue dome lights were spinning, illuminating the area and parked vehicles around them.

This place is like Fort Knox. It would take a battalion of Marines to get in.

Kolt could see the dead terrorist lying ahead, in the same contorted position that Kolt had left him in. Kolt slowed, taking it all in, assessing the situation.

The dead terrorist's head was bent at a sharp angle on a neck that might be broken. He was facedown in a large puddle of blood. The weapon, the pumps that had penetrated the lower portion of his cranium with every bit of their three-inch heels, sat just a few feet away.

Kolt reached down to pick up the high heel and noticed the large orange and rust-colored cast iron manhole cover sitting off kilter at the top of its circular drainage hole. Kolt dropped the pump and moved to the manhole cover, reaching down and grabbing it with both hands. It was heavy, and Kolt struggled a bit but was able to slide it out of the way to reveal the vertical line in the catch basin.

Kolt dropped to his knees and leaned over the hole, looking down past the rusted ladder rungs secured to the side of the basin and into total darkness. He pulled out the Ruger SR9, checked to ensure he had one in the pipe, and then pulled his cell off his hip. He thumbed the screen and pulled up the flashlight app on his iPhone and tapped it. Moving to his belly and over the open basin, he aimed the pistol and the light into the hole. It was fairly deep, maybe ten to fifteen feet.

Kolt's stomach hollowed out. Was there more to the attack? He needed to know. He turned around and dropped both legs into the basin, finding the ladder rungs with his feet. He secured his phone and descended the ladder with one hand, keeping the pistol at a low ready. At the bottom, he turned the flashlight back on. The horizontal pipe was definitely big enough for a human to crawl through, with plenty of freeboard and maybe six inches of water at the bottom.

As Kolt stooped down to get a better look, his knee came down on something hard. He winced in pain and turned the light toward the bottom.

Crow bar!

Kolt's stomach lurched. He knew immediately what he was facing. The nuke plot was more than just two vehicle bombs. The terrorists weren't settling for simple terrorism on this one. Cherokee was probably only a test. They'd be watching for how America responded, what security features were in place, what would be modified in the attack's wake, what local law enforcement would do, and whether the president activated the National Guard. At Cherokee, terrorism was the simple goal.

At Yellow Creek, it was so much more: the goal was radiological sabotage and the indiscriminate killing of thousands of people, who still had no idea that the second nuke plot by al Qaeda operatives had come to their hometown. Residents within a ten-mile radius would likely be awake by now. The wailing sirens reached that far and were too annoying to ignore. After waking up, they would be waiting for a phone call, remaining in their homes, closing all windows, doors, and sources of outside air. But if Kolt didn't stop the attack, folks inside the ten-mile radius from the power plant would have a ton to worry about.

Instantly, Kolt recalled again what Hawk had said about air bottles and small tanks.

That's it! The pool! Those bastards are going after the spent-fuel pool!

Kolt stowed his pistol and cell before frantically climbing the ladder rungs and crawling out of the catch basin.

Now on his feet, he looked to enter the protected area through the main entrance facility. His site-issued badge provided access up to the vital area of the power block, but he would be unable to enter the radiological controlled area. From there he would have to figure out how to get through the magnetically locked high-security doors when he got to them. Kolt instinctively tapped his chest, looking for his site-access picture badge. Nothing.

Kolt looked at the ground around his feet, then turned fast to look at the route he had taken. No sign of it. He jumped back over to the catch basin and looked back into the hole. It was too dark to see if he had dropped it in there or not.

You're wasting time here, Kolt!

Kolt had to decide. Did he really need to be a damn hero again? Did he really need to enter the power block? Hell, Yellow Creek has a sound protective strategy. They have sufficient defense in depth to thwart any attack. They have a lot of guns all around the outside perimeter, all protected by elevated bullet-resistant enclosures. Moreover, inside the buildings, more armed responders waited for any adversary attempting to enter and reach vital plant equipment.

They have a shit ton of guns here!

Kolt arched his back and drew in a deep breath. Why not just let the normal armed response handle it? Call it an op, let the cops help if they can. The popo are swarming all over the place. Yellow Creek is good to go. They will survive.

Shit, Kolt, just walk over to the ambulance and check on Hawk's status.

Kolt turned to look back toward the flashing ambulance lights, to where he had carried Hawk and turned her over to the paramedics. They were just as much heroes as the armed officers inside. Everyone had a part to play. It was a team effort.

Kolt heard the PA announcement again. "CODE RED, CODE RED. INTRUDERS HALT. DEADLY FORCE AUTHORIZED," the only interruption to the incredibly annoying and loud wail of the emergency siren.

Hawk's last words came back to him again. "Air bottles. Small ones." Yes, that's what she said. He was sure of it. That's exactly what she whispered from inside the Durango.

Son of a bitch! Those bastards are going to come up from the underground and get in behind the security force. *What if the highly trained armed officers don't detect the terrorists before they reach the spent-fuel pool?*

Aww, hell!

The decision had been made. Fortune favors the bold!

TWENTY-NINE

Kolt took off for the breach in the fence made by Joma and his rabbit VBIED. He sprinted past the police officers and gathering crowd of plant employees, turned left beyond a tan-colored two-story sheet metal building, and saw the breach point. The fence had been crushed under the weight of the vehicle. If nothing else, Joma had at least created a positive breach in the protected area perimeter.

Kolt considered pulling out the Ruger but quickly reconsidered. He knew that would be the quickest way to get stitched by a responder in a tower position.

I'm not shooting a dang security officer out here. Think!

Kolt instinctively reached to his rear pocket and pulled out his credentials. He opened the black leather folder to expose his shiny gold badge, the one marking him as a federal agent with the U.S. Department of Energy. Sure, it was the shallowest cover imaginable and only meant to protect his true identity while he was at Yellow Creek.

It was fake as hell, but nobody besides Kolt knew the real deal.

Kolt raised the badge high in the air and took off at a dead sprint. He hit the first fence at full stride, keeping his knees pumping high to prevent tripping over the razor wire and intrusion-detection wire that were obviously entangled in the fencing. No response.

Kolt continued to the second, most inner fence, keeping the badge high in the air for all to see. Off to his left, out of the corner of his eye, the still-smoking black Durango sat on what looked like four flat tires. Joma's body would be nearby, but he didn't care to confirm it.

And, as before, when he made his way from the power block to the Durango, the distinct sound of supersonic .223 rounds, mixed with the wailing emergency sirens, cracked as they passed over his head. Other bullets skipped off the tarmac closer to his feet. Kolt dropped his arm, the badge obviously not fooling anybody, and increased his speed by pumping both arms in tandem with his legs. Kolt fully expected to take a through and through with each stride he took.

Kolt hit the revolving glass door leading into the four-story administration building at full speed, bouncing off the glass as it slowly rotated around. As soon as it opened to the inside, Kolt dove to the freshly mopped floor and scrambled behind the leather couch in the visitors' waiting area. He sat up, back to the couch, desperately trying to catch his breath and amazed he covered the distance without as much as a single flesh wound.

He waited about twenty seconds before he rolled to his knees and stood up. He paused to get his bearings, not wanting to head in the wrong direction, and looked to the hallway ahead of him.

Kolt drew the Ruger from the appendix area of his pants—how he wished he had secured another mag or two from the dead terrorist—then headed down the hallway toward the turbine building.

Entering through the unlocked red fire door, he noticed the posting requiring hearing protection from that point forward. As Kolt entered, he could hear the turbines whining as the plant obviously had not been scrammed yet. As much as the noise was irritating, he knew it would provide him some cover as he continued across the turbine deck toward the fuel-handling building.

Kolt crossed to the other side of the turbine deck, pistol at the low ready, then moved another rough two hundred feet, passing an arm's length from the two giant light-green turbines before eyeing the light-blue door he needed. Beyond that door, he recalled, was the quickest way.

Kolt stopped just short of the door, contemplating whether he should ease through it or go dynamic. Uncertain if an armed responder was on the other side or not, he knew the closer he moved to the vital equipment required for safe shutdown the more likely he was to have trouble with armed officers. And the ones outside would no doubt be doing their damnedest to alert everyone inside.

Kolt yanked the fire door open and sprinted to the first piece of cover he could see: a concrete column just seven or eight feet away. It wasn't pretty, but it would absorb bullets, for sure.

The first burst of .223 impacted the corner of the concrete column just as Kolt was sliding in behind it. Concrete chips peppered the area, leaving a small dust cloud floating in the air.

Shit! That was close.

"Cease fire! Cease fire!" Kolt yelled from behind the pillar.

The officer didn't comply; instead, he unloaded what must have been the rest of his thirty-round magazine. More chunks of the concrete broke away with each bullet's impact as Kolt turned away and covered his eyes with his left forearm. Kolt planned to wait for a lull in fire, when the officer would be reloading, but a ricochet found the meaty portion of his upper left shoulder, stamping a through and through that hurt like a bitch. A lull in fire.

"Dude. Cease fucking fire!" Kolt yelled. "I'm hit!"

"What's the running password?" the officer yelled, his voice muffled by the air filters and positively sealed gas mask.

Running password? How the hell . . .

Kolt knew a standard running password was a single word, something that could be remembered easily and recalled when things got a little crazy, like now. Usually they are well-known words like colors, or states, or even models of cars. Unfortunately, such passwords are changed every twelve hours, which meant whatever Kolt said would be a wild-ass guess.

"Chevrolet!" Kolt yelled. "Chevrolet!" Kolt hoped to either get lucky or maybe prompt the officer to think the guy behind the concrete pillar was close enough and maybe had just forgotten the password of the day. Any password with conviction, even a fake one, and the guy just might buy it.

"Wrong, sucker!" the muffled voice responded before letting loose another half-dozen .223 rounds toward Kolt's hiding position. "Drop your weapon and show yourself!"

Kolt pulled the pistol from his pants and slid it out into the open floor, hoping it would calm the officer by showing him he would not be armed once he stepped from behind cover. Kolt then yanked his creds out of his back pocket, put his hands up, stepped from around the concrete corner, and walked toward the man with his creds out, badge visible, and holding his wounded left shoulder.

"Officer, I'm a federal agent," Kolt said, continuing to close the distance. "How about pointing that rifle in a different direction?"

Kolt noticed the rifle wobbling, the muzzle drawing large figure 8s in the air, heavy in the stocky officer's hands. He watched the officer pull his black protective mask up off his face and rest it higher on his forehead, exposing his entire face. He was certainly scared shitless, and breathing extremely hard, two data points Kolt knew he needed to mind or he was going to be tasting lead in an instant.

"On your face, buddy!" the officer ordered. "Lay down!"

Kolt immediately dropped his hands and went to his knees. He placed his opened creds' case with his badge facing up on the floor next to him, hoping the officer would take the bait.

The officer came out from behind his V-wedge ballistic defensive position and cautiously moved toward the prone Kolt. Kolt had turned his face toward the officer, first seeing his fairly new tan Rocky assault boots, then working his eyes up the unbloused battleship-gray pants, past the man's black-mesh tactical vest and the obvious access badge at chest level hanging on a yellow lanyard. Kolt watched him sling his rifle behind his back. The officer stopped for a moment and struggled to slip the stowed handcuffs from the black pouch on his duty belt.

Kolt picked up on the officer's rifle falling off his shoulder, still hanging by the sling and sliding back toward his front as he leaned over to reach for Kolt's wrists.

In an instant, just at the point where the officer touched Kolt's wrist, Kolt launched.

He immediately rolled over, pinning the muzzle of the rifle under his body weight and forcing the officer to move closer to him as the sling controlled his momentum. In a half second, the two were chest to chest, mano a mano. Not a good place to be with Kolt Raynor.

Feeling the officer resist, pulling himself up and away, Kolt released the pressure off the rifle, simultaneously slipping in a tight ankle pick while controlling the officer's sleeve with his other hand. The officer continued his momentum up as Kolt yanked the right ankle off the gray-painted floor, sending the officer hard to his back.

Maintaining the sleeve grip and thus elbow control, Kolt palmed the dirty floor to raise his rear end up just enough to swing his left leg around the officer's raised left arm, letting his leg slam down over the officer's chest. Kolt slid his left hand a few inches up the controlled forearm and then grabbed the wrist with his right hand, rotating it clockwise to ensure the officer's thumb was pointing directly at Kolt's boots and that the elbow joint would lock.

Kolt leaned backward, maintaining leg pressure on the officer's chest and stomach, and completed the arm bar by bringing the controlled arm to his chest. The officer yelled out, obviously feeling the severe pain and anticipating having his arm broken. But Kolt simply held pressure, letting the officer scream out, and grabbed the handcuffs lying on the floor nearby.

With one hand, Kolt opened one cuff and slapped it on the controlled wrist, squeezing the metal ends together, ensuring they locked. Kolt pushed to a knee, eyed the pipe to his rear, and dragged the officer like a fresh trophy buck seven or eight feet before cuffing him to a silver conduit the circumference of a convenience-store energy shot.

The officer was breathing extremely hard, certainly not wanting any more of Kolt.

"Don't kill me, man!" the officer pleaded.

"Chill out, brother. I'm here to help," Kolt said as he cleverly unclipped the front sling swivel from the black rifle and unsnapped the officer's vital area–access badge from the neck lanyard, pulling both critical items of interest away from the supine officer.

Kolt looked at the photo badge for a second before shoving it in his front pant pocket. He then thumbed the mag-release button, dropped the mag, eyed the remaining bullets, and slipped the partial mag in his left rear pocket. The movement sent a sharp pain through his shoulder. Walking back toward the shot-up pillar, Kolt grabbed his creds and the Ruger and walked back to the tethered officer.

"Officer Polamalu? Am I pronouncing that correctly?" Kolt asked.

"Listen, I can't release you just yet, but I'll trade you this pistol for your fresh mags."

"I thought you were one of them," the officer said as he handed Kolt the only fresh thirty-round magazine he hadn't dumped yet.

"No worries. Aiming is a bitch when it's for real, isn't it?" Kolt said. "That should have been a chip shot for you at that range."

"Sorry about that," Officer Polamalu said, almost with a look of shock on his face.

"Look, man, have you seen anyone? Any of the attackers?"

"No, no, you were the first person I fi'"—

"Control room. Which way?" Kolt said, letting the officer know he was in a big hurry and didn't know exactly where he was.

"It's that way," the officer said, pointing behind Kolt and down a long, wide hallway.

"Where did you come from?" Kolt asks. "Where is the pool?"

"I came through the orange and blue door that way. But I was redirected to move here from the pool floor," the officer said, pointing to Kolt's right. "Maybe five minutes, tops."

Shit, gotta decide, control room or spent-fuel pool. Wasting time here.

"Did you look down into the pool?" Kolt asked, hoping Officer Polamalu could provide some guy-on-the-ground information, maybe a hint, or even a hunch.

"No, we never do!" the officer answered, obviously puzzled by the question.

Kolt laid the pistol on the floor a few feet from Officer Polamalu and turned to flow through the auxiliary building. After a series of turns that threatened to throw Kolt off course, he recognized a bright orange door with a light blue vertical stripe. Posted on the door was a sign in magenta and yellow, warning personnel that, beyond the door, was a "High Rad Area" requiring dosimetry to enter. Kolt knew that, although he was risking taking a dose of radiation if he entered the door, he risked a lot more by hastily pieing the open doors and cursorily clearing the corners. But, in this situation, he also knew that speed was security, particularly since he was losing a lot of blood and leaving a trail in his wake. He just had to accept the radiation risk or change his mind and head for the control room.

It was just a guess as to where the terrorists were now. They could be in front of the main control panel, dead plant operators scattered, setting explosive charges on the console. Kolt knew the only information he had to work with was what Hawk shared. He hadn't seen it with his own eyes, but Hawk said she did. Maybe she was delirious? She had lost a good amount of blood, was dehydrated from over a month of captivity, and was on the verge of going into shock. It wasn't too late to turn back, head to the control room. Maybe pick up Officer Polamalu en route, increase the odds, roll as a pair. If that's what Kolt's gut instinct told him, he would certainly audible the play.

Small bottles, air tanks . . . trust the guy on the ground.

At the door's card reader, Kolt swiped Officer Polamalu's access badge and waited for the red light to turn to green. A long second later, there was a click, signaling that the door's balanced magnetic switch successfully released. Kolt pulled the heavy door to him, stepped inside, and in three strides reached the radiological-controlled-area turnstiles, which he jumped. He kept on running through the radiation-portal monitors, which alarmed, and made for the blue double doors marked HIGH-RAD-FUEL-HANDLING BUILDING.

Swiping the badge again, Kolt stepped onto the lower floor. Years of training made his clearing procedure automatic and swift. *So far, so good.* Having cleared the area on his level, he raised his rifle to clear high, searching for targets.

C'mon, c'mon, where are they?

Now, just five feet inside the double doors, face-to-face with a massive three-story-high concrete wall, Kolt caught the first sign of movement. It was just beyond the bright yellow guardrail at the very top. Easing his rifle up, he tucked the stock against his right cheek, naturally centering the Trijicon's red dot. Thumbing the selector switch to fire, he squeezed his finger to take up the slack in the trigger.

Too late.

Damn!

Kolt lowered his rifle and quickly turned to the right and sprinted to the elevator door. His lungs were heaving by the time he reached it, and spots flashed before his eyes. He kicked off his black leather Doc Martens as he pulled out his creds and pushed the open button. The silver doors slid open as the elevator bell rang. Kolt set his boots inside the elevator, dress right, dress, and toes facing out. He then laid his creds down in front of the boots and pushed the button for the pool deck before stepping back out.

Kolt raced for the stairwell door. He knew he was running out of time. They all were.

He ignored all his training. The time for sound, close-quarter battle fundamentals was long gone. This was charge-of-the-fucking-light-brigade time. Throwing caution to wind, he took the stairs three at a time, a sudden thirst and numbing of his left arm growing more noticeable with each step. Blood loss was going to bring him down if he didn't hurry.

Kolt reached the stairwell door, huffing for breath. He gulped down some air and pushed the crash bar, opening the door enough to step through. The first thing that hit him was the odd smell, like a mix of chlorine and engine oil. It was coming from the massive pool of water used to cool the spent fusion rods. He didn't gag, but he came close. He looked to his left and saw a five-foot-tall piece of corner ballistic steel with a sliding gun port half-opened. On his right was the yellow guardrail he had seen from below.

Across the pool deck, an armed security officer stood with his back to Kolt in front of the open elevator door. He wore the same tan boots and black-over-tan dress as Officer Polamalu and was also armed with a rifle. This created a problem for Kolt. If the guy was in normal civilian clothing, he'd have lit him up, figuring he had to be one of the terrorists who'd taken Kolt's bait. But the Yellow Creek security officer uniform gave Kolt pause. He knew he wasn't going to kill another American. No, the burden was on Kolt to prove to the armed officers that *he* wasn't a terrorist, *not* the other way around. He had to discriminate.

"Hey, federal agent. Don't shoot!" Kolt yelled. That's when he noticed a pile of shoes, some odd gear, and a brown zippered bag just on the edge of the pool. A large puddle of water had settled on the surface nearby, at the pool's edge.

Shit! Am I too late? They're in the pool already.

The guard turned, raising what looked like an AK-47.

Terrorist!

"Allah u Akbar!"

There was no mistaking that running password! With no time to aim,

Kolt sprayed a couple of rounds toward the terrorist, preventing him from getting a shot off, while lunging for the safety of the corner steel. The ballistic position was slightly rusted at the connections and bolted areas, most likely a legacy position from an old protective strategy but never removed.

Kolt reached up to close the sliding port another inch or so as 7.62 mm rounds impacted all around it. The metal reverberated with each hit, adding to the ringing in his ears from the earlier explosion. Several bullets tore through the opening and punctured the thin-metal-skin stairwell door to his rear. Kolt ducked, then slid the opening closed. A ricochet from an AK-47 round could be lethal.

He leaned over to his right and extended his rifle muzzle slightly around the corner of the barrier. Kolt didn't have a lot of ammo to burn. He was down to less than a full mag now.

Kolt peeked and fired three rapid rounds. He exposed himself just long enough to see the terrorist behind his own piece of ballistic cover. They exchanged fire several more times, two and three rounds at a time, neither getting the better of the other.

Gotta do something, Kolt. Plan A ain't working.

Kolt continued the cat and mouse until his magazine ran dry. He dropped it, pulled the partial spare from his back pocket, press-checked it for the number of rounds remaining, which he figured to be no more than twelve, and then inserted it. He slapped the bolt release to load the top round and then paused to consider just what the hell to do next. He was wounded, terrorists were in the water pool, and time was running out. He took a breath, taking in the bitter smell of sawdust, nitroglycerin, and graphite that hung heavy in the air.

The terrorist snapped off two rounds and then a five-round burst, convincing Kolt that the terrorist was packing a lot more ammo than he was. This was it, then. The terrorist in the pool must be close to planting his explosives. He's probably already said his good-byes and is planning on a one-way trip. Safely back home for these terrorists meant moving on to the next plane of existence.

Fucking martyrdom in swim trunks.

Kolt blinked and shook his head. He was sitting, not acting. He shifted his legs underneath him and focused. A light above the stairwell door had been shot out. Without the light, the area he was in darkened significantly and shadows extended farther across the deck.

Kolt looked left and spied three more lights along the wall past the yellow guardrails. He quickly turned back to the right, looking around the corner to see another three lights on the far wall beyond the pool.

Six lights, twelve rounds. Kolt had his plan B, assuming he could determine his hold-off with a round or two using Officer Palomalu's rifle. Kolt turned back left, raised the rifle, and placed the red dot center mass of the first light, raised it roughly eight inches, and broke the trigger.

THIRTY

Spent-Fuel Deck, Yellow Creek

Hit!

He moved to the next light, farther down and center of the wall.

Hit.

The terrorist screamed something Kolt couldn't understand and snapped off another three-round burst. Kolt ducked, then lined up on the farthest light, just to the right of the elevator doors. Six, maybe seven inches hold-off and broke the shot.

Miss! Shot high.

Shit! Breathe, Kolt. Breathe!

Five inches hold off. Blading his body to prevent the terrorist from changing his plans again, Kolt steadied the rifle against the side of the corner steel. He broke the shot.

Hit! The left side was now in darkness.

Kolt turned quickly to service the lights on the far wall of the pool.

He remembered the holds, taking all three lights out. It was now much darker, with the only two lights remaining just behind the terrorist's steel position. Kolt pressed the mag release and yanked the mag out of his rifle. Too dark to see down in the mag, he tried to stick his forefinger inside the mag to get a good round count. No luck. Kolt quickly stripped the brass from the mag, careful not to drop any on the floor. One, two. Only two rounds remaining in the mag, with one in the pipe still. Three rounds. Three rounds to either take the two lights or try to take the terrorist.

Safely concealed by the dark side of the pool deck, Kolt noticed the terrorist was entirely backlit by the lights. If Kolt was patient, the terrorist would likely reveal himself, allowing Kolt to cut him down with a single shot to the cranium vault. However, killing him wouldn't stop the diver. Killing him wouldn't stop the spent-fuel wall from being breached, creating a massive hole that would cause the inventory, just over 270,000 gallons of cooling water, to drain faster than the spray lines could replace it. Once the water drained enough to expose the top of the nuclear fuel assemblies, the loss of water coolant would cause the fuel to overheat and melt, resulting in a major local zircalloy fire, and would cause a massive release of radiation to the atmosphere. The fire, after melting down the aluminum fuel assemblies containing fuel rods with millions of uranium dioxide fuel pellets, would not be able to be contained. It would snake quickly through the non-airtight doors, contaminate the hallways, and take the path of least resistance until it reached the open air, killing in short order tens of thousands of citizens in and around the area. Anyone—man, woman, or child—anywhere in the downwind-plum hazard path, would eventually die from a lethal dose of invisible radiation.

No time to wait. Gotta stop the crow in the pool.

Kolt abandoned the idea of trying to tag the terrorist. There just wasn't time to wait him out. He opted to take his vision instead. Kolt knew if he could only take all the lightbulbs, it would be as dark as three feet up a bull's ass, giving him the cloak he needed to take a swim. The terrorist wouldn't see him. Sure, he might hear him jump in the pool, but he risked killing his own man if he fired blindly into the water.

Kolt indexed on the light above and to the right of the terrorist's steel-protected position. He took a deep breath, exhaled halfway, and pressed the trigger.

Shit! Misfire! Not now.

Muscle memory took over as Kolt slapped up on the bottom of the magazine, two-fingered the charging handle. He sensed rather than saw the ejector grab the misfired round and eject it from the port. A glint showed the round tumbling through the air to skitter across the pool-deck floor.

The terrorist yelled more unintelligible threats and sprayed at least ten rounds in Kolt's direction.

"Easy, Sunshine, I'm coming," Kolt said, releasing the charging handle and tapping the forward assist on the right side of the rifle. Satisfied, he re-acquired his bright four-inch target.

Two rounds, two lights to go.

Kolt aimed, debating his hold off for several seconds, before breaking the shot.

Hit!

With a single 5.56 mm bullet standing between him and the possibility of saving upward of two hundred thousand people, Kolt transitioned to the last light, just above and to the right of the terrorist.

Before Kolt could take the only remaining light, AK–47 rounds slammed into the corner steel and wall behind him. Kolt took cover. A short lull in the fire and then another burst. Kolt knew the terrorist was on to plan B.

Kolt steadied himself and slowly took aim around the steel, several times stopping to blink his eyes and manage his breathing. This was to be the shot of Kolt's lifetime, and no shooter alive, given the same circumstances, would be cool as ice. Maybe the SEAL Team Six snipers on the USS *Bainbridge* 240 miles off the coast of Somalia, but not even they would be cool in the inner-most bowels of a Mississippi-based nuke plant.

Kolt felt his heart pounding. He didn't even bother himself with trying to think ahead to plan C. No, if it went there, with no ammunition, he was definitely going to come up short.

Kolt snapped the rifle up as he had done a million times before, indexed from muscle memory, held the dot with confidence, and broke the trigger.

Hit!

Kolt immediately unslung the rifle and placed it gently on the floor. He slipped around the corner steel on all fours. As he scrambled toward the edge of the pool, he suddenly wondered, what if the terrorist had night-vision goggles?

Little fucking late to think of that, he told himself. He took two deep breaths and slid headfirst into the water.

At 110 degrees Fahrenheit, the heat shocked Kolt's face and exposed hands immediately. In a second, once fully submerged, his entire body felt it, automatically making it difficult to hold his breath. No more noise, no more distinct smell of gunpowder, but, surprisingly, a lighted pathway. Subsurface lighting illuminated the top of the zircalloy-clad fuel assemblies that rested on the bottom of the pool, the very top of the assemblies roughly twenty-three feet under water.

After the bubbles from the initial plunge cleared the unoxygenated water around Kolt, he began breaststroking and frog kicking rapidly to descend, anticipating the terrorist still above on the fuel deck would be blindly pumping rounds into the pool. It was surprisingly clear underwater, not unlike the deep end of any Olympic swimming pool. Three rounds pierced the water at a steep angle, creating scattered minibubbles that quickly dissolved. Just off the left side of his head, the rounds prompted him to adjust his body to angle his dive closer to the painted concrete. Kolt knew the shooter was taking a big risk, since he might inadvertently strike his al Qaeda brother.

Three more hard pulls of breaststroke, and Kolt spotted a dark human-size figure below. As Kolt closed the distance, it was obvious that the gunfight on the fuel deck couldn't be heard from thirty feet below the water's surface. That, or the terrorist below simply ignored it, electing to remain focused on the primary task Allah expected of him.

As Kolt descended, his concern with the hot water lessened as he became increasingly spooked by the high radiation dose he was certainly receiving. The crimson blood filling the water from his winged shoulder was no defense against the deadly beta and gamma radiation emitting from both sides of the cladding. Water, or blood, offers exceptional shielding, but the longer he stayed underwater, the greater the dose he would absorb. The closer he moved to the stainless-clad spent-fuel assemblies, the chances of taking an accumulative lethal dose multiplied. Every two feet Kolt moved closer to the spent fuel assemblies he increased the radiation dose by a factor of 10. Worse, touching the assemblies would be certain death.

Is this worth it? I'm a dead man whether I stop this asshole or not.

Kolt took three more full strokes and frog kicks and spotted the submerged terrorist, a yellow scuba tank attached to his back, a belt of hard lead blocks surrounding his waist, the black hose regulator routed from the tank over his right shoulder. This terrorist was not worried about the radiation, knowing his soul was soon to be in paradise, knowing he had enough oxygen to ensure he got there.

Kolt couldn't be certain, but he saw what looked like some type of transmitter in both hands of the terrorist, still unaware of Kolt's presence. As Kolt did a free dive closer, he was able to make out the terrorist's right hand pushing buttons. A red light blinked three times on a dark square box attached to a circular pipe only a few feet from the terrorist. A strong swimmer on any other day, the heat, coupled with the adrenaline, forced Kolt's body to exhume what oxygen he had stored in his lungs. Kolt understood shallow-water blackout, where cerebral hypoxia could trigger loss of consciousness with little warning.

I hate the fucking water!

A second light, this one green, flashed and remained steady on the same dark object.

Decide, Kolt!

After one more full but powerless stroke, Kolt recognized the object wrapped in clear Bubble Wrap. Just to the right, four or five feet away, Kolt picked up on a second green light. A second package, wrapped the same but slightly smaller than the one closest to the terrorist, was attached to some type of basketball-size transfer valve.

Kolt understood the bastard's plan. One explosive charge on the stainless steel fuel assemblies, a second smaller one, most assuredly designed to destroy the crossover valve. The terrorists had done their homework; the damage would be irreversible.

Compromise this asshole's air source, or condemn myself to a watery grave.

Kolt swam in behind the terrorist, grabbing the top of both shoulders and wrapping his legs tightly around the terrorist's waist. The terrorist's reaction was instant panic. He dropped the transmitter from his hands and began flailing madly. Locked together, they began rolling over and over, Kolt's natural buoyancy not enough to counter the belt of weight around the terrorist.

Upside down and with bubbles moving up toward the surface, past the terrorist's bare feet, Kolt reached around and yanked the regulator from the bomber's mouth. As Kolt did so, he noticed the thin and black curly hair as it floated underwater. The terrorist turned his head, and Kolt recognized the high forehead.

Fucking Nadal!

On the extreme edge of passing out, Kolt shoved the regulator in his own mouth and took a deep hit of oxygen. He'd never enjoyed breathing as much as he did then. Invigorated, he squeezed his leg-lock tight around Nadal's torso as they rolled again, this time to the opposite direction, much like Tarzan would cling to a massive alligator.

The terrorist reached back with his right hand, grabbing ahold of the hose regulator and pulling it out of Kolt's mouth. Kolt could see the deformed hand, the one missing two fingers, confirming beyond any doubt that he had found Nadal the Romanian. Kolt reached up with both hands and put a tight kink in the hose before tying a double overhand noose in the hose. A sudden thought flashed in his mind—*now I know why SEALs do this kind of training.* Kolt grabbed the black knob and turned it hard clockwise, killing the air feed into the primary mouthpiece, just as a SEAL buddy of his had done to him one day while diving off the coast of Newport News. Kolt didn't think it was funny then, and he knew Nadal certainly wasn't finding it funny now.

Nadal whipped his head around to the right again. His eyes were wide with fear. Kolt knew that Nadal needed to escape his clutch, or he would die a failure. Kolt kept the pressure on, refusing to relent. He squeezed the scuba tank hard, keeping it to his front, not letting Nadal turn around inside the leg lock. With his right hand, Kolt wrapped the knotted black air hose twice around Nadal's skinny neck. Arching his back, Kolt pulled the hose as tight as he could.

Kolt tightened his grip as Nadal thrashed to get free. He was fighting longer and harder than Kolt anticipated for someone without oxygen. Kolt knew he needed air, too, but he was more focused on keeping Nadal between himself and the fuel assemblies to manage the radiation dose he was certainly receiving. Water and a human body were excellent shields from deadly radiation. Whether Kolt was receiving a lethal dose or not, they could continue to struggle for another ten seconds, fifteen max, before shallow-water blackout set in.

Kolt sensed the water pressure as a large splash shook the water above him and to his right rear. Something large had fallen into the pool. A body, the body of a security officer, or maybe the terrorist Kolt had exchanged a few mags with on the fuel deck earlier had joined the party. Just past the sinking man, small white spotlights criss-crossed above the water's surface. As the body sunk deeper and deeper, Kolt recognized the lifeless body of the other terrorist, blood contaminating the water near his back and left leg.

Kolt's leg lock finally forced Nadal to go limp, only a second before Kolt's vision grayed at the edges and then grew increasingly black. *I'm not going to make it,* Kolt realized, as all strength in his arms and legs melted away and he released his hold on Nadal. With all his dive gear, Nadal sunk a few feet deeper. Without equal buoyancy compensation, Kolt floated upward toward the surface, but he couldn't even lift his head to look up. What little air was left in his lungs was rapidly being replaced with pool water.

He was drowning.

His last thought brought a smile to his face even as he blacked out.

Should have worn water wings . . .

THIRTY-ONE

"Mr. Black just arrived with donut holes."

Kolt peered down at his iPad, reading the sliver of window that popped up on the top of the screen. Damn hard to read. Mr. Black brought Hawk donut holes? Any other time he might have thought it was code, but since he and Hawk were currently laid up a few rooms apart in a hospital, it made sense. He squinted and pecked away at the touchpad keys on the screen.

"Lucky you. Mr. White doesn't seem to need to eat or sleep," Kolt replied, referring to his security minder.

"You think HE is really coming today?" Hawk chatted.

"HE better," Kolt replied, his tongue sticking out of the corner of his mouth as he typed. "If not, I'm gonna roll my ass in to the nurses' station and administer the pain meds myself."

A week or so had passed since Kolt and Hawk saved the world. Well, Kolt allowed, maybe that's a stretch. What they pulled off at Yellow Creek was certainly something spectacular, easily saving tens of thousands of lives and stopping the largest attack on U.S. soil since 9/11 dead in its tracks. Both were laid up sorry now, trying to heal up and hope for release, somehow knowing that the decision would be made without their input.

At least Mr. Black and Mr. White had brought them iPads. Particularly since Cindy Bird was under strict doctor's orders to remain on the respirator and refrain from talking until her lungs had healed a little more.

Kolt looked up as a pair of nurses walked past his room. They didn't point; they didn't even look his way. He wasn't surprised. The doctors and nurses working shifts in medical office number 6, the high-security section of the Wound Treatment and Hyperbaric Medicine Center at Duke Raleigh Hospital, had no idea who he and Hawk were. Husband and wife, carjacking, and gunshot wounds were about all they'd been told. It was a solid cover. That sort of thing was pretty common in the south Raleigh area.

What wasn't common was the fuss being made over Kolt and Hawk—not by the medical staff who went about their jobs like the professionals they were, but by all the folks who weren't medical. Mr. Black and Mr. White, two large, silent, and determined gentlemen wearing earpieces, off-the-rack suits, and cold stares they must have practiced looking in a mirror. Carjacking victims didn't get security details. And they sure as hell weren't visited by the president of the United States during a nonelection year.

Kolt grimaced. He tried to locate the epicenter of the worst pain but gave up. His entire body hurt, and he was long past due for his next painkiller.

"I'm with ya," Hawk typed back. "I'm hoping these donuts are filled with jelly morphine."

Mr. White walked into Kolt's room and did a sweep. He didn't nod, didn't say hello, and didn't let on that Kolt was even there. Kolt watched him, looking for a pattern. Mr. White was good. He never started a sweep the same way. Sometimes he looked high then low. Other times, it was left to right, then right to left, and so on. Kolt admired brains that could focus like that and thanked God he didn't have one. Snipers and accountants and Mr. White.

"I thought I saw a nurse stuff a bale of marijuana in the sock drawer," Kolt said, motioning across the room.

"Top drawer?" Mr. White asked, completely ignoring Kolt's sense of humor.

"Middle," Kolt said, dropping his hand. Joking with Mr. White was a lot more fun under the effects of painkillers.

"I'll check them all," Mr. White said, proceeding to do just that.

They had been at Duke a week now, since the Air Evac Lifeteam helicopter out of Luka, Mississippi, landed on the roof and dropped off the injured couple, victims of random violence. Mr. White and Mr. Black had materialized at the hospital at the same time, and at least one of them had been there ever since. They weren't bad guys; in fact, Kolt knew these two to be good dudes. Kolt also understood and respected the importance of their mission to the national security of the United States.

Mr. Black and Mr. White had a specific job to do, and they took it as seriously as Kolt and Hawk took their jobs on target. Oreo, as Hawk had nicknamed the pair, had the sole mission of ensuring nobody administered any intravenous mind-boggling, hallucinogenic narcotics like pethidine and fentanyl to Hawk or Kolt that might get them too giddy and overly chatty. It was right out of a 60s spy novel, but the precaution was taken all the same. Kolt knew, and he knew Hawk did, too, that the way to avoid giving up a secret was to not talk about them and not think about them in a public setting. However, even Delta operators, if doped up, can make mistakes. And so Kolt and Hawk were currently suffering for national security because the president of the United States was coming to visit.

"Hit channel thirteen," Hawk messaged. "Your friend is on."

"Stand by!!!!!" Kolt replied, accidentally keeping his finger on the exclamation-point button.

"Clear," Mr. White said, closing up the last drawer.

Kolt looked at him. "Outstanding."

Mr. White turned and walked out of his room.

Kolt reached for the black channel changer sitting on the rolling over-bed table. He aimed it at the wall-mounted TV in the corner of the flowered-walled room, thumbed it on, and waited for the screen to show the current channel. He punched in one, three, and enter, finding a previously taped Fox News alert being aired and the attractive news anchor already into the script.

"Americans are awakening today to a White House announcement that the president of the United States has presented the Medal of Freedom to Ambassador William T. Mason, describing the former navy admiral as a 'national savior' at a private Roosevelt Room ceremony yesterday afternoon."

Kolt reached down to the side of his bed, found the push-button articulator, and pressed the up arrow to raise the back of his hospital bed in order to get a better look. Kolt watched as the president stepped in front of Bill Mason, accepted the medal by the blue and edged-white ribbon from an aide, and then delicately placed it around the ambassador's neck. Mason beamed.

The news anchor continued. "Confidential sources, including an anonymous senior administration official speaking off the record because they are unauthorized to disclose classified information, are telling Fox News that Ambassador Mason has been described as a 'hostage's best friend'." Here the anchor smiled. "Folks, if Timmy was down a well, forget about calling Lassie. American hero and patriot Ambassador Mason is who you want. His courage and skill thwarted last week's al Qaeda nuke plot and for that we all owe him our thanks."

Kolt stared at the television screen for a few more seconds before going back to Skype.

"Fuck up and move up!" Kolt messaged. "I'd say that's fair and balanced, wouldn't you?"

"Jealous?" Hawk replied.

Before Kolt could tell Hawk to kiss his ass, Mr. White stepped back into the room and did another sweep, walking to all four corners before stepping into the bathroom. He walked back out without a word.

"I think Mr. White has been sniffing too much glue lately," Kolt messaged before looking up to see the Delta commander Jeremy Webber enter the room. A moment later, the president of the United States walked in, shadowed by the Secret Service special agent in charge. Webber and the president both wore big smiles above their practically identical dark blue and pinstriped blazers, salmon-pink neckties, and splashed-white dress shirts, as if they were part of a Red Lobster staff about to sing "Happy Birthday" to an unsuspecting customer.

Kolt pulled his rear end back under him a bit, trying to appear more professional and worthy of the visit.

Webber motioned with his hand for the president to move to the right side of Kolt's bed, and the colonel followed him. Kolt turned away, back toward the door, to see Mr. Black pushing a raised surgical bed through the doorway. He was expecting Hawk, and it seemed perfectly coordinated for something he knew they had not rehearsed.

A second Secret Service agent stepped inside with a flat tray covered in bright green felt. Kolt knew the tray would be carrying the medals. Webber lifted the first one off the felt and handed it to the president.

The president stepped forward to the edge of Hawk's bed, smiled at her, and leaned over to pin the Purple Heart to Hawk's light blue hospital gown. He turned slightly toward Webber, accepting a second award, and turning back to Hawk.

"Staff Sergeant Cindy Bird, by my authority, and on behalf of a very grateful nation, you are hereby awarded the Distinguished Service Cross, for extraordinary actions in wartime against a known enemy of the United States."

The president leaned over to pin the imperial-blue and glory-red-edged DSC next to the Purple Heart.

"The American people are very proud of you, Staff Sergeant Bird," the president said as he reached down to squeeze her hand. Kolt could see Hawk nod in appreciation.

The president turned around to look at Kolt and took a few steps closer to the left side of his bed.

"Major Raynor, I can't say I was surprised to hear you were at the tip of the spear again."

"Hello, Mr. President. It's good to see you again," Kolt said.

The president stepped forward, shaking his head and smiling, and extended his hand. Kolt shook it as the president covered Kolt's right hand with both of his.

"Congratulations, Major, congratulations!" the president said.

"I didn't do anything, sir, really," Kolt said. "Sergeant Bird deserves all the credit."

The president looked at Colonel Webber for a moment, then back at Kolt.

"I assumed you'd say that, Major," the president said. "No medals this time. I was properly reminded about what you said last time."

Kolt thought back to the last time they had seen each other. It was the private award ceremony inside the West Wing, where the president presented Major Kolt Raynor his third Silver Star for gallantry in action after the American terrorist Daoud al-Amriki was killed. Kolt had tried to resist the award, even going so far as mentioning to the vice president, prior to the president's arriving, that medals should be reserved for the servicemen and women who had made the ultimate sacrifice.

"Medals for the dead," the president said. "Wasn't it?"

Kolt smiled, partly because the president actually remembered, but mostly because he had already meticulously prepared his dress uniform for the DA photo he needed before he could be considered for promotion to lieutenant colonel. The last thing he wanted was to have to fumble with adding another bronze oak-leaf cluster to his red, white, and blue Silver Star ribbon.

"What can I do for you instead, Major Raynor?" the president asked.

"Can't think of a thing, sir," Kolt said.

Just then, the president's SAIC stepped forward and whispered something in the president's ear. It appeared he was letting him know that they needed to get going to stay on their typically busy schedule.

Kolt realized there was something he did want from the president, actually. *Was this the right time and place?* Kolt was already speaking before he answered his own question.

Fuck it! I'll blame it on the meds!

"Sir, on second thought," Kolt said, "would you be willing to waive my mandatory attendance at yearlong advanced schooling? It's required to be promoted."

Webber gave Kolt a stern look. Kolt tried and failed to look suitably abashed. Webber turned to Mr. Black and Mr. White, standing near the doorway, giving them both the hairy eyeball. Kolt figured he was wondering if they had ensured the hallucinating drugs had been controlled properly.

"I'd like to be a Delta Force sabre squadron commander, sir," Kolt added.

"Done!" the president said as he quickly looked at his watch. "I'll have my staff see to it immediately."

Before Kolt could tell the president that he appreciated that, Hawk had raised her iPad in the air and the SAIC stepped up to accept it from her. He turned it right-side up, stepped back a few feet, turning toward the president and Colonel Webber, and read the typed message aloud.

"Mr. President, it seems Staff Sergeant Bird would like to be a Delta Force operator," the SAIC said before handing the iPad back to Hawk.

Even Kolt was shocked by Hawk's straightforwardness, and definitely impressed by her guts. She obviously was sincere, her bravery maybe prompted by the meds or that she didn't have to actually speak when asking for it, but she had to know that not even the president of the United States could grant that wish.

Kolt could see the president was taken a little aback by the request. He figured the president had no idea that there weren't female operators in the unit already. His support for females to attend the U.S. Army Ranger School and to serve in previously banned combat-arms duties like infantryman and tanker was well known throughout the armed services.

"I must say, your patriotism is unparalleled," the president said. "Colonel Webber, is that possible? Can we grant Staff Sergeant Bird her wish?"

Kolt detected a little fidgeting and agitation in Webber as he searched for the proper response. He knew Webber and other senior special forces leaders were in the middle of the Pentagon's two-year study and weren't even close to commenting yet. *How the hell does he answer that?*

Kolt noticed Hawk typing another message, this one much shorter than the first. *Don't push it, Hawk!*

"Mr. President, Delta Force selection is an ongoing process," Webber said. "Staff Sergeant Bird here has certainly demonstrated she deserves every consideration." It was clearly an effort for Webber to push the words out past his teeth.

"Excellent!" the president said, seeming to ignore Webber's noncommittal response. "I'll have my staff keep me apprised of the situation."

Bingo! Let's see you sweep it under the carpet now, Webber!

Webber swallowed and nodded. He looked straight at Kolt, and Kolt knew that Hawk's request was on him. Webber motioned for the president to follow him out of the room. The president nodded at Kolt and Hawk, and followed. The SAIC nodded to Kolt, gave a short wave to Hawk, and followed closely on the heels of his principal.

Mr. White unlocked Hawk's gurney wheels and moved to the head of the bed. Mr. Black took up the foot side, and together they maneuvered her through the doorway to take her back to her room down the hall.

Kolt looked down at his iPad. The screen saver was active, having gone to sleep since the party began. Kolt two-finger swiped the touch screen to unlock the tablet, still a little amazed at what just happened. *Did the president actually say all that?*

On the Skype chat screen, a parting message from Hawk awaited him. He tapped it to open.

"How's that for full assault mode?"